The CAPTAIN *of the* POLESTAR, LOT N^O. 249, *AND OTHER HORRORS*

The Best Weird Fiction and Ghost Stories of
SIR ARTHUR CONAN DOYLE

Edited, Annotated, and Illustrated By
M. GRANT KELLERMEYER, M.A.

— OLDSTYLE TALES PRESS —
Fort Wayne, Indiana

This edition published 2016 by
OLDSTYLE TALES PRESS
2424 N. Anthony Blvd
Fort Wayne, Indiana
46805-3604

For more information, or to request permission to reprint selections or illustrations from this book, write to the Editor at oldstyletales@gmail.com

Readers who are interested in further titles from Oldstyle Tales Press are invited to visit our website at

— WWW.OLDSTYLETALES.COM —

— TABLE *of* CONTENTS —

Concerning What You Are About to Read

UNQUESTIONABLY, Sir Arthur Conan Doyle is considered the most significant contributor to the detective story genre – what Verne and Wells are to science fiction, what Tolkein and Lewis are to fantasy, Doyle is to that genre. And yet – unlike his fellow sleuth writers Agatha Christie, Dorothy L. Sayers, and Rex Stout, his excursions in virtually every sub-genre of speculative fiction merit attention. Following in the tradition of the original detective story writers Edgar Allan Poe and Wilkie Collins, Doyle managed to infuse all of his fiction with a rich veneer of atmosphere and romance which easily translated over to science fiction, horror, or supernaturalism. In this wise a Sherlock Holmes story could steep in rich atmospherics which were entirely foreign to the more logic-focused exploits of Hercule Poirot, Miss Marple, and Nero Wolf. Holmes has always fostered a relationship with the supernatural (in spite of his famous injunction in the case of the Sussex vampire: "This agency stands flat-footed upon the ground, and there it must remain. The world is big enough for us. No ghosts need apply"): Holmes anthologies, fanfiction, pastiches, films, criticism, art, and general geekery has frequently been featured alongside (and sold along with) corresponding materials on Dracula, H. P. Lovecraft, H. G. Wells, Frankenstein, Jekyll and Hyde, and Carnacki the Ghost-finder. I can assure you that the fan fiction which pits Poirot or Lord Peter Wimsey against the forces of darkness is few and far between. For whatever reason, the fact that there are no stories of the supernatural in the Holmesian canon (*The Hound of the Baskervilles* and "The Sussex Vampire" are material Gothic detective stories, "The Creeping Man" is science fiction, and no other tale comes even close) Baker Street irregulars continue to crave a side of supernatural fiction with their Holmes, while many pastiche writers see fit to season the entrée liberally with spooks and monsters (Neil Gaiman's Lovecraftian "Study in Emerald" is a masterpiece of the form). But all of this talk of Holmes (who will continue to haunt this collection time and time again before materializing in "The Speckled Band," "The Devil's Foot," and "The Sussex Vampire") distracts us from the true focus of our attention today, and that is the speculative fiction of A. Conan Doyle – his horror and supernatural writings.

While Doyle spilled himself into dozens and dozens of detective stories, science fiction, and thrillers, his supernatural output was surprisingly compact (E. F. Bleiler puts him down for fourteen tales and four novels) considering both the wild breadth of his life's oeuvre (some 400 pieces of fiction), and his religious convictions as a Spiritualist. However, the batch left with us contain a variety of unique qualities which have ensured his legacy as a critical if concise contributor to speculative literature. His virtual creation of the mummy genre alone would secure his reputation, for what Stoker, Shelley, and Stevenson are to vampires, monsters, and werewolves, Doyle is to the malevolent mummy – a trope that didn't exist previous to his penning "Lot No. 249." This tale along with "The Ring of Thoth" were combined – the former being a Frankenstein-esque story of mad scientist employing a zombie assassin, and the later following the tragic love story of an immortal Egyptian desperately trying to reunite with his eons-dead lover – into the plot of Karl Freund's 1932 horror masterpiece, *The Mummy*. The film stared Boris Karloff who perfectly shifted between the roles of Doyle's sympathetic, lovelorn priest, the villainous Egyptologist Bellingham, and even Smith's grisly helpmate (although Karloff is on screen as the wrapped mummy for less than four minutes, his transformation is truly chilling and unforgettable). Before "Thoth" and "249" the few mummy stories in existence were almost exclusively romances, future-minded science fiction that crossed Frankenstein with *The Time Machine* (battery attached to physically preserved mummy equals time-traveler), or social satire (Poe's "Some Words with a Mummy" has disappointed thousands of young horror buffs, myself included, who read it expecting thrills only to find it to be a hysterical critique of modern society on par with Twain, Wilde, or Bierce in which a reanimated mummy is thoroughly unimpressed with anything in the nineteenth century except for cough drops. Horrifying, no. Hilarious, yes). Doyle saw the potential of the dried up corpse to be frightening rather than romantic or intellectual, and one of the great monsters of Western culture was born through his two visionary stories.

Doyle's greatest tales also dabbled with monsters and werewolves. "The Terror of Blue John Gap" follows the cryptozoological investigation into a blind, prehistoric "cave bear" living in an abandoned mineshaft. In "John Barrington Cowles" he uses a tremendous amount of creative restraint by merely implying what horrible being the narrator's friend's fiancée might be. Although the term "werewolf" is used, she could be a conventional vampire like Le Fanu's similarly sketched Carmilla (complete with hypnotic powers), a sadistic man killer like Keates' La Belle Dame Sans Merci, or a proto-Lovecraftian hybrid she-devil in the pattern of Arthur Machen's suicide-causing temptress Helen Vaughn in *The Great God Pan*. The story closely resembles *Pan* (both follow a mysterious society woman who leaves a wake of dead suitors in her path, implying a hideous, supernatural secret). As Machen would go on to write his magnum opus six years later, and as that work would be of foundational use to Lovecraft and his followers (compare to *The Dunwich Horror* which has been called a Machen pastiche by some critics), and Doyle's impact on horror fiction becomes even clearer. One of his greatest stories in the genre can be easily seen as a cozy transition from the ponderous science fiction of H. G. Wells to the cosmic terror of Lovecraft. "The Horror of the Heights" follows an aviator trying to break the altitude record all while suspecting that something hideous living in the clouds overhead has been responsible for a slew of recent pilot deaths. Written in the infancy of aviation, the story's beastly monsters pay homage to Well's squidlike, beaked Martians while presaging Lovecraft's amphibious, gelatinous Cthulhu, and the story often flips between science fiction and weird fiction seamlessly, leaving a lovely bookmark between Late Victorian horror a la *The War of the Worlds* and post-war weird tales a la *The Haunter of the Dark*. Complete with a blood-stained journal with half-mad last words scribbled onto it, a host of slimey, corpulent, fishlike monsters, and an unseen world of terror lurking just beyond human attention, the story had a doubtless impact on the American dean of weird fiction, and is one of Doyle's most innovative.

On the conventional side are Doyle's tales of ghosts and hauntings, which are no less artful and effective. Of particular mention is "The Captain of the *Polestar*," a haunting narrative that combines atmospheric elements of *Frankenstein*, "The Rime of the Ancient Mariner," and *The Narrative of Arthur Gordon Pym* in its polar wastes where a Byronic whaling captain (with strong hints of Ahab) risks his crew's lives to escape (or is it to find?) the ghost of his fiancée, a woman whose vague description leaves the nature of her untimely death a fascinating mystery (I present my pet theory in the notes). A genuinely beautiful ghost story complete with shivers, unease, and pathos, this is one of Doyle's best (and first) supernatural tales. Its level of humanity and feeling rival the best Victorian ghost stories of Elizabeth Gaskell, Mrs Oliphant, and Mrs Henry Wood. "The Bully of Brocas Court" is a phenomenal little spook tale written in the manner of J. Sheridan Le Fanu, the undisputed king of Victorian ghost tales, with its sense of sadism, moral decadence, physical fear, and blurring of boundaries between good and evil, living and dead, punished and punisher. Other tales follow haunted objects, like the genuinely chilling account of "The Leather Funnel," a torture device that brings with it dreams of its use in a manner which would titillate BDSM junkies, or the horrifying "Silver Hatchet" which causes its wielder to inadvertently chop to pieces the person they consider their best friend. Complete with homosexual subtext, a fascinating murder plot, and disturbing philosophical questions, "The Silver Hatchet" was quite ahead of its time. Similarly, "A Pastoral Horror" follows the movements of a serial killer, whose M.O. is shockingly modern (he ambushes his victims with his face hidden under a scarf and a wide-brimmed hat, wielding a pickaxe – very in kind with *Friday the 13th*, *I Know What You Did Last Summer*, etc.).

Doyle's supernatural fiction does not seem to have a unifying theme, ethos, or worldview. Unlike the oeuvres of Lovecraft, Stevenson, Le Fanu, Machen, Oliphant, Broughton, Blackwood, Hawthorne, or M. R. James, his stories do not connect to a higher philosophy other than a sense of chivalric, Nietzschean justice that permeates most of his fiction. Instead, his stories are simply good stories. They're tightly written, evocative, innovative, and above all entertaining. He was a showman, and knew how to grab an audience. Keenly aware of pathos, he used it to great effect in the Holmes stories, and with excellent attention in the best of his horror fiction ("Polestar," "Through the Veil," "Bully," "Ring of Thoth," and others are brilliant in their use of the emotional appeal). Sometimes his stories went too far into the eccentric or maudlin, and several of those were excluded from this anthology due to their lack of excellence, which so many other of his tales achieved. "The American's Tale" is a Wellsian (cf. "Valley of the Spiders") anecdote about a man-eating plant in the Wild West. "The Jappaned Box," often unfortunately anthologized in horror volumes, seems to be a ghost story (a widower locks himself in a room and a strange woman's voice is heard) until the big reveal: he is an alcoholic listening to a recording of his dead wife's encouraging voice in a bid for temperance. Even "Playing With Fire," included here, is somewhat ridiculous with its spectral unicorn (the story is only salvaged by having the beast fail to manifest to the reader). The cake is taken, however, by one of Doyle's most anthologized "horror" stories, a ludicrous tale called "J. Habakuk Jephson's Statement," which is mentionable only because of its contributions to the mythos of the *Mary Celeste* case – a derelict ship, the disappearance of whose crew in 1872 has never been explained. Doyle's story is rarely summarized online or in print, but it continues to be referenced liberally in both as if it is a classic. The story explains the mystery thus: a roving band of black supremacists murder the white passengers one by one before finally hijacking it from the survivors who are horrified to learn that the ship – bound for Portugal – has secretly been sailing to the African coast, where they are slaughtered as the blacks return to their motherland. The only survivor is saved because of a totem given to him by a slave during the Civil War, which *just so happens* to be the missing ear of an idol venerated by the tribe on shore. It is one of – and I say this seriously – one of the stupidest and most disappointing things I have read in all my life. After the buzz generated by so many references to the work, I now understand why I have never found a summary of the wholly unbelievable and pointless story which somehow finds its way into so many collections of Doyle's horror tales. We shall pass.

No discussion of Doyle's relationship to supernatural fiction could be complete without addressing his Spiritualism. "Through the Veil," "Playing with Fire," "De Profundis," and "How it Happened" are each episodes of psychic phenomena wherein the reincarnated souls of a Celt rapist and his Roman victim marry one another centuries later (to her eventual horror), a séance creates and summons a monster accidentally through reckless experimentation, a dead man appears to his wife as she sails over the spot his body was dumped, and a spirit recounts the story of his death – respectively. All of these tales involve either the theories or the practice of Spiritualism, a religion which focused primarily on investigating, celebrating, and utilizing psychic connections between the living world and that of the dead. Telepathy, ESP, hypnotism, premonitions, and mediums were their province, and Doyle was a devoted adherent, especially following the death of his wife from consumption, and that of his son and brother from Spanish flu contracted in World War One. Culminating in his impassioned defense on the existence of fairies, Doyle's faith caused him to become a public laughingstock, indeed, as E. F. Bleiler puts it, "in his old age his gullibility was pathetic." Harry Houdini, a devoted debunker, tried to prove to his friend that psychic powers could be tricks by performing one for him personally, then explaining how the trick was managed. Doyle refused to believe the explanation, arguing instead that Houdini was endowed with psychic powers and was denying it. The friendship was thenceforth terminated. The role of Spiritualism in his life affected his literature negatively, too. Spiritual belief is often important in how it manifests in a writer's work, whether they be believers (Machen, Blackwood, King), materialists (Lovecraft, Poe, Aickman), or open-minded agnostics (M.R. James, Onions, Gaiman). On one hand was Blackwood – like Doyle, a one-time member of the Society for Psychical Research – who believed in reincarnation, ghosts, and elementals. He infused his work with mystic wonder, awe, and madness derived from his feelings on the subject. On the other hand is Lovecraft, a devoted atheist who thought horror spoke best to the materialist because nothing could be more shattering than for an atheist to witness the supernatural; to him it was a genuine fear. Doyle, however, neither practiced awe or fear, rather accepting the spirit world as a scientific fact, often describing it in dully academic language. While many of his stories revel in romantic descriptions, moods, and settings, the more supernatural they are – with some exceptions (e.g. "Polestar") – the more tedious, preachy, and vapid they become. Doyle's tendency to invent words and scientific jargon in order to sound authoritative in his texts is something that plagues many of his stories, including the Holmes canon ("Shall I demonstrate your own ignorance? What do you know, pray, of Tapanuli fever? What do you know of the black Formosa corruption?" Watson is excused for never hearing of these things because Doyle made them up to sound good).

In spite of putting on airs, attempting to scientific-ate his prose, and shamelessly propagandizing on behalf of psychic frauds (in "Polestar" he essentially has the haunted captain say in defense of mediums "don't throw away the barrel because of one rotten apple"), Doyle's storytelling was masterful in most cases, and his gift for poetic justice made the conclusions of his horror stories especially effective. The tales that follow feature mummies, werewolves, vampires, zombies, reincarnations, serial killers, haunted axes, torture chambers, ether monsters, polar wastelands, booby-trapped treasure chests, psychedelic poisons, and yes, even a scary unicorn. They were created to entertain, to wonder at, and to give us some pause. I have confidence that they will perform exactly as designed.

M. Grant Kellermeyer
Fort Wayne, Walpurgis Night 2015

THE CAPTAIN OF THE POLESTAR, LOT NO. 249 & OTHERS

The Best Weird Fiction & Ghost Stories of

SIR ARTHUR CONAN DOYLE

DOYLE'S very first recorded short story – a rejected horror story called "The Haunted Grange of Goresthorpe" – was a ghost story written in the Victorian Gothic tradition about the ghost of a woman who is relentlessly haunting the ghost of her male killer. His first *published* supernatural tale – also about a man haunted by a woman – was similarly crafted with Victorian pathos and elegance, but this one became a masterpiece of the genre, commonly included in anthologies of classic bogey tales. It shares its principle features with other exemplars of the Victorian Gothic: the wild sublimity of the Brontës, the lonesome spiritual alienation of Charles Dickens, the otherworldly grotesqueness of J. S. Le Fanu, the domestic and romantic tensions of Nesbit, Braddon, and Broughton, and the humbling and horrible pathos of Edwards, Gaskell, and Oliphant. Doyle also linked himself with the cruder, Romantic tradition that immediately preceded polished, Victorian supernaturalism: the gloomy fantasies of Coleridge, Burns, Keats, Byron, Scott, and the Shelleys, and the uncanny tales of Poe, Hawthorne, Melville, and Irving. In many ways "The Captain of the 'Pole-Star'" is a vast homage to the 19th century's history of ghost stories – from the Romantics to the Victorians – carefully interweaving Shelley and Coleridge's wild wastes with Oliphant and Dickens' existential elegance. The story is one of a number of spook tales (*Frankenstein, Rime of the Ancient Mariner, The Mountains of Madness, Arthur Gordon Pym, The Shadow of a Shade*, etc.) which concern mankind's encroachment into the lonely Southern and Northern Poles. While most tend to feature the *Antarctic* wastelands, Doyle pastiches Frankenstein's diabolical pursuit of a supernatural being into the unpeopled North. The story is a classic, weighed down a touch by its lavish melodrama, but sustained by the author's dedication to holding sentiment and dread in a well-balanced tension, which prevents it from descending into a cheap horror story or maudlin romance. Instead, we are presented with a tale rife with mystery, wonder, and sadness.

The Captain of the "Pole-Star"
{1890}

[Being an extract from the singular journal of
JOHN M`ALISTER RAY, student of medicine.]

SEPTEMBER 11th. — Lat. 81° 40' N.; long. 2° E[1]. Still lying-to[2] amid enormous ice fields. The one which stretches away to the north of us, and to which our

---

[1] A hideously desolate location north of the craggy and icy Svalbard Islands and just south of Greenland's northern territories, quite near the North Pole

[2] To pause one's progress until conditions are more favorable

ice-anchor[1] is attached, cannot be smaller than an English county[2]. To the right and left unbroken sheets extend to the horizon. This morning the mate reported that there were signs of pack ice to the southward. Should this form of sufficient thickness to bar our return, we shall be in a position of danger, as the food, I hear, is already running somewhat short. It is late in the season, and the nights are beginning to reappear[3].

This morning I saw a star twinkling just over the fore-yard[4], the first since the beginning of May. There is considerable discontent among the crew, many of whom are anxious to get back home to be in time for the herring season, when labour always commands a high price upon the Scotch coast. As yet their displeasure is only signified by sullen countenances and black looks, but I heard from the second mate this afternoon that they contemplated sending a deputation to the Captain to explain their grievance. I much doubt how he will receive it, as he is a man of fierce temper, and very sensitive about anything approaching to an infringement of his rights. I shall venture after dinner to say a few words to him upon the subject. I have always found that he will tolerate from me what he would resent from any other member of the crew. Amsterdam Island, at the north-west corner of Spitzbergen[5], is visible upon our starboard quarter—a rugged line of volcanic rocks, intersected by white seams, which represent glaciers. It is curious to think that at the present moment there is probably no human being nearer to us than the Danish settlements in the south of Greenland—a good nine hundred miles as the crow flies. A captain takes a great responsibility upon himself when he risks his vessel under such circumstances. No whaler has ever remained in these latitudes till so advanced a period of the year[6].

9 P.M. — I have spoken to Captain Craigie, and though the result has been hardly satisfactory, I am bound to say that he listened to what I had to

---

[1] A bent bar whose prong is inserted into a hole drilled through ice used to prevent the ship from drifting

[2] Hampshire could be considered a decently sized county on England's southern coast. At 1,455 square miles, it is comparable in size to the state of Connecticut

[3] The northern latitudes experience days without night throughout the summer. Around September 21st the pole experiences pure twilight until mid-October when it sinks into endless night until the spring

[4] The lowest yard (a perpendicular spar which holds a sail) on the front-most (or "fore") mast

[5] A small, craggy island northwest of the main network of Svalbard Islands, once popular as a base camp for Arctic whalers and known as "Blubber Town" before being abandoned in 1660

[6] Unlike Walton in Frankenstein, this ambitious captain is no explorer or scientist, and the suggestion that a whaling captain would stray so near to the Pole is both outrageous and ridiculous – even an Arctic whaler. If he were to return home alive and sane, such a man would be arrested

say very quietly and even deferentially. When I had finished he put on that air of iron determination which I have frequently observed upon his face, and paced rapidly backwards and forwards across the narrow cabin for some minutes. At first I feared that I had seriously offended him, but he dispelled the idea by sitting down again, and putting his hand upon my arm with a gesture which almost amounted to a caress. There was a depth of tenderness too in his wild dark eyes which surprised me considerably. "Look here, Doctor," he said, "I'm sorry I ever took you—I am indeed —and I would give fifty pounds this minute to see you standing safe upon the Dundee quay[1]. It's hit or miss with me this time. There are fish[2] to the north of us. How dare you shake your head, sir, when I tell you I saw them blowing from the masthead[3]?"—this in a sudden burst of fury, though I was not conscious of having shown any signs of doubt. "Two-and-twenty fish in as many minutes as I am a living man, and not one under ten foot[4]. Now, Doctor, do you think I can leave the country when there is only one infernal strip of ice between me and my fortune? If it came on to blow from the north to-morrow we could fill the ship and be away before the frost could catch us. If it came on to blow from the south—well, I suppose the men are paid for risking their lives, and as for myself it matters but little to me, for I have more to bind me to the other world than to this one[5]. I confess that I am sorry for you, though. I wish I had old Angus Tait who was with me last voyage, for he was a man that would never be missed[6], and you—you said once that you were engaged, did you not?"

"Yes," I answered, snapping the spring of the locket which hung from my watch-chain, and holding up the little vignette of Flora[7].

"Curse you!" he yelled, springing out of his seat, with his very beard bristling with passion. "What is your happiness to me? What have I to do

---

[1] A harbor city on the eastern coast of Scotland. A quay is a dock or wharf

[2] Whaler slang for whales, which are – of course – mammals, not fish

[3] It truly is unlikely that whales would be spouting so far north other than narwhals and belugas which are not the sort of fare British whalers sought (bowheads, right whales, etc.)

[4] DOYLE'S NOTE: *A whale is measured among whalers not by the length of its body, but by the length of its whalebone.*

[5] A hideous thought. The captain suggests that if the wind blows in one direction they will make their fortune in whale oil, but if it goes in the other they will die, and it is no grave problem because such a crew knew there were risks. Any sane man would turn south and cut his losses. This is also the first time that a suggestion of supernatural involvement arises, as the captain claims to have more at stake in the afterlife than in the living world

[6] These words are practically murderous

[7] A suitable name for this story: the goddess of spring, flowers, nature, and fertility, the name suggests everything that the Pole is not, and provides a promise of warmth, love, life, and salvation if the ship manages to return

with her that you must dangle her photograph before my eyes[1]?" I almost thought that he was about to strike me in the frenzy of his rage, but with another imprecation he dashed open the door of the cabin and rushed out upon deck, leaving me considerably astonished at his extraordinary violence. It is the first time that he has ever shown me anything but courtesy and kindness. I can hear him pacing excitedly up and down overhead as I write these lines.

I should like to give a sketch of the character of this man, but it seems presumptuous to attempt such a thing upon paper, when the idea in my own mind is at best a vague and uncertain one. Several times I have thought that I grasped the clue which might explain it, but only to be disappointed by his presenting himself in some new light which would upset all my conclusions. It may be that no human eye but my own shall ever rest upon these lines, yet as a psychological study I shall attempt to leave some record of Captain Nicholas Craigie.

A man's outer case generally gives some indication of the soul within. The Captain is tall and well-formed, with dark, handsome face, and a curious way of twitching his limbs, which may arise from nervousness, or be simply an outcome of his excessive energy[2]. His jaw and whole cast of countenance is manly and resolute, but the eyes are the distinctive feature of his face. They are of the very darkest hazel, bright and eager, with a singular mixture of recklessness in their expression, and of something else which I have sometimes thought was more allied with horror than any other emotion[3]. Generally the former predominated, but on occasions, and more particularly when he was thoughtfully inclined, the look of fear would spread and deepen until it imparted a new character to his whole countenance. It is at these times that he is most subject to tempestuous fits of anger, and he seems to be aware of it, for I have known him lock himself up so that no one might approach him until his dark hour was passed. He sleeps badly[4], and I have heard him shouting during the night, but his cabin is some little distance from mine, and I could never distinguish the words which he said.

This is one phase of his character, and the most disagreeable one. It is only through my close association with him, thrown together as we are day

---

[1] The captain experiences guilt – both from seeing the doctor (his possible victim in the slowest, most complicated suicide attempt ever committed) further humanized, and (as we shall see) from being reminded of his fiancée, whose photograph he also treasures

[2] This portrait is one of the doomed, Byronic hero (compare to the dark and broody Captain Ahab): a man of singular talents and passions, whose greatest traits are also his greatest weaknesses. There is a suggestion of violent passion in the doctor's description

[3] Of course, the eyes are the windows of the soul, so this description is far more psychological than optometric: we see an emotional, spiritual, full-blooded man haunted, it would seem, by a horror from his past

[4] A literary sign of deep-felt guilt more than garden variety insomnia or stress (see: Hawthorne's sleep-troubled Reverend Dimmesdale)

after day, that I have observed it. Otherwise he is an agreeable companion, well-read and entertaining, and as gallant a seaman as ever trod a deck. I shall not easily forget the way in which he handled the ship when we were caught by a gale among the loose ice at the beginning of April. I have never seen him so cheerful, and even hilarious[1], as he was that night, as he paced backwards and forwards upon the bridge amid the flashing of the lightning and the howling of the wind[2]. He has told me several times that the thought of death was a pleasant one to him, which is a sad thing for a young man to say; he cannot be much more than thirty, though his hair and moustache are already slightly grizzled. Some great sorrow must have overtaken him and blighted his whole life. Perhaps I should be the same if I lost my Flora[3]—God knows! I think if it were not for her that I should care very little whether the wind blew from the north or the south to-morrow.

There, I hear him come down the companion, and he has locked himself up in his room, which shows that he is still in an unamiable mood. And so to bed, as old Pepys[4] would say, for the candle is burning down (we have to use them now since the nights are closing in), and the steward has turned in, so there are no hopes of another one.

September 12th. — Calm, clear day, and still lying in the same position. What wind there is comes from the south-east, but it is very slight. Captain is in a better humour, and apologised to me at breakfast for his rudeness. He still looks somewhat distrait, however, and retains that wild look in his eyes which in a Highlander would mean that he was "fey[5]" —at least so our chief engineer remarked to me, and he has some reputation among the Celtic portion of our crew as a seer and expounder of omens.

It is strange that superstition should have obtained such mastery over this hard-headed and practical race[6]. I could not have believed to what an extent it is carried had I not observed it for myself. We have had a perfect epidemic of it this voyage, until I have felt inclined to serve out rations of

---

[1] The connotation with "exceedingly amusing" only dates back to the 1920s. When this was penned, "hilarious" was more akin to hysterical, excessively cheerful, and manic

[2] A very Byronic atmosphere and very Romantic with its violent sublimity

[3] Whether ignorant of the situation or somehow unconsciously aware, the doctor hints at what is really at work in the captain's tormented soul: the loss of the woman he loved

[4] Samuel Pepys (1633-1703) was a naval administrator, diarist, and member of the British Parliament who rose to distinction in the Admiralty through hard work and talent in spite of having no sailing experience. A fitting idol for our green-horn doctor

[5] Scots: fated to die, doomed, marked by a foreboding of calamity; or crazy, touched, mad, haunted. All of these meanings work well for the doctor's purpose of describing a man who is losing his grip on the world of the living – whether through curses, hauntings, or insanity

[6] The Scots have a reputation for being both tremendously practical, sensible, and pragmatic all while continuing to nurse legends of the supernatural

sedatives and nerve-tonics[1] with the Saturday allowance of grog[2]. The first symptom of it was that shortly after leaving Shetland the men at the wheel used to complain that they heard plaintive cries and screams in the wake of the ship, as if something were following it and were unable to overtake it[3]. This fiction has been kept up during the whole voyage, and on dark nights at the beginning of the seal-fishing it was only with great difficulty that men could be induced to do their spell[4]. No doubt what they heard was either the creaking of the rudder-chains, or the cry of some passing sea-bird. I have been fetched out of bed several times to listen to it, but I need hardly say that I was never able to distinguish anything unnatural.

The men, however, are so absurdly positive upon the subject that it is hopeless to argue with them. I mentioned the matter to the Captain once, but to my surprise he took it very gravely, and indeed appeared to be considerably disturbed by what I told him. I should have thought that he at least would have been above such vulgar delusions.

All this disquisition upon superstition leads me up to the fact that Mr. Manson, our second mate, saw a ghost last night—or, at least, says that he did, which of course is the same thing[5]. It is quite refreshing to have some new topic of conversation after the eternal routine of bears and whales which has served us for so many months. Manson swears the ship is haunted, and that he would not stay in her a day if he had any other place to go to. Indeed the fellow is honestly frightened, and I had to give him some chloral and bromide of potassium[6] this morning to steady him down. He seemed quite indignant when I suggested that he had been having an extra glass the night before, and I was obliged to pacify him by keeping as grave a countenance as possible during his story, which he certainly narrated in a very straight-forward and matter-of-fact way.

"I was on the bridge[7]," he said, "about four bells in the middle watch[8], just when the night was at its darkest. There was a bit of a moon, but the clouds were blowing across it so that you couldn't see far from the ship.

---

1 Probably some solution of morphine, cocaine, opium, or lithium salts dissolved in quinine

2 Weak beer, lemon or lime juice, and rum, sometimes added to water. A fantastic concoction to raise spirits, lower scurvy, and prevent water-borne diseases on ship

3 A clue that whatever it is that is following the captain is chasing him – the captain is not running away *to* it, but *from* it

4 That is, their shifts or chores or watches

5 The doctor appears to be struggling with his skepticism "saw… says… same thing of course"

6 Chloral hydrate is an oily, organic compound used as a sedative or hypnotic substance. Bromide of potassium is a salt used as an anti-convulsant or sedative

7 The executive center of a vessel where the wheel, compass, and instrument are, and where the officers congregate. Typically an elevated deck at the rear of the vessel

8 Two in the morning

John M'Leod, the harpooner[1], came aft from the foc'sle-head[2] and reported a strange noise on the starboard bow[3].

I went forrard and we both heard it, sometimes like a bairn[4] crying and sometimes like a wench[5] in pain. I've been seventeen years to the country and I never heard seal, old or young, make a sound like that. As we were standing there on the foc'sle-head the moon came out from behind a cloud, and we both saw a sort of white figure moving across the ice field in the same direction that we had heard the cries. We lost sight of it for a while, but it came back on the port bow[6], and we could just make it out like a shadow on the ice. I sent a hand aft for the rifles, and M'Leod and I went down on to the pack, thinking that maybe it might be a bear. When we got on the ice I lost sight of M'Leod, but I pushed on in the direction where I could still hear the cries. I followed them for a mile or maybe more, and then running round a hummock[7] I came right on to the top of it standing and waiting for me seemingly. I don't know what it was. It wasn't a bear any way. It was tall and white and straight, and if it wasn't a man nor a woman, I'll stake my davy[8] it was something worse. I made for the ship as hard as I could run, and precious glad I was to find myself aboard. I signed articles to do my duty by the ship, and on the ship I'll stay, but you don't catch me on the ice again after sundown[9]."

That is his story, given as far as I can in his own words. I fancy what he saw must, in spite of his denial, have been a young bear erect upon its hind legs, an attitude which they often assume when alarmed. In the uncertain light this would bear a resemblance to a human figure, especially to a man whose nerves were already somewhat shaken. Whatever it may have been, the occurrence is unfortunate, for it has produced a most unpleasant effect upon the crew. Their looks are more sullen than before, and their discontent more open. The double grievance of being debarred from the herring fishing and of being detained in what they choose to call a haunted vessel, may lead them to do something rash. Even the harpooners, who are the oldest and steadiest among them, are joining in the general agitation.

Apart from this absurd outbreak of superstition, things are looking rather more cheerful. The pack which was forming to the south of us has partly cleared away, and the water is so warm as to lead me to believe that

---

[1] A strong and capable seaman tasked with hurling the harpoon spear into the whale

[2] The toilet in the ship's bows

[3] To the right and forward of the ship (if the bow is north, then northeast)

[4] Scots: baby, child, little one

[5] Woman, with a connotation of youth or low status – a young woman

[6] Moving towards the front and left (if the bow is north, then from northeast to northwest)

[7] Hump or ridge in an ice field

[8] A corruption of "affidavit," sometimes rendered "on my davy," or "so help my davy." Reputation

[9] A vow which will have increasing solemnity as each passing day grows shorter

we are lying in one of those branches of the gulf-stream which run up between Greenland and Spitzbergen. There are numerous small Medusse and sealemons[1] about the ship, with abundance of shrimps, so that there is every possibility of "fish" being sighted. Indeed one was seen blowing about dinner-time, but in such a position that it was impossible for the boats to follow it.

September 13th. — Had an interesting conversation with the chief mate, Mr. Milne, upon the bridge. It seems that our Captain is as great an enigma to the seamen, and even to the owners of the vessel, as he has been to me[2]. Mr. Milne tells me that when the ship is paid off, upon returning from a voyage, Captain Craigie disappears, and is not seen again until the approach of another season, when he walks quietly into the office of the company, and asks whether his services will be required. He has no friend in Dundee, nor does any one pretend to be acquainted with his early history. His position depends entirely upon his skill as a seaman, and the name for courage and coolness which he had earned in the capacity of mate, before being entrusted with a separate command. The unanimous opinion seems to be that he is not a Scotchman, and that his name is an assumed one[3]. Mr. Milne thinks that he has devoted himself to whaling simply for the reason that it is the most dangerous occupation which he could select, and that he courts death in every possible manner. He mentioned several instances of this, one of which is rather curious, if true. It seems that on one occasion he did not put in an appearance at the office, and a substitute had to be selected in his place. That was at the time of the last Russian and Turkish war[4]. When he turned up again next spring he had a puckered wound in the side of his neck which he used to endeavour to conceal with his cravat. Whether the mate's inference that he had been engaged in the war is true or not I cannot say. It was certainly a strange coincidence.

The wind is veering round in an easterly direction, but is still very slight. I think the ice is lying closer than it did yesterday. As far as the eye can reach on every side there is one wide expanse of spotless white, only broken by an occasional rift or the dark shadow of a hummock. To the south there is the narrow lane of blue water which is our sole means of escape, and

---

[1] Jelly fish and sea slugs, respectively

[2] The men have sailed with him before, and the owners have been in contract with him for years, so this is significant

[3] Craigie is a Scottish surname

[4] Fought from 1877-1878, the Russo-Turkish War was a conflict between a coalition of Eastern Orthodox states lead by Russia against the Ottoman Empire. The result was the liberation of the Slavic states (primarily Bulgaria, but also including Romania, Serbia, and Montenegro) and a Russian victory. Austria was awarded Bosnia as a result, and Britain occupied Cyprus

which is closing up every day[1]. The Captain is taking a heavy responsibility upon himself. I hear that the tank of potatoes has been finished, and even the biscuits are running short, but he preserves the same impassible countenance, and spends the greater part of the day at the crow's nest, sweeping the horizon with his glass. His manner is very variable, and he seems to avoid my society, but there has been no repetition of the violence which he showed the other night.

7.30 P.M. — My deliberate opinion is that we are commanded by a madman[2]. Nothing else can account for the extraordinary vagaries of Captain Craigie. It is fortunate that I have kept this journal of our voyage, as it will serve to justify us in case we have to put him under any sort of restraint, a step which I should only consent to as a last resource[3]. Curiously enough it was he himself who suggested lunacy and not mere eccentricity as the secret of his strange conduct. He was standing upon the bridge about an hour ago, peering as usual through his glass[4], while I was walking up and down the quarterdeck. The majority of the men were below at their tea, for the watches have not been regularly kept of late. Tired of walking, I leaned against the bulwarks[5], and admired the mellow glow cast by the sinking sun upon the great ice fields which surround us. I was suddenly aroused from the reverie into which I had fallen by a hoarse voice at my elbow, and starting round I found that the Captain had descended and was standing by my side. He was staring out over the ice with an expression in which horror, surprise, and something approaching to joy were contending for the mastery. In spite of the cold, great drops of perspiration were coursing down his forehead, and he was evidently fearfully excited.

His limbs twitched like those of a man upon the verge of an epileptic fit, and the lines about his mouth were drawn and hard.

"Look!" he gasped, seizing me by the wrist, but still keeping his eyes upon the distant ice, and moving his head slowly in a horizontal direction, as if following some object which was moving across the field of vision.

---

[1] Comparisons to *Frankenstein* – which are already extensive – are particularly acute here: the passionate captain has sailed recklessly into the Pole only for his crew to turn against him as they realize that the ice is closing around them and that escape may never come

[2] As a medical man (and one who seems to specialize in psychology and neurology), the doctor is very intentional about using the term "mad," and is making sure to stress the seriousness and professionalism of his accusation

[3] This was no small matter, and a tremendously illegal action that would have to be thoroughly justified to avoid a conviction of mutiny. Leadership on the high seas was critical, and international law was not merciful to mutineers who rebelled due to poor treatment, differences of temperament, or even poor leadership. Only madness, dereliction of duty, recklessness, piracy, or sabotage were acceptable reasons to usurp a ship's captain

[4] Telescope

[5] The sides of the ship that rise over the upper deck to provide a protective wall

"Look! There, man, there! Between the hummocks! Now coming out from behind the far one! You see her — you MUST see her! There still! Flying from me, by God, flying from me—and gone!"

He uttered the last two words in a whisper of concentrated agony which shall never fade from my remembrance. Clinging to the ratlines[1] he endeavoured to climb up upon the top of the bulwarks as if in the hope of obtaining a last glance at the departing object. His strength was not equal to the attempt, however, and he staggered back against the saloon skylights, where he leaned panting and exhausted. His face was so livid that I expected him to become unconscious, so lost no time in leading him down the companion, and stretching him upon one of the sofas in the cabin. I then poured him out some brandy, which I held to his lips, and which had a wonderful effect upon him, bringing the blood back into his white face and steadying his poor shaking limbs. He raised himself up upon his elbow, and looking round to see that we were alone, he beckoned to me to come and sit beside him.

"You saw it, didn't you?" he asked, still in the same subdued awesome tone so foreign to the nature of the man.

"No, I saw nothing."

His head sank back again upon the cushions. "No, he wouldn't without the glass," he murmured. "He couldn't. It was the glass that showed her to me, and then the eyes of love—the eyes of love[2]. I say, Doc, don't let the steward in! He'll think I'm mad. Just bolt the door, will you!"

I rose and did what he had commanded.

He lay quiet for a while, lost in thought apparently, and then raised himself up upon his elbow again, and asked for some more brandy.

"You don't think I am, do you, Doc?" he asked, as I was putting the bottle back into the after-locker. "Tell me now, as man to man, do you think that I am mad?"

"I think you have something on your mind," I answered, "which is exciting you and doing you a good deal of harm."

"Right there, lad!" he cried, his eyes sparkling from the effects of the brandy. "Plenty on my mind—plenty! But I can work out the latitude and the longitude, and I can handle my sextant and manage my logarithms[3]. You couldn't prove me mad in a court of law, could you, now?"

It was curious to hear the man lying back and coolly arguing out the question of his own sanity.

"Perhaps not," I said; "but still I think you would be wise to get home as soon as you can, and settle down to a quiet life for a while."

---

[1] Rope ladders which lead from the bulwark onto the masts

[2] Another important clue: the phantom chasing him was not hated in life, but adored

[3] The sextant was a tool used to gauge latitude by observing the movements of the sun, and then determining the ship's location on the map by a series of logarithms

"Get home, eh?" he muttered, with a sneer upon his face. "One word for me and two for yourself, lad. Settle down with Flora — pretty little Flora. Are bad dreams signs of madness?"

"Sometimes," I answered.

"What else? What would be the first symptoms?"

"Pains in the head, noises in the ears, flashes before the eyes, delusions—"

"Ah! what about them?" he interrupted. "What would you call a delusion?"

"Seeing a thing which is not there is a delusion."

"But she WAS there!" he groaned to himself. "She WAS there!" and rising, he unbolted the door and walked with slow and uncertain steps to his own cabin, where I have no doubt that he will remain until to-morrow morning. His system seems to have received a terrible shock, whatever it may have been that he imagined himself to have seen. The man becomes a greater mystery every day, though I fear that the solution which he has himself suggested is the correct one, and that his reason is affected. I do not think that a guilty conscience has anything to do with his behaviour. The idea is a popular one among the officers, and, I believe, the crew; but I have seen nothing to support it. He has not the air of a guilty man, but of one who has had terrible usage at the hands of fortune, and who should be regarded as a martyr rather than a criminal[1].

The wind is veering round to the south to-night. God help us if it blocks that narrow pass which is our only road to safety! Situated as we are on the edge of the main Arctic pack, or the "barrier" as it is called by the whalers, any wind from the north has the effect of shredding out the ice around us and allowing our escape, while a wind from the south blows up all the loose ice behind us and hems us in between two packs. God help us, I say again!

September 14th.—Sunday, and a day of rest. My fears have been confirmed, and the thin strip of blue water has disappeared from the southward. Nothing but the great motionless ice fields around us, with their weird hummocks and fantastic pinnacles[2]. There is a deathly silence over their wide expanse which is horrible. No lapping of the waves now, no cries of seagulls or straining of sails, but one deep universal silence in which the murmurs of the seamen, and the creak of their boots upon the white shining deck, seem discordant and out of place. Our only visitor was an

---

1 Although the doctor's characterization must be taken as a subjective response, not as authorial approval, it should be considered when attempting to determine what the captain's relationship is to his fiancée's death, and what her ghost's reason is for haunting him

2 *Weird* and *fantastic* had slightly different connotations at the time: "weird" meaning otherworldly, alien, supernatural, or witch-like and "fantastic" literally meaning "as of a fantasy"

Arctic fox, a rare animal upon the pack[1], though common enough upon the land. He did not come near the ship, however, but after surveying us from a distance fled rapidly across the ice. This was curious conduct, as they generally know nothing of man, and being of an inquisitive nature, become so familiar that they are easily captured. Incredible as it may seem, even this little incident produced a bad effect upon the crew. "Yon puir beastie kens mair, ay, an' sees mair nor you nor me[2]!" was the comment of one of the leading harpooners, and the others nodded their acquiescence. It is vain to attempt to argue against such puerile[3] superstition. They have made up their minds that there is a curse upon the ship, and nothing will ever persuade them to the contrary.

The Captain remained in seclusion all day except for about half an hour in the afternoon, when he came out upon the quarterdeck[4]. I observed that he kept his eye fixed upon the spot where the vision of yesterday had appeared, and was quite prepared for another outburst, but none such came. He did not seem to see me although I was standing close beside him. Divine service was read as usual by the chief engineer[5]. It is a curious thing that in whaling vessels the Church of England Prayer-book is always employed, although there is never a member of that Church among either officers or crew. Our men are all Roman Catholics or Presbyterians[6], the former predominating. Since a ritual is used which is foreign to both, neither can complain that the other is preferred to them, and they listen with all attention and devotion, so that the system has something to recommend it.

A glorious sunset, which made the great fields of ice look like a lake of blood[7]. I have never seen a finer and at the same time more weird effect. Wind is veering round. If it will blow twenty-four hours from the north all will yet be well.

September 15th. — To-day is Flora's birthday. Dear lass! It is well that she cannot see her boy, as she used to call me, shut up among the ice fields with a crazy captain and a few weeks' provisions. No doubt she scans the

---

[1] Certainly rare indeed, though the Arctic fox's hunting grounds extend as far north as there is land

[2] Scots and English: "That poor animal knows more – *true*, and sees more – than you, than me"

[3] Infantile, childlike

[4] The raised deck behind the mainmast where the bridge and poop deck are located

[5] Supervisor of all things relating to the steam engine that propels the ship

[6] Religious Scots are predominantly members of those two traditions – Catholics being more plentiful in the Highlands and Presbyterians in the Lowlands

[7] In one week the sun will disappear until mid-Spring. The sense that death and oblivion is creeping upon them all increases, and is highlighted by this beautiful but sinister vision of blood

shipping list in the Scotsman[1] every morning to see if we are reported from Shetland[2]. I have to set an example to the men and look cheery and unconcerned; but God knows, my heart is very heavy at times.

The thermometer is at nineteen Fahrenheit to-day. There is but little wind, and what there is comes from an unfavourable quarter[3]. Captain is in an excellent humour; I think he imagines he has seen some other omen or vision, poor fellow, during the night, for he came into my room early in the morning, and stooping down over my bunk, whispered, "It wasn't a delusion, Doc; it's all right!" After breakfast he asked me to find out how much food was left, which the second mate and I proceeded to do. It is even less than we had expected. Forward they have half a tank full of biscuits, three barrels of salt meat, and a very limited supply of coffee beans and sugar. In the after-hold and lockers there are a good many luxuries, such as tinned salmon, soups, haricot mutton, etc. , but they will go a very short way among a crew of fifty men. There are two barrels of flour in the store-room, and an unlimited supply of tobacco. Altogether there is about enough to keep the men on half rations for eighteen or twenty days[4]—certainly not more. When we reported the state of things to the Captain, he ordered all hands to be piped[5], and addressed them from the quarterdeck. I never saw him to better advantage. With his tall, well-knit figure, and dark animated face, he seemed a man born to command, and he discussed the situation in a cool sailor-like way which showed that while appreciating the danger he had an eye for every loophole of escape.

"My lads," he said, "no doubt you think I brought you into this fix, if it is a fix, and maybe some of you feel bitter against me on account of it. But you must remember that for many a season no ship that comes to the country has brought in as much oil-money as the old Pole-Star, and every one of you has had his share of it. You can leave your wives behind you in comfort while other poor fellows come back to find their lasses on the parish[6]. If you have to thank me for the one you have to thank me for the other, and we may call it quits. We've tried a bold venture before this and succeeded, so now that we've tried one and failed we've no cause to cry out about it. If the

---

1 *The Scotsman* was (and is) a periodical publication headquartered in Edinburgh founded in 1817. The shipping list is a record of what vessels have been sighted on their way home, which ones have disappeared, and which ones have been confirmed lost. Most major newspapers and business journals included them both for the sakes of family members and for businessmen and speculators whose investments rode on the waves

2 A subarctic archipelago northeast of Scotland which would be the first stop for the *Polestar* on its way home

3 One which would hinder the sails during their push southward, either by blowing against them, or across them

4 A little more than the time than it would take them to landfall at the Shetlands

5 Called together (by piping a whistle)

6 Being supported by donations to the church poor box – 19th century welfare

worst comes to the worst, we can make the land across the ice[1], and lay in a stock of seals which will keep us alive until the spring. It won't come to that, though, for you'll see the Scotch coast again before three weeks are out. At present every man must go on half rations, share and share alike, and no favour to any. Keep up your hearts and you'll pull through this as you've pulled through many a danger before. "These few simple words of his had a wonderful effect upon the crew. His former unpopularity was forgotten[2], and the old harpooner whom I have already mentioned for his superstition, led off three cheers, which were heartily joined in by all hands.

September 16th. — The wind has veered round to the north during the night, and the ice shows some symptoms of opening out. The men are in a good humour in spite of the short allowance upon which they have been placed. Steam is kept up in the engine-room, that there may be no delay should an opportunity for escape present itself[3]. The Captain is in exuberant spirits, though he still retains that wild "fey" expression which I have already remarked upon. This burst of cheerfulness puzzles me more than his former gloom. I cannot understand it. I think I mentioned in an early part of this journal that one of his oddities is that he never permits any person to enter his cabin, but insists upon making his own bed, such as it is, and performing every other office for himself[4]. To my surprise he handed me the key to-day and requested me to go down there and take the time by his chronometer while he measured the altitude of the sun at noon. It is a bare little room, containing a washing-stand and a few books, but little else in the way of luxury, except some pictures upon the walls. The majority of these are small cheap oleographs[5], but there was one water-colour sketch of the head of a young lady which arrested my attention. It was evidently a portrait, and not one of those fancy types of female beauty which sailors particularly affect. No artist could have evolved from his own mind such a curious mixture of character and weakness[6]. The languid, dreamy eyes, with their drooping

---

[1] He suggests walking across the ice to the islands, a last-chance strategy that usually ends in death but that proved effective for Ernest Shackleton's failed Antarctic expedition

[2] Like a classic Byronic hero, the Captain is charismatic, even hypnotic, easily rallying admiration through his willful character. It is a trait that might be important when trying to interpret his tragic background and the fate of his fiancée

[3] Should the ice loosen and the engine be off, a fire would have to be stoked and nurtured for some time while the steam pressure built slowly in the boiler. By the time the engine was ready to turn the propeller, the ice may have shifted back, so the crew are keeping the fire going at all times in case they need to have steam ready

[4] Very unusual, as the captain was typically attended to by a cabin boy

[5] Colored lithographs printed on cloth to look like oil paintings

[6] A critical note: "weakness" in Victorian terms referred to sexual restraint and personal self-control. The woman is not a tramp or a harlot because she appears to have strong character, but she is cursed by a moral weakness that is evident in the painting (again, this

lashes, and the broad, low brow, unruffled by thought or care, were in strong contrast with the clean-cut, prominent jaw, and the resolute set of the lower lip[1]. Underneath it in one of the corners was written, "M. B. , aet. 19[2]." That any one in the short space of nineteen years of existence could develop such strength of will as was stamped upon her face seemed to me at the time to be well-nigh incredible. She must have been an extraordinary woman. Her features have thrown such a glamour[3] over me that, though I had but a fleeting glance at them, I could, were I a draughtsman, reproduce them line for line upon this page of the journal. I wonder what part she has played in our Captain's life. He has hung her picture at the end of his berth[4], so that his eyes continually rest upon it. Were he a less reserved man I should make some remark upon the subject. Of the other things in his cabin there was nothing worthy of mention—uniform coats, a camp-stool, small looking-glass, tobacco-box, and numerous pipes, including an oriental hookah—which, by-the-bye, gives some colour to Mr. Milne's story about his participation in the war, though the connection may seem rather a distant one.

11.20 P.M. — Captain just gone to bed after a long and interesting conversation on general topics. When he chooses he can be a most fascinating companion, being remarkably well-read, and having the power of expressing his opinion forcibly without appearing to be dogmatic[5]. I hate to have my intellectual toes trod upon. He spoke about the nature of the soul, and sketched out the views of Aristotle and Plato[6] upon the subject in

---

is a literary world, not a real one, so such physiological evidence -- which moderns would reject as ludicrous -- is admissible).

[1] Doyle adored phrenological and physiological details, peppering his stories with supposedly germane details about his characters' skulls, chins, noses, and foreheads as if those details were sufficient to explain their character. According to this description, the woman represented is: given to fantasy, imaginative, romantic, lazy, impulsive, driven, determined, stubborn, placid, despondent, somewhat stupid, driven by desire, unintellectual, noble, resolute, proud, and arrogant. Her dichotomous personality is boiled down to her lip and chin with her brow and eyes: the prominent jaw and firm lip represent a strong will, and the low brow (hence the expression) and dreamy eyes indicate intellectual weakness and poor judgment. What Doyle describes here – especially when her beauty is considered – is a proud, arrogant, woman with poor judgment and impulsive tendencies. Such a person might be suspected of being prone to uninhibited sexual expression

[2] *Aet.* is an abbreviation for "at the age of" (Latin: *aetatis*)

[3] Spell, bewitching, hypnosis

[4] Sleeping space, typically an alcove where a mattress and blankets were stowed

[5] The comparisons to Melville's Ahab are immense. Every Byronic hero from Frankenstein's Creature to Rochester to Raskolnikov have the habit of being both very passionate and very well read

[6] Plato believed in a tripartite soul which did not die with the body, but was reincarnated. His soul was divided into three parts: reason, emotion, and desire. Aristotle saw the soul

a masterly manner. He seems to have a leaning for metempsychosis[1] and the doctrines of Pythagoras[2]. In discussing them we touched upon modern spiritualism, and I made some joking allusion to the impostures of Slade[3], upon which, to my surprise, he warned me most impressively against confusing the innocent with the guilty[4], and argued that it would be as logical to brand Christianity as an error because Judas, who professed that religion, was a villain. He shortly afterwards bade me good-night and retired to his room.

The wind is freshening up, and blows steadily from the north. The nights are as dark now as they are in England[5]. I hope to-morrow may set us free from our frozen fetters.

September 17th. — The Bogie[6] again. Thank Heaven that I have strong nerves! The superstition of these poor fellows, and the circumstantial accounts which they give, with the utmost earnestness and self-conviction, would horrify any man not accustomed to their ways. There are many versions of the matter, but the sum-total of them all is that something uncanny has been flitting round the ship all night, and that Sandie M'Donald of Peterhead and "lang" Peter Williamson of Shetland saw it[7], as

---

as existing within the physical body, not apart from it: soul was form and function without immortality. Some commentators interpret Aristotle as believing that the "active mind," or the intellect, was nonetheless immortal.

[1] Metempsychosis – literally "change expressed in the soul" – is the transmigration, after death, of the soul of a human into another body through reincarnation or possession. This may be used to explain the strange appearance of the Arctic fox, although Doyle may have intended this to be a purely natural event

[2] Pythagoras -- -- was a fervent believer in metempsychosis, believing in reincarnation as a series of stages that ultimately led to immortality. He claimed to have recollections of four previous lives, including a beautiful courtesan. In one famous anecdote, Pythagoras claimed to have heard the call of a deceased friend in a dog's bark

[3] Henry Slade (1835 – 1905) was a fraudulent medium whose spectacular hoaxes bordered on the ingenious: playing an accordion with one hand under a table, writing messages on slates with his toes, etc. Exposed multiple times, he was a notorious huckster who attracted the attention of skeptics and magicians who loved to analyze and reproduce his purported powers

[4] Doyle, of course, was a great lover of mediums, and his voice bleeds through here as he warns against forsaking all psychics because of one faker. And I will end here without lecturing on the idiocy of his campaign to defend and elevate this ludicrous profession of frauds

[5] Once "night" becomes like night in the majority of the earth's countries – black and light-less – it will rapidly consume the rest of the daylight and rein alone

[6] Scots: a ghost, monster, or other supernatural creature (hence, bogeyman or boogeyman)

[7] Consummate Highlanders: Peterhead is the easternmost point on the Scottish coast, and the Shetlands, of course, are its northernmost territory. "Lang," incidentally is Scots for "tall"

also did Mr. Milne on the bridge—so, having three witnesses, they can make a better case of it than the second mate did. I spoke to Milne after breakfast, and told him that he should be above such nonsense, and that as an officer he ought to set the men a better example. He shook his weatherbeaten head ominously, but answered with characteristic caution, "Mebbe aye, mebbe na, Doctor," he said; "I didna ca' it a ghaist. I canna' say I preen my faith in sea-bogles an' the like, though there's a mony as claims to ha' seen a' that and waur. I'm no easy feared, but maybe your ain bluid would run a bit cauld, mun, if instead o' speerin' aboot it in daylicht ye were wi' me last night, an' seed an awfu' like shape, white an' gruesome, whiles here, whiles there, an' it greetin' and ca'ing in the darkness like a bit lambie that hae lost its mither. Ye would na' be sae ready to put it a' doon to auld wives' clavers then, I'm thinkin'[1]." I saw it was hopeless to reason with him, so contented myself with begging him as a personal favour to call me up the next time the spectre appeared — a request to which he acceded with many ejaculations expressive of his hopes that such an opportunity might never arise.

As I had hoped, the white desert behind us has become broken by many thin streaks of water which intersect it in all directions. Our latitude to-day was 80° 52' N[2]. , which shows that there is a strong southerly drift upon the pack. Should the wind continue favourable it will break up as rapidly as it formed. At present we can do nothing but smoke and wait and hope for the best. I am rapidly becoming a fatalist. When dealing with such uncertain factors as wind and ice a man can be nothing else. Perhaps it was the wind and sand of the Arabian deserts which gave the minds of the original followers of Mahomet their tendency to bow to kismet[3].

These spectral alarms have a very bad effect upon the Captain. I feared that it might excite his sensitive mind, and endeavoured to conceal the absurd story from him, but unfortunately he overheard one of the men making an allusion to it, and insisted upon being informed about it. As I had expected, it brought out all his latent lunacy in an exaggerated form. I can hardly believe that this is the same man who discoursed philosophy last night with the most critical acumen and coolest judgment. He is pacing backwards and forwards upon the quarterdeck like a caged tiger, stopping now and again to throw out his hands with a yearning gesture, and stare

---

[1] A translation of the Scots English: "Maybe yes, maybe no, Doctor. I didn't call it a ghost. I cannot say I attach my faith to sea-ghosts and the like, though there's many who claim to have seen all that and worse. I'm not easily frightened, but maybe your own blood would run a bit cold, my friend, if instead of peering about in the daylight you were with me last night and saw an awful shape – white and gruesome – sometimes here and sometimes there – and it weeping and calling in the darkness like a little lamb that has lost its mother. You wouldn't be so ready to rationalize it as old wives' prattle then, I'm thinking"

[2] Since their original latitude of Lat. 81° 40' N, they have begun to inch their way back southward

[3] From the Arabic *kismat*, meaning a portion or allowance, the concept of divine fate or destiny

impatiently out over the ice. He keeps up a continual mutter to himself, and once he called out, "But a little time, love—but a little time[1]!" Poor fellow, it is sad to see a gallant seaman and accomplished gentleman reduced to such a pass, and to think that imagination and delusion can cow a mind to which real danger was but the salt of life. Was ever a man in such a position as I, between a demented captain and a ghost-seeing mate? I sometimes think I am the only really sane man aboard the vessel—except perhaps the second engineer, who is a kind of ruminant, and would care nothing for all the fiends in the Red Sea so long as they would leave him alone and not disarrange his tools[2].

The ice is still opening rapidly, and there is every probability of our being able to make a start to-morrow morning. They will think I am inventing when I tell them at home all the strange things that have befallen me.

12 P.M. — I have been a good deal startled, though I feel steadier now, thanks to a stiff glass of brandy. I am hardly myself yet, however, as this handwriting will testify. The fact is, that I have gone through a very strange experience, and am beginning to doubt whether I was justified in branding every one on board as madmen because they professed to have seen things which did not seem reasonable to my understanding. Pshaw! I am a fool to let such a trifle unnerve me; and yet, coming as it does after all these alarms, it has an additional significance, for I cannot doubt either Mr. Manson's story or that of the mate, now that I have experienced that which I used formerly to scoff at.

After all it was nothing very alarming—a mere sound, and that was all. I cannot expect that any one reading this, if any one ever should read it, will sympathise with my feelings, or realise the effect which it produced upon me at the time. Supper was over, and I had gone on deck to have a quiet pipe before turning in. The night was very dark—so dark that, standing under the quarter-boat[3], I was unable to see the officer upon the bridge[4]. I

---

[1] Another clue. The captain is putting something off with his ghostly companion. If it is death, that conflicts with his apparent death wish, although he seems more reckless than suicidal having never taken the plunge with bullet or noose that we know of. Speculation on this point is purely theoretical, though it seems impossible to argue the point that the spirit is longing to be reunited and that the captain is avoiding this rendezvous for whatever reason, though not without acknowledging its necessity

[2] We may presume that this man is meant to be a Lowlander, who are stereotyped as the pragmatic, rational, materialist, orderly, sensible, stubborn, and stingy brand of Scot

[3] A small boat suspended from the rear flank of the ship by pulleys on davits, or wooden arms which rotated out over the sea and in over the deck depending on whether the boat was being lowered

[4] An officer would always be on the bridge at all hours to supervise and to be present in the case of an emergency. At night this was typically a mate (first, second, or third) while the captain slept

think I have already mentioned the extraordinary silence which prevails in these frozen seas. In other parts of the world, be they ever so barren, there is some slight vibration of the air—some faint hum, be it from the distant haunts of men, or from the leaves of the trees, or the wings of the birds, or even the faint rustle of the grass that covers the ground. One may not actively perceive the sound, and yet if it were withdrawn it would be missed. It is only here in these Arctic seas that stark, unfathomable stillness obtrudes itself upon you in all its gruesome reality. You find your tympanum[1] straining to catch some little murmur, and dwelling eagerly upon every accidental sound within the vessel. In this state I was leaning against the bulwarks when there arose from the ice almost directly underneath me a cry, sharp and shrill, upon the silent air of the night, beginning, as it seemed to me, at a note such as prima donna never reached, and mounting from that ever higher and higher until it culminated in a long wail of agony, which might have been the last cry of a lost soul[2]. The ghastly scream is still ringing in my ears. Grief, unutterable grief, seemed to be expressed in it, and a great longing, and yet through it all there was an occasional wild note of exultation[3]. It shrilled out from close beside me, and yet as I glared into the darkness I could discern nothing. I waited some little time, but without hearing any repetition of the sound, so I came below, more shaken than I have ever been in my life before. As I came down the companion I met Mr. Milne coming up to relieve the watch. "Weel, Doctor," he said, "maybe that's auld wives' clavers tae? Did ye no hear it skirling? Maybe that's a supersteetion? What d'ye think o't noo[4]?" I was obliged to

---

[1] The drum-like (hence the name) membrane of the ear which translates vibrations to sound

[2] The spectre most closely resembles the Celtic myth of the banshee, an Irish spirit whose hideous cry warns of impending doom, or the death of a member of the family they have attached to. In Scottish lore (since this is a very Scottish story), the corresponding visitant is called the *Bean nighe* (pronounced ben-nee-YUH, it means “washer woman” and is etymologically related to the banshee, which – in Irish – is *Bean sí*, or “woman of the graves/barrows”). The *Bean nighe* is either a hideous witch with pendulous breasts and webbed feet and one nostril, or a beautiful girl. Said to be the spirits of women who die in childbirth, the washer woman is said to haunt the living until the day when they would have otherwise died under normal circumstances. They are seen bending over rivers and washing the blood out of the garments of those who are about to die (especially in battle or by murder). If approached politely, she will grant wishes, provide protection, or surrender the names of those about to die. While there is no overt connection to the *Bean nighe* spirit in the text, the concept of a woman dying in childbirth may prove a possible explanation for the captain’s misery: has the fiancée died after being premaritally impregnated by the passionate captain? Has she died through a dalliance with another lover? All are possibilities

[3] Grief, longing, exultation. Like the stormy captain the spectre is characterized by wild shifts in emotion, passion, and fiery sensibilities

[4] “Well, Doctor, maybe that’s a bunch of old wives’ gossip too, eh? Did you not hear it screeching? Maybe that’s a superstition, eh? What you think of it now?”

apologise to the honest fellow, and acknowledge that I was as puzzled by it as he was. Perhaps to-morrow things may look different. At present I dare hardly write all that I think. Reading it again in days to come, when I have shaken off all these associations, I should despise myself for having been so weak.

September 18th[1]. — Passed a restless and uneasy night, still haunted by that strange sound. The Captain does not look as if he had had much repose either, for his face is haggard and his eyes bloodshot. I have not told him of my adventure of last night, nor shall I. He is already restless and excited, standing up, sitting down, and apparently utterly unable to keep still.

A fine lead[2] appeared in the pack this morning, as I had expected, and we were able to cast off our ice-anchor, and steam about twelve miles in a west- sou'-westerly direction[3]. We were then brought to a halt by a great floe as massive as any which we have left behind us. It bars our progress completely, so we can do nothing but anchor again and wait until it breaks up, which it will probably do within twenty-four hours, if the wind holds. Several bladder-nosed seals were seen swimming in the water, and one was shot, an immense creature more than eleven feet long. They are fierce, pugnacious animals, and are said to be more than a match for a bear. Fortunately they are slow and clumsy in their movements, so that there is little danger in attacking them upon the ice.

The Captain evidently does not think we have seen the last of our troubles, though why he should take a gloomy view of the situation is more than I can fathom, since every one else on board considers that we have had a miraculous escape, and are sure now to reach the open sea.

"I suppose you think it's all right now, Doctor?" he said, as we sat together after dinner.

"I hope so," I answered.

"We mustn't be too sure—and yet no doubt you are right. We'll all be in the arms of our own true loves before long, lad, won't we[4]? But we mustn't be too sure—we mustn't be too sure. "

He sat silent a little, swinging his leg thoughtfully backwards and forwards. "Look here," he continued; "it's a dangerous place this, even at its best—a treacherous, dangerous place. I have known men cut off very suddenly in a land like this. A slip would do it sometimes—a single slip, and down you go through a crack, and only a bubble on the green water to show

---

[1] In four days night will be reigning endlessly in the Arctic

[2] Meaning a pathway through the ice, or a crack or series of rends suggesting the creation of a pathway

[3] Being just slightly south of due-west, heading SWS would be sending them towards the Greenland coastline. After a hundred miles of steaming in this direction they could steer due south for Scotland

[4] Obviously dripping with morbid implications for himself

where it was that you sank. It's a queer thing," he continued with a nervous laugh, "but all the years I've been in this country I never once thought of making a will—not that I have anything to leave in particular, but still when a man is exposed to danger he should have everything arranged and ready—don't you think so?"

"Certainly," I answered, wondering what on earth he was driving at.

"He feels better for knowing it's all settled," he went on. "Now if anything should ever befall me, I hope that you will look after things for me. There is very little in the cabin, but such as it is I should like it to be sold, and the money divided in the same proportion as the oil-money among the crew. The chronometer[1] I wish you to keep yourself as some slight remembrance of our voyage. Of course all this is a mere precaution, but I thought I would take the opportunity of speaking to you about it. I suppose I might rely upon you if there were any necessity?"

"Most assuredly," I answered; "and since you are taking this step, I may as well—" "You! you!" he interrupted. "YOU'RE all right. What the devil is the matter with YOU? There, I didn't mean to be peppery, but I don't like to hear a young fellow, that has hardly began life, speculating about death[2]. Go up on deck and get some fresh air into your lungs instead of talking nonsense in the cabin, and encouraging me to do the same. "

The more I think of this conversation of ours the less do I like it. Why should the man be settling his affairs at the very time when we seem to be emerging from all danger? There must be some method in his madness. Can it be that he contemplates suicide? I remember that upon one occasion he spoke in a deeply reverent manner of the heinousness of the crime[3] of self-destruction. I shall keep my eye upon him, however, and though I cannot obtrude upon the privacy of his cabin, I shall at least make a point of remaining on deck as long as he stays up.

Mr. Milne pooh-poohs my fears, and says it is only the "skipper's little way." He himself takes a very rosy view of the situation. According to him

---

[1] A large (and frankly very expensive) clock which is used as a navigational tool. The marine chronometer was so precise and reliable that it was used to measure longitude, since time was the only means of figuring how far the ship had moved across the earth's longitudinal axes. Along with the sextant (used to configure latitude), the compass (direction), the barometer (weather changes), and the charts, it was one of the key elements of any ship's successful voyage

[2] The captain presaged that the doctor was about to communicate his bequests in return, a step which sets him off, leading one to suspect that he is thoroughly optimistic about the ship's safe return, and that his precaution is not one of pessimism (if the ship doesn't make it; if we hit a storm; if I starve; if I sicken and die; if I fall overboard) but one of intended suicide

[3] Indeed: suicide was illegal in Britain until 1961, in fact it was a felony according to *felo de se* (felon against himself) laws, though most coroner's juries ruled suicides as *non compos mentis* (not of sound mind), and ruled in favor of temporary insanity – what we today simply call depression

we shall be out of the ice by the day after to-morrow, pass Jan Meyen[1] two days after that, and sight Shetland in little more than a week. I hope he may not be too sanguine. His opinion may be fairly balanced against the gloomy precautions of the Captain, for he is an old and experienced seaman, and weighs his words well before uttering them.

ℵ

The long-impending catastrophe has come at last. I hardly know what to write about it. The Captain is gone. He may come back to us again alive, but I fear me—I fear me[2]. It is now seven o'clock of the morning of the 19th of September. I have spent the whole night traversing the great ice-floe in front of us with a party of seamen in the hope of coming upon some trace of him, but in vain. I shall try to give some account of the circumstances which attended upon his disappearance. Should any one ever chance to read the words which I put down, I trust they will remember that I do not write from conjecture or from hearsay, but that I, a sane and educated man, am describing accurately what actually occurred before my very eyes. My inferences are my own, but I shall be answerable for the facts.

The Captain remained in excellent spirits after the conversation which I have recorded. He appeared to be nervous and impatient, however, frequently changing his position, and moving his limbs in an aimless choreic[3] way which is characteristic of him at times. In a quarter of an hour he went upon deck seven times, only to descend after a few hurried paces. I followed him each time, for there was something about his face which confirmed my resolution of not letting him out of my sight. He seemed to observe the effect which his movements had produced, for he endeavoured by an over-done hilarity, laughing boisterously at the very smallest of jokes, to quiet my apprehensions.

After supper he went on to the poop once more, and I with him. The night was dark and very still, save for the melancholy soughing of the wind among the spars. A thick cloud was coming up from the northwest, and the ragged tentacles which it threw out in front of it were drifting across the face of the moon, which only shone now and again through a rift in the wrack. The Captain paced rapidly backwards and forwards, and then seeing me still dogging him, he came across and hinted that he thought I should be better below—which, I need hardly say, had the effect of strengthening my resolution to remain on deck.

I think he forgot about my presence after this, for he stood silently leaning over the taffrail[4], and peering out across the great desert of snow,

---

[1] A rosy prognosis indeed: Jan Meyen is a Norwegian island and outpost some 750 miles from Iceland, and 1600 miles from the British coast

[2] Meaning: "But I am afraid," or "But I worry," not "I fear myself"

[3] Spasmodic, fitful, jerking

[4] Railing on the rear of a ship

part of which lay in shadow, while part glittered mistily in the moonlight. Several times I could see by his movements that he was referring to his watch, and once he muttered a short sentence, of which I could only catch the one word "ready." I confess to having felt an eerie feeling creeping over me as I watched the loom of his tall figure through the darkness, and noted how completely he fulfilled the idea of a man who is keeping a tryst[1]. A tryst with whom? Some vague perception began to dawn upon me as I pieced one fact with another, but I was utterly unprepared for the sequel.

By the sudden intensity of his attitude I felt that he saw something. I crept up behind him. He was staring with an eager questioning gaze at what seemed to be a wreath of mist, blown swiftly in a line with the ship. It was a dim, nebulous body, devoid of shape[2], sometimes more, sometimes less apparent, as the light fell on it. The moon was dimmed in its brilliancy at the moment by a canopy of thinnest cloud, like the coating of an anemone.

"Coming, lass, coming," cried the skipper, in a voice of unfathomable tenderness and compassion[3], like one who soothes a beloved one by some favour long looked for, and as pleasant to bestow as to receive.

What followed happened in an instant. I had no power to interfere.

He gave one spring to the top of the bulwarks, and another which took him on to the ice[4], almost to the feet of the pale misty figure. He held out his hands as if to clasp it, and so ran into the darkness with outstretched arms and loving words. I still stood rigid and motionless, straining my eyes after his retreating form, until his voice died away in the distance. I never thought to see him again, but at that moment the moon shone out brilliantly through a chink in the cloudy heaven, and illuminated the great field of ice. Then I saw his dark figure already a very long way off, running with prodigious speed across the frozen plain[5]. That was the last glimpse

---

[1] A discreet appointment, especially between lovers

[2] While we may not appreciate it, Doyle succeeds in avoiding the Gothic tropes of the time by presenting us with a strange, ethereal, non-form rather than a woman wrapped in a cloak holding a blue lantern, etc. His phantom is surprising, modern, and eerie, and stands out as one of the more original spectres of Victorian supernatural fiction, bringing to mind such ghosts as the twirling dust in Bernard Capes "An Eddy on the Floor," the clammy touch in Braddon's "The Cold Embrace," the colorless monstrosity in Ambrose Bierce's "The Damned Thing"

[3] Again, the emotions are bizarre: compliant, tender, and eager, he seems to court death, yet seems to have been avoiding it. The captain both has a death wish and a stubborn resistance to destruction (otherwise he would have killed himself years ago), but they coalesce and harmonize in this scene where he finally finds himself ready to surrender to the call of his dead lover

[4] Impossible to say how he managed to do this without shattering his ankles or shins: the jump from the quarterdeck bulwark to the ice below would have been a good ten to twenty feet

[5] Running from, running with, or running towards? It is unclear here, but we may assume the later of the three

which we caught of him—perhaps the last we ever shall. A party was organised to follow him, and I accompanied them, but the men's hearts were not in the work, and nothing was found. Another will be formed within a few hours. I can hardly believe I have not been dreaming, or suffering from some hideous nightmare, as I write these things down.

7.30 P.M. — Just returned dead beat and utterly tired out from a second unsuccessful search for the Captain. The floe is of enormous extent, for though we have traversed at least twenty miles of its surface, there has been no sign of its coming to an end. The frost has been so severe of late that the overlying snow is frozen as hard as granite, otherwise we might have had the footsteps to guide us. The crew are anxious that we should cast off and steam round the floe and so to the southward, for the ice has opened up during the night, and the sea is visible upon the horizon. They argue that Captain Craigie is certainly dead, and that we are all risking our lives to no purpose by remaining when we have an opportunity of escape. Mr. Milne and I have had the greatest difficulty in persuading them to wait until to-morrow night, and have been compelled to promise that we will not under any circumstances delay our departure longer than that. We propose therefore to take a few hours' sleep, and then to start upon a final search.

September 20th, evening. — I crossed the ice this morning with a party of men exploring the southern part of the floe, while Mr. Milne went off in a northerly direction.We pushed on for ten or twelve miles without seeing a trace of any living thing except a single bird, which fluttered a great way over our heads, and which by its flight I should judge to have been a falcon[1]. The southern extremity of the ice field tapered away into a long narrow spit which projected out into the sea. When we came to the base of this promontory, the men halted, but I begged them to continue to the extreme end of it, that we might have the satisfaction of knowing that no possible chance had been neglected.

---

[1] Two points of interest here: firstly, a bird, especially a high-flying bird is a symbol of the spirit, freedom, and immortality. Birds are often used in scenes of a releasing death (as of one who has been suffering and has now found peace), or in scenes of hauntings. Owls, ravens, albatrosses, songbirds, and birds of prey are commonly employed to stand in for, represent, or manifest as the spirit of a dead person. *The Rime of the Ancient Mariner* famously employed an albatross to represent the spiritual innocence of the south pole, while J. Sheridan Le Fanu included judgmental owls to project guilt, Edgar Allan Poe's raven represented the spiritual gulf between the remembered dead and the lonely living, and Bram Stoker used the mammalian aerial counterpart, the bat, to represent a perversion of the innocence often represented by symbolic birds. Secondly, given the captain's obsession with reincarnation, combined with the strange appearance of the fox, it is not beyond the realm of possibility to suggest that the falcon may *literally* be the captain's newly freed soul escaping its earthly sufferings

We had hardly gone a hundred yards before M'Donald of Peterhead cried out that he saw something in front of us, and began to run. We all got a glimpse of it and ran too. At first it was only a vague darkness against the white ice, but as we raced along together it took the shape of a man, and eventually of the man of whom we were in search. He was lying face downwards upon a frozen bank. Many little crystals of ice and feathers of snow had drifted on to him as he lay, and sparkled upon his dark seaman's jacket. As we came up some wandering puff of wind caught these tiny flakes in its vortex, and they whirled up into the air, partially descended again, and then, caught once more in the current, sped rapidly away in the direction of the sea. To my eyes it seemed but a snow-drift, but many of my companions averred that it started up in the shape of a woman, stooped over the corpse and kissed it, and then hurried away across the floe. I have learned never to ridicule any man's opinion, however strange it may seem. Sure it is that Captain Nicholas Craigie had met with no painful end, for there was a bright smile upon his blue pinched features, and his hands were still outstretched as though grasping at the strange visitor which had summoned him away into the dim world that lies beyond the grave[1].

We buried him the same afternoon with the ship's ensign around him[2], and a thirty-two pound shot at his feet[3]. I read the burial service, while the rough sailors wept like children, for there were many who owed much to his kind heart, and who showed now the affection which his strange ways had repelled during his lifetime. He went off the grating with a dull, sullen splash, and as I looked into the green water I saw him go down, down, down until he was but a little flickering patch of white hanging upon the outskirts of eternal darkness. Then even that faded away, and he was gone. There he shall lie, with his secret and his sorrows and his mystery all still buried in his breast, until that great day when the sea shall give up its dead[4], and Nicholas Craigie come out from among the ice with the smile upon his face, and his stiffened arms outstretched in greeting[5]. I pray that his lot may be a happier one in that life than it has been in this.

---

[1] Indeed, this appears to be the situation – the captain has followed his phantom into the icy wastes, wherein he joined her spirit after freezing to death in the elements

[2] The flag denoting the ship's nationality – in this case, a scarlet flag with the British union flag tucked in the top corner, or canton. It is probable that Doyle means the flag was draped over him before he was dropped into the sea, sewed into a shroud made from sailcloth. To bury him with the flag would have been an extreme act of unpatriotic disrespect

[3] A cannonball meant to ensure that his body sank

[4] He is paraphrasing from the Anglican hominy for the dead: *"We therefore commit his body to the deep, to be turned into corruption, looking for the resurrection of the body, (when the Sea shall give up her dead,) and the life of the world to come, through our Lord Jesus Christ; who at his coming shall change our vile body, that it may be like his glorious body, according to the mighty working, whereby he is able to subdue all things to himself"*

[5] A rather grisly fantasy, but such are the morbid thoughts of the grieving

I shall not continue my journal. Our road to home lies plain and clear before us, and the great ice field will soon be but a remembrance of the past. It will be some time before I get over the shock produced by recent events. When I began this record of our voyage I little thought of how I should be compelled to finish it. I am writing these final words in the lonely cabin, still starting at times and fancying I hear the quick nervous step of the dead man upon the deck above me. I entered his cabin to-night, as was my duty, to make a list of his effects in order that they might be entered in the official log. All was as it had been upon my previous visit, save that the picture which I have described as having hung at the end of his bed had been cut out of its frame, as with a knife, and was gone[1]. With this last link in a strange chain of evidence I close my diary of the voyage of the *Pole-Star*[2].

ဢ

[NOTE by Dr. John M'Alister Ray, senior. — I have read over the strange events connected with the death of the Captain of the Pole-Star, as narrated in the journal of my son. That everything occurred exactly as he describes it. I have the fullest confidence, and, indeed, the most positive certainty, for I know him to be a strong-nerved and unimaginative man, with the strictest regard for veracity. Still, the story is, on the face of it, so vague and so improbable, that I was long opposed to its publication[3]. Within the last few days, however, I have had independent testimony upon the subject which throws a new light upon it. I had run down to Edinburgh to attend a meeting of the British Medical Association[4], when I chanced to come across Dr. P—, an old college chum of mine, now practising at Saltash[5], in Devonshire. Upon my telling him of this experience of my son's, he declared to me that he was familiar with the man, and proceeded, to my no small surprise, to give me a description of him, which tallied remarkably well with that given in the journal, except that he depicted him as a younger man[6]. According to his account, he had been engaged to a young lady of singular

---

1 The captain has unquestionably taken this with him to the grave. Had they searched him (as they should have) it would probably appeared in his breast pocket or tucked in his shirt. It is not a mutilation or a desecration, but a release: he has cut her free of her frame – free from the fixed, dead place where she was imprisoned in his heart – just as he has been cut free from life

2 The doctor means to imply an undeniable connection between the captain's behavior, disappearance, and death, and the girl in the portrait. While it may seem obvious to us from a literary standpoint, Doyle does well to underscore this at the conclusion in order to drive home the relationship between this unknown woman and the dead captain

3 Lest it discredit his son's sanity, credibility, or professionalism

4 Founded in 1832, a trade union for medical professionals

5 A small city of 16,000 in southwest England. It is in Cornwall, not Devonshire, though just barely

6 Ergo, this story comes from the captain's youth

beauty residing upon the Cornish coast[1]. During his absence at sea[2] his betrothed had died under circumstances of peculiar horror[3].]

---

[1] The wild, romantic, rugged terrain of Cornwall in southwest England is a fitting origin to this stormy, Byronic lover

[2] This important detail precludes some of the most obvious theories, such as murder, although the mystery is made thicker as a result, since it seems to absolve him of responsibility (not necessarily)

[3] "Circumstance of peculiar horror..." So much to unpack from so few details. As has been mentioned earlier, the possibilities seem to hinge principally on the doctor's phrenological observations, which painted the picture of a passionate and impulsive woman of poor judgment and great beauty. A sexual undertone is impossible to remove from these interpretations, and while there may be other valid backstories, I find it unlikely. The causes include murder, suicide, death in childbirth, suicide due to pregnancy, murder or suicide resulting from an affair, or some sort of physical affliction caused by guilt. Of the captain we have been led to doubt that he is somehow guilty, but rather a victim. Of the girl we find that her spirit follows him imploringly. Concerning their relationship we find it to be tragic but loving, seemingly more fired by loss and heartache than guilt. Upon analysis I find that there are four principle possibilities – four narratives that seem to make the most sense, all of which hinge on the fiancée's characterization as impulsively passionate:

1. TRAGEDY. In this narrative the loss is deeply colored by pathos and heartbreak. The girl and the captain each suffer from hot temperments which lead to the consummation of their relationship before marriage, followed by a pregnancy. While the captain is at sea he does not know that his fiancée has been impregnated, and upon his return he learns that she has either died in childbirth (like a *Bean nighe*), or through a botched abortion, or through suicide at the thought of her shame. This explains the guiltless sorrow that hangs over the captain, flavored nonetheless with a sharp sense of penance. He has not killed her, nor has she betrayed him, but they did violate their society's mores, and the result has been her death. He feels responsible – though not necessarily guilty – and is shamed by the death, which almost certainly led to the demise of the child (either naturally or through an abortion), which found him alone and their relationship thoroughly dead upon his return. I personally advocate this view.

2. BETRAYAL. This version views the woman's death as resulting from her affair with another man. The captain is devoted to her, but her judgment is poor and spontaneous, and her spirit is wild and hungry. Alone during his absence, she begins an affair with another man. This affair ends horribly. Perhaps the lover murders her for becoming pregnant (a common plot in British folksongs), or for refusing to continue their relationship, or perhaps she dies during childbirth, from an abortion, or as a result of suicide.

3. MURDER. This is the least likely of the three, and it follows the theory that number two is also accurate, and that the captain murders his lover for her infidelity. Following the logic of Sherlock Holmes, it is entirely possible to murder a person without being in the room with the person. She may have been killed by an accumulating poison (like in Agatha Christie's *The Mysterious Affair at Styles*), or by some trap devised by him, or by a hired agent. In this scenario, both are guilty – one of infidelity, one of murder – and those there

IT is entirely reasonable to be suspicious of the good captain's involvement in his fiancée's death, and regular readers of both Arthur Conan Doyle and Victorian ghost stories will have plenty of precedent to suggest that he is not merely a heartbroken lover. Mary E. Braddon's "The Cold Embrace," Elizabeth Gaskell's "The Old Nurse's Story," Mary E. Wilkins Freeman's "The Shadow's on the Wall," Jerome K. Jerome's "The Man of Science," Kipling's "The End of the Passage," and Henry James' "The Romance of Certain Old Clothes" are exemplars of the genre, and each feature a similar set-up: a person responsible – either directly or indirectly – for the death or ruin of another person are haunted to the point of extinction by their victim. The last six words of the story suggests something of the sinister beyond mere disease, and Doyle demonstrates a tremendous (and, considering the melodrama that often overwhelmed the genre, applaud-able) amount of restraint by remaining vague to the point of confusion about his hero's backstory. Precedent does imply foul play, but – as Doyle's silence on the matter suggests – this is ultimately immaterial. My personal thoughts on the matter – my theory if you like – is that both parties bear guilt of some kind, and I am disinclined to suspect the captain of murder, though that is one of four possibilities I have identified. Without going into too much detail, it seems most probable to me that the headstrong and impulsive fiancée was either murdered by the captain or a lover, died from a hideous disease, or expired during childbirth as a result of extramarital sex – again either with the captain or a lover. An expanded over view of these four theories can be read in the final note to this story. Like Shelley (Frankenstein) and Coleridge (Rime of the Ancient Mariner), Doyle banishes his protagonist to the polar wastelands as a means of penance – penance for murder, for sexual seduction, for abandonment, for abuse, or for simply failing to be there for her at her death. Whether responsible for the death or merely depressed by it, this Captain Ahab has shunned society, begrudging romantic bliss (like that of his surgeon) in pursuit of spiritual absolution. By putting his body is peril (both in the frozen Arctic floes and the blistering Turkish battlefields), he hopes to atone for his sins, and ultimately – at the cost of his life in an act of self-execution – he receives his dearly sought

is no animosity on the part of the ghost, while the captain seems tormented – she has paid for her sin in her killing, while he still suffers for his.

4. DISEASE. Least likely and dullest of all – devoid of any dramatic tension or literary necessity – is the boring suggestion that she died of a disease during his absence, and he is simply sad that he wasn't there to be with her. This doesn't explain the mysterious "horror" of her demise, however, and I doubt that Doyle with his love of sensation and crime would mean to imply this possibility in lieu of one of the previous three. I strongly advocate for the first solution, but each reader is responsible for their own opinion

extreme unction and appears to die in the presence of a peace that life forbade him. Doyle's story is swept with grand but understated Romanticism in the elegant tradition of Melville, Shelley, and Coleridge which is difficult to find except in the very best examples of Victorian supernaturalism, which was often either sere and ambiguous (á la Henry James) or garish and vulgar (á la Varney the Vampire). Here is truly a disciplined, artistic masterwork of the genre, a pleasant surprise from such an unseasoned writer.

HERE Doyle provides us with a fine, chilly little ghost story written in the Irish Gothic tradition. It reads very much like a genuine folk tale: lacking the finer points of a literary story, but somewhat purer and more direct as a result. He makes no buts about it: this is a bogey tale, and like the spooky writings of M. R. James, E. F. Benson, or Bram Stoker, it seeks to do very little other than to present a pleasantly eerie narrative for our amusement. The story is effective at its mission, and sounds astonishingly like a typical Victorian ghost story in the tradition of Rhoda Broughton, Edith Nesbit, Amelia B. Edwards, and especially J. Sheridan Le Fanu. In fact, the tale bears a number of obvious similarities to Le Fanu's straight forward ghost episodes, particularly "The Village Bully," and in various ways to "Mr Justice Harbottle," "Ghost Stories of the Tiled House," "Ultor de Lacy," "Squire Toby's Will," "The Dead Sexton," "Sir Dominick's Bargain," and The Haunted Baronet. It follows the somber exploit of a boxer who is waylaid on his way to duel a champion in London, but rapidly finds himself confronted with a much worthier (and gruesome) opponent.

The Bully of Brocas Court

{1921}

THAT year — it was in 1878 — the South Midland Yeomanry were out near Luton, and the real question which appealed to every man in the great camp was not how to prepare for a possible European war, but the far more vital one how to get a man who could stand up for ten rounds to Farrier-Sergeant Burton. Slogger Burton was a fine upstanding fourteen stone of bone and brawn, with a smack in either hand which would leave any ordinary mortal senseless. A match must be found for him somewhere or his head would outgrow his dragoon helmet. Therefore Sir Fred Milburn, better known as Mumbles, was dispatched to London to find if among the fancy there was no one who would make a journey in order to take down the number of the bold dragoon.

They were bad days, those, in the prize-ring. The old knuckle-fighting had died out in scandal and disgrace, smothered by the pestilent crowd of betting men and ruffians of all sorts who hung upon the edge of the movement and brought disgrace and ruin upon the decent fighting men, who were often humble heroes whose gallantry has never been surpassed. An honest sportsman who desired to see a fight was usually set upon by villains, against whom he had no redress, since he was himself engaged on what was technically an illegal action. He was stripped in the open Street, his purse taken, and his head split open if he ventured to resist. The ring-side could only be reached by men who were prepared to fight their way there with cudgels and hunting crops. No wonder that the classic sport was attended now by those only who had nothing to lose.

On the other hand, the era of the reserved building and the legal glove-fight had not yet arisen, and the cult was in a strange intermediate condition. It was impossible to regulate it, and equally impossible to abolish it, since nothing appeals more directly and powerfully to the average Briton. Therefore there were scrambling contests in stableyards and barns, hurried visits to France, secret meetings at dawn in wild parts of the country, and all manner of evasions and experiments. The men themselves became as unsatisfactory as their surroundings. There could be no honest open contest, and the loudest bragger talked his way to the top of the list. Only across the Atlantic had the huge figure of John Lawrence Sullivan appeared, who was destined to be the last of the earlier system and the first of the later one.

Things being in this condition, the sporting Yeomanry Captain found it no easy matter among the boxing saloons and sporting pubs of London to find a man who could be relied upon to give a good account of the huge Farrier-Sergeant. Heavy-weights were at a premium. Finally his choice fell upon Alf Stevens of Kentish Town, an excellent rising middle-weight who had never yet known defeat and had indeed some claims to the championship. His professional experience and craft would surely make up for the three stone of weight which separated him from the formidable dragoon. It was in this hope that Sir Fred Milburn engaged him, and proceeded to convey him in his dog-cart behind a pair of spanking greys to the camp of the Yeomen. They were to start one evening, drive up the Great North Road, sleep at St. Albans, and finish their journey next day.

The prize-fighter met the sporting Baronet at the Golden Cross, where Bates, the little groom, was standing at the head of the spirited horses. Stevens, a pale-faced, clean-cut young fellow, mounted beside his employer and waved his hand to a little knot of fighting men, rough, collarless, reefer-coated fellows who had gathered to bid their comrade good-bye. "Good luck, Alf!" came in a hoarse chorus as the boy released the horses' heads and sprang in behind, while the high dog-cart swung swiftly round the curve into Trafalgar Square.

Sir Frederick was so busy steering among the traffic in Oxford Street and the Edgware Road that he had little thought for anything else, but when he got into the edges of the country near Hendon, and the hedges had at last taken the place of that endless panorama of brick dwellings, he let his horses go easy with a loose rein while he turned his attention to the young man at his side. He had found him by correspondence and recommendation, so that he had some curiosity now in looking him over. Twilight was already falling and the light dim, but what the Baronet saw pleased him well. The man was a fighter every inch, clean-cut, deep-chested, with the long straight cheek and deep-set eye which goes with an obstinate courage. Above all, he was a man who had never yet met his master and was still upheld by the deep sustaining confidence which is never quite the same after a single defeat. The Baronet chuckled as he realized what a surprise packet was being carried north for the Farrier-Sergeant.

"I suppose you are in some sort of training, Stevens?" he remarked, turning to his companion. "Yes, sir; I am fit to fight for my life."

"So I should judge by the look of you."

"I live regular all the time, sir, but I was matched against Mike Connor for this last week-end and scaled down to eleven four. Then he paid forfeit, and here I am at the top of my form." "That's lucky. You'll need it all against a man who has a pull of three stone and four inches." The young man smiled.

"I have given greater odds than that, sir."

"I dare say. But he's a game man as well."

"Well, sir, one can but do one's best."

The Baronet liked the modest but assured tone of the young pugilist. Suddenly an amusing thought struck him, and he burst out laughing.

"By Jove!" he cried. "What a lark if the Bully is out to-night!"

Alf Stevens pricked up his ears.

"Who might he be, sir?"

"Well, that's what the folk are asking. Some say they've seen him, and some say he's a fairy tale, but there's good evidence that he is a real man with a pair of rare good fists that leave their marks behind him."

"And where might he live?"

"On this very road. It's between Finchley and Elstree, as I've beard. There are two chaps, and they come out on nights when the moon is at full and challenge the passers-by to fight in the old style. One fights and the other picks up. By George! the fellow can fight, too, by all accounts. Chaps have been found in the morning with their faces all cut to ribbons to show that the Bully had been at work upon them."

Alf Stevens was full of interest.

"I've always wanted to try an old-style battle, sir, but it never chanced to come my way. I believe it would suit me better than the gloves."

"Then you won't refuse the Bully?"

"Refuse him! I'd go ten miles to meet him."

"By George! it would be great!" cried the Baronet. "Well, the moon is at the full, and the place should be about here."

"If he's as good as you say," Stevens remarked, "he should be known in the ring, unless he is just an amateur who amuses himself like that."

"Some think he's an ostler, or maybe a racing man from the training stables over yonder. Where there are horses there is boxing. If you can believe the accounts, there is something a bit queer and outlandish about the fellow. Hi! Look out, damn you, look out!"

The Baronet's voice had risen to a sudden screech of surprise and of anger. At this point the road dips down into a hollow, heavily shaded by trees, so that at night it arches across like the mouth of a tunnel. At the foot of the slope there stand two great stone pillars, which, as viewed by daylight, are lichen-stained and weathered, with heraldic devices on each which are so mutilated by time that they are mere protuberances of stone. An iron gate of elegant design, hanging loosely upon rusted hinges, proclaims both the past glories and the present decay of Brocas Old Hall, which lies at the end of the weed-encumbered avenue. It was from the shadow of this ancient gateway that an active figure had sprung suddenly into the centre of the road and had, with great dexterity, held up the horses, who ramped and pawed as they forced back upon their haunches.

"Here, Rowe, you 'old the tits, will ye?" cried a high strident voice. "I've a little word to say to this 'ere slap-up Corinthian before 'e goes any farther."

A second man had emerged from the shadows and without a word took hold of the horses' heads. He was a short, thick fellow, dressed in a curious brown many-caped overcoat, which came to his knees, with gaiters and boots beneath it. He wore no hat, and those in the dog-cart had a view, as he came in front of the side-lamps, of a surly red face with an ill-fitting lower lip clean shaven, and a high black cravat swathed tightly under the chin. As he gripped the leathers his more active comrade sprang forward and rested a bony hand upon the side of the splashboard while he looked keenly up with a pair of fierce blue eyes at the faces of the two travellers, the light beating full upon his own features. He wore a hat low upon his brow, but in spite of its shadow both the Baronet and the pugilist could see enough to shrink from him, for it was an evil face, evil but very formidable, stern, craggy, high-nosed, and fierce, with an inexorable mouth which bespoke a nature which would neither ask for mercy nor grant it. As to his age, one could only say for certain that a man with such a face was young enough to have all his virility and old enough to have experienced all the wickedness of life. The cold, savage eyes took a deliberate survey, first of the Baronet and then of the young man beside him.

"Aye, Rowe, it's a slap-up Corinthian, same as I said," he remarked over his shoulder to his companion. "But this other is a likely chap. If 'e isn't a millin' cove 'e ought to be. Any'ow, we'll try 'im out."

"Look here," said the Baronet, "I don't know who you are, except that you are a damned impertinent fellow. I'd put the lash of my whip across your face for two pins!"

"Stow that gammon, gov'nor! It ain't safe to speak to me like that."

"I've heard of you and your ways!" cried the angry soldier. "I'll teach you to stop my horses on the Queen's high road! You've got the wrong men this time, my fine fellow, as you will soon learn."

"That's as it may be," said the stranger. "May'ap, master, we may all learn something before we part. One or other of you 'as got to get down and put up your 'ands before you get any farther."

Stevens had instantly sprung down into the road.

"If you want a fight you've come to the right shop," said he; "it's my trade, so don't say I took you unawares."

The stranger gave a cry of satisfaction.

"Blow my dickey!" he shouted. "It is a millin' cove, Joe, same as I said. No more chaw-bacons for us, but the real thing. Well, young man, you've met your master to-night. Happen you never 'eard what Lord Longmore said o' me? 'A man must be made special to beat you,' says 'e. That's wot Lord Longmore said."

"That was before the Bull came along," growled the man in front, speaking for the first time. "Stow your chaffing, Joe! A little more about the Bull and you and me will quarrel. 'E bested me once, but it's all betters and no takers that I glut 'im if ever we meet again. Well, young man, what d'ye think of me?"

"I think you've got your share of cheek."

"Cheek. Wot's that?"

"Impudence, bluff—gas, if you like."

The last word had a surprising effect upon the stranger. He smote his leg with his hand and broke out into a high neighing laugh, in which he was joined by his gruff companion.

"You've said the right word, my beauty," cried the latter, "Gas is the word and no error. Well, there's a good moon, but the clouds are comin' up. We had best use the light while we can."

Whilst this conversation had been going on the Baronet had been looking with an ever-growing amazement at the attire of the stranger. A good deal of it confirmed his belief that he was connected with some stables, though making every allowance for this his appearance was very eccentric and old-fashioned. Upon his head he wore a yellowish-white top-hat of long-haired beaver, such as is still affected by some drivers of four-in-hands, with a bell crown and a curling brim. His dress consisted of a shortwaisted swallow-tail coat, snuff- coloured, with steel buttons. It opened in front to show a vest of striped silk, while his legs were encased in buff knee breeches with blue stockings and low shoes. The figure was angular and hard, with a great suggestion of wiry activity. This Bully of Brocas was clearly a very great character, and the young dragoon officer chuckled as he thought what a glorious story he would carry back to the mess of this queer old-world figure and the thrashing which he was about to receive from the famous London boxer.

Billy, the little groom, had taken charge of the horses, who were shivering and sweating.

"This way!" said the stout man, turning towards the gate. It was a sinister place, black and weird, with the crumbling pillars and the heavy arching trees. Neither the Baronet nor the pugilist liked the look of it.

"Where are you going, then?"

"This is no place for a fight," said the stout man. "We've got as pretty a place as ever you saw inside the gate here. You couldn't beat it on Molesey Hurst."

"The road is good enough for me," said Stevens.

"The road is good enough for two Johnny Raws," said the man with the beaver hat. "It ain't good enough for two slap-up millin' coves like you an' me. You ain't afeard, are you?" "Not of you or ten like you," said Stevens, stoutly.

"Well, then, come with me and do it as it ought to be done."

Sir Frederick and Stevens exchanged glances.

"I'm game," said the pugilist.

"Come on, then."

The little party of four passed through the gateway. Behind them in the darkness the horses stamped and reared, while the voice of the boy could be heard as he vainly tried to soothe them. After walking fifty yards up the grass- grown drive the guide turned to the right through a thick belt of trees, and they came out upon a circular plot of grass, white and clear in the moonlight. It had a raised bank, and on the farther side was one of those little pillared stone summer-houses beloved by the early Georgians.

"What did I tell you?" cried the stout man, triumphantly. "Could you do better than this within twenty mile of town? It was made for it. Now, Tom, get to work upon him, and show us what you can do."

It had all become like an extraordinary dream. The strange men, their odd dress, their queer speech, the moonlit circle of grass, and the pillared summer- house all wove themselves into one fantastic whole. It was only the sight of Alf Stevens's ill-fitting tweed suit, and his homely English face surmounting it, which brought the Baronet back to the workaday world. The thin stranger had taken off his beaver hat, his swallow-tailed coat, his silk waistcoat, and finally his shirt had been drawn over his head by his second. Stevens in a cool and leisurely fashion kept pace with the preparations of his antagonist. Then the two fighting men turned upon each other.

But as they did so Stevens gave an exclamation of surprise and horror. The removal of the beaver hat had disclosed a horrible mutilation of the head of his antagonist. The whole upper forehead had fallen in, and there seemed to be a broad red weal between his close-cropped hair and his heavy brows.

"Good Lord," cried the young pugilist. "What's amiss with the man?" The question seemed to rouse a cold fury in his antagonist.

"You look out for your own head, master," said he. "You'll find enough to do, I'm thinkin', without talkin' about mine."

This retort drew a shout of hoarse laughter from his second. "Well said, my Tommy!" he cried. "It's Lombard Street to a China orange on the one and only."

The man whom he called Tom was standing with his hands up in the centre of the natural ring. He looked a big man in his clothes, but he seemed bigger in the buff, and his barrel chest, sloping shoulders, and loosely-slung muscular arms were all ideal for the game. His grim eyes gleamed fiercely beneath his misshapen brows, and his lips were set in a fixed hard smile, more menacing than a scowl. The pugilist confessed, as he approached him, that he had never seen a more formidable figure. But his bold heart rose to the fact that he had never yet found the man who could master him, and that it was hardly credible that he would appear as an old-fashioned stranger on a country road. Therefore, with an answering smile, he took up his position and raised his hands.

But what followed was entirely beyond his experience. The stranger feinted quickly with his left, and sent in a swinging hit with his right, so quick and hard that Stevens had barely time to avoid it and to counter with a short jab as his opponent rushed in upon him. Next instant the man's bony arms were round him, and the pugilist was hurled into the air in a whirling cross buttock, coming down with a heavy thud upon the grass. The stranger stood back and folded his arms while Stevens scrambled to his feet with a red flush of anger upon his cheeks.

"Look here," he cried. "What sort of game is this?"

"We claim foul!" the Baronet shouted.

"Foul be damned! As clean a throw as ever I saw!" said the stout man. "What rules do you fight under?"

"Queensberry, of course."

"I never heard of it. It's London prize-ring with us."

"Come on, then!" cried Stevens, furiously. "I can wrestle as well as another. You won't get me napping again."

Nor did he. The next time that the stranger rushed in Stevens caught him in as strong a grip, and after swinging and swaying they came down together in a dog-fall. Three times this occurred, and each time the stranger walked across to his friend and seated himself upon the grassy bank before he recommenced.

"What d'ye make of him?" the Baronet asked, in one of these pauses.

Stevens was bleeding from the ear, but otherwise showed no sign of damage.

"He knows a lot," said the pugilist. "I don't know where he learned it, but he's had a deal of practice somewhere. He's as strong as a lion and as hard as a board, for all his queer face." "Keep him at out-fighting. I think you are his master there."

"I'm not so sure that I'm his master anywhere, but I'll try my best."

It was a desperate fight, and as round followed round it became clear, even to the amazed Baronet, that the middle-weight champion had met his match. The stranger had a clever draw and a rush which, with his springing hits, made him a most dangerous foe. His head and body seemed insensible

to blows, and the horribly malignant smile never for one instant flickered from his lips. He hit very hard with fists like flints, and his blows whizzed up from every angle. He had one particularly deadly lead, an uppercut at the jaw, which again and again nearly came home, until at last it did actually fly past the guard and brought Stevens to the ground. The stout man gave a whoop of triumph.

"The whisker hit, by George! It's a horse to a hen on my Tommy! Another like that, lad, and you have him beat."

"I say, Stevens, this is going too far," said the Baronet, as he supported his weary man. "What will the regiment say if I bring you up all knocked to pieces in a bye-battle! Shake hands with this fellow and give him best, or you'll not be fit for your job."

"Give him best? Not I!" cried Stevens, angrily. "I'll knock that damned smile off his ugly mug before I've done."

"What about the Sergeant?"

"I'd rather go back to London and never see the Sergeant than have my number taken down by this chap."

"Well, 'ad enough?" his opponent asked, in a sneering voice, as he moved from his seat on the bank.

For answer young Stevens sprang forward and rushed at his man with all the strength that was left to him. By the fury of his onset he drove him back, and for a long minute had all the better of the exchanges. But this iron fighter seemed never to tire. His step was as quick and his blow as hard as ever when this long rally had ended. Stevens had eased up from pure exhaustion. But his opponent did not ease up. He came back on him with a shower of furious blows which beat down the weary guard of the pugilist. Alf Stevens was at the end of his strength and would in another instant have sunk to the ground but for a singular intervention.

It has been said that in their approach to the ring the party had passed through a grove of trees. Out of these there came a peculiar shrill cry, a cry of agony, which might be from a child or from some small woodland creature in distress. It was inarticulate, high-pitched, and inexpressibly melancholy. At the sound the stranger, who had knocked Stevens on to his knees, staggered back and looked round him with an expression of helpless horror upon his face. The smile had left his lips and there only remained the loose-lipped weakness of a man in the last extremity of terror.

"It's after me again, mate!" he cried.

"Stick it out, Tom! You have him nearly beat! It can't hurt you."

"It can 'urt me! It will 'urt me!" screamed the fighting man. "My God! I can't face it! Ah, I see it! I see it!"

With a scream of fear he turned and bounded off into the brushwood. His companion, swearing loudly, picked up the pile of clothes and darted after him, the dark shadows swallowing up their flying figures.

Stevens, half-senselessly, had staggered back and lay upon the grassy bank, his head pillowed upon the chest of the young Baronet, who was holding his flask of brandy to his lips. As they sat there they were both aware that the cries had become louder and shriller. Then from among the bushes there ran a small white terrier, nosing about as if following a trail and yelping most piteously. It squattered across the grassy sward, taking no notice of the two young men. Then it also vanished into the shadows. As it did so the two spectators sprang to their feet and ran as hard as they could tear for the gateway and the trap. Terror had seized them—a panic terror far above reason or control. Shivering and shaking, they threw themselves into the dog- cart, and it was not until the willing horses had put two good miles between that ill-omened hollow and themselves that they at last ventured to speak.

"Did you ever see such a dog?" asked the Baronet.

"No," cried Stevens. "And, please God, I never may again."

Late that night the two travellers broke their journey at the Swan Inn, near Harpenden Common. The landlord was an old acquaintance of the Baronet's, and gladly joined him in a glass of port after supper. A famous old sport was Mr. Joe Homer, of the Swan, and he would talk by the hour of the legends of the ring, whether new or old. The name of Alf Stevens was well known to him, and he looked at him with the deepest interest.

"Why, sir, you have surely been fighting," said he. "I hadn't read of any engagement in the papers."

"Enough said of that," Stevens answered, in a surly voice.

"Well, no offence! I suppose"—his smiling face became suddenly very serious—"I suppose you didn't, by chance, see anything of him they call the Bully of Brocas as you came north?"

"Well, what if we did?"

The landlord was tense with excitement.

"It was him that nearly killed Bob Meadows. It was at the very gate of Brocas Old Hall that he stopped him. Another man was with him. Bob was game to the marrow, but he was found hit to pieces on the lawn inside the gate where the summer-house stands."

The Baronet nodded.

"Ah, you've been there!" cried the landlord.

"Well, we may as well make a clean breast of it," said the Baronet, looking at Stevens. "We have been there, and we met the man you speak of —an ugly customer he is, too!"

"Tell me!" said the landlord, in a voice that sank to a whisper. "Is it true what Bob Meadows says, that the men are dressed like our grandfathers, and that the fighting man has his head all caved in?"

"Well, he was old-fashioned, certainly, and his head was the queerest ever I saw."

"God in Heaven!" cried the landlord. "Do you know, sir, that Tom Hickman, the famous prize fighter, together with his pal, Joe Rowe, a silversmith of the City, met his death at that very point in the year 1822, when he was drunk, and tried to drive on the wrong side of a wagon? Both were killed and the wheel of the wagon crushed in Hickman's forehead."

"Hickman! Hickman!" said the Baronet. "Not the gasman?"

"Yes, sir, they called him Gas. He won his fights with what they called the 'whisker hit,' and no one could stand against him until Neate—him that they called the Bristol Bull—brought him down."

Stevens had risen from the table as white as cheese.

"Let's get out of this, sir. I want fresh air. Let us get on our way." The landlord clapped him on the back.

"Cheer up, lad! You've held him off, anyhow, and that's more than anyone else has ever done. Sit down and have another glass of wine, for if a man in England has earned it this night it is you. There's many a debt you would pay if you gave the Gasman a welting, whether dead or alive. Do you know what he did in this very room?"

The two travellers looked round with startled eyes at the lofty room, stone-flagged and oak panelled, with great open grate at the farther end.

"Yes, in this very room. I had it from old Squire Scotter, who was here that very night. It was the day when Shelton beat Josh Hudson out St. Albans way, and Gas had won a pocketful of money on the fight. He and his pal Rowe came in here upon their way, and he was mad-raging drunk. The folk fairly shrunk into the corners and under the tables, for he was stalkin' round with the great kitchen poker in his hand, and there was murder behind the smile upon his face. He was like that when the drink was in him—cruel, reckless, and a terror to the world. Well, what think you that he did at last with the poker? There was a little dog, a terrier as I've heard, coiled up before the fire, for it was a bitter December night. The Gasman broke its back with one blow of the poker. Then he burst out laughin', flung a curse or two at the folk that shrunk away from him, and so out to his high gig that was waiting outside. The next we heard was that he was carried down to Finchley with his head ground to a jelly by the wagon wheel. Yes, they do say the little dog with its bleeding skin and its broken back has been seen since then, crawlin' and yelpin' about Brocas Corner, as if it were bookin' for the swine that killed it. So you see, Mr. Stevens, you were fightin' for more than yourself when you put it across the Gasman."

"Maybe so," said the young prize-fighter, "but I want no more fights like that. The Farrier Sergeant is good enough for me, sir, and if it is the same to you, we'll take a railway train back to town."

GHOST stories function in a slightly different way from a conventional horror story (say, like "The Cask of Amontillado"). They are parables of a collective conscience, and are usually more interested in making social, cultural, or moral prognoses than they are in conveying simple thrills. The theory of the classic ghost story is that society has attempt to suppress, repress, or deny a fact of human nature, and that that fact manifests itself in hauntings. These manifestations usually involve our baser, cruder, more primitive inclinations, and often are represented by an act of malice, brutality, or vice. The Gasman was not so evil as a serial killer or so heartless as a blackmailer, but there is a genuine wickedness in his spirit that the "civilized" Victorians might hope to forget – a wickedness that cannot be avoided, lurking in the shadows and around the corners. It is very significant that Doyle sets his tale smack-dab in heart of the Victorian Era, the very height of the British Empire. Written in 1921 – after the epicurean revels of the Edwardians, and the soul-rending miseries of the Great War – Doyle was thoroughly aware that the postwar generation was only all too acquainted with human depravity. The ideal person to be taught these lessons was not a member of the cynical Lost Generation, but one of Doyle's idealistic Victorian peers. Set in 1878, when he was himself only 19 years old, there is a conflicting tension between cynicism and nostalgia in this tale, and there is a sense that, as Doyle moved on from the war and the deaths of his son and brother, he wrote this ghost story (and set in in the era of his youth) as a retroactive message to himself. It's lesson seems to be that as much as we may appear to have grown and progressed – as noble as we may fancy ourselves, and as civilized as we may imagine our societies – there will always be demons which haunt us in our darkest travels, shadowing our victories and chilling our peace.

"THE Leather Funnel" is a very unsettling tale, presaging the queasy fiction of Algernon Blackwood ("The Insanity of Jones"), M. R. James ("The Rose Garden"), and Oliver Onions ("Io"). The stories I've associated with these Edwardian masters of the macabre all bear a somber similarity to "The Leather Funnel," in that they concern visions of the past being forced onto the consciousness of a hapless victim – either by their proximity to the supernatural, the loss of their senses, or (in the worst cases) both. The tale is particularly Jamesian, with its repulsive descriptions of the eponymous medieval torture device – the grisly bridge by which the violent woes of the past can cross to invade the bourgeois doldrums of the present – and in one other important respect: its mastery of authorial control. Doyle demonstrates extreme discipline in what he broods on and in what he avoids, choosing to create atmospheric mood rather than reveling in physical gore. But rest assured, there is still something particularly icky about this tale, which successfully conveys the uneasiness that can be generated when the illusion of our relatively humane civilization is shattered by a visitor from the barbaric past: a simple museum piece that requires no supernatural intervention to imbue its observers with bad dreams and terrors in the night.

The Leather Funnel

{1902}

MY friend, Lionel Dacre, lived in the Avenue de Wagram, Paris. His house was that small one, with the iron railings and grass plot in front of it, on the left-hand side as you pass down from the Arc de Triomphe. I fancy that it had been there long before the avenue was constructed, for the grey tiles were stained with lichens, and the walls were mildewed and discoloured with age. It looked a small house from the street, five windows in front, if I remember right, but it deepened into a single long chamber at the back. It was here that Dacre had that singular library of occult literature, and the fantastic curiosities which served as a hobby for himself, and an amusement for his friends. A wealthy man of refined and eccentric tastes, he had spent much of his life and fortune in gathering together what was said to be a unique private collection of Talmudic, cabalistic, and magical works, many of them of great rarity and value. His tastes leaned toward the marvellous and the monstrous, and I have heard that his experiments in the direction of the unknown have passed all the bounds of civilization and of decorum. To his English friends he never alluded to such matters, and took the tone of the student and virtuoso; but a Frenchman whose tastes were of the same nature has assured me that the worst excesses of the black mass have been perpetrated in that large and lofty hall, which is lined with the shelves of his books, and the cases of his museum.

Dacre's appearance was enough to show that his deep interest in these psychic matters was intellectual rather than spiritual. There was no trace of asceticism upon his heavy face, but there was much mental force in his huge, dome-like skull, which curved upward from amongst his thinning locks, like a snowpeak above its fringe of fir trees. His knowledge was greater than his wisdom, and his powers were far superior to his character. The small bright eyes, buried deeply in his fleshy face, twinkled with intelligence and an unabated curiosity of life, but they were the eyes of a sensualist and an egotist. Enough of the man, for he is dead now, poor devil, dead at the very time that he had made sure that he had at last discovered the elixir of life. It is not with his complex character that I have to deal, but with the very strange and inexplicable incident which had its rise in my visit to him in the early spring of the year '82.

I had known Dacre in England, for my researches in the Assyrian Room of the British Museum had been conducted at the time when he was endeavouring to establish a mystic and esoteric meaning in the Babylonian tablets, and this community of interests had brought us together. Chance remarks had led to daily conversation, and that to something verging upon friendship. I had promised him that on my next visit to Paris I would call upon him. At the time when I was able to fulfil my compact I was living in a cottage at Fontainebleau, and as the evening trains were inconvenient, he asked me to spend the night in his house.

"I have only that one spare couch," said he, pointing to a broad sofa in his large salon; "I hope that you will manage to be comfortable there."

It was a singular bedroom, with its high walls of brown volumes, but there could be no more agreeable furniture to a bookworm like myself, and there is no scent so pleasant to my nostrils as that faint, subtle reek which comes from an ancient book. I assured him that I could desire no more charming chamber, and no more congenial surroundings.

"If the fittings are neither convenient nor conventional, they are at least costly," said he, looking round at his shelves. "I have expended nearly a quarter of a million of money upon these objects which surround you. Books, weapons, gems, carvings, tapestries, images--there is hardly a thing here which has not its history, and it is generally one worth telling."

He was seated as he spoke at one side of the open fire-place, and I at the other. His reading-table was on his right, and the strong lamp above it ringed it with a very vivid circle of golden light. A half-rolled palimpsest lay in the centre, and around it were many quaint articles of bric-a-brac. One of these was a large funnel, such as is used for filling wine casks. It appeared to be made of black wood, and to be rimmed with discoloured brass.

"That is a curious thing," I remarked. "What is the history of that?"

"Ah!" said he, "it is the very question which I have had occasion to ask myself. I would give a good deal to know. Take it in your hands and examine it."

I did so, and found that what I had imagined to be wood was in reality leather, though age had dried it into an extreme hardness. It was a large funnel, and might hold a quart when full. The brass rim encircled the wide end, but the narrow was also tipped with metal.

"What do you make of it?" asked Dacre.

"I should imagine that it belonged to some vintner or maltster in the Middle Ages," said I. "I have seen in England leathern drinking flagons of the seventeenth century--'black jacks' as they were called--which were of the same colour and hardness as this filler."

"I dare say the date would be about the same," said Dacre, "and, no doubt, also, it was used for filling a vessel with liquid. If my suspicions are correct, however, it was a queer vintner who used it, and a very singular cask which was filled. Do you observe nothing strange at the spout end of the funnel."

As I held it to the light I observed that at a spot some five inches above the brass tip the narrow neck of the leather funnel was all haggled and scored, as if someone had notched it round with a blunt knife. Only at that point was there any roughening of the dead black surface.

"Someone has tried to cut off the neck."

"Would you call it a cut?"

"It is torn and lacerated. It must have taken some strength to leave these marks on such tough material, whatever the instrument may have been. But what do you think of it? I can tell that you know more than you say."

Dacre smiled, and his little eyes twinkled with knowledge.

"Have you included the psychology of dreams among your learned studies?" he asked.

"I did not even know that there was such a psychology."

"My dear sir, that shelf above the gem case is filled with volumes, from Albertus Magnus onward, which deal with no other subject. It is a science in itself."

"A science of charlatans!"

"The charlatan is always the pioneer. From the astrologer came the astronomer, from the alchemist the chemist, from the mesmerist the experimental psychologist. The quack of yesterday is the professor of tomorrow. Even such subtle and elusive things as dreams will in time be reduced to system and order. When that time comes the researches of our friends on the bookshelf yonder will no longer be the amusement of the mystic, but the foundations of a science."

"Supposing that is so, what has the science of dreams to do with a large, black, brass-rimmed funnel?"

"I will tell you. You know that I have an agent who is always on the look-out for rarities and curiosities for my collection. Some days ago he heard of a dealer upon one of the Quais who had acquired some old rubbish found in a cupboard in an ancient house at the back of the Rue Mathurin, in the Quartier Latin. The dining-room of this old house is decorated with a coat of arms, chevrons, and bars rouge upon a field argent, which prove, upon inquiry, to be the shield of Nicholas de la Reynie, a high official of King Louis XIV. There can be no doubt that the other articles in the cupboard date back to the early days of that king. The inference is, therefore, that they were all the property of this Nicholas de la Reynie, who was, as I understand, the gentleman specially concerned with the maintenance and execution of the Draconic laws of that epoch."

"What then?"

"I would ask you now to take the funnel into your hands once more and to examine the upper brass rim. Can you make out any lettering upon it?"

There were certainly some scratches upon it, almost obliterated by time. The general effect was of several letters, the last of which bore some resemblance to a B.

"You make it a B?"

"Yes, I do."

"So do I. In fact, I have no doubt whatever that it is a B."

"But the nobleman you mentioned would have had R for his initial."

"Exactly! That's the beauty of it. He owned this curious object, and yet he had someone else's initials upon it. Why did he do this?"

"I can't imagine; can you?"

"Well, I might, perhaps, guess. Do you observe something drawn a little farther along the rim?"

"I should say it was a crown."

"It is undoubtedly a crown; but if you examine it in a good light, you will convince yourself that it is not an ordinary crown. It is a heraldic crown--a badge of rank, and it consists of an alternation of four pearls and strawberry leaves, the proper badge of a marquis. We may infer, therefore, that the person whose initials end in B was entitled to wear that coronet."

"Then this common leather filler belonged to a marquis?"

Dacre gave a peculiar smile.

"Or to some member of the family of a marquis," said he. "So much we have clearly gathered from this engraved rim."

"But what has all this to do with dreams?" I do not know whether it was from a look upon Dacre's face, or from some subtle suggestion in his manner, but a feeling of repulsion, of unreasoning horror, came upon me as I looked at the gnarled old lump of leather.

"I have more than once received important information through my dreams," said my companion in the didactic manner which he loved to affect. "I make it a rule now when I am in doubt upon any material point to place the article in question beside me as I sleep, and to hope for some enlightenment. The process does not appear to me to be very obscure, though it has not yet received the blessing of orthodox science. According to my theory, any object which has been intimately associated with any supreme paroxysm of human emotion, whether it be joy or pain, will retain a certain atmosphere or association which it is capable of communicating to a sensitive mind. By a sensitive mind I do not mean an abnormal one, but such a trained and educated mind as you or I possess."

"You mean, for example, that if I slept beside that old sword upon the wall, I might dream of some bloody incident in which that very sword took part?"

"An excellent example, for, as a matter of fact, that sword was used in that fashion by me, and I saw in my sleep the death of its owner, who perished in a brisk skirmish, which I have been unable to identify, but which occurred at the time of the wars of the Frondists. If you think of it, some of our popular observances show that the fact has already been recognized by our ancestors, although we, in our wisdom, have classed it among superstitions."

"For example?"

"Well, the placing of the bride's cake beneath the pillow in order that the sleeper may have pleasant dreams. That is one of several instances which you will find set forth in a small brochure which I am myself writing upon the subject. But to come back to the point, I slept one night with this funnel beside me, and I had a dream which certainly throws a curious light upon its use and origin."

"What did you dream?"

"I dreamed----" He paused, and an intent look of interest came over his massive face. "By Jove, that's well thought of," said he. "This really will be an exceedingly interesting experiment. You are yourself a psychic subject--with nerves which respond readily to any impression."

"I have never tested myself in that direction."

"Then we shall test you tonight. Might I ask you as a very great favour, when you occupy that couch tonight, to sleep with this old funnel placed by the side of your pillow?"

The request seemed to me a grotesque one; but I have myself, in my complex nature, a hunger after all which is bizarre and fantastic. I had not the faintest belief in Dacre's theory, nor any hopes for success in such an experiment; yet it amused me that the experiment should be made. Dacre, with great gravity, drew a small stand to the head of my settee, and placed the funnel upon it. Then, after a short conversation, he wished me good night and left me.

I sat for some little time smoking by the smouldering fire, and turning over in my mind the curious incident which had occurred, and the strange experience which might lie before me. Sceptical as I was, there was something impressive in the assurance of Dacre's manner, and my extraordinary surroundings, the huge room with the strange and often sinister objects which were hung round it, struck solemnity into my soul. Finally I undressed, and turning out the lamp, I lay down. After long tossing I fell asleep. Let me try to describe as accurately as I can the scene which came to me in my dreams. It stands out now in my memory more clearly than anything which I have seen with my waking eyes. There was a room which bore the appearance of a vault. Four spandrels from the corners ran up to join a sharp, cup-shaped roof. The architecture was rough, but very strong. It was evidently part of a great building.

Three men in black, with curious, top-heavy, black velvet hats, sat in a line upon a red-carpeted dais. Their faces were very solemn and sad. On the left stood two long-gowned men with port-folios in their hands, which seemed to be stuffed with papers. Upon the right, looking toward me, was a small woman with blonde hair and singular, light-blue eyes--the eyes of a child. She was past her first youth, but could not yet be called middle-aged. Her figure was inclined to stoutness and her bearing was proud and confident. Her face was pale, but serene. It was a curious face, comely and yet feline, with a subtle suggestion of cruelty about the straight, strong little mouth and chubby jaw. She was draped in some sort of loose, white gown. Beside her stood a thin, eager priest, who whispered in her ear, and continually raised a crucifix before her eyes. She turned her head and looked fixedly past the crucifix at the three men in black, who were, I felt, her judges.

As I gazed the three men stood up and said something, but I could distinguish no words, though I was aware that it was the central one who was speaking. They then swept out of the room, followed by the two men with the papers. At the same instant several rough-looking fellows in stout jerkins came bustling in and removed first the red carpet, and then the boards which formed the dais, so as to entirely clear the room. When this screen was removed I saw some singular articles of furniture behind it. One looked like a bed with wooden rollers at each end, and a winch handle to regulate its length. Another was a wooden horse. There were several other curious objects, and a number of swinging cords which played over pulleys. It was not unlike a modern gymnasium.

When the room had been cleared there appeared a new figure upon the scene. This was a tall, thin person clad in black, with a gaunt and austere face. The aspect of the man made me shudder. His clothes were all shining with grease and mottled with stains. He bore himself with a slow and impressive dignity, as if he took command of all things from the instant of his entrance. In spite of his rude appearance and sordid dress, it was now his business, his room, his to command. He carried a coil of light ropes over his left forearm. The lady looked him up and down with a searching glance, but her expression was unchanged. It was confident--even defiant. But it was very different with the priest. His face was ghastly white, and I saw the moisture glisten and run on his high, sloping forehead. He threw up his hands in prayer and he stooped continually to mutter frantic words in the lady's ear.

The man in black now advanced, and taking one of the cords from his left arm, he bound the woman's hands together. She held them meekly

toward him as he did so. Then he took her arm with a rough grip and led her toward the wooden horse, which was little higher than her waist. On to this she was lifted and laid, with her back upon it, and her face to the ceiling, while the priest, quivering with horror, had rushed out of the room. The woman's lips were moving rapidly, and though I could hear nothing I knew that she was praying. Her feet hung down on either side of the horse, and I saw that the rough varlets in attendance had fastened cords to her ankles and secured the other ends to iron rings in the stone floor.

My heart sank within me as I saw these ominous preparations, and yet I was held by the fascination of horror, and I could not take my eyes from the strange spectacle. A man had entered the room with a bucket of water in either hand. Another followed with a third bucket. They were laid beside the wooden horse. The second man had a wooden dipper--a bowl with a straight handle--in his other hand. This he gave to the man in black. At the same moment one of the varlets approached with a dark object in his hand, which even in my dream filled me with a vague feeling of familiarity. It was a leathern filler. With horrible energy he thrust it--but I could stand no more. My hair stood on end with horror. I writhed, I struggled, I broke through the bonds of sleep, and I burst with a shriek into my own life, and found myself lying shivering with terror in the huge library, with the moonlight flooding through the window and throwing strange silver and black traceries upon the opposite wall. Oh, what a blessed relief to feel that I was back in the nineteenth century--back out of that mediaeval vault into a world where men had human hearts within their bosoms. I sat up on my couch, trembling in every limb, my mind divided between thankfulness and horror. To think that such things were ever done--that they could be done without God striking the villains dead. Was it all a fantasy, or did it really stand for something which had happened in the black, cruel days of the world's history? I sank my throbbing head upon my shaking hands. And then, suddenly, my heart seemed to stand still in my bosom, and I could not even scream, so great was my terror. Something was advancing toward me through the darkness of the room.

It is a horror coming upon a horror which breaks a man's spirit. I could not reason, I could not pray; I could only sit like a frozen image, and glare at the dark figure which was coming down the great room. And then it moved out into the white lane of moonlight, and I breathed once more. It was Dacre, and his face showed that he was as frightened as myself.

"Was that you? For God's sake what's the matter?" he asked in a husky voice.

"Oh, Dacre, I am glad to see you! I have been down into hell. It was dreadful."

"Then it was you who screamed?"

"I dare say it was."

"It rang through the house. The servants are all terrified." He struck a match and lit the lamp. "I think we may get the fire to burn up again," he added, throwing some logs upon the embers. "Good God, my dear chap, how white you are! You look as if you had seen a ghost."

"So I have--several ghosts."

"The leather funnel has acted, then?"

"I wouldn't sleep near the infernal thing again for all the money you could offer me."

Dacre chuckled.

"I expected that you would have a lively night of it," said he. "You took it out of me in return, for that scream of yours wasn't a very pleasant sound at two in the morning. I suppose from what you say that you have seen the whole dreadful business."

"What dreadful business?"

"The torture of the water--the 'Extraordinary Question,' as it was called in the genial days of 'Le Roi Soleil.' Did you stand it out to the end?"

"No, thank God, I awoke before it really began."

"Ah! it is just as well for you. I held out till the third bucket. Well, it is an old story, and they are all in their graves now, anyhow, so what does it matter how they got there? I suppose that you have no idea what it was that you have seen?"

"The torture of some criminal. She must have been a terrible malefactor indeed if her crimes are in proportion to her penalty."

"Well, we have that small consolation," said Dacre, wrapping his dressing-gown round him and crouching closer to the fire. "They WERE in proportion to her penalty. That is to say, if I am correct in the lady's identity."

"How could you possibly know her identity?"

For answer Dacre took down an old vellum-covered volume from the shelf.

"Just listen to this," said he; "it is in the French of the seventeenth century, but I will give a rough translation as I go. You will judge for yourself whether I have solved the riddle or not.

"'The prisoner was brought before the Grand Chambers and Tournelles of Parliament, sitting as a court of justice, charged with the murder of Master Dreux d'Aubray, her father, and of her two brothers, MM. d'Aubray, one being civil lieutenant, and the other a counsellor of Parliament. In person it seemed hard to believe that she had really done such wicked deeds, for she was of a mild appearance, and of short stature, with a fair skin and blue eyes. Yet the Court, having found her guilty, condemned her to the ordinary and to the extraordinary question in order that she might be forced to name her accomplices, after which she should be carried in a cart to the Place de Greve, there to have her head cut off, her body being afterwards burned and her ashes scattered to the winds.'

"The date of this entry is July 16, 1676."

"It is interesting," said I, "but not convincing. How do you prove the two women to be the same?"

"I am coming to that. The narrative goes on to tell of the woman's behaviour when questioned. 'When the executioner approached her she recognized him by the cords which he held in his hands, and she at once held out her own hands to him, looking at him from head to foot without uttering a word.' How's that?"

"Yes, it was so."

"'She gazed without wincing upon the wooden horse and rings which had twisted so many limbs and caused so many shrieks of agony. When her eyes fell upon the three pails of water, which were all ready for her, she said with a smile, "All that water must have been brought here for the purpose of drowning me, Monsieur. You have no idea, I trust, of making a person of my small stature swallow it all."' Shall I read the details of the torture?"

"No, for Heaven's sake, don't."

"Here is a sentence which must surely show you that what is here recorded is the very scene which you have gazed upon tonight: 'The good Abbe Pirot, unable to contemplate the agonies which were suffered by his penitent, had hurried from the room.' Does that convince you?"

"It does entirely. There can be no question that it is indeed the same event. But who, then, is this lady whose appearance was so attractive and whose end was so horrible?"

For answer Dacre came across to me, and placed the small lamp upon the table which stood by my bed. Lifting up the ill-omened filler, he turned the brass rim so that the light fell full upon it. Seen in this way the engraving seemed clearer than on the night before.

"We have already agreed that this is the badge of a marquis or of a marquise," said he. "We have also settled that the last letter is B."

"It is undoubtedly so."

"I now suggest to you that the other letters from left to right are, M, M, a small d, A, a small d, and then the final B."

"Yes, I am sure that you are right. I can make out the two small d's quite plainly."

"What I have read to you tonight," said Dacre, "is the official record of the trial of Marie Madeleine d'Aubray, Marquise de Brinvilliers, one of the most famous poisoners and murderers of all time."

I sat in silence, overwhelmed at the extraordinary nature of the incident, and at the completeness of the proof with which Dacre had exposed its real meaning. In a vague way I remembered some details of the woman's career, her unbridled debauchery, the cold-blooded and protracted torture of her sick father, the murder of her brothers for motives of petty gain. I recollected also that the bravery of her end had done something to atone for the horror of her life, and that all Paris had sympathized with her last moments, and blessed her as a martyr within a few days of the time when they had cursed her as a murderess. One objection, and one only, occurred to my mind.

"How came her initials and her badge of rank upon the filler? Surely they did not carry their mediaeval homage to the nobility to the point of decorating instruments of torture with their titles?"

"I was puzzled with the same point," said Dacre, "but it admits of a simple explanation. The case excited extraordinary interest at the time, and nothing could be more natural than that La Reynie, the head of the police, should retain this filler as a grim souvenir. It was not often that a marchioness of France underwent the extraordinary question. That he should engrave her initials upon it for the information of others was surely a very ordinary proceeding upon his part."

"And this?" I asked, pointing to the marks upon the leathern neck.

"She was a cruel tigress," said Dacre, as he turned away. "I think it is evident that like other tigresses her teeth were both strong and sharp."

IN his groundbreaking *Danse Macabre* – a philosophical treatise on fictional horror, and a successful response to H. P. Lovecraft's 1927 *Supernatural Horror in Literature* – Stephen King dissected the emotional and psychological effects of horror fiction into three distinct appeals: where rhetoric has been split into *logos, ethos,* and *pathos*, speculative fiction, he claims, can be divided into *terror, horror*, and *revulsion*. Terror, like logos, is the finest element – it is the creeping dread of doom, of confrontation. It is a primarily psychological feature that is more atmospheric than visual. Horror follows soon behind. It is the lurking, unseen *source* of the terror – the big reveal, the "shock value of the dread" manifested in a monster or mutilation. Lastly, there is revulsion, or – as King calls it both disparagingly and affectionately – the "gross-out." Blood and gore, nauseating and primal. Today the gross-out tends to be king in the theatres, with horror and terror revolving around a steady stream of gouged eyes, chewed glass, and sexually-infused body torture. In "The Leather Funnel," Doyle stands head and shoulders above many lesser writers who would have relished describing the water swelling Brinvilliers' belly, the vomit splashing on the cobblestones, the cries and moans as her nubile body becomes drenched in water with her white shift clinging to her flesh and turning pink and transparent. People do *love* that stuff. But that's the thing of BDSM erotica, not artful horror fiction intended to plague the psyche rather than feed the libido. Doyle was not a prude, and he does not pull back out of shame or modesty. This was the *Edwardian* Era after all, not the *Victorian*. Oscar Wilde was dead, but his scandalous "Salome" had captured imaginations; the Decadence Movement was still churning out erotic literature and art; and while obscenity laws were still in existence, the shock factor of depicting a woman's kinky torture was not what it had been during the days of Walter Scott or even Victor Hugo. Doyle focuses on the revulsion of *psychological* trials, not *physical* ones. His disgust rests on the fact that through careful preservation a tool of such savagery should reunite modern man with his primal past – and stand as a reminder of his latent, cruel potential. It is worth noting that Madame de Brinvilliers is an entirely historical person, and that Doyle's account is thoroughly accurate. This lends a certain potency to his story: that the torture of such a vile woman – a serial killer and patricide – could evoke a deep and sincere disgust. It remains one of Doyle's most humane and disturbing tales, haunting its readers long after the set it down – not unlike a worn, leather funnel left on a bed stand.

NO collection of Victorian Era ghost stories would be complete without a glance into the troubling relationship between Britain and her colonies. Rudyard Kipling's "At the End of the Passage" and B.M. Croker's "'To Let'" are brilliant examples of how invading a foreign culture can conjure the ghosts of guilt and regret in a heart once thirsty for wealth or adventure. Doyle was keenly aware of the disasters incurred by empire. Try to think of a single Sherlock Holmes adventure that didn't somehow feature people or events from a current (*The Sign of Four*, "The Speckled Band," "The Crooked Man") or former (*A Study in Scarlet*, "The Dancing Men," "The Five Orange Pips") British colony: the dangers Holmes faces are almost always caused by the shadowy relationship between Britain and one of her overseas colonies (cf. "Abbey Grange," "The Resident Patient," "The Blanched Soldier"), her project of imperial expansion (cf. "The Second Stain," "The Naval Treaty," "The Bruce-Partington Plans"), or immigrants from poorer countries (cf. "The Greek Interpreter," "Wisteria Lodge," "The Six Napoleons"). Dabbling in the affairs of another culture transforms the interloping British intruder – for better or worse – and the colonizer stands to become haunted by the ghosts of shame and rage that work their way back home. This story (despite its anglicized spellings and misconceptions (see footnotes)) is a rich study in colonial sins haunting its guilt-burdened malefactor, all in the bucolic safety of the English countryside. The only cure for imperial crimes, Doyle suggests, is complete reimbursement, or – if the transgression is otherwise irredeemable – a "reasonable compromise."

The Story of the Brown Hand[1]

{1899}

EVERYONE knows that Sir Dominick Holden, the famous Indian surgeon, made me his heir, and that his death changed me in an hour from a hard-working and impecunious young man to a well-to-do landed proprietor Many know also that there were at least five people between the inheritance and me, and that Sir Dominick's selection appeared to be altogether arbitrary and whimsical. I can assure them, however, that they are quite mistaken, and that, although I only knew Sir Dominick in the closing years of his life, there were, none the less, very real reasons why he should show his goodwill towards me. As a matter of fact, though I say it myself, no man

1 No further than the title and race has become an issue worth probing. Much like his similarly titled and hugely unpopular Sherlock Holmes tale, "The Yellow Face" (1893), Doyle immediately leaps to otherness in a bid to attract readership. There are very, very few Holmes stories that do not use either the colonies or former colonies to add an effect of drama to their plots. And yet, it is unfair to brand Doyle a blatant racist: this haunting does little to enhance the glory of British imperialism and much to decry it

ever did more for another than I did for my Indian uncle. I cannot expect the story to be believed, but it is so singular[1] that I should feel that it was a breach of duty if I did not put it upon record—so here it is, and your belief or incredulity is your own affair.

Sir Dominick Holden, C.B., K.C.S.I.[2], and I don't know what besides, was the most distinguished Indian surgeon of his day. In the Army originally, he afterwards settled down into civil practice in Bombay[3], and visited, as a consultant, every part of India. His name is best remembered in connection with the Oriental Hospital, which he founded and supported. The time came, however, when his iron constitution began to show signs of the long strain to which he had subjected it, and his brother practitioners (who were not, perhaps, entirely disinterested upon the point) were unanimous in recommending him to return to England. He held on so long as he could, but at last he developed nervous symptoms of a very pronounced character, and so came back, a broken man, to his native county of Wiltshire[4]. He bought a considerable estate with an ancient manor-house upon the edge of Salisbury Plain[5], and devoted his old age to the study of Comparative Pathology[6], which had been his learned hobby all his life, and in which he was a foremost authority.

We of the family were, as may be imagined, much excited by the news of the return of this rich and childless uncle to England. On his part, although by no means exuberant in his hospitality, he showed some sense of his duty to his relations, and each of us in turn had an invitation to visit him. From the accounts of my cousins it appeared to be a melancholy business, and it was with mixed feelings that I at last received my own summons to appear at Rodenhurst. My wife was so carefully excluded in the invitation that my first impulse was to refuse it, but the interests of the children had to be considered, and so, with her consent, I set out one October afternoon upon my visit to Wiltshire, with little thought of what that visit was to entail.
My uncle's estate was situated where the arable[7] land of the plains begins to swell upwards into the rounded chalk hills which are characteristic of the county. As I drove from Dinton Station in the waning light of that autumn day, I was impressed by the weird[8] nature of the scenery. The few scattered cottages of the peasants were so dwarfed by the huge evidences of prehistoric life that the present appeared to be a dream and the past to be

---

[1] A favorite Holmesian term of Doyle's – unique, unparalleled, bizarre
[2] Knighthoods. C.B. represents a Companion of the Order of Bath. K.C.S.I. represents a Knight Commander of the Order of the Star of India
[3] Mumbai. Located on the east coast of central India on the Arabian Sea
[4] Grassy, rolling county in southern England – due west of London – home to the town of Salisbury and the nearby prehistoric monoliths of Stonehenge
[5] No more purely English – and simultaneously foreboding – setting could be imagined
[6] The comparative study of diseases across types and classes
[7] Suitable for farming
[8] Evoking the mystical, bizarre, and supernatural

the obtrusive and masterful reality. The road wound through the valleys, formed by a succession of grassy hills, and the summit of each was cut and carved into the most elaborate fortifications, some circular, and some square, but all on a scale which has defied the winds and the rains of many centuries. Some call them Roman and some British, but their true origin and the reasons for this particular tract of country being so interlaced with entrenchments have never been finally made clear[1]. Here and there on the long, smooth, olive-coloured slopes there rose small, rounded barrows or tumuli[2]. Beneath them lie the cremated ashes of the race which cut so deeply into the hills, but their graves tell us nothing save that a jar full of dust represents the man who once laboured under the sun[3].

It was through this weird country that I approached my uncle's residence of Rodenhurst, and the house was, as I found, in due keeping with its surroundings. Two broken and weather-stained pillars, each surmounted by a mutilated heraldic emblem[4], flanked the entrance to a neglected drive. A cold wind whistled through the elms which lined it, and the air was full of the drifting leaves. At the far end, under the gloomy arch of trees, a single yellow lamp burned steadily. In the dim half-light of the coming night I saw a long, low building stretching out two irregular wings, with deep eaves, a sloping gambrel roof[5], and walls which were criss-crossed with timber balks in the fashion of the Tudors. The cheery light of a fire flickered in the broad, latticed window to the left of the low-porched door, and this, as it proved, marked the study of my uncle, for it was thither that I was led by his butler in order to make my host's acquaintance.

He was cowering over his fire, for the moist chill of an English autumn had set him shivering. His lamp was unlit, and I only saw the red glow of the embers beating upon a huge, craggy face, with a Red Indian[6] nose and cheek, and deep furrows and seams from eye to chin, the sinister marks of hidden volcanic fires. He sprang up at my entrance with something of an old-world courtesy and welcomed me warmly to Rodenhurst. At the same time I was conscious, as the lamp was carried in, that it was a very critical pair of light-blue eyes which looked out at me from under shaggy eyebrows, like scouts beneath a bush, and that this outlandish uncle of mine was carefully reading off my character with all the ease of a practised observer and an experienced man of the world.

---

[1] Both early Britons and Roman legions constructed earthwork fortifications along the coasts of Britain. The Roman fort of Cunetio was discovered in Wiltshire in 1940 after an aerial photograph of farmland revealed its traces

[2] Prehistoric mounds of earth covering burial plots

[3] A melancholy meditation indeed – the theme of works (such as Sir Dominick's charity) as being worthless is already drumming loudly

[4] A family crest or other design

[5] A roof typical of a Dutch colonial house or an American barn, with two sloping sides

[6] American Indian, that is to say

For my part I looked at him, and looked again, for I had never seen a man whose appearance was more fitted to hold one's attention. His figure was the framework of a giant, but he had fallen away until his coat dangled straight down in a shocking fashion from a pair of broad and bony shoulders. All his limbs were huge yet emaciated, and I could not take my gaze from his knobby wrists, and long, gnarled hands. But his eyes—those peering, light-blue eyes—they were the most arrestive of any of his peculiarities. It was not their colour alone, nor was it the ambush of hair in which they lurked; but it was the expression which I read in them. For the appearance and bearing of the man were masterful, and one expected a certain corresponding arrogance in his eyes, but instead of that I read the look which tells of a spirit cowed and crushed, the furtive[1], expectant look of the dog whose master has taken the whip from the rack. I formed my own medical diagnosis upon one glance at those critical and yet appealing eyes. I believed that he was stricken with some mortal ailment, that he knew himself to be exposed to sudden death, and that he lived in terror of it. Such was my judgment—a false one, as the event showed; but I mention it that it may help you to realize the look which I read in his eyes.

My uncle's welcome was, as I have said, a courteous one, and in an hour or so I found myself seated between him and his wife at a comfortable dinner, with curious, pungent delicacies upon the table, and a stealthy, quick-eyed Oriental waiter behind his chair. The old couple had come round to that tragic imitation of the dawn of life when husband and wife, having lost or scattered all those who were their intimates, find themselves face to face and alone once more, their work done, and the end nearing fast. Those who have reached that stage in sweetness and love, who can change their winter into a gentle, Indian summer[2], have come as victors through the ordeal of life. Lady Holden was a small, alert woman with a kindly eye, and her expression as she glanced at him was a certificate of character to her husband. And yet, though I read a mutual love in their glances, I read also mutual horror, and recognized in her face some reflection of that stealthy fear which I had detected in his. Their talk was sometimes merry and sometimes sad, but there was a forced note in their merriment and a naturalness in their sadness which told me that a heavy heart beat upon either side of me.

We were sitting over our first glass of wine, and the servants had left the room, when the conversation took a turn which produced a remarkable effect upon my host and hostess. I cannot recall what it was which started the topic of the supernatural, but it ended in my showing them that the abnormal in psychical experiences was a subject to which I had, like many neurologists, devoted a great deal of attention. I concluded by narrating my

---

1 Secretive

2 A term that refers to an autumn where a pleasant heat wave appears after the first frost

experiences when, as a member of the Psychical Research Society[1], I had formed one of a committee of three who spent the night in a haunted house. Our adventures were neither exciting nor convincing, but, such as it was, the story appeared to interest my auditors in a remarkable degree. They listened with an eager silence, and I caught a look of intelligence between them which I could not understand. Lady Holden immediately afterwards rose and left the room.

Sir Dominick pushed the cigar-box over to me, and we smoked for some little time in silence. That huge, bony hand of his was twitching as he raised it with his cheroot[2] to his lips, and I felt that the man's nerves were vibrating like fiddle-strings. My instincts told me that he was on the verge of some intimate confidence, and I feared to speak lest I should interrupt it. At last he turned towards me with a spasmodic gesture like a man who throws his last scruple to the winds.

"From the little that I have seen of you it appears to me, Dr. Hardacre," said he, "that you are the very man I have wanted to meet."

"I am delighted to hear it, sir."

"Your head seems to be cool and steady. You will acquit me of any desire to flatter you, for the circumstances are too serious to permit of insincerities. You have some special knowledge upon these subjects, and you evidently view them from that philosophical standpoint which robs them of all vulgar[3] terror. I presume that the sight of an apparition would not seriously discompose you?"

"I think not, sir."

"Would even interest you, perhaps?"

"Most intensely."

"As a psychical observer, you would probably investigate it in as impersonal a fashion as an astronomer investigates a wandering comet?"

"Precisely."

He gave a heavy sigh.

"Believe me, Dr. Hardacre, there was a time when I could have spoken as you do now. My nerve was a byword in India. Even the Mutiny[4] never shook

---

[1] Formed in 1882, this society of paranormal investigators included Doyle, Sigmund Freud, W.B. Yeats, Carl Jung, and many other luminaries. Its self-proclaimed mission was to understand "events and abilities commonly described as psychic or paranormal by promoting and supporting important research in this area" and to "examine allegedly paranormal phenomena in a scientific and unbiased way"

[2] A large cigar with both ends cut flush rather than tapering. They are traditionally associated with India and, in particular, Burma, where they remain popular

[3] Lower-classed, uneducated

[4] The Indian Rebellion of 1857 occurred when Indian soldiers in service to the British East India Company mutinied. It began over a rumor that the paper cartridges soldiers had to bite off to load their rifles were greased in pig and cow fat – offensive to both Muslims and Hindus respectively. The conflict was far from civil, being vicious, bloody, and

it for an instant. And yet you see what I am reduced to—the most timorous[1] man, perhaps, in all this county of Wiltshire. Do not speak too bravely upon this subject, or you may find yourself subjected to as long-drawn a test as I am—a test which can only end in the madhouse or the grave."

I waited patiently until he should see fit to go farther in his confidence. His preamble had, I need not say, filled me with interest and expectation.

"For some years, Dr. Hardacre," he continued, "my life and that of my wife have been made miserable by a cause which is so grotesque that it borders upon the ludicrous. And yet familiarity has never made it more easy to bear—on the contrary, as time passes my nerves become more worn and shattered by the constant attrition. If you have no physical fears, Dr. Hardacre, I should very much value your opinion upon this phenomenon which troubles us so."

"For what it is worth my opinion is entirely at your service. May I ask the nature of the phenomenon?"

"I think that your experiences will have a higher evidential value if you are not told in advance what you may expect to encounter. You are yourself aware of the quibbles of unconscious cerebration and subjective impressions with which a scientific sceptic may throw a doubt upon your statement. It would be as well to guard against them in advance[2]."

"What shall I do, then?"

"I will tell you. Would you mind following me this way?" He led me out of the dining-room and down a long passage until we came to a terminal door. Inside there was a large, bare room fitted as a laboratory, with numerous scientific instruments and bottles. A shelf ran along one side, upon which there stood a long line of glass jars containing pathological and anatomical specimens[3].

"You see that I still dabble in some of my old studies," said Sir Dominick. "These jars are the remains of what was once a most excellent collection, but unfortunately I lost the greater part of them when my house was burned down in Bombay in '92. It was a most unfortunate affair for me—in more ways than one. I had examples of many rare conditions, and my splenic collection was probably unique. These are the survivors."

I glanced over them, and saw that they really were of a very great value and rarity from a pathological point of view: bloated organs, gaping cysts, distorted bones, odious parasites—a singular exhibition of the products of

---

inhuman. Massacres of surrendered garrisons, torture, and mass executions clouded the year with unforgettable violence

[1] Nervous, timid

[2] Rhetoric undoubtedly lifted from the SPR's playbook – applying scientific process to supernaturalism naturally assists in developing veracity, respect, and credibility

[3] Tumors, diseased organs, deformed fetuses, and anatomical anomalies are likely candidates

India[1].

"There is, as you see, a small settee[2] here," said my host. "It was far from our intention to offer a guest so meagre an accommodation, but since affairs have taken this turn, it would be a great kindness upon your part if you would consent to spend the night in this apartment. I beg that you will not hesitate to let me know if the idea should be at all repugnant to you."

"On the contrary," I said, "it is most acceptable."

"My own room is the second on the left, so that if you should feel that you are in need of company a call would always bring me to your side."

"I trust that I shall not be compelled to disturb you."

"It is unlikely that I shall be asleep. I do not sleep much. Do not hesitate to summon me."

And so with this agreement we joined Lady Holden in the drawing-room and talked of lighter things. It was no affectation upon my part to say that the prospect of my night's adventure was an agreeable one. I have no pretence to greater physical courage than my neighbours, but familiarity with a subject robs it of those vague and undefined terrors which are the most appalling to the imaginative mind. The human brain is capable of only one strong emotion at a time, and if it be filled with curiosity or scientific enthusiasm, there is no room for fear. It is true that I had my uncle's assurance that he had himself originally taken this point of view, but I reflected that the break-down of his nervous system might be due to his forty years in India as much as to any psychical experiences which had befallen him. I at least was sound in nerve and brain, and it was with something of the pleasurable thrill of anticipation with which the sportsman takes his position beside the haunt of his game that I shut the laboratory door behind me, and partially undressing, lay down upon the rug-covered settee.

It was not an ideal atmosphere for a bedroom. The air was heavy with many chemical odours, that of methylated spirit[3] predominating. Nor were the decorations of my chamber very sedative[4]. The odious line of glass jars with their relics of disease and suffering[5] stretched in front of my very eyes.

---

[1] The "products of India" are repulsive, hateful, parasitic deformities – Doyle seems to suggest that Britain's dalliances in colonialism (and in India's case, brutal colonialism) have come back to haunt the national conscience, and that, like Indian parasites revoltingly pickled in a British study, these moral shames have not remained neatly behind in their country of origin

[2] Comfortable seat for two persons

[3] Denatured alcohol; ethanol laced with caustic additives to discourage drinking, with many uses in the industrial, medical, commercial, and janitorial fields – in this case, pickling tissue

[4] Relaxing, conducive to sleep

[5] "relics of disease and suffering…" once more we are reminded that the impact of colonialism in India has not been one-sided – the British public is conscious of their shame and guilt

There was no blind to the window, and a three-quarter moon streamed its white light into the room, tracing a silver square with filigree[1] lattices upon the opposite wall. When I had extinguished my candle this one bright patch in the midst of the general gloom had certainly an eerie and discomposing aspect. A rigid and absolute silence reigned throughout the old house, so that the low swish of the branches in the garden came softly and smoothly to my ears. It may have been the hypnotic lullaby of this gentle susurrus[2], or it may have been the result of my tiring day, but after many dozings and many efforts to regain my clearness of perception, I fell at last into a deep and dreamless sleep.

I was awakened by some sound in the room, and I instantly raised myself upon my elbow on the couch. Some hours had passed, for the square patch upon the wall had slid downwards and sideways until it lay obliquely at the end of my bed. The rest of the room was in deep shadow. At first I could see nothing, presently, as my eyes became accustomed to the faint light, I was aware, with a thrill which all my scientific absorption could not entirely prevent, that something was moving slowly along the line of the wall. A gentle, shuffling sound, as of soft slippers, came to my ears, and I dimly discerned a human figure walking stealthily from the direction of the door. As it emerged into the patch of moonlight I saw very clearly what it was and how it was employed. It was a man, short and squat, dressed in some sort of dark-grey gown, which hung straight from his shoulders to his feet. The moon shone upon the side of his face, and I saw that it was chocolate-brown in colour, with a ball of black hair like a woman's at the back of his head. He walked slowly, and his eyes were cast upwards towards the line of bottles which contained those gruesome remnants of humanity. He seemed to examine each jar with attention, and then to pass on to the next. When he had come to the end of the line, immediately opposite my bed, he stopped, faced me, threw up his hands with a gesture of despair, and vanished from my sight.

I have said that he threw up his hands, but I should have said his arms, for as he assumed that attitude of despair I observed a singular peculiarity about his appearance. He had only one hand! As the sleeves drooped down from the upflung arms I saw the left plainly, but the right ended in a knobby and unsightly[3] stump. In every other way his appearance was so natural, and I had both seen and heard him so clearly, that I could easily have believed that he was an Indian servant of Sir Dominick's who had come into my room in search of something. It was only his sudden disappearance which suggested anything more sinister to me. As it was I

---

1 Delicate metalwork

2 Whimpering, murmuring noise

3 *Unsightly*. Once more, Doyle evinces feelings of discomfort, shame, repulsion, and "unsightliness" that could be compared to the national conscience of the United Kingdom in the later stages of British imperialism

sprang from my couch, lit a candle, and examined the whole room carefully. There were no signs of my visitor, and I was forced to conclude that there had really been something outside the normal laws of Nature in his appearance. I lay awake for the remainder of the night, but nothing else occurred to disturb me.

I am an early riser, but my uncle was an even earlier one, for I found him pacing up and down the lawn at the side of the house. He ran towards me in his eagerness when he saw me come out from the door.

"Well, well!" he cried. "Did you see him?"

"An Indian with one hand?"

"Precisely."

"Yes, I saw him"—and I told him all that occurred. When I had finished, he led the way into his study.

"We have a little time before breakfast," said he. "It will suffice to give you an explanation of this extraordinary affair—so far as I can explain that which is essentially inexplicable. In the first place, when I tell you that for four years I have never passed one single night, either in Bombay, aboard ship, or here in England without my sleep being broken by this fellow, you will understand why it is that I am a wreck of my former self. His programme[1] is always the same. He appears by my bedside, shakes me roughly by the shoulder, passes from my room into the laboratory, walks slowly along the line of my bottles, and then vanishes. For more than a thousand times he has gone through the same routine."

"What does he want?"

"He wants his hand."

"His hand?"

"Yes, it came about in this way. I was summoned to Peshawur[2] for a consultation some ten years ago, and while there I was asked to look at the hand of a native who was passing through with an Afghan caravan. The fellow came from some mountain tribe living away at the back of beyond somewhere on the other side of Kaffiristan[3]. He talked a bastard Pushtoo[4], and it was all I could do to understand him. He was suffering from a soft sarcomatous[5] swelling of one of the metacarpal[6] joints, and I made him realize that it was only by losing his hand that he could hope to save his life. After much persuasion he consented to the operation, and he asked me, when it was over, what fee I demanded. The poor fellow was almost a beggar, so that the idea of a fee was absurd, but I answered in jest that my

---

[1] Schedule, agenda, routine

[2] *Peshawar* is a city situated in northeast Pakistan, near the Afghani border

[3] *Kāfiristān* is a historical region in southeastern Afghanistan

[4] *Pashto* is a central Asian language also loosely called Afghani

[5] A malignant tumor rising from connective tissues

[6] Situated between the wrist and fingers

fee should be his hand, and that I proposed to add it to my pathological collection.

"To my surprise he demurred very much to the suggestion, and he explained that according to his religion it was an all-important matter that the body should be reunited after death, and so make a perfect dwelling for the spirit. The belief is, of course, an old one, and the mummies of the Egyptians arose from an analogous superstition. I answered him that his hand was already off, and asked him how he intended to preserve it. He replied that he would pickle it in salt and carry it about with him. I suggested that it might be safer in my keeping than in his, and that I had better means than salt for preserving it. On realizing that I really intended to carefully keep it, his opposition vanished instantly. 'But remember, sahib[1],' said he, 'I shall want it back when I am dead.' I laughed at the remark, and so the matter ended. I returned to my practice, and he no doubt in the course of time was able to continue his journey to Afghanistan.

"Well, as I told you last night, I had a bad fire in my house at Bombay. Half of it was burned down, and, amongst other things, my pathological collection was largely destroyed. What you see are the poor remains of it. The hand of the hillman went with the rest, but I gave the matter no particular thought at the time. That was six years ago.

"Four years ago—two years after the fire—I was awakened one night by a furious tugging at my sleeve. I sat up under the impression that my favourite mastiff was trying to arouse me. Instead of this, I saw my Indian patient of long ago, dressed in the long, grey gown which was the badge of his people. He was holding up his stump and looking reproachfully at me. He then went over to my bottles, which at that time I kept in my room, and he examined them carefully, after which he gave a gesture of anger and vanished. I realized that he had just died, and that he had come to claim my promise that I should keep his limb in safety for him.

"Well, there you have it all, Dr. Hardacre. Every night at the same hour for four years this performance has been repeated. It is a simple thing in itself, but it has worn me out like water dropping on a stone. It has brought a vile insomnia with it, for I cannot sleep now for the expectation of his coming. It has poisoned my old age and that of my wife, who has been the sharer in this great trouble. But there is the breakfast gong, and she will be waiting impatiently to know how it fared with you last night. We are both much indebted to you for your gallantry, for it takes something from the weight of our misfortune when we share it, even for a single night, with a friend, and it reassures us to our sanity, which we are sometimes driven to question."

This was the curious narrative which Sir Dominick confided to me—a story which to many would have appeared to be a grotesque impossibility, but which, after my experience of the night before, and my previous

---

[1] South Indian address to a respectable man (cf. *mynheer, mein Herr, monsieur, senior*)

knowledge of such things, I was prepared to accept as an absolute fact. I thought deeply over the matter, and brought the whole range of my reading and experience to bear over it. After breakfast, I surprised my host and hostess by announcing that I was returning to London by the next train. "My dear doctor," cried Sir Dominick in great distress, "you make me feel that I have been guilty of a gross breach of hospitality in intruding this unfortunate matter upon you. I should have borne my own burden."

"It is, indeed, that matter which is taking me to London," I answered; "but you are mistaken, I assure you, if you think that my experience of last night was an unpleasant one to me. On the contrary, I am about to ask your permission to return in the evening and spend one more night in your laboratory. I am very eager to see this visitor once again."

My uncle was exceedingly anxious to know what I was about to do, but my fears of raising false hopes prevented me from telling him. I was back in my own consulting-room a little after luncheon, and was confirming my memory of a passage in a recent book upon occultism which had arrested my attention when I read it.

"In the case of earth-bound spirits," said my authority, "some one dominant idea obsessing them at the hour of death is sufficient to hold them in this material world. They are the amphibia of this life and of the next, capable of passing from one to the other as the turtle passes from land to water. The causes which may bind a soul so strongly to a life which its body has abandoned are any violent emotion. Avarice, revenge, anxiety, love, and pity have all been known to have this effect. As a rule it springs from some unfulfilled wish, and when the wish has been fulfilled the material bond relaxes. There are many cases upon record which show the singular persistence of these visitors, and also their disappearance when their wishes have been fulfilled, or in some cases when a reasonable compromise has been effected."[1]

"*A reasonable compromise effected*"—those were the words which I had brooded over all the morning, and which I now verified in the original. No actual atonement could be made here—but a reasonable compromise! I made my way as fast as a train could take me to the Shadwell Seamen's Hospital, where my old friend Jack Hewett was house-surgeon. Without explaining the situation I made him understand what it was that I wanted.

"A brown man's hand!" said he, in amazement. "What in the world do you want that for?"

"Never mind. I'll tell you some day. I know that your wards are full of Indians."

"I should think so. But a hand—" He thought a little, and then struck a bell.

---

[1] This is a very excellent summarization of the principle theory – both in literature and among 19th century spiritualists – of who ghosts are and why they remain. A more concise but exhaustive explanation could not be hoped for

"Travers," said he to a student-dresser, "what became of the hands of the Lascar[1] which we took off yesterday? I mean the fellow from the East India Dock who got caught in the steam winch."

"They are in the *post-mortem* room, sir."

"Just pack one of them in antiseptics and give it to Dr. Hardacre."

And so I found myself back at Rodenhurst before dinner with this curious outcome of my day in town. I still said nothing to Sir Dominick, but I slept that night in the laboratory, and I placed the Lascar's hand in one of the glass jars at the end of my couch.

So interested was I in the result of my experiment that sleep was out of the question. I sat with a shaded lamp beside me and waited patiently for my visitor. This time I saw him clearly from the first. He appeared beside the door, nebulous[2] for an instant, and then hardening into as distinct an outline as any living man. The slippers beneath his grey gown were red and heelless, which accounted for the low, shuffling sound which he made as he walked. As on the previous night he passed slowly along the line of bottles until he paused before that which contained the hand. He reached up to it, his whole figure quivering with expectation, took it down, examined it eagerly, and then, with a face which was convulsed with fury and disappointment, he hurled it down on the floor. There was a crash which resounded throughout the house, and when I looked up the mutilated Indian had disappeared. A moment later my door flew open and Sir Dominick rushed in.

"You are not hurt?" he cried.

"No—but deeply disappointed."

He looked in astonishment at the splinters of glass, and the brown hand lying upon the floor.

"Good God!" he cried. "What is this?"

I told him my idea and its wretched sequel. He listened intently, but shook his head.

"It was well thought of," said he, "but I fear that there is no such easy end to my sufferings. But one thing I now insist upon. It is that you shall never again upon any pretext occupy this room. My fears that something might have happened to you—when I heard that crash—have been the most acute of all the agonies which I have undergone. I will not expose myself to a repetition of it."

He allowed me, however, to spend the remainder of the night where I was, and I lay there worrying over the problem and lamenting my own failure. With the first light of morning there was the Lascar's hand still lying upon the floor to remind me of my fiasco. I lay looking at it—and as I lay suddenly an idea flew like a bullet through my head and brought me quivering with excitement out of my couch. I raised the grim relic from

---

[1] A southeast Indian menial worker – in this case, a sailor

[2] Unclear, hazy

where it had fallen. Yes, it was indeed so. The hand was the *left* hand of the Lascar.

By the first train I was on my way to town, and hurried at once to the Seamen's Hospital. I remembered that both hands of the Lascar had been amputated, but I was terrified lest the precious organ which I was in search of might have been already consumed in the crematory[1]. My suspense was soon ended. It had still been preserved in the *post-mortem* room. And so I returned to Rodenhurst in the evening with my mission accomplished and the material for a fresh experiment.

But Sir Dominick Holden would not hear of my occupying the laboratory again. To all my entreaties he turned a deaf ear. It offended his sense of hospitality, and he could no longer permit it. I left the hand, therefore, as I had done its fellow the night before, and I occupied a comfortable bedroom in another portion of the house, some distance from the scene of my adventures.

But in spite of that my sleep was not destined to be uninterrupted. In the dead of night my host burst into my room, a lamp in his hand. His huge, gaunt figure was enveloped in a loose dressing-gown, and his whole appearance might certainly have seemed more formidable to a weak-nerved man than that of the Indian of the night before. But it was not his entrance so much as his expression which amazed me. He had turned suddenly younger by twenty years at the least. His eyes were shining, his features radiant, and he waved one hand in triumph over his head. I sat up astounded, staring sleepily at this extraordinary visitor. But his words soon drove the sleep from my eyes.

"We have done it! We have succeeded!" he shouted. "My dear Hardacre, how can I ever in this world repay you?"

"You don't mean to say that it is all right?"

"Indeed I do. I was sure that you would not mind being awakened to hear such blessed news."

"Mind! I should think not indeed. But is it really certain?"

"I have no doubt whatever upon the point. I owe you such a debt, my dear nephew, as I have never owed a man before, and never expected to. What can I possibly do for you that is commensurate[2]? Providence must have sent you to my rescue. You have saved both my reason and my life, for another six months of this must have seen me either in a cell[3] or a coffin. And my wife—it was wearing her out before my eyes. Never could I have believed that any human being could have lifted this burden off me." He seized my hand and wrung it in his bony grip.

"It was only an experiment—a forlorn hope—but I am delighted from my heart that it has succeeded. But how do you know that it is all right? Have

---

[1] Furnace where unclaimed bodies were cremated

[2] A proportional favor in return

[3] At a madhouse

you seen something?"

He seated himself at the foot of my bed.

"I have seen enough," said he. "It satisfies me that I shall be troubled no more. What has passed is easily told. You know that at a certain hour this creature always comes to me. To-night he arrived at the usual time, and aroused me with even more violence than is his custom. I can only surmise that his disappointment of last night increased the bitterness of his anger against me. He looked angrily at me, and then went on his usual round. But in a few minutes I saw him, for the fist time since this persecution began, return to my chamber. He was smiling. I saw the gleam of his white teeth through the dim light. He stood facing me at the end of my bed, and three times he made the low Eastern salaam[1] which is their solemn leave-taking. And the third time that he bowed he raised his arms over his head, and I saw his *two* hands outstretched in the air. So he vanished, and, as I believe, for ever."

So that is the curious experience which won me the affection and the gratitude of my celebrated uncle, the famous Indian surgeon. His anticipations were realised, and never again was he disturbed by the visits of the restless hillman in search of his lost member. Sir Dominick and Lady Holden spent a very happy old age, unclouded, so far as I know, by any trouble, and they finally died during the great influenza epidemic[2] within a few weeks of each other. In his lifetime he always turned to me for advice in everything which concerned that English life of which he knew so little; and I aided him also in the purchase and development of his estates. It was no great surprise to me, therefore, that I found myself eventually promoted over the heads of five exasperated cousins, and changed in a single day from a hard-working country doctor into the head of an important Wiltshire family. I, at least, have reason to bless the memory of the man with the brown hand, and the day when I was fortunate enough to relieve Rodenhurst of his unwelcome presence.

---

[1] A deep bow with the right hand on the forehead commonly practiced in Muslim cultures, *salām* meaning "peace" in Arabic

[2] The Russian Flu of 1889-1890 swept across Europe, the Americas, and Asia taking the lives of some one million people. It remains the earliest flu pandemic in recorded history

BY 1857 the experiment of the British Empire had run into the most cataclysmic colonial misadventure since the Black Hole of Calcutta. That year's Indian Mutiny was a costly conflict drenched in gore and noted for its civilian massacres, moral travesties, and grisly retributions. Blood was spilled liberally on both sides, and all parties were guilty of crimes against humanity. When the British finally squelched the rebellion, their public image and national identity had been damaged irreparably. By the time this story was published, British atrocities in Africa, China, India, and South America had continued to plague the public imagination, haunting the sense of national pride and morality with the ghosts of guilt, shame, and disgust. It was a haunting which Doyle chose to tackle more than once, but none go quite so far in their exploration of colonial trauma, distrust, and reparations than "The Brown Hand." Infusing his ghost tale with a Holmesian seasoning of logic and deduction, Doyle provides a solution to the disastrous race relations in the British Empire: making symbolic reparations in place of the irredeemable losses incurred by the Anglo-Saxon colonial ventures. Life and limb may not be replaceable, but suitable compensations and national gestures of apology can be made. Other Doyle ghost stories have far grimmer plots, but this one attempts to exorcise a social ill rather than taking the pessimistic stance that many colonial ghost stories (see: Kipling) strike. Images of decayed invaders feature prominently even in the story's English landscape with its Roman ruins, foreshadowing the British Empire's ghostly fate if left unaltered, draping the plot in a dreary pall of constricting doom. While the specter is certainly not duped into believing the replacement hand to be the original, it responds to a respectful effort to right the wrong. After this the suffocating vapors dissipate from the English countryside. A similar effort, Doyle suggests, could exorcise the demons of the spiritually anemic Victorian society.

DOYLE fostered a deep fascination with the duality of man and the frequent hypocrisy which came with power and prestige – the same troubling concepts which launched Robert Louis Stevenson's *Dr Jekyll and Mr Hyde* into household fame. Doyle's villains are sometimes low-born parasites, pathetic crooks, and dim-witted aspirants, but they are much more often men of acclaim and authority. We need only think of the well-bred, widely-esteemed villains of "The Creeping Man," "Charles Augustus Milverton," "The Empty House," "The Speckled Band," "Wisteria Lodge," "The Red-Headed League," and "The Illustrious Client," not to mention Professor James Moriarty. Doyle was always a bit of a renegade, and despite his knighthood, his idealism, and his chivalric character, he demonstrated a profound distrust in institutions and authority figures. The great *ideas* of mankind – like patriotism and humanitarianism – were far more attractive to him than the great *men*. His was a world where mercy trumped legal justice, and individual genius outperformed official appointments. Indeed, Holmes and Watson committed innumerable misdemeanors, felonies – and perhaps several manslaughters – in the name of a Nietzschean pursuit of personal justice. Authorities are subject to corruption, stupidity, and complacency in his fiction, and the most trusted man in a community may very well be the greatest tripwire to the pursuit of justice, or the source of evildoing itself (e.g., the judge in "The Greek Interpreter" who hesitates to sign the search warrant due to his unflinching devotion to constitutional rights – a delay which results in the death of a kidnapped man). The following tale bears much similarity to "The Silver Hatchet," but with one major exception: this killer is possessed by nothing other than a vendetta against humanity, and an unquestionable position of trust in the community – a Hyde in Jekyll's clothing.

A Pastoral Horror

{1890}

FAR above the level of the Lake of Constance, nestling in a little corner of the Tyrolese Alps, lies the quiet town of Feldkirch. It is remarkable for nothing save for the presence of a large and well-conducted Jesuit school and for the extreme beauty of its situation. There is no more lovely spot in the whole of the Vorarlberg. From the hills which rise behind the town, the great lake glimmers some fifteen miles off, like a broad sea of quicksilver. Down below in the plains the Rhine and the Danube prattle along, flowing swiftly and merrily, with none of the dignity which they assume as they grow from brooks into rivers. Five great countries or principalities,—Switzerland, Austria, Baden, Wurtemburg, and Bavaria—are visible from the plateau of Feldkirch.

Feldkirch is the centre of a large tract of hilly and pastoral country. The main road runs through the centre of the town, and then on as far as Anspach, where it divides into two branches, one of which is larger than the other. This more important one runs through the valleys across Austrian Tyrol into Tyrol proper, going as far, I believe, as the capital of Innsbruck. The lesser road runs for eight or ten miles amid wild and rugged glens to the village of Laden, where it breaks up into a network of sheep-tracks. In this quiet spot, I, John Hudson, spent nearly two years of my life, from the June of '65 to the March of '67, and it was during that time that those events occurred which for some weeks brought the retired hamlet into an unholy prominence, and caused its name for the first, and probably for the last time, to be a familiar word to the European press. The short account of these incidents which appeared in the English papers was, however, inaccurate and misleading, besides which, the rapid advance of the Prussians, culminating in the battle of Sadowa, attracted public attention away from what might have moved it deeply in less troublous times. It seems to me that the facts may be detailed now, and be new to the great majority of readers, especially as I was myself intimately connected with the drama, and am in a position to give many particulars which have never before been made public.

And first a few words as to my own presence in this out of the way spot. When the great city firm of Sprynge, Wilkinson, and Spragge failed, and paid their creditors rather less than eighteen-pence in the pound, a number of humble individuals were ruined, including myself. There was, however, some legal objection which held out a chance of my being made an exception to the other creditors, and being paid in full. While the case was being brought out I was left with a very small sum for my subsistance.

I determined, therefore, to take up my residence abroad in the interim, since I could live more economically there, and be spared the mortification of meeting those who had known me in my more prosperous days. A friend of mine had described Laden to me some years before as being the most isolated place which he had ever come across in all his experience, and as isolation and cheap living are usually synonymous, I bethought use of his words. Besides, I was in a cynical humour with my fellow-man, and desired to see as little of him as possible for some time to come. Obeying, then, the guidances of poverty and of misanthropy, I made my way to Laden, where my arrival created the utmost excitement among the simple inhabitants. The manners and customs of the red- bearded Englander, his long walks, his check suit, and the reasons which had led him to abandon his fatherland, were all fruitful sources of gossip to the topers who frequented the Gruner Mann and the Schwartzer Bar—the two alehouses of the village.

I found myself very happy at Laden. The surroundings were magnificent, and twenty years of Brixton had sharpened my admiration for nature as an olive improves the flavour of wine. In my youth I had been a fair German scholar, and I found myself able, before I had been many months abroad, to converse even on scientific and abstruse subjects with the new curé of the parish.

This priest was a great godsend to me, for he was a most learned man and a brilliant conversationalist. Father Verhagen—for that was his name—though little more than forty years of age, had made his reputation as an author by a brilliant monograph upon the early Popes—a work which eminent critics have compared favourably with Von Ranke's. I shrewdly suspect that it was owing to some rather unorthodox views advanced in this book that Verhagen was relegated to the obscurity of Laden. His opinions upon every subject were ultra-Liberal, and in his fiery youth he had been ready to vindicate them, as was proved by a deep scar across his chin, received from a dragoon's sabre in the abortive insurrection at Berlin. Altogether the man was an interesting one, and though he was by nature somewhat cold and reserved, we soon established an acquaintanceship.

The atmosphere of morality in Laden was a very rarefied one. The position of Intendant Wurms and his satellites had for many years been a sinecure. Non-attendance at church upon a Sunday or feast-day was about the deepest and darkest crime which the most advanced of the villagers had attained to. Occasionally some hulking Fritz or Andreas would come lurching home at ten o'clock at night, slightly under the influence of Bavarian beer, and might even abuse the wife of his bosom if she ventured to remonstrate, but such cases were rare, and when they occurred the Ladeners looked at the culprit for some time in a half admiring, half horrified manner, as one who had committed a gaudy sin and so asserted his individuality.

It was in this peaceful village that a series of crimes suddenly broke out which astonished all Europe, and for atrocity and for the mystery which surrounded them surpassed anything of which I have ever heard or read. I shall endeavour to give a succinct account of these events in the order of their sequence, in which I am much helped by the fact that it has been my custom all my life to keep a journal—to the pages of which I now refer.

It was, then, I find upon the 19th of May in the spring of 1866, that my old landlady, Frau Zimmer, rushed wildly into the room as I was sipping my morning cup of chocolate and informed me that a murder had been committed in the village. At first I could hardly believe the news, but as she persisted in her statement, and was evidently terribly frightened, I put on my hat and went out to find the truth. When I came into the main street of the village I saw several men hurrying along in front of me, and following them I came upon an excited group in front of the little stadthaus or town hall—a barn-like edifice which was used for all manner of public gatherings. They were collected round the body of one Maul, who had formerly been a steward upon one of the steamers running between Lindau and Fredericshaven, on the Lake of Constance. He was a harmless, inoffensive little man, generally popular in the village, and, as far as was known, without an enemy in the world. Maul lay upon his face, with his fingers dug into the earth, no doubt in his last convulsive struggles, and his hair all matted together with blood, which had streamed down over the collar of his coat. The body had been discovered nearly two hours, but no one appeared to know what to do or whither to convey it. My arrival, however, together with that of the curé, who came almost simultaneously, infused some vigour into the crowd. Under our direction the corpse was carried up the steps, and laid on the floor of the town hall, where, having made sure that life was extinct, we proceeded to examine the injuries, in conjunction with Lieutenant Wurms, of the police. Maul's face was perfectly placid, showing that he had had no thought of danger until the fatal blow was struck. His watch and purse had not been taken. Upon washing the clotted blood from the back of his head a singular triangular wound was found, which had smashed the bone and penetrated deeply into the brain. It had evidently been inflicted by a heavy blow from a sharp-pointed pyramidal instrument. I believe that it was Father Verhagen, the curé, who suggested the probability of the weapon in question having been a short mattock or small pickaxe, such as are to be found in every Alpine cottage. The Intendant, with praiseworthy promptness, at once obtained one and striking a turnip, produced just such a curious gap as was to be seen in poor Maul's head. We felt that we had come upon the first link of a chain which might guide us to the assassin. It was not long before we seemed to grasp the whole clue.

A sort of inquest was held upon the body that same afternoon, at which Pfiffor, the maire, presided, the curé, the Intendant, Freckler, of the post office, and myself forming ourselves into a sort of committee of investigation. Any villager who could throw a light upon the case or give an account of the movements of the murdered man upon the previous evening was invited to attend. There was a fair muster of witnesses, and we soon gathered a connected series of facts. At half-past eight o'clock Maul had entered the Gruner Mann public-house, and had called for a flagon of beer. At that time there were sitting in the tap-room Waghorn, the butcher of the village, and an Italian pedlar named Cellini, who used to come three times a year to Laden with cheap jewellery and other wares. Immediately after his entrance the landlord had seated himself with his customers, and the four had spent the evening together, the common villagers not being admitted beyond the bar. It seemed from the evidence of the landlord and of Waghorn, both of whom were most respectable and trustworthy men, that shortly after nine o'clock a dispute arose between the deceased and the pedlar. Hot words had been exchanged, and the Italian had eventually left the room, saying that he would not stay any longer to hear his country decried. Maul remained for nearly an hour, and being somewhat elated at having caused his adversary's retreat, he drank rather more than was usual with him. One witness had met him walking towards his home, about ten o'clock, and deposed to his having been slightly the worse for drink. Another had met him just a minute or so before he reached the spot in front of the stadthaus where the deed was done. This man's evidence was most important. He swore confidently that while passing the town hall, and before meeting Maul, he had seen a figure standing in the shadow of the building, adding that the person appeared to him, as far as he could make him out, to be not unlike the Italian.

Up to this point we had then established two facts—that the Italian had left the Gruner Mann before Maul, with words of anger on his lips; the second, that some unknown individual had been seen lying in wait on the road which the ex-steward would have to traverse. A third, and most important, was reached when the woman with whom the Italian lodged deposed that he had not returned the night before until half-past ten, an unusually late hour for Laden. How had he employed the time, then, from shortly after nine, when he left the public-house, until half-past ten, when he returned to his rooms? Things were beginning to look very black, indeed, against the pedlar.

It could not be denied, however, that there were points in the man's favour, and that the case against him consisted entirely of circumstantial evidence. In the first place, there was no sign of a mattock or any other instrument which could have been used for such a purpose among the Italian's goods; nor was it easy to understand how he could come by any such a weapon, since he did not go home between the time of the quarrel and his final return. Again, as the curé pointed out, since Cellini was a comparative stranger in the village, it was very unlikely that he would know which road Maul would take in order to reach his home. This objection was weakened, however, by the evidence of the dead man's servant, who deposed that the pedlar had been hawking his wares in front of their house the day before, and might very possibly have seen the owner at one of the windows. As to the prisoner himself, his attitude at first had been one of defiance, and even of amusement; but when he began to realise the weight of evidence against him, his manner became cringing, and he wrung his hands hideously, loudly proclaiming his innocence. His defence was that after leaving the inn, he had taken a long walk down the Anspach-road in order to cool down his excitement, and that this was the cause of his late return. As to the murder of Maul, he knew no more about it than the babe unborn.

I have dwelt at some length upon the circumstances of this case, because there are events in connection with it which makes it peculiarly interesting. I intend now to fall back upon my diary, which was very fully kept during this period, and indeed during my whole residence abroad. It will save me trouble to quote from it, and it will be a teacher for the accuracy of facts.

May 20th.—Nothing thought of and nothing talked of but the recent tragedy. A hunt has been made among the woods and along the brook in the hope of finding the weapon of the assassin. The more I think of it, the more convinced I am that Cellini is the man. The fact of the money being untouched proves that the crime was committed from motives of revenge, and who would bear more spite towards poor innocent Maul except the vindictive hot-blooded Italian whom he had just offended. I dined with Pfiffor in the evening, and he entirely agreed with me in my view of the case.

May 21st.—Still no word as far as I can hear which throws any light upon the murder. Poor Maul was buried at twelve o'clock in the neat little village churchyard. The curé led the service with great feeling, and his audience, consisting of the whole population of the village, were much moved, interrupting him frequently by sobs and ejaculations of grief. After the painful ceremony was over I had a short walk with our good priest. His naturally excitable nature has been considerably stirred by recent events. His hand trembles and his face is pale.

"My friend," said he, taking me by the hand as we walked together, "you know something of medicine." (I had been two years at Guy's). "I have been far from well of late."

"It is this sad affair which has upset you," I said.

"No," he answered, "I have felt it coming on for some time, but it has been worse of late. I have a pain which shoots from here to there," he put his hand to his temples. "If I were struck by lightning, the sudden shock it causes me could not be more great. At times when I close my eyes flashes of light dart before them, and my ears are for ever ringing. Often I know not what I do. My fear is lest I faint some time when performing the holy offices."

"You are overworking yourself," I said, "you must have rest and strengthening tonics. Are you writing just now? And how much do you do each day?"

"Eight hours," he answered. "Sometimes ten, sometimes even twelve, when the pains in my head do not interrupt me."

"You must reduce it to four," I said authoritatively. "You must also take regular exercise. I shall send you some quinine which I have in my trunk, and you can take as much as would cover a gulden in a glass of milk every morning and night."

He departed, vowing that he would follow my directions.

I hear from the maire that four policemen are to be sent from Anspach to remove Cellini to a safer gaol.

May 22nd.—To say that I was startled would give but a faint idea of my mental state. I am confounded, amazed, horrified beyond all expression. Another and a more dreadful crime has been committed during the night. Freckler has been found dead in his house—the very Freckler who had sat with me on the committee of investigation the day before. I write these notes after a long and anxious day's work, during which I have been endeavouring to assist the officers of the law. The villagers are so paralysed with fear at this fresh evidence of an assassin in their midst that there would be a general panic but for our exertions. It appears that Freckler, who was a man of peculiar habits, lived alone in an isolated dwelling. Some curiosity was aroused this morning by the fact that he had not gone to his work, and that there was no sign of movement about the house. A crowd assembled, and the doors were eventually forced open. The unfortunate Freckler was found in the bed-room upstairs, lying with his head in the fireplace. He had met his death by an exactly similar wound to that which had proved fatal to Maul, save that in this instance the injury was in front. His hands were clenched, and there was an indescribable look of horror, and, as it seemed to me, of surprise upon his features. There were marks of muddy footsteps upon the stairs, which must have been caused by the murderer in his ascent, as his victim had put on his slippers before retiring to his bed-room. These prints, however, were too much blurred to enable us to get a trustworthy outline of the foot. They were only to be found upon every third step, showing with what fiendish swiftness this human tiger had rushed upstairs in search of his victim. There was a considerable sum of money in the house, but not one farthing had been touched, nor had any of the drawers in the bed-room been opened.

As the dismal news became known the whole population of the village assembled in a great crowd in front of the house—rather, I think, from the gregariousness of terror than from mere curiosity. Every man looked with suspicion upon his neighbour. Most were silent, and when they spoke it was in whispers, as if they feared to raise their voices. None of these people were allowed to enter the house, and we, the more enlightened members of the community, made a strict examination of the premises. There was absolutely nothing, however, to give the slightest clue as to the assassin. Beyond the fact that he must be an active man, judging from the manner in which he ascended the stairs, we have gained nothing from this second tragedy. Intendant Wurms pointed out, indeed, that the dead man's rigid right arm was stretched out as if in greeting, and that, therefore, it was probable that this late visitor was someone with whom Freckler was well acquainted. This, however, was, to a large extent, conjecture. If anything could have added to the horror created by the dreadful occurrence, it was the fact that the crime must have been committed at the early hour of half-past eight in the evening—that being the time registered by a small cuckoo clock, which had been carried away by Freckler in his fall.

No one, apparently, heard any suspicious sounds or saw any one enter or leave the house. It was done rapidly, quietly, and completely, though many people must have been about at the time. Poor Pfiffor and our good curé are terribly cut up by the awful occurrence, and, indeed, I feel very much depressed myself now that all the excitement is over and the reaction set in. There are very few of the villagers about this evening, but from every side is heard the sound of hammering—the peasants fitting bolts and bars upon the doors and windows of their houses. Very many of them have been entirely unprovided with anything of the sort, nor were they ever required until now. Frau Zimmer has manufactured a huge fastening which would be ludicrous if we were in a humour for laughter.

I hear to-night that Cellini has been released, as, of course, there is no possible pretext for detaining him now; also that word has been sent to all the villages near for any police that can be spared.

My nerves have been so shaken that I remained awake the greater part of the night, reading Gordon's translation of Tacitus by candlelight. I have got out my navy revolver and cleaned it, so as to be ready for all eventualities.

Mary 23rd.—The police force has been recruited by three more men from Anspach and two from Thalstadt at the other side of the hills. Intendant Wurms has established an efficient system of patrols, so that we may consider ourselves reasonably safe. To-day has cast no light upon the murders. The general opinion in the village seems to be that they have been done by some stranger who lies concealed among the woods. They argue that they have all known each other since childhood, and that there is no one of their number who would be capable of such actions. Some of the more daring of them have made a hunt among the pine forests to-day, but without success.

May 24th.—Events crowd on apace. We seem hardly to have recovered from one horror when something else occurs to excite the popular imagination. Fortunately, this time it is not a fresh tragedy, although the news is serious enough.

The murderer has been seen, and that upon the public road, which proves that his thirst for blood has not been quenched yet, and also that our reinforcements of police are not enough to guarantee security. I have just come back from hearing Andreas Murch narrate his experience, though he is still in such a state of trepidation that his story is somewhat incoherent. He was belated among the hills, it seems, owing to mist. It was nearly eleven o'clock before he struck the main road about a couple of miles from the village. He confesses that he felt by no means comfortable at finding himself out so late after the recent occurrences. However, as the fog had cleared away and the moon was shining brightly, he trudged sturdily along. Just about a quarter of a mile from the village the road takes a very sharp bend. Andreas had got as far as this when he suddenly heard in the still night the sound of footsteps approaching rapidly round this curve. Overcome with fear, he threw himself into the ditch which skirts the road, and lay there motionless in the shadow, peering over the side. The steps came nearer and nearer, and then a tall dark figure came round the corner at a swinging pace, and passing the spot where the moon glimmered upon the white face of the frightened peasant, halted in the road about twenty yards further on, and began probing about among the reeds on the roadside with an instrument which Andreas Murch recognised with horror as being a long mattock. After searching about in this way for a minute or so, as if he suspected that someone was concealed there, for he must have heard the sound of the footsteps, he stood still leaning upon his weapon. Murch describes him as a tall, thin man, dressed in clothes of a darkish colour. The lower part of his face was swathed in a wrapper of some sort, and the little which was visible appeared to be of a ghastly pallor. Murch could not see enough of his features to identify him, but thinks that it was no one whom he had ever seen in his life before. After standing for some little time, the man with the mattock had walked swiftly away into the darkness, in the direction in which he imagined the fugitive had gone. Andreas, as may be supposed, lost little time in getting safely into the village, where he alarmed the police. Three of them, armed with carbines, started down the road, but saw no signs of the miscreant. There is, of course, a possibility that Murch's story is exaggerated and that his imagination has been sharpened by fear. Still, the whole incident cannot be trumped up, and this awful demon who haunts us is evidently still active.

There is an ill-conditioned fellow named Hiedler, who lives in a hut on the side of the Spiegelberg, and supports himself by chamois hunting and by acting as guide to the few tourists who find their way here. Popular suspicion has fastened on this man, for no better reason than that he is tall, thin, and known to be rough and brutal. His chalet has been searched to-day, but nothing of importance found. He has, however, been arrested and confined in the same room which Cellini used to occupy.

☙

At this point there is a gap of a week in my diary, during which time there was an entire cessation of the constant alarms which have harassed us lately. Some explained it by supposing that the terrible unknown had moved on to some fresh and less guarded scene of operations. Others imagine that we have secured the right man in the shape of the vagabond Hiedler. Be the cause what it may, peace and contentment reign once more in the village, and a short seven days have sufficed to clear away the cloud of care from men's brows, though the police are still on the alert. The season for rifle shooting is beginning, and as Laden has, like every other Tyrolese village, butts of its own, there is a continual pop, pop, all day. These peasants are dead shots up to about four hundred yards. No troops in the world could subdue them among their native mountains.

My friend Verhagen, the curé, and Pfiffor, the maire, used to go down in the afternoon to see the shooting with me. The former says that the quinine has done him much good and that his appetite is improved. We all agree that it is good policy to encourage the amusements of the people so that they may forget all about this wretched business. Vaghorn, the butcher, won the prize offered by the maire. He made five bulls, and what we should call a magpie out of six shots at 100 yards. This is English prize-medal form.

June 2nd.—Who could have imagined that a day which opened so fairly could have so dark an ending? The early carrier brought me a letter by which I learned that Spragge and Co. have agreed to pay my claim in full, although it may be some months before the money is forthcoming. This will make a difference of nearly £400 a year to me—a matter of moment when a man is in his seven-and-fortieth year.

And now for the grand events of the hour. My interview with the vampire who haunts us, and his attempt upon Frau Bischoff, the landlady of the Gruner Mann—to say nothing of the narrow escape of our good curé. There seems to be something almost supernatural in the malignity of this unknown fiend, and the impunity with which he continues his murderous course. The real reason of it lies in the badly lit state of the place—or rather the entire absence of light—and also in the fact that thick woods stretch right down to the houses on every side, so that escape is made easy. In spite of this, however, he had two very narrow escapes to-night—one from my pistol, and one from the officers of the law. I shall not sleep much, so I may spend half an hour in jotting down these strange doings in my dairy. I am no coward, but life in Laden is becoming too much for my nerves. I believe the matter will end in the emigration of the whole population.

To come to my story, then. I felt lonely and depressed this evening, in spite of the good news of the morning. About nine o'clock, just as night began to fall, I determined to stroll over and call upon the curé, thinking that a little intellectual chat might cheer me up. I slipped my revolver into my pocket, therefore—a precaution which I never neglected—and went out, very much against the advice of good Frau Zimmer. I think I mentioned some months ago in my diary that the curé's house is some little way out of the village upon the brow of a small hill. When I arrived there I found that he had gone out—which, indeed, I might have anticipated, for he had complained lately of restlessness at night, and I had recommended him to take a little exercise in the evening. His housekeeper made me very welcome, however, and having lit the lamp, left me in the study with some books to amuse me until her master's return.

I suppose I must have sat for nearly half an hour glancing over an odd volume of Klopstock's poems, when some sudden instinct caused me to raise my head and look up. I have been in some strange situations in my life, but never have I felt anything to be compared to the thrill which shot through me at that moment. The recollection of it now, hours after the event, makes me shudder. There, framed in one of the panes of the window, was a human face glaring in, from the darkness, into the lighted room—the face of a man so concealed by a cravat and slouch hat that the only impression I retain of it was a pair of wild-beast eyes and a nose which was whitened by being pressed against the glass. It did not need Andreas Murch's description to tell me that at last I was face to face with the man with the mattock. There was murder in those wild eyes. For a second I was so unstrung as to be powerless; the next I cocked my revolver and fired straight at the sinister face. I was a moment too late. As I pressed the trigger I saw it vanish, but the pane through which it had looked was shattered to pieces. I rushed to the window, and then out through the front door, but everything was silent. There was no trace of my visitor. His intention, no doubt, was to attack the curé, for there was nothing to prevent his coming through the folding window had he not found an armed man inside.

As I stood in the cool night air with the curé's frightened housekeeper beside me, I suddenly heard a great hubbub down in the village. By this time, alas! such sounds were so common in Laden that there was no doubting what it forboded. Some fresh misfortune had occurred there. To-night seemed destined to be a night of horror. My presence might be of use in the village, so I set off there, taking with me the trembling woman, who positively refused to remain behind. There was a crowd round the Gruner Mann public-house, and a dozen excited voices were explaining the circumstances to the curé, who had arrived just before us. It was as I had thought, though happily without the result which I had feared. Frau Bischoff, the wife of the proprietor of the inn, had, it seems, gone some twenty minutes before a few yards from her door to draw some water, and had been at once attacked by a tall disguised man, who had cut at her with some weapon. Fortunately he had slipped, so that she was able to seize him by the wrist and prevent his repeating his attempt, while she screamed for help. There were several people about at the time, who came running towards them, on which the stranger wrested himself free, and dashed off into the woods, with two of our police after him. There is little hope of their overtaking or tracing him, however, in such a dark labyrinth. Frau Bischoff had made a bold attempt to hold the assassin, and declares that her nails made deep furrows in his right wrist. This, however, must be mere conjecture, as there was very little light at the time. She knows no more of the man's features than I do. Fortunately she is entirely unhurt. The curé was horrified when I informed him of the incident at his own house. He was returning from his walk, it appears, when hearing cries in the village, he had hurried down to it. I have not told anyone else of my own adventure, for the people are quite excited enough already.

As I said before, unless this mysterious and bloodthirsty villain is captured, the place will become deserted. Flesh and blood cannot stand such a strain. He is either some murderous misanthrope who has declared a vendetta against the whole human race, or else he is an escaped maniac. Clearly after the unsuccessful attempt upon Frau Bischoff he had made at once for the curé's house, bent upon slaking his thirst for blood, and thinking that its lonely situation gave hope of success. I wish I had fired at him through the pocket of my coat. The moment he saw the glitter of the weapon he was off.

June 3rd.—Everybody in the village this morning has learned about the attempt upon the curé last night. There was quite a crowd at his house to congratulate him on his escape, and when I appeared they raised a cheer and hailed me as the "tapferer Englander." It seems that his narrow shave must have given the ruffian a great start, for a thick woollen muffler was

found lying on the pathway leading down to the village, and later in the day the fatal mattock was discovered close to the same place. The scoundrel evidently threw those things down and then took to his heels. It is possible that he may prove to have been frightened away from the neighbourhood altogether. Let us trust so!

June 4th.—A quiet day, which is as remarkable a thing in our annals as an exciting one elsewhere. Wurms has made strict inquiry, but cannot trace the muffler and mattock to any inhabitant. A description of them has been printed, and copies sent to Anspach and neighbouring villages for circulation among the peasants, who may be able to throw some light upon the matter. A thanksgiving service is to be held in the church on Sunday for the double escape of the pastor and of Martha Bischoff. Pfiffer tells me that Herr von Weissendorff, one of the most energetic detectives in Vienna, is on his way to Laden. I see, too, by the English papers sent me, that people at home are interested in the tragedies here, although the accounts which have reached them are garbled and untrustworthy.

How well I can recall the Sunday morning following upon the events which I have described, such a morning as it is hard to find outside the Tyrol! The sky was blue and cloudless, the gentle breeze wafted the balsamic odour of the pine woods through the open windows, and away up on the hills the distant tinkling of the cow bells fell pleasantly upon the ear, until the musical rise and fall which summoned the villagers to prayer drowned their feebler melody. It was hard to believe, looking down that peaceful little street with its quaint topheavy wooden houses and old-fashioned church, that a cloud of crime hung over it which had horrified Europe. I sat at my window watching the peasants passing with their picturesquely dressed wives and daughters on their way to church. With the kindly reverence of Catholic countries, I saw them cross themselves as they went by the house of Freckler and the spot where Maul had met his fate. When the bell had ceased to toll and the whole population had assembled in the church, I walked up there also, for it has always been my custom to join in the religious exercises of any people among whom I may find myself.

When I arrived at the church I found that the service had already begun. I took my place in the gallery which contained the village organ, from which I had a good view of the congregation. In the front seat of all was stationed Frau Bischoff, whose miraculous escape the service was intended to celebrate, and beside her on one side was her worthy spouse, while the maire occupied the other. There was a hush through the church as the curé turned from the altar and ascended the pulpit. I have seldom heard a more magnificent sermon. Father Verhagen was always an eloquent preacher, but on that occasion he surpassed himself. He chose for his text:—"In the midst of life we are in death," and impressed so vividly upon our minds the thin veil which divides us from eternity, and how unexpectedly it may be rent, that he held his audience spell-bound and horrified. He spoke next with tender pathos of the friends who had been snatched so suddenly and so dreadfully from among us, until his words were almost drowned by the sobs of the women, and, suddenly turning he compared their peaceful existence in a happier land to the dark fate of the gloomy- minded criminal, steeped in blood and with nothing to hope for either in this world or the next—a man solitary among his fellows, with no woman to love him, no child to prattle at his knee, and an endless torture in his own thoughts. So skilfully and so powerfully did he speak that as he finished I am sure that pity for this merciless demon was the prevailing emotion in every heart.

The service was over, and the priest, with his two acolytes before him, was leaving the altar, when he turned, as was his custom, to give his blessing to the congregation. I shall never forget his appearance. The summer sunshine shining slantwise through the single small stained glass window which adorned the little church threw a yellow lustre upon his sharp intellectual features with their dark haggard lines, while a vivid crimson spot reflected from a ruby- coloured mantle in the window quivered over his uplifted right hand. There was a hush as the villagers bent their heads to receive their pastor's blessing—a hush broken by a wild exclamation of surprise from a woman who staggered to her feet in the front pew and gesticulated frantically as she pointed at Father Verhagen's uplifted arm. No need for Frau Bischoff to explain the cause of that sudden cry, for there—there in full sight of his parishioners, were lines of livid scars upon the cure's white wrist—scars which could be left by nothing on earth but a desperate woman's nails. And what woman save her who had clung so fiercely to the murderer two days before!

That in all this terrible business poor Verhagen was the man most to be pitied I have no manner of doubt. In a town in which there was good medical advice to be had, the approach of the homicidal mania, which had undoubtedly proceeded from overwork and brain worry, and which assumed such a terrible form, would have been detected in time and he would have been spared the awful compunction with which he must have been seized in the lucid intervals between his fits—if, indeed, he had any lucid intervals. How could I diagnose with my smattering of science the existence of such a terrible and insidious form of insanity, especially from the vague symptoms of which he informed me. It is easy now, looking back, to think of many little circumstances which might have put us on the right scent; but what a simple thing is retrospective wisdom! I should be sad indeed if I thought that I had anything with which to reproach myself.

We were never able to discover where he had obtained the weapon with which he had committed his crimes, nor how he managed to secrete it in the interval. My experience proved that it had been his custom to go and come through his study window without disturbing his housekeeper. On the occasion of the attempt on Frau Bischoff he had made a dash for home, and then, finding to his astonishment that his room was occupied, his only resource was to fling away his weapon and muffler, and to mix with the crowd in the village. Being both a strong and an active man, with a good knowledge of the footpaths through the woods, he had never found any difficulty in escaping all observation.

Immediately after his apprehension, Verhagen's disease took an acute form, and he was carried off to the lunatic asylum at Feldkirch. I have heard that some months afterwards he made a determined attempt upon the life of one of his keepers, and afterwards committed suicide. I cannot be positive of this, however, for I heard it quite accidentally during a conversation in a railway carriage.

As for myself, I left Laden within a few months, having received a pleasing intimation from my solicitors that my claim had been paid in full. In spite of my tragic experience there, I had many a pleasing recollection of the little Tyrolese village, and in two subsequent visits I renewed my acquaintance with the maire, the Intendant, and all my old friends, on which occasion, over long pipes and flagons of beer, we have taken a grim pleasure in talking with bated breath of that terrible month in the quiet Vorarlberg hamlet.

"YOU look at these scattered houses, and you are impressed by their beauty. I look at them, and the only thought which comes to me is a feeling of their isolation and of the impunity with which crime may be committed there... It is my belief, Watson, founded upon my experience, that the lowest and vilest alleys in London do not present a more dreadful record of sin than does the smiling and beautiful countryside..." Holmes' famous cynicism in regards to country living is presaged in "A Pastoral Horror." Doyle was at heart a romantic – far more of a Watson than a Holmes – and he loved the countryside, being an ardent sportsman who hunted in the moors of Devon, golfed in Egypt and Vermont, motored the country lanes of England, and single-handedly introduced Switzerland to skiing (yes, this is true: before his move there in 1893 skiing was unknown to the Alps, being a predominantly Scandinavian pastime). Doyle was able to relish the beauty, freedom, and loneliness of the countryside without forgetting its deadly potential – remote and insular, it was a perfect breeding ground for successful crimes. But it is not the literal countryside that this story is concerned with so much as the metaphorical Eden of civilization. By the 1890s humanity had advanced more in fifty years than it had in the past four hundred. Society was civil, educated, well-bred, and driven by the supply and demand of a healthy, upwardly mobile middle class. There was hope in mankind's condition, and an expectation that war, disease, and crime would eventually go by the wayside. But as Doyle suggests in this somber tale of murder without cause, madness and death can run rampant in any scenario, and a civilization without avarice, resentment, or rage can still be afflicted by random violence. "Misery is manifold," Poe wrote, and despite his inborn optimism, Doyle writes to remind us that there is *no* Eden, and that our best hope for peace is to conduct our lives *peaceably*, for there is no guarantee that disaster will spare us when it is sowed so haphazardly by fate.

PERHAPS the most famous short story featuring the Great Detective – second only to "A Scandal in Bohemia" if at all – "The Speckled Band" was also Doyle's favorite. When he compiled a list of his twelve favorites, it stood at the top, and remained there when he expanded the list to nineteen several years later. In the twentieth century, Doyle even adapted it into a stage play with some minor differences, and it continues to be one of the most anthologized of Holmes' episode. Today it continues to be rated number one on a variety of polls of Holmesian societies and literary salons (trailed at varying intervals by "Scandal in Bohemia," "Red-Headed League," "Silver Blaze," and "Blue Carbuncle"). It is often seen as the epitome or exemplar of Doyle's famous first collection, "The Adventures of Sherlock Holmes," with its general emphasis on conspiracies, dread, and horrible secrets. The grotesque details of Miss Stoner's experiences – from her sister's inexplicable death in her nightgown to her seemingly erratic horror at the sound of a low whistle – Roylott's menacing figure as a vulgar tyrant (capable of violence, murder, and possibly the molestation of his stepdaughters), and Holmes' emotionally-charged, white-knuckle nighttime vigil all combine to a story with an uncommon power over the imagination. Where classics like "The Red-headed League" and "The Blue Carbuncle" are alternatively humorous and thrilling – tales of adventure and fun – "The Speckled Band" is chilling and sinister from beginning to end – a secular horror story. It remains one of Holmes' most utterly Gothic adventures, rivalling "The Copper Beeches," "The Yellow Face," "The Sussex Vampire," and *The Hound of the Baskervilles* in its sustained tone of dread, use of Gothic stocks, and grisly finale, and the tale has been featured in all three editions of *The Oxford Book of Gothic Tales* as an example of an exemplary study in the grotesque. Like all of Holmes' forays, the dangers encountered here are not supernatural, but they are chilling, and they do springboard off of the conventions established a century previous – those of Lewis and Walpole: crumbling manors, dysfunctional aristocratic families on their way to extinction, exotic murders, locked room killings, stepfathers seeking the destruction of their wards, and starless nights torn asunder by the cries of a dying woman. Doyle plunges us into such a world, and while it is not plagued by spectral knights, bloody nuns, or phantom portraits, it is haunted in a far more palpable way: by greed and murder and evil.

The Adventure of the Speckled Band
{1891}

ON GLANCING over my notes of the seventy odd cases[1] in which I have during the last eight years[2] studied the methods of my friend Sherlock Holmes, I find many tragic, some comic[3], a large number merely strange, but none commonplace; for, working as he did rather for the love of his art than for the acquirement of wealth, he refused to associate himself with any investigation which did not tend towards the unusual, and even the fantastic. Of all these varied cases, however, I cannot recall any which presented more singular features than that which was associated with the well-known Surrey[4] family of the Roylotts of Stoke Moran. The events in question occurred in the early days of my association with Holmes, when we were sharing rooms as bachelors in Baker Street[5]. It is possible that I might have placed them upon record before, but a promise of secrecy was made at the time, from which I have only been freed during the last month by the untimely death of the lady to whom the pledge was given[6]. It is perhaps as well that the facts should now come to light, for I have reasons to know that there are widespread rumours as to the death of Dr. Grimesby Roylott which tend to make the matter even more terrible than the truth[7].

It was early in April in the year '83 that I woke one morning to find Sherlock Holmes standing, fully dressed, by the side of my bed. He was a late riser, as a rule, and as the clock on the mantelpiece showed me that it was only a quarter-past seven, I blinked up at him in some surprise, and perhaps just a little resentment, for I was myself regular in my habits.

---

1 Before his 1903 retirement, Holmes is estimated to have had roughly 1,700 cases

2 Having first met one another in 1881

3 The Red-Headed League springs to mind

4 A county in southern England, just west of Greater London, renowned for its beautiful countryside and wealth, historically being the site of many London aristocrats' country retreats, particularly popular with the booming nouveau riche and industrialists who wanted to remain close to Town – a suburb of suburbs

5 Prior, then, to Watson's first marriage – sandwiched between the events of the first two novels "A Study in Scarlet" and "The Sign of the Four"

6 This passing note has attracted wild attention from Sherlockians who speculate that either Holmes got the wrong crook, nabbed only one member of a conspiracy (perhaps we should be suspicious of a pact between Roylott and the fiancée), or ignored Miss Stoner's perfidious role in her sister's death (implying a guilt-induced suicide). Of course, the likeliest reason for her death is her shattered health following these experiences, but this theory is less fun

7 Also a comment which has attracted speculation. What are the rumors? Primarily we are lead to suppose that there are rumblings that Holmes killed Roylott, that there was an inappropriate – even incestuous – relationship between Roylott and his daughter (more later), or that there has been a conspiracy to cash in on Roylott's inheritance

"Very sorry to knock you up, Watson," said he, "but it's the common lot this morning. Mrs. Hudson has been knocked up, she retorted upon me, and I on you."

"What is it, then -- a fire?"[1]

"No; a client. It seems that a young lady has arrived in a considerable state of excitement, who insists upon seeing me. She is waiting now in the sitting-room. Now, when young ladies wander about the metropolis at this hour of the morning, and knock sleepy people up out of their beds, I presume that it is something very pressing which they have to communicate. Should it prove to be an interesting case, you would, I am sure, wish to follow it from the outset. I thought, at any rate, that I should call you and give you the chance."

"My dear fellow, I would not miss it for anything."

I had no keener pleasure than in following Holmes in his professional investigations, and in admiring the rapid deductions, as swift as intuitions, and yet always founded on a logical basis with which he unraveled the problems which were submitted to him. I rapidly threw on my clothes and was ready in a few minutes to accompany my friend down to the sitting-room. A lady dressed in black and heavily veiled[2], who had been sitting in the window, rose as we entered.

"Good-morning, madam," said Holmes cheerily. "My name is Sherlock Holmes. This is my intimate friend and associate, Dr. Watson, before whom you can speak as freely as before myself. Ha! I am glad to see that Mrs. Hudson has had the good sense to light the fire. Pray draw up to it, and I shall order you a cup of hot coffee, for I observe that you are shivering[3]."

"It is not cold which makes me shiver," said the woman in a low voice, changing her seat as requested.

"What, then?"

"It is fear, Mr. Holmes. It is terror." She raised her veil as she spoke, and we could see that she was indeed in a pitiable state of agitation, her face all drawn and gray, with restless frightened eyes, like those of some hunted animal[4]. Her features and figure were those of a woman of thirty, but her hair was shot with premature gray, and her expression was weary and haggard. Sherlock Holmes ran her over with one of his quick, all comprehensive glances.

---

[1] While some actors (David Burke for example) have played this line straight, most critics detect sarcasm and annoyance in Watson's retort

[2] This is no mere disguise – she is in deep mourning for her sister, breaking the convention of three months' mourning period

[3] Holmes unquestionably knows that her shivers are caused by emotions rather than feelings, but playfully uses this observation to draw forth her narrative

[4] Animals, as we known, play a significant role in this story, and the theme of prey/predator runs throughout it, challenging the definitions of who is human and who is animal

"You must not fear," said he soothingly, bending forward and patting her forearm. "We shall soon set matters right, I have no doubt. You have come in by train this morning, I see."

"You know me, then?"

"No, but I observe the second half of a return ticket in the palm of your left glove. You must have started early, and yet you had a good drive in a dog-cart[1], along heavy roads, before you reached the station."

The lady gave a violent start and stared in bewilderment at my companion.

"There is no mystery, my dear madam," said he, smiling. "The left arm of your jacket is spattered with mud in no less than seven places. The marks are perfectly fresh. There is no vehicle save a dog-cart which throws up mud in that way, and then only when you sit on the left-hand side of the driver."

"Whatever your reasons may be, you are perfectly correct," said she. "I started from home before six, reached Leatherhead at twenty past, and came in by the first train to Waterloo[2]. Sir, I can stand this strain no longer; I shall go mad if it continues. I have no one to turn to -- none, save only one, who cares for me, and he, poor fellow, can be of little aid. I have heard of you, Mr. Holmes; I have heard of you from Mrs. Farintosh, whom you helped in the hour of her sore need. It was from her that I had your address. Oh, sir, do you not think that you could help me, too, and at least throw a little light through the dense darkness which surrounds me? At present it is out of my power to reward you for your services, but in a month or six weeks I shall be married, with the control of my own income, and then at least you shall not find me ungrateful."

Holmes turned to his desk and, unlocking it, drew out a small case-book, which he consulted.

"Farintosh," said he. "Ah yes, I recall the case; it was concerned with an opal tiara. I think it was before your time, Watson[3]. I can only say, madam, that I shall be happy to devote the same care to your case as I did to that of your friend. As to reward, my profession is its own reward; but you are at liberty to defray whatever expenses I may be put to, at the time which suits

---

1 A two-wheeled horse-drawn cart, with cross seats back to back

2 Famously among Sherlockians, this is impossible according to the Bradshaws of the period. Rather than "play the game," I'll merely note that Conan Doyle made a mistake here

3 Sherlockians pore over this inconsistency, too (how could she know his address if the case was before Watson and he and Watson rented 221B together!!??). The solution is ridiculously simple: Holmes is now a famous consultant, so perhaps she has read of his new address; or maybe she double checked his address before giving it out; or maybe she found it because she needed to pay his bill after he moved; or maybe he already lived there but Watson hadn't yet begun shadowing Holmes yet (Holmes had some cases at 221B before Watson was caught up in the "Study" affair). Really, people...

you best[1]. And now I beg that you will lay before us everything that may help us in forming an opinion upon the matter."

"Alas!" replied our visitor, "the very horror of my situation lies in the fact that my fears are so vague, and my suspicions depend so entirely upon small points, which might seem trivial to another, that even he to whom of all others I have a right to look for help and advice looks upon all that I tell him about it as the fancies of a nervous woman. He does not say so, but I can read it from his soothing answers and averted eyes. But I have heard, Mr. Holmes, that you can see deeply into the manifold wickedness of the human heart. You may advise me how to walk amid the dangers which encompass me."

"I am all attention, madam."

"My name is Helen Stoner, and I am living with my stepfather, who is the last survivor of one of the oldest Saxon[2] families in England, the Roylotts of Stoke Moran, on the western border of Surrey[3]."

Holmes nodded his head. "The name is familiar to me," said he.

"The family was at one time among the richest in England, and the estates extended over the borders into Berkshire in the north, and Hampshire in the west[4]. In the last century, however, four successive heirs were of a dissolute and wasteful disposition, and the family ruin was eventually completed by a gambler in the days of the Regency[5]. Nothing was left save a few acres of ground, and the two-hundred-year-old house, which is itself crushed under a heavy mortgage. The last squire dragged out his existence there, living the horrible life of an aristocratic pauper; but his only son, my stepfather, seeing that he must adapt himself to the new

---

[1] Holmes' generosity and his policies of payment constantly seem to change. Sometimes he has a set fee, other times he waives it, asks only for reimbursement, or demands a high commission. This is, of course, dependent on the apparent means of the client – and frequently their gender (stony perhaps, but Holmes was always a soft touch with the ladies)

[2] Britain was – at the time – primarily populated by three main ethnicities: the original Celts/Britons who were forced into the highlands of Wales and Scotland by the Saxons, the invading Saxons and Angles (whence we derive "Anglo" and "England" and "English" or "Anglish") who were Germanic and Danish sea raiders – the enemies of the Briton King Arthur – who took over Britain during the so-called Dark Ages, and the Normans – the enemies of the Saxon Robin Hood – who invaded Britain in 1066, becoming the new British aristocracy

[3] Possibly based on Stoke d'Abernon – a village of 6,000 in the same proximity: three miles from Leatherhead in western Surrey

[4] Berkshire is on Surrey's northwest border, Hampshire to its southwest

[5] The glamourous 1810s popularized by Jane Austen and renowned as a time when fashion, excess, and debauchery were popularized by the example of the Prince Regent – the future George IV – who reigned while his father, George III, was debilitated by insanity

conditions[1], obtained an advance from a relative, which enabled him to take a medical degree and went out to Calcutta, where, by his professional skill and his force of character, he established a large practice. In a fit of anger, however, caused by some robberies which had been perpetrated in the house, he beat his native butler to death and narrowly escaped a capital sentence. As it was, he suffered a long term of imprisonment and afterwards returned to England a morose and disappointed man.

"When Dr. Roylott was in India he married my mother, Mrs. Stoner, the young widow of Major-General[2] Stoner, of the Bengal Artillery[3]. My sister Julia and I were twins, and we were only two years old at the time of my mother's re-marriage. She had a considerable sum of money -- not less than 1000 pounds[4] a year -- and this she bequeathed to Dr. Roylott entirely while we resided with him, with a provision that a certain annual sum should be allowed to each of us in the event of our marriage. Shortly after our return to England my mother died -- she was killed eight years ago in a railway accident near Crewe[5]. Dr. Roylott then abandoned his attempts to establish himself in practice in London and took us to live with him in the old ancestral house at Stoke Moran. The money which my mother had left was enough for all our wants, and there seemed to be no obstacle to our happiness.

"But a terrible change came over our stepfather about this time. Instead of making friends and exchanging visits with our neighbours, who had at first been overjoyed to see a Roylott of Stoke Moran back in the old family seat[6], he shut himself up in his house and seldom came out save to indulge in ferocious quarrels with whoever might cross his path. Violence of temper approaching to mania has been hereditary in the men of the family, and in my stepfather's case it had, I believe, been intensified by his long residence

---

[1] A Saxon aristocrat wouldn't be expected to enter a trade – not even medicine, which we consider distinguished today – unless he was terribly hard up for cash

[2] Socially, a major general of common birth was probably the equal of an impoverished squire – both have deficits and both have recommendations

[3] A unit of field and garrison artillery officered by British commanders and manned by Indian sepoys

[4] In the 1870s, before her death in 1875, this would be comparable to $100,000 in 2017 currency. By 1883, the sum was worth nigh on half a million

[5] Home of the Rolls Royce, a major train hub in western England. Much eyebrow raising has been caused by this accident (or WAS it!?), but it seems fairly unlikely that such a major event could be plotted by a man whose idea of murder is changing your stepdaughter's sleep quarters and training a snake to slither into it each night for two weeks

[6] Having the local manor inhabited by its ancestral heir has historically been good for the local economy and the prestige of the area – it brings business, visitors, and civic pride. Not so with this lout

in the tropics[1]. A series of disgraceful brawls took place, two of which ended in the police court, until at last he became the terror of the village, and the folks would fly at his approach, for he is a man of immense strength, and absolutely uncontrollable in his anger.

"Last week he hurled the local blacksmith[2] over a parapet into a stream, and it was only by paying over all the money which I could gather together that I was able to avert another public exposure. He had no friends at all save the wandering gypsies, and he would give these vagabonds leave to encamp upon the few acres of bramble-covered land which represent the family estate, and would accept in return the hospitality of their tents, wandering away with them sometimes for weeks on end. He has a passion also for Indian animals, which are sent over to him by a correspondent, and he has at this moment a cheetah[3] and a baboon[4], which wander freely over his grounds and are feared by the villagers almost as much as their master.

"You can imagine from what I say that my poor sister Julia and I had no great pleasure in our lives. No servant would stay with us, and for a long time we did all the work of the house. She was but thirty at the time of her death, and yet her hair had already begun to whiten, even as mine has[5]."

"Your sister is dead, then?"

"She died just two years ago, and it is of her death that I wish to speak to you. You can understand that, living the life which I have described, we were little likely to see anyone of our own age and position. We had, however, an aunt, my mother's maiden sister, Miss Honoria Westphail, who lives near Harrow[6], and we were occasionally allowed to pay short visits at this lady's house. Julia went there at Christmas two years ago, and met there a half-pay major[7] of marines[8], to whom she became engaged. My stepfather

---

[1] In virtually EVERY case that Holmes conducted, the danger comes from Britain's colonization of a foreign power or its relationships with foreign countries. Almost every villain has some connection to "the tropics," Britain's African colonies, or former colonies like the United States. In this case it is India that provides the fatal germ of crime

[2] Typically the strongest, burliest man in each village – an occupational side effect of pounding iron all day long

[3] Actually a fairly gentle animal – unlike the aggressive leopard – cheetahs can still be intimidating to English villagers who have no familiarity with the breed

[4] Baboons are native to Indonesia, not India, but Stoner is probably using the word "Indian" loosely to mean the Asian tropics bordering the Indian Ocean

[5] This favorite literary trope – one used by Doyle's favorite writer, Poe, in "A Descent into the Maelstrom" – is impossible. Prematurely white hair is genetic, not caused by stress or fear, although stress can cause hair loss, which may render gray hairs more prominent

[6] A London suburb northwest of Town

[7] Watson was himself a half-pay officer during his convalescence. Essentially a pension, half-pay was given to officers who were not in active-duty: they could either sell the commission to an up and comer, or accept half-pay and await reassignment or the next war

[8] Amphibious soldiers who were assigned to ships. They frequently acted as temporary garrisons to foreign posts, or as landing parties in naval actions against fortifications

learned of the engagement when my sister returned and offered no objection to the marriage; but within a fortnight of the day which had been fixed for the wedding, the terrible event occurred which has deprived me of my only companion."

Sherlock Holmes had been leaning back in his chair with his eyes closed and his head sunk in a cushion, but he half opened his lids now and glanced across at his visitor.

"Pray be precise as to details," said he.

"It is easy for me to be so, for every event of that dreadful time is seared into my memory. The manor-house is, as I have already said, very old, and only one wing is now inhabited. The bedrooms in this wing are on the ground floor, the sitting-rooms being in the central block of the buildings. Of these bedrooms the first is Dr. Roylott's, the second my sister's, and the third my own. There is no communication between them, but they all open out into the same corridor. Do I make myself plain?"

"Perfectly so."

"The windows of the three rooms open out upon the lawn. That fatal night Dr. Roylott had gone to his room early, though we knew that he had not retired to rest, for my sister was troubled by the smell of the strong Indian cigars[1] which it was his custom to smoke. She left her room, therefore, and came into mine, where she sat for some time, chatting about her approaching wedding. At eleven o'clock she rose to leave me, but she paused at the door and looked back.

" 'Tell me, Helen,' said she, 'have you ever heard anyone whistle in the dead of the night?'

" 'Never,' said I.

" 'I suppose that you could not possibly whistle, yourself, in your sleep?'

" 'Certainly not. But why?'

" 'Because during the last few nights I have always, about three in the morning, heard a low, clear whistle. I am a light sleeper, and it has awakened me. I cannot tell where it came from perhaps from the next room, perhaps from the lawn. I thought that I would just ask you whether you had heard it.'

" 'No, I have not. It must be those wretched gypsies in the plantation.'

" 'Very likely. And yet if it were on the lawn, I wonder that you did not hear it also.'

" 'Ah, but I sleep more heavily than you.'

" 'Well, it is of no great consequence, at any rate.' She smiled back at me, closed my door, and a few moments later I heard her key turn in the lock."

---

[1] Like Holmes, the doctor has a predilection for strong tobacco. Doyle usually uses this as a motif to suggest intelligence and craft: upon hearing that his antagonist smokes strong tobacco, Holmes probably recognizes a foe to contend with – one cerebral of mind and (a requirement if he can bear the powerful fumes) brawny of body

"Indeed," said Holmes. "Was it your custom always to lock yourselves in at night?"

"Always."

"And why?"

"I think that I mentioned to you that the doctor kept a cheetah and a baboon. We had no feeling of security unless our doors were locked[1]."

"Quite so. Pray proceed with your statement."

"I could not sleep that night. A vague feeling of impending misfortune impressed me. My sister and I, you will recollect, were twins, and you know how subtle are the links which bind two souls which are so closely allied. It was a wild night. The wind was howling outside, and the rain was beating and splashing against the windows. Suddenly, amid all the hubbub of the gale, there burst forth the wild scream of a terrified woman. I knew that it was my sister's voice. I sprang from my bed, wrapped a shawl round me, and rushed into the corridor. As I opened my door I seemed to hear a low whistle, such as my sister described, and a few moments later a clanging sound, as if a mass of metal had fallen. As I ran down the passage, my sister's door was unlocked, and revolved slowly upon its hinges. I stared at it horror-stricken, not knowing what was about to issue from it[2]. By the light of the corridor-lamp I saw my sister appear at the opening, her face blanched with terror, her hands groping for help , her whole figure swaying to and fro like that of a drunkard. I ran to her and threw my arms round her, but at that moment her knees seemed to give way and she fell to the ground. She writhed as one who is in terrible pain, and her limbs were dreadfully convulsed. At first I thought that she had not recognized me, but as I bent over her she suddenly shrieked out in a voice which I shall never forget, 'Oh, my God! Helen! It was the band! The speckled band![3]' There was

---

[1] Most commentators view this as an excuse (and Holmes' "Quite so" as a polite recognition of the fact): no cheetah or baboon will open a door, unlocked or otherwise. It is most likely Roylott – who manhandles Stoner – whom they fear. The specter of sexual abuse lingers over this story like a fog

[2] Her sister is the obvious answer, but it is interesting that she expects someone else. Again, I sense that she half expects to see her stepfather sally forth from the room, tucking his shirt into his loose drawers

[3] Many have shaken their heads at this indictment. Why not "it was a snake! A snake just bit me!" The solution may be that she was bitten while asleep, and awakened by the symptoms of the poison. Stumbling up, struggling to breathe, she lights a candle and sees a strange spotted band next to her pillow. In the darkness she doesn't recognize a snake, but assumes it to be an article of clothing or belt and rushes outside, horrified to think someone has been in her bed. As her brain fogs with death, she can only remember to shout out the one thing that she remembers seeing. At her cry, Roylott recalls the snake, and there is nothing for Stoner to discover in her room. The meaning of the cry might be an attempt to justify a suspicion. "He was in my bed with me!" she is trying to say, but all she can get out is her reason for suspecting it: "It was the band that told me; it was the

something else which she would fain have said, and she stabbed with her finger into the air in the direction of the doctor's room, but a fresh convulsion seized her and choked her words[1]. I rushed out, calling loudly for my stepfather, and I met him hastening from his room in his dressing-gown. When he reached my sister's side she was unconscious, and though he poured brandy down her throat and sent for medical aid from the village, all efforts were in vain, for she slowly sank and died without having recovered her consciousness. Such was the dreadful end of my beloved sister."

One moment," said Holmes, "are you sure about this whistle and metallic sound? Could you swear to it?"

"That was what the county coroner asked me at the inquiry. It is my strong impression that I heard it, and yet, among the crash of the gale and the creaking of an old house, I may possibly have been deceived."

"Was your sister dressed?"

"No, she was in her night-dress. In her right hand was found the charred stump of a match, and in her left a match-box."

"Showing that she had struck a light and looked about her when the alarm took place. That is important. And what conclusions did the coroner come to?"

"He investigated the case with great care, for Dr. Roylott's conduct had long been notorious in the county, but he was unable to find any satisfactory cause of death[2]. My evidence showed that the door had been fastened upon the inner side, and the windows were blocked by old-fashioned shutters with broad iron bars, which were secured every night. The walls were carefully sounded, and were shown to be quite solid all round, and the flooring was also thoroughly examined, with the same result. The chimney is wide, but is barred up by four large staples. It is certain, therefore, that my sister was quite alone when she met her end. Besides, there were no marks of any violence upon her."

"How about poison?"

"The doctors examined her for it, but without success."

"What do you think that this unfortunate lady died of, then?"

"It is my belief that she died of pure fear and nervous shock, though what it was that frightened her I cannot imagine[3]."

---

band I saw that proved to me that he was there – my own stepfather, before my wedding!"

[1] Many critics argue that – like Sir Charles Baskerville – Julia is slain not BY the animal sent to her, but by her own terror. Already preternaturally nervous, she is never bitten, but shocked into cardiac arrest, which explains her symptoms far more than a snake bite. It is also worth noting that she survives for a minute or so after the encounter while Roylott himself is paralyzed immediately by the creature, and dies sitting in his chair

[2] Again, it is probable that the snake never bit her since such a potent venom would surely cause extreme swelling. Instead, she probably died of the shock of suspecting that her stepfather had violated her in her sleep

[3] I agree

"Were there gypsies in the plantation at the time?"

"Yes, there are nearly always some there."

"Ah, and what did you gather from this allusion to a band -- a speckled band?"

"Sometimes I have thought that it was merely the wild talk of delirium[1], sometimes that it may have referred to some band of people, perhaps to these very gypsies in the plantation. I do not know whether the spotted handkerchiefs which so many of them wear over their heads might have suggested the strange adjective which she used."

Holmes shook his head like a man who is far from being satisfied.

"These are very deep waters," said he; "pray go on with your narrative."

"Two years have passed since then, and my life has been until lately lonelier than ever. A month ago, however, a dear friend, whom I have known for many years, has done me the honour to ask my hand in marriage. His name is Armitage -- Percy Armitage -- the second son of Mr. Armitage, of Crane Water, near Reading. My stepfather has offered no opposition to the match, and we are to be married in the course of the spring. Two days ago some repairs were started in the west wing of the building, and my bedroom wall has been pierced, so that I have had to move into the chamber in which my sister died, and to sleep in the very bed in which she slept. Imagine, then, my thrill of terror when last night, as I lay awake, thinking over her terrible fate, I suddenly heard in the silence of the night the low whistle which had been the herald of her own death. I sprang up and lit the lamp, but nothing was to be seen in the room. I was too shaken to go to bed again, however, so I dressed, and as soon as it was daylight I slipped down, got a dog-cart at the Crown Inn, which is opposite, and drove to Leatherhead, from whence I have come on this morning with the one object of seeing you and asking your advice."

"You have done wisely," said my friend. "But have you told me all?"

"Yes, all."

"Miss Roylott, you have not. You are screening your stepfather."

"Why, what do you mean?"

For answer Holmes pushed back the frill of black lace which fringed the hand that lay upon our visitor's knee. Five little livid spots, the marks of four fingers and a thumb, were printed upon the white wrist.

"You have been cruelly used[2]," said Holmes.

---

[1] That is, hysteria – hysterical fear

[2] "Used" is the precise word. Or perhaps "forced." Why would a man in his sixties bruise the arm of his thirthy-something daughter – a grown woman who is engaged? What, did she steal a cookie from the jar, or refuse to stop throwing a tantrum in the toy aisle, or play with matches in her playroom? There is no logical reason for two genteel people – a squire and a cultured lady – to have an interaction like this unless it was sexual: unless Roylott grabbed her and refused to let her go until he had derived the pleasure he sought from her body. I don't necessarily suggest rape, but certainly sexual molestation. No adult

The lady coloured deeply and covered over her injured wrist. "He is a hard man," she said, "and perhaps he hardly knows his own strength[1]."

There was a long silence, during which Holmes leaned his chin upon his hands and stared into the crackling fire.

"This is a very deep business," he said at last. "There are a thousand details which I should desire to know before I decide upon our course of action. Yet we have not a moment to lose. If we were to come to Stoke Moran to-day, would it be possible for us to see over these rooms without the knowledge of your stepfather?"

"As it happens, he spoke of coming into town to-day upon some most important business. It is probable that he will be away all day, and that there would be nothing to disturb you. We have a housekeeper now, but she is old and foolish, and I could easily get her out of the way."

"Excellent. You are not averse to this trip, Watson?"

"By no means."

"Then we shall both come. What are you going to do yourself?"

"I have one or two things which I would wish to do now that I am in town. But I shall return by the twelve o'clock train, so as to be there in time for your coming."

"And you may expect us early in the afternoon. I have myself some small business matters to attend to. Will you not wait and breakfast?"

"No, I must go. My heart is lightened already since I have confided my trouble to you. I shall look forward to seeing you again this afternoon." She dropped her thick black veil over her face and glided from the room.

"And what do you think of it all, Watson?" asked Sherlock Holmes, leaning back in his chair.

"It seems to me to be a most dark and sinister business."

"Dark enough and sinister enough."

"Yet if the lady is correct in saying that the flooring and walls are sound, and that the door, window, and chimney are impassable, then her sister must have been undoubtedly alone when she met her mysterious end."

"What becomes, then, of these nocturnal whistles, and what of the very peculiar words of the dying woman?"

"I cannot think."

"When you combine the ideas of whistles at night, the presence of a band of gypsies who are on intimate terms with this old doctor, the fact that we have every reason to believe that the doctor has an interest in preventing his stepdaughter's marriage, the dying allusion to a band, and, finally, the fact that Miss Helen Stoner heard a metallic clang, which might have been caused by one of those metal bars that secured the shutters falling back into

---

woman of breeding need be gripped so, especially so polite and shy a woman – not to be reprimanded – unless the aim was to restrain her during a violent pass

[1] A chilling comment. The language of an abused woman – "it's okay, he didn't know it was hurting me"

its place, I think that there is good ground to think that the mystery may be cleared along those lines."

"But what, then, did the gypsies do?"

"I cannot imagine."

"I see many objections to any such theory."

"And so do I. It is precisely for that reason that we are going to Stoke Moran this day. I want to see whether the objections are fatal, or if they may be explained away. But what in the name of the devil!"

The ejaculation had been drawn from my companion by the fact that our door had been suddenly dashed open, and that a huge man had framed himself in the aperture. His costume was a peculiar mixture of the professional and of the agricultural[1], having a black top-hat, a long frock-coat[2], and a pair of high gaiters[3], with a hunting-crop[4] swinging in his hand. So tall was he that his hat actually brushed the cross bar of the- doorway, and his breadth seemed to span it across from side to side. A large face, seared with a thousand wrinkles, burned yellow with the sun, and marked with every evil passion, was turned from one to the other of us, while his deep-set, bile-shot eyes, and his high, thin, fleshless nose, gave him somewhat the resemblance to a fierce old bird of prey.

"Which of you is Holmes?" asked this apparition.

"My name, sir; but you have the advantage of me," said my companion quietly.

"I am Dr. Grimesby Roylott, of Stoke Moran."

"Indeed, Doctor," said Holmes blandly. "Pray take a seat."

"I will do nothing of the kind. My stepdaughter has been here. I have traced her[5]. What has she been saying to you?"

"It is a little cold for the time of the year," said Holmes.

"What has she been saying to you?" screamed the old man furiously.

"But I have heard that the crocuses promise well," continued my companion imperturbably.

"Ha! You put me off, do you?" said our new visitor, taking a step forward and shaking his hunting-crop. "I know you, you scoundrel! I have heard of you before. You are Holmes, the meddler."

My friend smiled.

---

1 In other words, the costume of a country squire – one who is simultaneously expected to be a refined gentleman and a rugged sportsman

2 A fashionable, knee-length coat – worn by urban gentlemen (as opposed to the rural shooting jacket or tweeds)

3 Canvas leggings that covered the shoe tops and calves (up to the knee) – protecting it from mud, briars, and brush during country romps

4 A small cane made of heavy wood used to urge horses to ride harder during a hunt

5 Remember what I said about how this stories ponders the idea of predators and prey, about humans who are treated like animals or act like animals? Donning elements of a hunting outfit, the doctor bursts in claiming to have tracked his daughter like a slinking fox to its hole

"Holmes, the busybody!"

His smile broadened.

"Holmes, the Scotland Yard Jack-in-office[1]!"

Holmes chuckled heartily. "Your conversation is most entertaining," said he. "When you go out close the door, for there is a decided draught."

"I will go when I have said my say. Don't you dare to meddle with my affairs. I know that Miss Stoner has been here. I traced her! I am a dangerous man to fall foul of! See here." He stepped swiftly forward, seized the poker, and bent it into a curve with his huge brown hands[2].

"See that you keep yourself out of my grip," he snarled, and hurling the twisted poker into the fireplace he strode out of the room.

"He seems a very amiable person," said Holmes, laughing. "I am not quite so bulky, but if he had remained I might have shown him that my grip was not much more feeble than his own." As he spoke he picked up the steel poker and, with a sudden effort, straightened it out again.

"Fancy his having the insolence to confound me with the official detective force! This incident gives zest to our investigation, however, and I only trust that our little friend will not suffer from her imprudence in allowing this brute to trace her. And now, Watson, we shall order breakfast, and afterwards I shall walk down to Doctors' Commons[3], where I hope to get some data which may help us in this matter."

☙

It was nearly one o'clock when Sherlock Holmes returned from his excursion. He held in his hand a sheet of blue paper, scrawled over with notes and figures.

"I have seen the will of the deceased wife," said he. "To determine its exact meaning I have been obliged to work out the present prices of the investments with which it is concerned. The total income, which at the time of the wife's death was little short of 1100 pounds, is now, through the fall in agricultural prices, not more than 750 pounds. Each daughter can claim an income of 250 pounds[4], in case of marriage. It is evident, therefore, that if both girls had married, this beauty would have had a mere pittance, while even one of them would cripple him to a very serious extent. My morning's work has not been wasted, since it has proved that he has the very strongest motives for standing in the way of anything of the sort. And now, Watson,

---

[1] A petty official – Roylott accuses Holmes of being a half-baked detective whom Scotland Yard drags out when it has no one better to call on

[2] One commentator experimented with his wife's poker and proclaimed the task to be "a not inconsiderable though not Herculean feat." It is not impossible for a healthy man to do this, but it does take a good deal of brawn

[3] A legal building on the Strand which housed a wide range of public records in its archives

[4] Still a respectable sum: about $30,000 in 2017 currency

this is too serious for dawdling, especially as the old man is aware that we are interesting ourselves in his affairs; so if you are ready, we shall call a cab and drive to Waterloo. I should be very much obliged if you would slip your revolver into your pocket. An Eley's No. 2[1] is an excellent argument with gentlemen who can twist steel pokers into knots. That and a tooth-brush are, I think all that we need."

At Waterloo we were fortunate in catching a train for Leatherhead, where we hired a trap[2] at the station inn and drove for four or five miles through the lovely Surrey lanes. It was a perfect day, with a bright sun and a few fleecy clouds in the heavens. The trees and wayside hedges were just throwing out their first green shoots, and the air was full of the pleasant smell of the moist earth. To me at least there was a strange contrast between the sweet promise of the spring and this sinister quest upon which we were engaged. My companion sat in the front of the trap, his arms folded, his hat pulled down over his eyes, and his chin sunk upon his breast, buried in the deepest thought. Suddenly, however, he started, tapped me on the shoulder, and pointed over the meadows

"Look there!" said he.

A heavily timbered park stretched up in a gentle slope, thickening mto a grove at the highest point. From amid the branches there jutted out the gray gables and high roof-tree of a very old mansion.

"Stoke Moran?" said he.

"Yes, sir, that be the house of Dr. Grimesby Roylott," remarked the driver.

"There is some building going on there," said Holmes; "that is where we are going."

"There's the village," said the driver, pointing to a cluster of roofs some distance to the left; "but if you want to get to the house, you'll find it shorter to get over this stile, and so by the foot-path over the fields. There it is, where the lady is walking."

"And the lady, I fancy, is Miss Stoner," observed Holmes, shading his eyes. "Yes, I think we had better do as you suggest."

We got off, paid our fare, and the trap rattled back on its way to Leatherhead.

"I thought it as well," said Holmes as we climbed the stile, "that this fellow should think we had come here as architects, or on some definite business. It may stop his gossip. Good-afternoon, Miss Stoner. You see that we have been as good as our word."

---

1 A popular sidearm among officers, the Webley revolver took .320 bore, No. 2 rounds which were produced by Eley's – an arms manufacturer whose name would be on the ammunition box (although the round is technically a Webley No. 2)

2 A speedy, one-horse, two-wheeled carriage – not unlike a dog cart, but sportier and less messy

Our client of the morning had hurried forward to meet us with a face which spoke her joy. "I have been waiting so eagerly for you," she cried, shaking hands with us warmly. "All has turned out splendidly. Dr. Roylott has gone to town, and it is unlikely that he will be back before evening."

"We have had the pleasure of making the doctor's acquaintance," said Holmes, and in a few words he sketched out what had occurred. Miss Stoner turned white to the lips as she listened.

"Good heavens!" she cried, "he has followed me, then."

"So it appears."

"He is so cunning that I never know when I am safe from him. What will he say when he returns?"

"He must guard himself, for he may find that there is someone more cunning than himself upon his track. You must lock yourself up from him to-night. If he is violent, we shall take you away to your aunt's at Harrow. Now, we must make the best use of our time, so kindly take us at once to the rooms which we are to examine."

The building was of gray, lichen-blotched stone, with a high central portion and two curving wings, like the claws of a crab, thrown out on each side. In one of these wings the windows were broken and blocked with wooden boards, while the roof was partly caved in, a picture of ruin[1]. The central portion was in little better repair, but the right-hand block was comparatively modern, and the blinds in the windows, with the blue smoke curling up from the chimneys, showed that this was where the family resided. Some scaffolding had been erected against the end wall, and the stone-work had been broken into, but there were no signs of any workmen at the moment of our visit. Holmes walked slowly up and down the ill-trimmed lawn and examined with deep attention the outsides of the windows.

"This, I take it, belongs to the room in which you used to sleep, the centre one to your sister's, and the one next to the main building to Dr. Roylott's chamber?"

"Exactly so. But I am now sleeping in the middle one."

"Pending the alterations, as I understand. By the way, there does not seem to be any very pressing need for repairs at that end wall."

"There were none. I believe that it was an excuse to move me from my room[2]."

"Ah! that is suggestive. Now, on the other side of this narrow wing runs the corridor from which these three rooms open. There are windows in it, of course?"

"Yes, but very small ones. Too narrow for anyone to pass through."

---

[1] An apt metaphor for the depraved, decayed House of Roylott

[2] A very clever woman – Stoner continues a trend in "The Adventures of Sherlock Holmes" of stories hosting intelligent and perceptive female clients

"As you both locked your doors at night, your rooms were unapproachable from that side. Now, would you have the kindness to go into your room and bar your shutters?"

Miss Stoner did so, and Holmes, after a careful examination through the open window, endeavoured in every way to force the shutter open, but without success. There was no slit through which a knife could be passed to raise the bar. Then with his lens he tested the hinges, but they were of solid iron, built firmly into the massive masonry. "Hum!" said he, scratching his chin in some perplexity, "my theory certainly presents some difficulties. No one could pass these shutters if they were bolted. Well, we shall see if the inside throws any light upon the matter."

A small side door led into the whitewashed corridor from which the three bedrooms opened. Holmes refused to examine the third chamber, so we passed at once to the second, that in which Miss Stoner was now sleeping, and in which her sister had met with her fate. It was a homely little room, with a low ceiling and a gaping fireplace, after the fashion of old country-houses. A brown chest of drawers stood in one corner, a narrow white counterpaned[1] bed in another, and a dressing-table on the left-hand side of the window. These articles, with two small wicker-work chairs, made up all the furniture in the room save for a square of Wilton carpet[2] in the centre. The boards round and the paneling of the walls were of brown, worm-eaten oak, so old and discoloured that it may have dated from the original building of the house. Holmes drew one of the chairs into a corner and sat silent, while his eyes travelled round and round and up and down, taking in every detail of the apartment.

"Where does that bell communicate with[3]?" he asked at last pointing to a thick belt-rope which hung down beside the bed, the tassel actually lying upon the pillow.

"It goes to the housekeeper's room."

"It looks newer than the other things?"

"Yes, it was only put there a couple of years ago."

"Your sister asked for it, I suppose?"

"No, I never heard of her using it. We used always to get what we wanted for ourselves."

"Indeed, it seemed unnecessary to put so nice a bell-pull there. You will excuse me for a few minutes while I satisfy myself as to this floor." He threw himself down upon his face with his lens in his hand and crawled swiftly backward and forward, examining minutely the cracks between the boards. Then he did the same with the wood-work with which the chamber was

---

[1] A quilt

[2] Made of woven wool – from Wilton in Wiltshire. Try saying that, Henry Higgins

[3] Made of embroidered cloth bands or corded velvet, ending in a pert tassel, bell pulls tugged on a wire that communicated with a bell in the servants' quarters, alerting servants to a need in the room whose bell rings out

paneled. Finally he walked over to the bed and spent some time in staring at it and in running his eye up and down the wall. Finally he took the bell-rope in his hand and gave it a brisk tug.

"Why, it's a dummy," said he.

"Won't it ring?"

"No, it is not even attached to a wire. This is very interesting. You can see now that it is fastened to a hook just above where the little opening for the ventilator is."

"How very absurd! I never noticed that before[1]."

"Very strange!" muttered Holmes, pulling at the rope. "There are one or two very singular points about this room. For example, what a fool a builder must be to open a ventilator into another room, when, with the same trouble, he might have communicated with the outside air!"

"That is also quite modern," said the lady.

"Done about the same time as the bell-rope?" remarked Holmes.

"Yes, there were several little changes carried out about that time."

"They seem to have been of a most interesting character -- dummy bell-ropes, and ventilators which do not ventilate. With your permission, Miss Stoner, we shall now carry our researches into the inner apartment."

Dr. Grimesby Roylott's chamber was larger than that of his stepdaughter, but was as plainly furnished. A camp-bed[2], a small wooden shelf full of books, mostly of a technical character an armchair beside the bed, a plain wooden chair against the wail, a round table, and a large iron safe were the principal things which met the eye. Holmes walked slowly round and examined each and all of them with the keenest interest.

"What's in here?" he asked, tapping the safe.

"My stepfather's business papers."

"Oh! you have seen inside, then?"

"Only once, some years ago. I remember that it was full of papers."

"There isn't a cat in it, for example?"

"No. What a strange idea!"

"Well, look at this!" He took up a small saucer of milk which stood on the top of it.

"No; we don't keep a cat. But there is a cheetah and a baboon."

"Ah, yes, of course! Well, a cheetah is just a big cat, and yet a saucer of milk does not go very far in satisfying its wants, I daresay. There is one point

---

[1] This seems unlikely, but given her pattern of self reliance, Roylott may have trusted that it would never be used, and while we have no picture of the way it is fastened to the hook, it may be obscured by angles or beams to the point where you would have to go out of your way to peer at it before it was seen

[2] A cot used by soldiers. Cheap to the point of eccentricity, Roylott rebukes a comfortable bed either for the cost or in order to replicate his Indian experiences as realistically as possible – hence the baboon and cheetah whom he delights in setting free on his lands

which I should wish to determine." He squatted down in front of the wooden chair and examined the seat of it with the greatest attention.

"Thank you. That is quite settled," said he, rising and putting his lens in his pocket. "Hello! Here is something interesting!"

The object which had caught his eye was a small dog lash[1] hung on one corner of the bed. The lash, however, was curled upon itself and tied so as to make a loop of whipcord.

"What do you make of that, Watson?"

"It's a common enough lash. But I don't know why if should be tied."

"That is not quite so common, is it? Ah, me! it's a wicked world, and when a clever man[2] turns his brains to crime it is the worst of all. I think that I have seen enough now, Miss Stoner, and with your permission we shall walk out upon the lawn."

I had never seen my friend's face so grim or his brow so dark as it was when we turned from the scene of this investigation. We had walked several times up and down the lawn, neither Miss Stoner nor myself liking to break in upon his thoughts before he roused himself from his reverie.

"It is very essential, Miss Stoner," said he, "that you should absolutely follow my advice in every respect."

"I shall most certainly do so."

"The matter is too serious for any hesitation. Your life may depend upon your compliance."

"I assure you that I am in your hands."

"In the first place, both my friend and I must spend the night in your room."

Both Miss Stoner and I gazed at him in astonishment[3].

"Yes, it must be so. Let me explain. I believe that that is the village inn over there?"

"Yes, that is the Crown."

"Very good. Your windows would be visible from there?"

"Certainly."

"You must confine yourself to your room, on pretence of a headache, when your stepfather comes back. Then when you hear him retire for the night, you must open the shutters of your window, undo the hasp, put your lamp there as a signal to us, and then withdraw quietly with everything which you are likely to want into the room which you used to occupy. I have no doubt that, in spite of the repairs, you could manage there for one night."

---

[1] That is, a "leash"

[2] Everything we have seen points to low intelligence – his squalid lifestyle, eccentric habits, and bizarre belongings. Holmes is no doubt pondering that predilection for strong, intellectual tobacco

[3] Not having yet mentioned that she would not be there during their slumber party, Holmes has led Watson and Stoner to balk at the impropriety of such a suggestion – one that pokes yet again at the sexual undertones of this very erotic – but subtly erotic – story

"Oh, yes, easily."

"The rest you will leave in our hands."

"But what will you do?"

"We shall spend the night in your room, and we shall investigate the cause of this noise which has disturbed you."

"I believe, Mr. Holmes, that you have already made up your mind," said Miss Stoner, laying her hand upon my companion's sleeve.

"Perhaps I have."

"Then, for pity's sake, tell me what was the cause of my sister's death."

"I should prefer to have clearer proofs before I speak."

"You can at least tell me whether my own thought is correct, and if she died from some sudden fright."

"No, I do not think so. I think that there was probably some more tangible cause. And now, Miss Stoner, we must leave you for if Dr. Roylott returned and saw us our journey would be in vain. Good-bye, and be brave, for if you will do what I have told you you may rest assured that we shall soon drive away[1] the dangers that threaten you."

Sherlock Holmes and I had no difficulty in engaging a bedroom and sitting-room at the Crown Inn. They were on the upper floor, and from our window we could command a view of the avenue gate, and of the inhabited wing of Stoke Moran Manor House. At dusk we saw Dr. Grimesby Roylott drive past, his huge form looming up beside the little figure of the lad who drove him. The boy had some slight difficulty in undoing the heavy iron gates, and we heard the hoarse roar of the doctor's voice and saw the fury with which he shook his clinched fists at him. The trap drove on, and a few minutes later we saw a sudden light spring up among the trees as the lamp was lit in one of the sitting-rooms.

"Do you know, Watson," said Holmes as we sat together in the gathering darkness, "I have really some scruples as to taking you to-night. There is a distinct element of danger."

"Can I be of assistance?"

"Your presence might be invaluable."

"Then I shall certainly come."

"It is very kind of you."

"You speak of danger. You have evidently seen more in these rooms than was visible to me."

"No, but I fancy that I may have deduced a little more[2]. I imagine that you saw all that I did."

"I saw nothing remarkable save the bell-rope, and what purpose that could answer I confess is more than I can imagine."

---

[1] Quite *literally* he *will* "drive [them] away" – with his cane

[2] A dominant theme in Holmes and Watson's relationship. While Watson ultimately grows capable of deducing in Holmes manner – as seen in the opening sequence of "Hound of the Baskervilles" – he never quite gets the knack of deducing *correctly*

"You saw the ventilator, too?"

"Yes, but I do not think that it is such a very unusual thing to have a small opening between two rooms. It was so small that a rat could hardly pass through."

"I knew that we should find a ventilator before ever we came to Stoke Moran."

"My dear Holmes!"

"Oh, yes, I did. You remember in her statement she said that her sister could smell Dr. Roylott's cigar. Now, of course that suggested at once that there must be a communication between the two rooms. It could only be a small one, or it would have been remarked upon at the coroner's inquiry. I deduced a ventilator."

"But what harm can there be in that?"

"Well, there is at least a curious coincidence of dates. A ventilator is made, a cord is hung, and a lady who sleeps in the bed dies. Does not that strike you?"

"I cannot as yet see any connection."

"Did you observe anything very peculiar about that bed?"

"No."

"It was clamped to the floor[1]. Did you ever see a bed fastened like that before?"

"I cannot say that I have."

"The lady could not move her bed. It must always be in the same relative position to the ventilator and to the rope -- or so we may call it, since it was clearly never meant for a bell-pull."

"Holmes," I cried, "I seem to see dimly what you are hinting at. We are only just in time to prevent some subtle and horrible crime."

"Subtle enough and horrible enough. When a doctor does go wrong he is the first of criminals. He has nerve and he has knowledge. Palmer and Pritchard[2] were among the heads of their profession. This man strikes even deeper, but I think, Watson, that we shall be able to strike deeper still. But we shall have horrors enough before the night is over; for goodness' sake let us have a quiet pipe and turn our minds for a few hours to something more cheerful."

ᘓ

---

1 This comment always sends a chill down my spine. It broods with sinister suggestion, but Holmes maintains the tension by refusing to clarify his deduction. It is certainly a ghastly idea to clamp down a person's bed so that she is forced to sleep in such a way that while she is most vulnerable, she is in the line of some intended fire

2 Edward William Palmer and Edward William Pritchard were two Victorian doctors convicted of poisoning respective family members. Holmes's comment that they were "among the heads of their profession" is intended to be ironic, since the only profession either excelled at was murder

About nine o'clock the light among the trees was extinguished, and all was dark in the direction of the Manor House. Two hours passed slowly away, and then, suddenly, just at the stroke of eleven, a single bright light shone out right in front of us.

"That is our signal," said Holmes, springing to his feet; "it comes from the middle window."

As we passed out he exchanged a few words with the landlord, explaining that we were going on a late visit to an acquaintance, and that it was possible that we might spend the night there. A moment later we were out on the dark road, a chill wind blowing in our faces, and one yellow light twinkling in front of us through the gloom to guide us on our sombre errand.

There was little difficulty in entering the grounds, for unrepaired breaches gaped in the old park wall. Making our way among the trees, we reached the lawn, crossed it, and were about to enter through the window when out from a clump of laurel bushes there darted what seemed to be a hideous and distorted child, who threw itself upon the grass with writhing limbs and then ran swiftly across the lawn into the darkness.

"My God!" I whispered; "did you see it?"

Holmes was for the moment as startled as I. His hand closed like a vise upon my wrist in his agitation. Then he broke into a low laugh and put his lips to my ear.

"It is a nice household," he murmured. "That is the baboon."

I had forgotten the strange pets which the doctor affected. There was a cheetah, too; perhaps we might find it upon our shoulders at any moment[1]. I confess that I felt easier in my mind when, after following Holmes's example and slipping off my shoes, I found myself inside the bedroom. My companion noiselessly closed the shutters, moved the lamp onto the table, and cast his eyes round the room. All was as we had seen it in the daytime. Then creeping up to me and making a trumpet of his hand, he whispered into my ear again so gently that it was all that I could do to distinguish the words:

"The least sound would be fatal to our plans."

I nodded to show that I had heard.

"We must sit without light. He would see it through the ventilator."

I nodded again.

[1] Again, Watson is mistaking the personality of the docile cheetah with that of the truly vicious leopard

"Do not go asleep; your very life may depend upon it. Have your pistol ready in case we should need it. I will sit on the side of the bed, and you in that chair."

I took out my revolver and laid it on the corner of the table.

Holmes had brought up a long thin cane[1], and this he placed upon the bed beside him. By it he laid the box of matches and the stump of a candle[2]. Then he turned down the lamp, and we were left in darkness.

How shall I ever forget that dreadful vigil? I could not hear a sound, not even the drawing of a breath, and yet I knew that my companion sat open-eyed, within a few feet of me, in the same state of nervous tension in which I was myself. The shutters cut off the least ray of light, and we waited in absolute darkness. From outside came the occasional cry of a night-bird, and once at our very window a long drawn catlike whine, which told us that the cheetah was indeed at liberty. Far away we could hear the deep tones of the parish clock, which boomed out every quarter of an hour. How long they seemed, those quarters! Twelve struck, and one and two and three, and still we sat waiting silently for whatever might befall.

Suddenly there was the momentary gleam of a light up in the direction of the ventilator, which vanished immediately, but was succeeded by a strong smell of burning oil and heated metal. Someone in the next room had lit a dark-lantern[3]. I heard a gentle sound of movement, and then all was silent once more, though the smell grew stronger. For half an hour I sat with straining ears. Then suddenly another sound became audible -- a very gentle, soothing sound, like that of a small jet of steam escaping continually from a kettle. The instant that we heard it, Holmes sprang from the bed, struck a match, and lashed furiously with his cane at the bell-pull.

"You see it, Watson?" he yelled. "You see it?"

But I saw nothing. At the moment when Holmes struck the light I heard a low, clear whistle, but the sudden glare flashing into my weary eyes made it impossible for me to tell what it was at which my friend lashed so savagely. I could, however, see that his face was deadly pale and filled with horror and loathing.-

He had ceased to strike and was gazing up at the ventilator when suddenly there broke from the silence of the night the most horrible cry to which I have ever listened. It swelled up louder and louder, a hoarse yell of

---

[1] Presumably made of bamboo – a popular material for canes used during casual rural outings like picnics and river excursions. The original illustration suggests this, with the cane bending pliably in Holmes' backswing

[2] Jeremy Brett interprets this moment beautifully in the Granada adaptation: his hands tremble as he lays them out precisely, and you can see his eyes wince at the physical proof of his own personal terror

[3] A lantern with a metal visor that could be closed around it to prevent light from escaping, while keeping the flame lit and ready for use at any moment – always a very sinister tool to have: the companion of murderers and grave robbers

pain and fear and anger all mingled in the one dreadful shriek. They say that away down in the village, and even in the distant parsonage, that cry raised the sleepers from their beds[1]. It struck cold to our hearts, and I stood gazing at Holmes, and he at me, until the last echoes of it had died away into the silence from which it rose.

"What can it mean?" I gasped.

"It means that it is all over," Holmes answered. "And perhaps, after all, it is for the best. Take your pistol[2], and we will enter Dr. Roylott's room."

With a grave face he lit the lamp and led the way down the corridor. Twice he struck at the chamber door without any reply from within. Then he turned the handle and entered, I at his heels, with the cocked pistol in my hand.

It was a singular sight which met our eyes. On the table stood a dark-lantern with the shutter half open, throwing a brilliant beam of light upon the iron safe, the door of which was ajar. Beside this table, on the wooden chair, sat Dr. Grimesby Roylott clad in a long gray dressing-gown, his bare ankles protruding beneath, and his feet thrust into red heelless Turkish slippers. Across his lap lay the short stock with the long lash which we had noticed during the day. His chin was cocked upward and his eyes were fixed in a dreadful, rigid stare at the corner of the ceiling. Round his brow he had a peculiar yellow band, with brownish speckles, which seemed to be bound tightly round his head. As we entered he made neither sound nor motion.

"The band! the speckled band!" whispered Holmes.

I took a step forward. In an instant his strange headgear began to move, and there reared itself from among his hair the squat diamond-shaped head and puffed neck[3] of a loathsome serpent.

"It is a swamp adder[4]!" cried Holmes; "the deadliest snake in India. He has died within ten seconds of being bitten[5]. Violence does, in truth, recoil upon the violent, and the schemer falls into the pit which he digs for another. Let us thrust this creature back into its den, and we can then

---

[1] They say so, but they are lying. It definitely woke sleepers in the house, but come on...

[2] In case the snake is so irate that it can't be corralled – presumably Roylott has been given up for dead (although he is probably only paralyzed)

[3] Verifying some relation to the cobra

[4] Of course this monster is fictitious, and dozens of real-life snakes have been suggested. Rather than list them all off, I'll give you the likeliest contender according to Doyle's description: the *Naja naja*, or cobra. Like the snake described here, it is Indian, has rapid-acting venom, can climb and rear, is yellow with brown speckles, has a diamond shaped head, and has a neck frill – or hood – that puffs when agitated

[5] Proving that he is incorrect about Julia's death by snake bite: though delirious, Julia lived for at least a minute or two after being attacked. Most critics agree that – scientifically speaking – Roylott is probably entirely conscious and aware of the conversation in front of him: he is merely paralyzed and slowing dying; his heart will probably stop in around twenty minutes to an hour

remove Miss Stoner to some place of shelter and let the county police know what has happened."

As he spoke he drew the dog-whip swiftly from the dead man's lap, and throwing the noose round the reptile's neck he drew it from its horrid perch and, carrying it at arm's length, threw it into the iron safe, which he closed upon it.

Such are the true facts of the death of Dr. Grimesby Roylott, of Stoke Moran. It is not necessary that I should prolong a narrative which has already run to too great a length by telling how we broke the sad news to the terrified girl, how we conveyed her by the morning train to the care of her good aunt at Harrow, of how the slow process of official inquiry came to the conclusion that the doctor met his fate while indiscreetly playing with a dangerous pet. The little which I had yet to learn of the case was told me by Sherlock Holmes as we travelled back next day.

"I had," said he, "come to an entirely erroneous conclusion which shows, my dear Watson, how dangerous it always is to reason from insufficient data. The presence of the gypsies, and the use of the word 'band,' which was used by the poor girl, no doubt to explain the appearance which she had caught a hurried glimpse of by the light of her match, were sufficient to put me upon an entirely wrong scent. I can only claim the merit that I instantly reconsidered my position when, however, it became clear to me that whatever danger threatened an occupant of the room could not come either from the window or the door. My attention was speedily drawn, as I have already remarked to you, to this ventilator, and to the bell-rope which hung down to the bed. The discovery that this was a dummy, and that the bed was clamped to the floor, instantly gave rise to the suspicion that the rope was there as a bridge for something passing through the hole and coming to the bed. The idea of a snake instantly occurred to me, and when I coupled it with my knowledge that the doctor was furnished with a supply of creatures from India, I felt that I was probably on the right track. The idea of using a form of poison which could not possibly be discovered by any chemical test was just such a one as would occur to a clever and ruthless man who had had an Eastern training. The rapidity with which such a poison would take effect would also, from his point of view, be an advantage. It would be a sharp-eyed coroner, indeed, who could distinguish the two little dark punctures which would show where the poison fangs had done their work[1]. Then I thought of the whistle. Of course he must recall the snake before the morning light revealed it to the victim[2]. He had trained it[3], probably by the

[1] As a doctor, Doyle should have known that such a bite would be immediately obvious. Again, I must insist on a verdict of death by heart failure in a moment of acute shock

[2] Snakes don't have hearing. They can detect vibrations, but they are deaf to sounds

[3] Snakes don't respond well to training

use of the milk[1] which we saw, to return to him when summoned[2]. He would put it through this ventilator at the hour that he thought best, with the certainty that it would crawl down the rope and land on the bed. It might or might not bite the occupant, perhaps she might escape every night for a week, but sooner or later she must fall a victim.

"I had come to these conclusions before ever I had entered his room. An inspection of his chair showed me that he had been in the habit of standing on it, which of course would be necessary in order that he should reach the ventilator. The sight of the safe, the saucer of milk, and the loop of whipcord were enough to finally dispel any doubts which may have remained. The metallic clang heard by Miss Stoner was obviously caused by her stepfather hastily closing the door of his safe upon its terrible occupant. Having once made up my mind, you know the steps which I took in order to put the matter to the proof. I heard the creature hiss as I have no doubt that you did also, and I instantly lit the light and attacked it."

"With the result of driving it through the ventilator."

"And also with the result of causing it to turn upon its master at the other side. Some of the blows of my cane came home and roused its snakish temper, so that it flew upon the first person it saw. In this way I am no doubt indirectly responsible for Dr. Grimesby Roylott's death, and I cannot say that it is likely to weigh very heavily upon my conscience[3]."

---

[1] Snakes don't drink milk. At all. They drink water and eat rodents

[2] Snakes cannot climb up things as smooth and narrow as a rope. A tree? Yes. A bell pull? No. In the Granada version, it is apparent that the snake in question is being filmed *from above* slithering *on top of* a rope – not coiling around it and ascending as one might see in a cartoon

[3] Probably due to the bandied about sexual subtext of this story: Holmes is probably convinced that Roylott sexually harassed – probably assaulted, possibly raped – both of his stepdaughters. The Freudian symbolism of the phallic snake protruding into the girls' sleeping room through the vulnerable hold in the wall is enough to raise some red flags, and some critics think the whole snake story is a mere fabrication used to disguise what Watson and Holmes really found: they slipped into the room to find Roylott angrily raping his daughter, killed him, and invented this outlandish story full of scientific holes. This is the rumor, then, that Watson points to at the beginning

ROYLOTT is perhaps one of Holmes' most imposing adversaries, and his demise is one of the most relished of all the Sherlockian villains. Unlike Moriarty, who, though wicked, is still little more than a crime world CEO, or the many schemers who litter the tales with their elaborate plans to cheat innocent women out of their inheritances, to abscond with priceless riches, or to sell state secrets, Roylott is truly loathsome: a filicidal sociopath. He isn't craven or shifty, but bold and determined, and he would rather see his stepdaughters dead than allow them to leave him with their dowries. This places him on par with Jack Stapleton who brilliantly schemes to slaughter his kinsmen in a bid to pocket the family inheritance. As you may have already noticed, Doyle was fascinated by human degradation and evil – the types of men and women who carefully design the destruction of their fellow human beings. Roylott is indifferent to human suffering, and only hopes to profit from it. One of the most chilling subtexts of the tale – one that (as Watson puts it) we only "dimly see what [Doyle is] hinting at" – is that of sexual molestation and incest. In a tidy Victorian way, Doyle gives us only a few clues that something even less savory than murder-by-snake is happen at Stoke Moran: Miss Stoner's bruised wrist (hidden by her glove in a classic sign of the embarrassment which victims of abuse often suffer), the suggestive death of her sister (staggering out of her bedroom in a nightgown, swaying and convulsing lewdly), and the phallic nature of the snake. Indeed, the more symbolic nature of the speckled serpent might be the predatory danger of the lust-driven man, whose actual penis might be expected to be leprous with syphilitic ulcers. While some may consider this reading into the snake motif too much, there is little question that the tale has a low-boiling sexual subtext, with the sisters coming into danger on the eves of their wedding night – robbed from their bridal beds in their maidenhood while dreaming of matrimony in the warm comfort of their boudoirs. Even if Roylott has not been raping his stepdaughters, the stench of his phallic cigars perfuming their rooms, the leering flash of his lamp through the adjoining vent-hole, and his domination of their beds (possessively clamped as they are to the floor) are rife with uncomfortable innuendo.

II.

It is just one more example of the brooding, shadowy atmosphere that has made this tale Holmes' most popular short case. The story might not have the gore of "Black Peter" with its harpoon blood bath, or the Gothic tropes of "The Copper Beeches" with its madwoman in the attic, or "The Sussex Vampire" and *The Hound of the Baskervilles* with their recitations of supernatural mythology, but once Holmes and Watson hear the story of Miss Stoner's long-suffered terror – of her sister's nighttime demise with its enigmatic clues – and once Roylott storms their quarters with threats of physical destruction, the mood has been set, and our heartbeats up their tempo while the duo wait in the darkness – first for the silent signal of the lamp, and then for some nameless horror which Holmes tantalizingly keeps to himself. The atmosphere is as thick with dread and terror as 221B's is with blue smoke during a three pipe problem, and our terror finally gives birth to horror at the description of Roylott's bloated head cradled in his snake's possessive grip. To make matters worse, experts (who by the way will also inform us that swamp adders are pure fiction, that snakes are deaf, cannot climb ropes, and do not drink milk – leading many players of the Sherlockian "game" to think up slews of creative lizard/snake hybrids) have assured the reading public that, while fatal, it is highly unlikely that Roylott would be dead at the time that Holmes and Watson find him. It is likelier – fictional snake or not – that even the most potent of poisons had merely paralyzed him, leaving him speechless and immobile as the poison leeched its way into his organs and shut them down one after another. Worse yet, although justifiably, some have argued that Holmes intentionally drove the snake to kill his master, that he would have known full well that Roylott – though moribund and doomed – was still alive based on his research, and that he lied about the villain's condition to prevent Watson from attempting to resuscitate him, effectively allowing him to expire while a doctor stood and watched. In any case, the death would have been a very fitting one: like his step-daughters who quietly, hopelessly, and defenselessly suffered his abuses, he is felled by the serpent he sent to snuff them, and is then paralyzed and killed by the same creature, forced to die their death – quietly, hopelessly, and defenselessly.

THE following tale is one of the first to reveal Doyle's taste for crime fiction, but it is a case far better suited for Carnacki the Ghost-finder rather than Sherlock Holmes, for – unlike the feigned devilry of *The Hound of the Baskervilles* or "The Sussex Vampire" – the supernatural powers that haunt these victims are all too genuine. The format is one to which Doyle would return several times, most notably in "The Leather Funnel" which also features a medieval relic with a macabre past and a malign influence. Doyle was certainly drawn to the narrative of the commonplace world being invaded by sinister and exotic forces, and most of his horror stories feature just such a concept. And he was not alone: there is something about this plot that distinctly presages the spirit of M. R. James' tales: an artifact haunted by a supernatural spell, a scroll hidden within it which carries a death sentence to those it impacts (cf. "Casting the Runes," "Stalls of Barchester Cathedral," etc.), and a clueless professor horribly killed as a result of impetuous curiousity. H. P. Lovecraft, too, seems to have an ancestor in this academic tale, as Dr. Hopstein bears a strong resemblance to "The Call of Cthulhu's" ill-starred Professor Angell. But this story is pure Doyle: written in an affable, journalistic style that attempts to relate facts in a thorough but appealing way, "The Silver Hatchet" paves the path for many more macabre mysteries and, specifically, for the most famous of Doyle's crime chroniclers – Dr. John H. Watson – whose debut adventure was a mere three years away.

The Silver Hatchet

{1883}

ON the 3rd of December 1861, Dr. Otto von Hopstein, Regius Professor of Comparative Anatomy of the University of Budapest, and Curator of the Academical Museum, was foully and brutally murdered within a stone-throw of the entrance to the college quadrangle.

Besides the eminent position of the victim and his popularity amongst both students and towns-folk, there were other circumstances which excited public interest very strongly, and drew general attention throughout Austria and Hungary to this murder. The *Peshter Abendblatt* of the following day had an article upon it, which may still be consulted by the curious, and from which I translate a few passages giving a succinct account of the circumstances under which the crime was committed, and the peculiar features in the case which puzzled the Hungarian police.

"It appears," said that very excellent paper, "that Professor von Hopstein left the University about half-past four in the afternoon, in order to meet the train which is due from Vienna at three minutes after five. He was accompanied by his old and dear friend, Herr Wilhelm Schlessinger, sub-Curator of the Museum and Privat-docent of Chemistry. The object of these two gentlemen in meeting this particular train was to receive the legacy bequeathed by Graf von Schulling to the University of Budapest. It is well known that this unfortunate nobleman, whose tragic fate is still fresh in the recollection of the public, left his unique collection of mediaeval weapons, as well as several priceless black-letter editions, to enrich the already celebrated museum of his Alma Mater. The worthy Professor was too much of an enthusiast in such matters to intrust the reception or care of this valuable legacy to any subordinate; and, with the assistance of Herr Schlessinger, he succeeded in removing the whole collection from the train, and stowing it away in a light cart which had been sent by the University authorities. Most of the books and more fragile articles were packed in cases of pine-wood, but many of the weapons were simply done round with straw, so that considerable labour was involved in moving them all. The Professor was so nervous, however, lest any of them should be injured, that he refused to allow any of the railway employes (Eisenhahndiener) to assist. Every article was carried across the platform by Herr Schlessinger, and handed to Professor von Hopstein in the cart, who packed it away. When everything was in, the two gentlemen, still faithful to their charge, drove back to the University, the Professor being in excellent spirits, and not a little proud of the physical exertion which he had shown himself capable of. He made some joking allusion to it to Reinmaul, the janitor, who, with his friend Schiffer, a Bohemian Jew, met the cart on its return and unloaded the contents. Leaving his curiosities safe in the storeroom, and locking the door, the Professor handed the key to his sub-curator, and, bidding every one good evening, departed in the direction of his lodgings. Schlessinger took a last look to reassure himself that all was right, and also went off, leaving Reinmaul and his friend Schiffer smoking in the janitor's lodge.

"At eleven o'clock, about an hour and a half after Von Hopstein's departure, a soldier of the 14th regiment of Jager, passing the front of the University on his way to barracks, came upon the lifeless body of the Professor lying a little way from the side of the road. He had fallen upon his face, with both hands stretched out. His head was literally split in two halves by a tremendous blow, which, it is conjectured, must have been struck from behind, there remaining a peaceful smile upon the old man's face, as if he had been still dwelling upon his new archaeological acquisition when death had overtaken him. There is no other mark of violence upon the body, except a bruise over the left patella, caused probably by the fall. The most mysterious part of the affair is that the Professor's purse, containing forty-three gulden, and his valuable watch have been untouched. Robbery cannot, therefore, have been the incentive to the deed, unless the assassins were disturbed before they could complete their work.

"This idea is negatived by the fact that the body must have lain at least an hour before any one discovered it. The whole affair is wrapped in mystery. Dr. Langemann, the eminent medico-jurist, has pronounced that the wound is such as might have been inflicted by a heavy sword-bayonet wielded by a powerful arm. The police are extremely reticent upon the subject, and it is suspected that they are in possession of a clue which may lead to important results."

Thus far the Pesther Abendblatt. The researches of the police failed, however, to throw the least glimmer of light upon the matter. There was absolutely no trace of the murderer, nor could any amount of ingenuity invent any reason which could have induced any one to commit the dreadful deed. The deceased Professor was a man so wrapped in his own studies and pursuits that he lived apart from the world, and had certainly never raised the slightest animosity in any human breast. It must have been some fiend, some savage, who loved blood for its own sake, who struck that merciless blow.

Though the officials were unable to come to any conclusions upon the matter, popular suspicion was not long in pitching upon a scapegoat. In the first published accounts of the murder the name of one Schiffer had been mentioned as having remained with the janitor after the Professor's departure. This man was a Jew, and Jews have never been popular in Hungary. A cry was at once raised for Schiffer's arrest; but as there was not the slightest grain of evidence against him, the authorities very properly refused to consent to so arbitrary a proceeding. Reinmaul, who was an old and most respected citizen, declared solemnly that Schiffer was with him until the startled cry of the soldier had caused them both to run out to the scene of the tragedy. No one ever dreamed of implicating Reinmaul in such a matter; but still, it was rumoured that his ancient and well-known friendship for Schiffer might have induced him to tell a falsehood in order to screen him. Popular feeling ran very high upon the subject, and there seemed a danger of Schiffer's being mobbed in the street, when an incident occurred which threw a very different light upon the matter.

On the morning of the 12th of December, just nine days after the mysterious murder of the Professor, Schiffer the Bohemian Jew was found lying in the north-western corner of the Grand Platz stone dead, and so mutilated that he was hardly recognisable. His head was cloven open in very much the same way as that of Von Hopstein, and his body exhibited numerous deep gashes, as if the murderer had been so carried away and transported with fury that he had continued to hack the lifeless body. Snow had fallen heavily the day before, and was lying at least a foot deep all over the square; some had fallen during the night, too, as was evidenced by a thin layer lying like a winding-sheet over the murdered man. It was hoped at first that this circumstance might assist in giving a clue by enabling the footsteps of the assassin to be traced; but the crime had been committed, unfortunately, in a place much frequented during the day, and there were innumerable tracks in every direction. Besides, the newly-fallen snow had blurred the footsteps to such an extent that it would have been impossible to draw trustworthy evidence from them.

In this case there was exactly the same impenetrable mystery and absence of motive which had characterised the murder of Professor von Hopstein. In the dead man's pocket there was found a notebook containing a considerable sum in gold and several very valuable bills, but no attempt had been made to rifle him. Supposing that any one to whom he had lent money (and this was the first idea which occurred to the police) had taken this means of evading his debt, it was hardly conceivable that he would have left such a valuable spoil untouched. Schiffer lodged with a widow named Gruga, at 49 Marie Theresa Strasse, and the evidence of his landlady and her children showed that he had remained shut up in his room the whole of the preceding day in a state of deep dejection, caused by the suspicion which the populace had fastened upon him. She had heard him go out about eleven o'clock at night for his last and fatal walk, and as he had a latch-key she had gone to bed without waiting for him. His object in choosing such a late hour for a ramble obviously was that he did not consider himself safe if recognised in the streets.

The occurrence of this second murder so shortly after the first threw not only the town of Budapest, but the whole of Hungary, into a terrible state of excitement, and even of terror. Vague dangers seemed to hang over the head of every man. The only parallel to this intense feeling was to be found in our own country at the time of the Williams murders described by De Quincey. There were so many resemblances between the cases of Von Hopstein and of Schiffer that no one could doubt that there existed a connection between the two. The absence of object and of robbery, the utter want of any clue to the assassin, and, lastly, the ghastly nature of the wounds, evidently inflicted by the same or a similar weapon, all pointed in one direction. Things were in this state when the incidents which I am now about to relate occurred, and in order to make them intelligible I must lead up to them from a fresh point of departure.

Otto von Schlegel was a younger son of the old Silesian family of that name. His father had originally destined him for the army, but at the advice of his teachers, who saw the surprising talent of the youth, had sent him to the University of Budapest to be educated in medicine. Here young Schlegel carried everything before him, and promised to be one of the most brilliant graduates turned out for many a year. Though a hard reader, he was no bookworm, but an active, powerful young fellow, full of animal spirits and vivacity, and extremely popular among his fellow-students.

The New Year examinations were at hand, and Schlegel was working hard—so hard that even the strange murders in the town, and the general excitement in men's minds, failed to turn his thoughts from his studies. Upon Christmas Eve, when every house was illuminated, and the roar of drinking songs came from the Bierkeller in the Student-quartier, he refused the many invitations to roystering suppers which were showered upon him, and went off with his books under his arm to the rooms of Leopold Strauss, to work with him into the small hours of the morning.

Strauss and Schlegel were bosom friends. They were both Silesians, and had known each other from boyhood. Their affection had become proverbial in the University. Strauss was almost as distinguished a student as Schlegel, and there had been many a tough struggle for academic honours between the two fellow-countrymen, which had only served to strengthen their friendship by a bond of mutual respect. Schlegel admired the dogged pluck and never-failing good temper of his old playmate; while the latter considered Schlegel, with his many talents and brilliant versatility, the most accomplished of mortals.

The friends were still working together, the one reading from a volume on anatomy, the other holding a skull and marking off the various parts mentioned in the text, when the deep-toned bell of St. Gregory's church struck the hour of midnight.

"Hark to that!" said Schlegel, snapping up the book and stretching out his long legs towards the cheery fire. "Why, it's Christmas morning, old friend! May it not be the last that we spend together!"

"May we have passed all these confounded examinations before another one comes!" answered Strauss. "But see here, Otto, one bottle of wine will not be amiss. I have laid one up on purpose;" and with a smile on his honest South German face, he pulled out a long-necked bottle of Rhenish from amongst a pile of books and bones in the corner.

"It is a night to be comfortable indoors," said Otto von Schlegel, looking out at the snowy landscape, "for 'tis bleak and bitter enough outside. Good health, Leopold!"

"Lebe hoch!" replied his companion. "It is a comfort indeed to forget sphenoid bones and ethmoid bones, if it be but for a moment. And what is the news of the corps, Otto? Has Graube fought the Swabian?"

"They fight to-morrow," said Von Schlegel. "I fear that our man will lose his beauty, for he is short in the arm. Yet activity and skill may do much for him. They say his hanging guard is perfection."

"And what else is the news amongst the students?" asked Strauss.

"They talk, I believe, of nothing but the murders. But I have worked hard of late, as you know, and hear little of the gossip."

"Have you had time," inquired Strauss, "to look over the books and the weapons which our dear old Professor was so concerned about the very day he met his death? They say they are well worth a visit."

"I saw them to-day," said Schlegel, lighting his pipe. "Reinmaul, the janitor, showed me over the store-room, and I helped to label many of them from the original catalogue of Graf Schulling's museum. As far as we can see, there is but one article missing of all the collection."

"One missing!" exclaimed Strauss. "That would grieve old Von Hopstein's ghost. Is it anything of value?"

"It is described as an antique hatchet, with a head of steel and a handle of chased silver. We have applied to the railway company, and no doubt it will be found."

"I trust so," echoed Strauss; and the conversation drifted off into other channels. The fire was burning low and the bottle of Rhenish was empty before the two friends rose from their chairs, and Von Schlegel prepared to depart.

"Ugh! It's a bitter night!" he said, standing on the doorstep and folding his cloak round him. "Why, Leopold, you have your cap on. You are not going out, are you?"

"Yes, I am coming with you," said Strauss, shutting the door behind him. "I feel heavy," he continued, taking his friend's arm, and walking down the street with him. "I think a walk as far as your lodgings, in the crisp frosty air, is just the thing to set me right."

The two students went down Stephen Strasse together and across Julien Platz, talking on a variety of topics. As they passed the corner of the Grand Platz, however, where Schiffer had been found dead, the conversation turned naturally upon the murder.

"That's where they found him," remarked Von Schlegel, pointing to the fatal spot

"Perhaps the murderer is near us now," said Strauss. "Let us hasten on."

They both turned to go, when Von Schlegel gave a sudden cry of pain and stooped down.

"Something has cut through my boot!" he cried; and feeling about with his hand in the snow, he pulled out a small glistening battle-axe, made apparently entirely of metal. It had been lying with the blade turned slightly upwards, so as to cut the foot of the student when he trod upon it.

"The weapon of the murderer!" he ejaculated.

"The silver hatchet from the museum!" cried Strauss in the same breath.

There could be no doubt that it was both the one and the other. There could not be two such curious weapons, and the character of the wounds was just such as would be inflicted by a similar instrument. The murderer had evidently thrown it aside after committing the dreadful deed, and it had lain concealed in the snow some twenty metres from the spot ever since. It was extraordinary that of all the people who had passed and repassed none had discovered it; but the snow was deep, and it was a little off the beaten track.

"What are we to do with it? said Von Schlegel, holding it in his hand. He shuddered as he noticed by the light of the moon that the head of it was all dabbled with dark-brown stains.

"Take it to the Commissary of Police," suggested Strauss.

"He'll be in bed now. Still, I think you are right. But it is nearly four o'clock. I will wait until morning, and take it round before breakfast Meanwhile, I must carry it with me to my lodgings."

"That is the best plan," said his friend; and the two walked on together talking of the remarkable find which they had made. When they came to Schlegel's door, Strauss said good-bye, refusing an invitation to go in, and walked briskly down the street in the direction of his own lodgings.

Schlegel was stooping down putting the key into the lock, when a strange change came over him. He trembled violently, and dropped the key from his quivering fingers. His right hand closed convulsively round the handle of the silver hatchet, and his eye followed the retreating figure of his friend with a vindictive glare. In spite of the coldness of the night the perspiration streamed down his face. For a moment he seemed to struggle with himself, holding his hand up to his throat as if he were suffocating. Then, with crouching body and rapid, noiseless steps, he crept after his late companion.

Strauss was plodding sturdily along through the snow, humming snatches of a student song, and little dreaming of the dark figure which pursued him. At the Grand Platz it was forty yards behind him; at the Julien Platz it was but twenty; in Stephen Strasse it was ten, and gaining on him with panther-like rapidity. Already it was almost within arm's length of the unsuspecting man, and the hatchet glittered coldly in the moonlight, when some slight noise must have reached Strauss's ears, for he faced suddenly round upon his pursuer. He started and uttered an exclamation as his eye met the white set face, with flashing eyes and clenched teeth, which seemed to be suspended in the air behind him.

"What, Otto!" he exclaimed, recognising his friend. "Art thou ill? You look pale. Come with me to my Ah! hold, you madman, hold! Drop that axe! Drop it, I say, or by heaven I'll choke you!"

Von Schlegel had thrown himself upon him with a wild cry and uplifted weapon; but the student was stout-hearted and resolute. He rushed inside the sweep of the hatchet and caught his assailant round the waist, narrowly escaping a blow which would have cloven his head. The two staggered for a moment in, a deadly wrestle, Schlegel endeavouring to shorten his weapon; but Strauss with a desperate wrench managed to bring him to the ground, and they rolled together in the snow, Strauss clinging to the other's right arm and shouting frantically for assistance. It was as well that he did so, for Schlegel would certainly have succeeded in freeing his arm had it not been for the arrival of two stalwart gendarmes, attracted by the uproar. Even then the three of them found it difficult to overcome the maniacal strength of Schlegel, and they were utterly unable to wrench the silver hatchet from his grasp. One of the gendarmes, however, had a coil of rope round his waist, with which he rapidly secured the student's arms to his sides. In this way, half pushed, half dragged, he was conveyed, in spite of furious cries and frenzied struggles, to the central police station.

Strauss assisted in coercing his former friend, and accompanied the police to the station; protesting loudly at the same time against any

unnecessary violence, and giving it as his opinion that a lunatic asylum would be a more fitting place for the prisoner. The events of the last half-hour had been so sudden and inexplicable that he felt quite dazed himself. What did it all mean? It was certain that his old friend from boyhood had attempted to murder him, and had nearly succeeded. Was Von Schlegel then the murderer of Professor von Hopstein and of the Bohemian Jew? Strauss felt that it was impossible, for the Jew was not even known to him, and the Professor had been his especial favourite. He followed mechanically to the police station, lost in grief and amazement.

Inspector Baumgarten, one of the most energetic and best known of the police officials, was on duty in the absence of the Commissary. He was a wiry little active man, quiet and retiring in his habits, but possessed of great sagacity and a vigilance which never relaxed. Now, though he had had a six hours' vigil, he sat as erect as ever, with his pen behind his ear, at his official desk, while his friend, Sub-inspector Winkel, snored in a chair at the side of the stove. Even the inspector's usually immovable features betrayed surprise, however, when the door was flung open and Von Schlegel was dragged in with pale face and disordered clothes, the silver hatchet still grasped firmly in his hand. Still more surprised was he when Strauss and the gendarmes gave their account, which was duly entered in the official register.

"Young man, young man," said Inspector Baumgarten, laying down his pen and fixing his eyes sternly upon the prisoner, "this is pretty work for Christmas morning; why have you done this thing?"

"God knows!" cried Von Schlegel, covering his face with his hands and dropping the hatchet. A change had come over him, his fury and excitement were gone, and he seemed utterly prostrated with grief.

"You have rendered yourself liable to a strong suspicion of having committed the other murders which have disgraced our city."

"No, no, indeed!" said Von Schlegel earnestly. "God forbid!"

"At least you are guilty of attempting the life of Herr Leopold Strauss."

"The dearest friend I have in the world," groaned the student. "Oh, how could I! How could I!"

"His being your friend makes your crime ten times more heinous," said the inspector severely. "Remove him for the remainder of the night to the But steady! Who comes here?"

The door was pushed open, and a man came into the room, so haggard and careworn that he looked more like a ghost than a human being. He tottered as he walked, and had to clutch at the backs of the chairs as he approached the inspector's desk. It was hard to recognise in this miserable-looking object the once cheerful and rubicund sub-curator of the museum and privat-docent of chemistry, Herr Wilhelm Schlessinger. The practised eye of Baumgarten, however, was not to be baffled by any change.

"Good morning, mein herr," he said; "you are up early. No doubt the reason is that you have heard that one of your students, Von Schlegel, is arrested for attempting the life of Leopold Strauss?"

"No; I have come for myself," said Schlessinger, speaking huskily, and putting his hand up to his throat. "I have come to ease my soul of the weight of a great sin, though, God knows, an unmeditated one. It was I who— But, merciful heavens! there it is—the horrid thing! Oh, that I had never seen it!"

He shrank back in a paroxysm of terror, glaring at the silver hatchet where it lay upon the floor, and pointing at it with his emaciated hand.

"There it lies!" he yelled. "Look at it! It has come to condemn me. See that brown rust on it! Do you know what that is? That is the blood of my dearest, best friend. Professor von Hopstein. I saw it gush over the very handle as I drove the blade through his brain. Mein Gott, I see it now!"

"Sub-inspector Winkel," said Baumgarten, endeavouring to preserve his official austerity, "you will arrest this man, charged on his own confession with the murder of the late Professor. I also deliver into your hands Von Schlegel here, charged with a murderous assault upon Herr Strauss. You will also keep this hatchet"—here he picked it from the floor—"which has apparently been used for both crimes."

Wilhelm Schlessinger had been leaning against the table, with a face of ashy paleness. As the inspector ceased speaking, he looked up excitedly.

"What did you say?" he cried. "Von Schlegel attack Strauss! The two dearest friends in the college! I slay my old master! It is magic, I say; it is a charm! There is a spell upon us! It is—Ah, I have it! It is that hatchet—that thrice accursed hatchet!" and he pointed convulsively at the weapon which Inspector Baumgarten still held in his hand.

The inspector smiled contemptuously.

"Restrain yourself, mein herr," he said. "You do but make your case worse by such wild excuses for the wicked deed you confess to. Magic and charms are not known in the legal vocabulary, as my friend Winkel will assure you."

"I know not," remarked his sub-inspector, shrugging his broad shoulders. "There are many strange things in the world. Who knows but that—"

"What!" roared Inspector Baumgarten furiously. "You would undertake to contradict me! You would set up your opinion! You would be the champion of these accursed murderers! Fool, miserable fool, your hour has come!" and rushing at the astounded Winkel, he dealt a blow at him with the silver hatchet which would certainly have justified his last assertion had it not been that, in his fury, he overlooked the lowness of the rafters above his head. The blade of the hatchet struck one of these, and remained there quivering, while the handle was splintered into a thousand pieces.

"What have I done?" gasped Baumgarten, falling back into his chair. "What have I done?"

"You have proved Herr Schlessinger's words to be correct," said Von Schlegel, stepping forward, for the astonished policemen had let go their grasp of him. "That is what you have done. Against reason, science, and everything else though it be, there is a charm at work. There must be! Strauss, old boy, you know I would not, in my right senses, hurt one hair of your head. And you, Schlessinger, we both know you loved the old man who is dead. And you, Inspector Baumgarten, you would not willingly have struck your friend the sub-inspector?"

"Not for the whole world," groaned the inspector, covering his face with his hands.

"Then is it not clear? But now, thank Heaven, the accursed thing is broken, and can never do harm again. But see, what is that?"

Right in the centre of the room was lying a thin brown cylinder of parchment. One glance at the fragments of the handle of the weapon showed that it had been hollow. This roll of paper had apparently been hidden away inside the metal case thus formed, having been introduced through a small hole, which had been afterwards soldered up. Von Schlegel opened the document. The writing upon it was almost illegible from age; but as far as they could make out it stood thus, in mediaeval German—

"DIESE WAFFE BENUTZTE MAX VON ERLICHINGEN, UM JOANNA BODECK ZU ERMORDEN; DESHALB BESCHULDIGE ICH, JOHANN BODECK, MITTELST DER MACHT, WELCHE MIR ALS MITGLIED DES CONCILS DES ROTHEN KREUZES VERLIEHEN WURDE, DIESELBE MIT DIESER UNTHAT. MAG SIE ANDEREN DENSELBEN SCHMERZ VERURSACHEN, DEN SIE MIR VERURSACHT HAT. MAG JEDE HAND, DIE SIE ERGREIFT, MIT DEM BLUT EINES FREUNDES GERÖTHET SEIN.

“IMMER ÜBEL, NIEMALS GUT, GERÖTHET MIT DES FREUNDES BLUT.'"

Which may be roughly translated—

"THIS WEAPON WAS USED BY MAX VON ERLICHINGEN FOR THE MURDER OF JOANNA BODECK. THEREFORE DO I, JOHANN BODECK, ACCUSE IT BY THE POWER WHICH HAS BEEN BEQUEATHED TO ME AS ONE OF THE COUNCIL OF THE ROSY CROSS. MAY IT DEAL TO OTHERS THE GRIEF WHICH IT HAS DEALT TO ME! MAY EVERY HAND THAT GRASPS IT BE REDDENED IN THE BLOOD OF A FRIEND!
"'EVER EVIL, NEVER GOOD, REDDENED WITH A LOVED ONE'S BLOOD.'"

There was a dead silence in the room when Von Schlegel had finished spelling out this strange document. As he put it down Strauss laid his hand affectionately upon his arm.

"No such proof is needed by me, old friend," he said. "At the very moment that you struck at me I forgave you in my heart. I well know that if the poor Professor were in the room he would say as much to Herr Wilhelm Schlessinger."

"Gentlemen," remarked the inspector, standing up and resuming his official tones, "this affair, strange as it is, must be treated according to rule and precedent Sub-inspector Winkel, as your superior officer, I command you to arrest me upon a charge of murderously assaulting you. You will commit me to prison for the night, together with Herr von Schlegel and Herr Wilhelm Schlessinger. We shall take our trial at the coming sitting of the judges. In the meantime take care of that piece of evidence —pointing to the piece of parchment—"and, while I am away, devote your time and energy to utilising the clue you have obtained in discovering who it was who slew Herr Schiffer, the Bohemian Jew."

The one missing link in the chain of evidence was soon supplied. On the 28th of December the wife of Reinmaul the janitor, coming into the bedroom after a short absence, found her husband hanging lifeless from a hook in the wall. He had tied a long bolster-case round his neck and stood upon a chair in order to commit the fatal deed. On the table was a note in which he confessed to the murder of Schiffer the Jew, adding that the deceased had been his oldest friend, and that he had slain him without premeditation, in obedience to some incontrollable impulse. Remorse and grief, he said, had driven him to self-destruction; and he wound up his confession by commending his soul to the mercy of Heaven.

The trial which ensued was one of the strangest which ever occurred in the whole history of jurisprudence. It was in vain that the prosecuting council urged the improbability of the explanation offered by the prisoners, and deprecated the introduction of such an element as magic into a nineteenth-century law-court. The chain of facts was too strong, and the prisoners were unanimously acquitted. "This silver hatchet," remarked the judge in his summing up, "has hung untouched upon the wall in the mansion of the Graf von Schulling for nearly two hundred years. The shocking manner in which he met his death at the hands of his favourite house steward is still fresh in your recollection. It has come out in evidence that, a few days before the murder, the steward had overhauled the old weapons and cleaned them. In doing this he must have touched the handle of this hatchet. Immediately afterwards he slew his master, whom he had served faithfully for twenty years. The weapon then came, in conformity with the Count's will, to Budapest, where, at the station, Herr Wilhelm Schlessinger grasped it, and, within two hours, used it against the person of the deceased Professor. The next man whom we find touching it is the janitor Reinmaul, who helped to remove the weapons from the cart to the store-room. At the first opportunity he buried it in the body of his friend Schiffer. We then have the attempted murder of Strauss by Schlegel, and of Winkel by Inspector Baumgarten, all immediately following the taking of the hatchet into the hand. Lastly, comes the providential discovery of the extraordinary document which has been read to you by the clerk of the court. I invite your most careful consideration, gentlemen of the jury, to this chain of facts, knowing that you will find a verdict according to your consciences without fear and without favour."

Perhaps the most interesting piece of evidence to the English reader, though it found few supporters among the Hungarian audience, was that of Dr. Langemann, the eminent medico-jurist, who has written text-books upon metallurgy and toxicology. He said—

"I am not so sure, gentlemen, that there is need to fall back upon necromancy or the black art for an explanation of what has occurred. What I say is merely a hypothesis, without proof of any sort, but in a case so extraordinary every suggestion may be of value. The Rosicrucians, to whom allusion is made in this paper, were the most profound chemists of the early Middle Ages, and included the principal alchemists whose names have descended to us. Much as chemistry has advanced, there are some points in which the ancients were ahead of us, and in none more so than in the manufacture of poisons of subtle and deadly action. This man Bodeck, as one of the elders of the Rosicrucians, possessed, no doubt, the recipe of many such mixtures, some of which, like the aqua tofana of the Medicis, would poison by penetrating through the pores of the skin. It is conceivable that the handle of this silver hatchet has been anointed by some preparation which is a diffusible poison, having the effect upon the human body of bringing on sudden and acute attacks of homicidal mania. In such attacks it is well known that the madman's rage is turned against those whom he loved best when sane. I have, as I remarked before, no proof to support me in my theory, and simply put it forward for what it is worth."

With this extract from the speech of the learned and ingenious professor, we may close the account of this famous trial.

The broken pieces of the silver hatchet were thrown into a deep pond, a clever poodle being employed to carry them in his mouth, as no one would touch them for fear some of the infection might still hang about them. The piece of parchment was preserved in the museum of the University. As to Strauss and Schlegel, Winkel and Baumgarten, they continued the best of friends, and are so still for all I know to the contrary. Schlessinger became surgeon of a cavalry regiment; and was shot at the battle of Sadowa five years later, while rescuing the wounded under a heavy fire. By his last injunctions his little patrimony was to be sold to erect a marble obelisk over the grave of Professor von Hopstein.

FROM an early point in his career, Doyle became keenly interested in the concept of the "homosocial relationship" - particularly the platonic affection of two male friends. During the Victorian Age, while emotional familiarity was restricted and regulated by convention and custom, public displays of affection were common between men, and hardly ever excited attention or speculation. Men linked arms and even snuggled cozily one against another without risking accusations of homosexuality. But the last decades of the Victorian era would increasingly cast a shadow over the brotherly warmth that many men - straight and gay - felt comfortable publicly expressing. The Cleveland Street Scandal, the trial of Oscar Wilde, the 1871 trial of two cross-dressing socialites called "Fanny" and "Stella," and the reckless hedonism of the Decadent Movement posed a threat to the open affection that men at that time felt free to express towards one another - a public warmth that would have been scandalous had it been shared with a woman, even a wife. Suddenly motives were being called into question and the nature of male friendships were now poised under the same suspicion and scrutiny that opposite sex relationships had suffered. Although the scandals of the 1890s were still a-ways off at the time this tale was published, there remains a proto-Freudian discomfort with the very close, affectionate relationships which these men share. What lies beneath them - whether emotional, sexual, or criminal - is suddenly a matter of distrust, suspicion, and anxiety. Are they chums who can comfortably trust one another's motives and fidelity, or is there something rapacious and violent stalking behind the screen of public affection?

TERROR was never an alien element to the adventures of Mr Sherlock Holmes and Dr John H. Watson. Early on it haunted the duo in the grisly affairs chronicled in *A Study in Scarlet* and *The Sign of Four*, later it stalked them in "The Speckled Band," "The Five Orange Pips," "The Cooper Beeches," "The Cardboard Box," "Black Peter," "The Sussex Vampire," "The Veiled Lodger," "The Lion's Mane," and of course *The Hound of the Baskervilles*. One story, however, dealt more intimately with horror than any other, since it – rather than a bullet, snake, or harpoon – was the murder weapon. And what a weapon. When listing his twelve favorite Holmes stories, Doyle ranked this one as ninth, and it is not terribly difficult to see why: the murder is horrific, the mood grim, the tone Gothic, and the mystery truly baffling – one of the great locked room murders in the annals of English detective fiction. Holmes had seen terror employed as a modus of murder in previous cases – it was used to incite Sir Charles Baskerville's fatal heart attack for instance – but never in such a cruel and horrendous manner: the idea is not to burst a dying heart with a shock, but to plainly drive three young people to the furthest reaches of sanity with horror: to very literally frighten them to death.

The Adventure of the Devil's Foot
{1910}

IN RECORDING from time to time some of the curious experiences and interesting recollections which I associate with my long and intimate friendship with Mr. Sherlock Holmes, I have continually been faced by difficulties caused by his own aversion to publicity. To his sombre and cynical spirit all popular applause was always abhorrent, and nothing amused him more at the end of a successful case than to hand over the actual exposure to some orthodox official, and to listen with a mocking smile to the general chorus of misplaced congratulation. It was indeed this attitude upon the part of my friend and certainly not any lack of interesting material which has caused me of late years to lay very few of my records before the public. My participation in some if his adventures was always a privilege which entailed discretion and reticence upon me.

It was, then, with considerable surprise that I received a telegram from Homes last Tuesday—he has never been known to write where a telegram would serve—in the following terms:

Why not tell them of the Cornish horror—strangest case I have handled.

I have no idea what backward sweep of memory had brought the matter fresh to his mind, or what freak had caused him to desire that I should recount it; but I hasten, before another cancelling telegram may arrive, to hunt out the notes which give me the exact details of the case and to lay the narrative before my readers.

It was, then, in the spring of the year 1897 that Holmes's iron constitution showed some symptoms of giving way in the face of constant hard work of a most exacting kind, aggravated, perhaps, by occasional indiscretions of his own. In March of that year Dr. Moore Agar, of Harley Street, whose dramatic introduction to Holmes I may some day recount, gave positive injunctions that the famous private agent lay aside all his cases and surrender himself to complete rest if he wished to avert an absolute breakdown. The state of his health was not a matter in which he himself took the faintest interest, for his mental detachment was absolute, but he was induced at last, on the threat of being permanently disqualified from work, to give himself a complete change of scene and air. Thus it was that in the early spring of that year we found ourselves together in a small cottage near Poldhu Bay, at the further extremity of the Cornish peninsula.

It was a singular spot, and one peculiarly well suited to the grim humour of my patient. From the windows of our little whitewashed house, which stood high upon a grassy headland, we looked down upon the whole sinister semicircle of Mounts Bay, that old death trap of sailing vessels, with its fringe of black cliffs and surge-swept reefs on which innumerable seamen have met their end. With a northerly breeze it lies placid and sheltered, inviting the storm-tossed craft to tack into it for rest and protection.

Then come the sudden swirl round of the wind, the blistering gale from the south-west, the dragging anchor, the lee shore, and the last battle in the creaming breakers. The wise mariner stands far out from that evil place.

On the land side our surroundings were as sombre as on the sea. It was a country of rolling moors, lonely and dun-colored, with an occasional church tower to mark the site of some old-world village. In every direction upon these moors there were traces of some vanished race which had passed utterly away, and left as it sole record strange monuments of stone, irregular mounds which contained the burned ashes of the dead, and curious earthworks which hinted at prehistoric strife. The glamour and mystery of the place, with its sinister atmosphere of forgotten nations, appealed to the imagination of my friend, and he spent much of his time in long walks and solitary meditations upon the moor. The ancient Cornish language had also arrested his attention, and he had, I remember, conceived the idea that it was akin to the Chaldean, and had been largely derived from the Phoenician traders in tin. He had received a consignment of books upon philology and was settling down to develop this thesis when suddenly, to my sorrow and to his unfeigned delight, we found ourselves, even in that land of dreams, plunged into a problem at our very doors which was more intense, more engrossing, and infinitely more mysterious than any of those which had driven us from London. Our simple life and peaceful, healthy routine were violently interrupted, and we were precipitated into the midst of a series of events which caused the utmost excitement not only in Cornwall but throughout the whole west of England. Many of my readers may retain some recollection of what was called at the time "The Cornish Horror," though a most imperfect account of the matter reached the London press. Now, after thirteen years, I will give the true details of this inconceivable affair to the public.

I have said that scattered towers marked the villages which dotted this part of Cornwall. The nearest of these was the hamlet of Tredannick Wollas, where the cottages of a couple of hundred inhabitants clustered round an ancient, moss-grown church. The vicar of the parish, Mr. Roundhay, was something of an archaeologist, and as such Holmes had made his acquaintance. He was a middle-aged man, portly and affable, with a considerable fund of local lore. At his invitation we had taken tea at the vicarage and had come to know, also, Mr. Mortimer Tregennis, an independent gentleman, who increased the clergyman's scanty resources by taking rooms in his large, straggling house. The vicar, being a bachelor, was glad to come to such an arrangement, though he had little in common with his lodger, who was a thin, dark, spectacled man, with a stoop which gave the impression of actual, physical deformity. I remember that during our short visit we found the vicar garrulous, but his lodger strangely reticent, a sad-faced, introspective man, sitting with averted eyes, brooding apparently upon his own affairs.

These were the two men who entered abruptly into our little sitting-room on Tuesday, March the 16th, shortly after our breakfast hour, as we were smoking together, preparatory to our daily excursion upon the moors.

"Mr. Holmes," said the vicar in an agitated voice, "the most extraordinary and tragic affair has occurred during the night. It is the most unheard-of business. We can only regard it as a special Providence that you should chance to be here at the time, for in all England you are the one man we need."

I glared at the intrusive vicar with no very friendly eyes; but Holmes took his pipe from his lips and sat up in his chair like an old hound who hears the view-halloa. He waved his hand to the sofa, and our palpitating visitor with his agitated companion sat side by side upon it. Mr. Mortimer Tregennis was more self-contained than the clergyman, but the twitching of his thin hands and the brightness of his dark eyes showed that they shared a common emotion.

"Shall I speak or you?" he asked of the vicar.

"Well, as you seem to have made the discovery, whatever it may be, and the vicar to have had it second-hand, perhaps you had better do the speaking," said Holmes.

I glanced at the hastily clad clergyman, with the formally dressed lodger seated beside him, and was amused at the surprise which Holmes's simple deduction had brought to their faces.

"Perhaps I had best say a few words first," said the vicar, "and then you can judge if you will listen to the details from Mr. Tregennis, or whether we should not hasten at once to the scene of this mysterious affair. I may explain, then, that our friend here spent last evening in the company of his two brothers, Owen and George, and of his sister Brenda, at their house of Tredannick Wartha, which is near the old stone cross upon the moor. He left them shortly after ten o'clock, playing cards round the dining-room table, in excellent health and spirits. This morning, being an early riser, he walked in that direction before breakfast and was overtaken by the carriage of Dr. Richards, who explained that he had just been sent for on a most urgent call to Tredannick Wartha. Mr. Mortimer Tregennis naturally went with him. When he arrived at Tredannick Wartha he found an extraordinary state of things. His two brothers and his sister were seated round the table exactly as he had left them, the cards still spread in front of them and the candles burned down to their sockets. The sister lay back stone-dead in her chair, while the two brothers sat on each side of her laughing, shouting, and singing, the senses stricken clean out of them. All three of them, the dead woman and the two demented men, retained upon their faces an expression of the utmost horror—a convulsion of terror which was dreadful to look upon. There was no sign of the presence of anyone in the house, except Mrs. Porter, the old cook and housekeeper, who declared that she had slept deeply and heard no sound during the night. Nothing had been stolen or disarranged, and there is absolutely no explanation of what the horror can be which has frightened a woman to death and two strong men out of their senses. There is the situation, Mr. Holmes, in a nutshell, and if you can help us to clear it up you will have done a great work."

I had hoped that in some way I could coax my companion back into the quiet which had been the object of our journey; but one glance at his intense face and contracted eyebrows told me how vain was now the expectation. He sat for some little time in silence, absorbed in the strange drama which had broken in upon our peace.

"I will look into this matter," he said at last. "On the face of it, it would appear to be a case of a very exceptional nature. Have you been there yourself, Mr. Roundhay?"

"No, Mr. Holmes. Mr. Tregennis brought back the account to the vicarage, and I at once hurried over with him to consult you."

"How far is it to the house where this singular tragedy occurred?"

"About a mile inland."

"Then we shall walk over together. But before we start I must ask you a few questions, Mr. Mortimer Tregennis."

The other had been silent all this time, but I had observed that his more controlled excitement was even greater than the obtrusive emotion of the clergyman. He sat with a pale, drawn face, his anxious gaze fixed upon Holmes, and his thin hands clasped convulsively together. His pale lips quivered as he listened to the dreadful experience which had befallen his family, and his dark eyes seemed to reflect something of the horror of the scene.

"Ask what you like, Mr. Holmes," said he eagerly. "It is a bad thing to speak of, but I will answer you the truth."

"Tell me about last night."

"Well, Mr. Holmes, I supped there, as the vicar has said, and my elder brother George proposed a game of whist afterwards. We sat down about nine o'clock. It was a quarter-past ten when I moved to go. I left them all round the table, as merry as could be."

"Who let you out?"

"Mrs. Porter had gone to bed, so I let myself out. I shut the hall door behind me. The window of the room in which they sat was closed, but the blind was not drawn down. There was no change in door or window this morning, or any reason to think that any stranger had been to the house. Yet there they sat, driven clean mad with terror, and Brenda lying dead of fright, with her head hanging over the arm of the chair. I'll never get the sight of that room out of my mind so long as I live."

"The facts, as you state them, are certainly most remarkable," said Holmes. "I take it that you have no theory yourself which can in any way account for them?"

"It's devilish, Mr. Holmes, devilish!" cried Mortimer Tregennis. "It is not of this world. Something has come into that room which has dashed the light of reason from their minds. What human contrivance could do that?"

"I fear," said Holmes, "that if the matter is beyond humanity it is certainly beyond me. Yet we must exhaust all natural explanations before we fall back upon such a theory as this. As to yourself, Mr. Tregennis, I take it you were divided in some way from your family, since they lived together and you had rooms apart?"

"That is so, Mr. Holmes, though the matter is past and done with. We were a family of tin-miners at Redruth, but we sold our venture to a company, and so retired with enough to keep us. I won't deny that there was some feeling about the division of the money and it stood between us for a time, but it was all forgiven and forgotten, and we were the best of friends together."

"Looking back at the evening which you spent together, does anything stand out in your memory as throwing any possible light upon the tragedy? Think carefully, Mr. Tregennis, for any clue which can help me."

"There is nothing at all, sir."

"Your people were in their usual spirits?"

"Never better."

"Were they nervous people? Did they ever show any apprehension of coming danger?"

"Nothing of the kind."

"You have nothing to add then, which could assist me?"

Mortimer Tregennis considered earnestly for a moment.

"There is one thing occurs to me," said he at last. "As we sat at the table my back was to the window, and my brother George, he being my partner at cards, was facing it. I saw him once look hard over my shoulder, so I turned round and looked also. The blind was up and the window shut, but I could just make out the bushes on the lawn, and it seemed to me for a moment that I saw something moving among them. I couldn't even say if it was man or animal, but I just thought there was something there. When I asked him what he was looking at, he told me that he had the same feeling. That is all that I can say."

"Did you not investigate?"

"No; the matter passed as unimportant."

"You left them, then, without any premonition of evil?"

"None at all."

"I am not clear how you came to hear the news so early this morning."

"I am an early riser and generally take a walk before breakfast. This morning I had hardly started when the doctor in his carriage overtook me. He told me that old Mrs. Porter had sent a boy down with an urgent message. I sprang in beside him and we drove on. When we got there we looked into that dreadful room. The candles and the fire must have burned out hours before, and they had been sitting there in the dark until dawn had broken. The doctor said Brenda must have been dead at least six hours. There were no signs of violence. She just lay across the arm of the chair with that look on her face. George and Owen were singing snatches of songs and gibbering like two great apes. Oh, it was awful to see! I couldn't stand it, and the doctor was as white as a sheet. Indeed, he fell into a chair in a sort of faint, and we nearly had him on our hands as well."

"Remarkable—most remarkable!" said Holmes, rising and taking his hat. "I think, perhaps, we had better go down to Tredannick Wartha without further delay. I confess that I have seldom known a case which at first sight presented a more singular problem."

Our proceedings of that first morning did little to advance the investigation. It was marked, however, at the outset by an incident which left the most sinister impression upon my mind. The approach to the spot at which the tragedy occurred is down a narrow, winding, country lane. While we made our way along it we heard the rattle of a carriage coming towards us and stood aside to let it pass. As it drove by us I caught a glimpse through the closed window of a horribly contorted, grinning face glaring out at us. Those staring eyes and gnashing teeth flashed past us like a dreadful vision.

"My brothers!" cried Mortimer Tregennis, white to his lips. "They are taking them to Helston."

We looked with horror after the black carriage, lumbering upon its way. Then we turned our steps towards this ill-omened house in which they had met their strange fate.

It was a large and bright dwelling, rather a villa than a cottage, with a considerable garden which was already, in that Cornish air, well filled with spring flowers. Towards this garden the window of the sitting-room fronted, and from it, according to Mortimer Tregennis, must have come that thing of evil which had by sheer horror in a single instant blasted their minds. Holmes walked slowly and thoughtfully among the flower-plots and along the path before we entered the porch. So absorbed was he in his thoughts, I remember, that he stumbled over the watering-pot, upset its contents, and deluged both our feet and the garden path. Inside the house we were met by the elderly Cornish housekeeper, Mrs. Porter, who, with the aid of a young girl, looked after the wants of the family. She readily answered all Holmes's questions. She had heard nothing in the night. Her employers had all been in excellent spirits lately, and she had never known them more cheerful and prosperous. She had fainted with horror upon entering the room in the morning and seeing that dreadful company round the table. She had, when she recovered, thrown open the window to let the morning air in, and had run down to the lane, whence she sent a farm-lad for the doctor. The lady was on her bed upstairs if we cared to see her. It took four strong men to get the brothers into the asylum carriage. She would not herself stay in the house another day and was starting that very afternoon to rejoin her family at St. Ives.

We ascended the stairs and viewed the body. Miss Brenda Tregennis had been a very beautiful girl, though now verging upon middle age. Her dark, clear-cut face was handsome, even in death, but there still lingered upon it something of that convulsion of horror which had been her last human emotion. From her bedroom we descended to the sitting-room, where this strange tragedy had actually occurred. The charred ashes of the overnight fire lay in the grate. On the table were the four guttered and burned-out candles, with the cards scattered over its surface. The chairs had been moved back against the walls, but all else was as it had been the night before. Holmes paced with light, swift steps about the room; he sat in the various chairs, drawing them up and reconstructing their positions. He tested how much of the garden was visible; he examined the floor, the ceiling, and the fireplace; but never once did I see that sudden brightening of his eyes and tightening of his lips which would have told me that he saw some gleam of light in this utter darkness.

"Why a fire?" he asked once. "Had they always a fire in this small room on a spring evening?"

Mortimer Tregennis explained that the night was cold and damp. For that reason, after his arrival, the fire was lit. "What are you going to do now, Mr. Holmes?" he asked.

My friend smiled and laid his hand upon my arm. "I think, Watson, that I shall resume that course of tobacco-poisoning which you have so often and so justly condemned," said he. "With your permission, gentlemen, we will

now return to our cottage, for I am not aware that any new factor is likely to come to our notice here. I will turn the facts over in my mid, Mr, Tregennis, and should anything occur to me I will certainly ommunicate with you and the vicar. In the meantime I wish you both good-morning."

It was not until long after we were back in Poldhu Cottage that Holmes broke his complete and absorbed silence. He sat coiled in his armchair, his haggard and ascetic face hardly visible amid the blue swirl of his tobacco smoke, his black brows drawn down, his forehead contracted, his eyes vacant and far away. Finally he laid down his pipe and sprang to his feet.

"It won't do, Watson!" said he with a laugh. "Let us walk along the cliffs together and search for flint arrows. We are more likely to find them than clues to this problem. To let the brain work without sufficient material is like racing an engine. It racks itself to pieces. The sea air, sunshine, and patience, Watson—all else will come.

"Now, let us calmly define our position, Watson," he continued as we skirted the cliffs together. "Let us get a firm grip of the very little which we *do* know, so that when fresh facts arise we may be ready to fit them into their places. I take it, in the first place, that neither of us is prepared to admit diabolical intrusions into the affairs of men. Let us begin by ruling that entirely out of our minds. Very good. There remain three persons who have been grievously stricken by some conscious or unconscious human agency. That is firm ground. Now, when did this occur? Evidently, assuming his narrative to be true, it was immediately after Mr. Mortimer Tregennis had left the room. That is a very important point. The presumption is that it was within a few minutes afterwards. The cards still lay upon the table. It was already past their usual hour for bed. Yet they had not changed their position or pushed back their chairs. I repeat, then, that the occurrence was immediately after his departure, and not later than eleven o'clock last night.

"Our next obvious step is to check, so far as we can, the movements of Mortimer Tregennis after he left the room. In this there is no difficulty, and they seem to be above suspicion. Knowing my methods as you do, you were, of course, conscious of the somewhat clumsy water-pot expedient by which I obtained a clearer impress of his foot than might otherwise have been possible. The wet, sandy path took it admirably. Last night was also wet, you will remember, and it was not difficult—having obtained a sample print—to pick out his track among others and to follow his movements. He appears to have walked away swiftly in the direction of the vicarage.

"If, then, Mortimer Tregennis disappeared from the scene, and yet some outside person affected the card-players, how can we reconstruct that person, and how was such an impression of horror conveyed? Mrs. Porter may be eliminated. She is evidently harmless. Is there any evidence that someone crept up to the garden window and in some manner produced so terrific an effect that he drove those who saw it out of their senses? The only suggestion in this direction comes from Mortimer Tregennis himself, who says that his brother spoke about some movement in the garden. That is certainly remarkable, as the night was rainy, cloudy, and dark. Anyone who had the design to alarm these people would be compelled to place his very face against the glass before he could be seen. There is a three-foot flower-border outside this window, but no indication of a footmark. It is difficult to imagine, then, how an outsider could have made so terrible an impression upon the company, nor have we found any possible motive for so strange and elaborate an attempt. You perceive our difficulties, Watson?"

"They are only too clear," I answered with conviction.

"And yet, with a little more material, we may prove that they are not insurmountable," said Holmes. "I fancy that among your extensive archives, Watson, you may find some which were nearly as obscure. Meanwhile, we shall put the case aside until more accurate data are available, and devote the rest of our morning to the pursuit of neolithic man."

I may have commented upon my friend's power of mental detachment, but never have I wondered at it more than upon that spring morning in Cornwall when for two hours he discoursed upon celts, arrowheads, and shards, as lightly as if no sinister mystery were waiting for his solution. It was not until we had returned in the afternoon to our cottage that we found a visitor awaiting us, who soon brought our minds back to the matter in hand. Neither of us needed to be told who that visitor was. The huge body, the craggy and deeply seamed face with the fierce eyes and hawk-like nose, the grizzled hair which nearly brushed our cottage ceiling, the beard—golden at the fringes and white near the lips, save for the nicotine stain from his perpetual cigar—all these were as well known in London as in Africa, and could only be associated with the tremendous personality of Dr. Leon Sterndale, the great lion-hunter and explorer.

We had heard of his presence in the district and had once or twice caught sight of his tall figure upon the moorland paths. He made no advances to us, however, nor would we have dreamed of doing so to him, as it was well known that it was his love of seclusion which caused him to spend the greater part of the intervals between his journeys in a small bungalow buried in the lonely wood of Beauchamp Arriance. Here, amid his books and his maps, he lived an absolutely lonely life, attending to his own simple wants and paying little apparent heed to the affairs of his neighbours. It was a surprise to me, therefore, to hear him asking Holmes in an eager voice whether he had made any advance in his reconstruction of this mysterious episode. "The county police are utterly at fault," said he, "but perhaps your wider experience has suggested some conceivable explanation. My only claim to being taken into your confidence is that during my many residences here I have come to know this family of Tregennis very well—indeed, upon my Cornish mother's side I could call them cousins—and their strange fate has naturally been a great shock to me. I may tell you that I had got as far as Plymouth upon my way to Africa, but the news reached me this morning, and I came straight back again to help in the inquiry."

Holmes raised his eyebrows.

"Did you lose your boat through it?"

"I will take the next."

"Dear me! that is friendship indeed."

"I tell you they were relatives."

"Quite so—cousins of your mother. Was your baggage aboard the ship?"

"Some of it, but the main part at the hotel."

"I see. But surely this event could not have found its way into the Plymouth morning papers."

"No, sir; I had a telegram."

"Might I ask from whom?"

A shadow passed over the gaunt face of the explorer.

"You are very inquisitive, Mr. Holmes."

"It is my business."

With an effort Dr. Sterndale recovered his ruffled composure.

"I have no objection to telling you," he said. "It was Mr. Roundhay, the vicar, who sent me the telegram which recalled me."

"Thank you," said Holmes. "I may say in answer to your original question that I have not cleared my mind entirely on the subject of this case, but that I have every hope of reaching some conclusion. It would be premature to say more."

"Perhaps you would not mind telling me if your suspicions point in any particular direction?"

"No, I can hardly answer that."

"Then I have wasted my time and need not prolong my visit." The famous doctor strode out of our cottage in considerable ill-humour, and within five minutes Holmes had followed him. I saw him no more until the evening, when he returned with a slow step and haggard face which assured me that he had made no great progress with his investigation. He glanced at a telegram which awaited him and threw it into the grate.

"From the Plymouth hotel, Watson," he said. "I learned the name of it from the vicar, and I wired to make certain that Dr. Leon Sterndale's account was true. It appears that he did indeed spend last night there, and that he has actually allowed some of his baggage to go on to Africa, while he returned to be present at this investigation. What do you make of that, Watson?"

"He is deeply interested."

"Deeply interested—yes. There is a thread here which we had not yet grasped and which might lead us through the tangle. Cheer up, Watson, for I am very sure that our material has not yet all come to hand. When it does we may soon leave our difficulties behind us."

Little did I think how soon the words of Holmes would be realized, or how strange and sinister would be that new development which opened up an entirely fresh line of investigation. I was shaving at my window in the morning when I heard the rattle of hoofs and, looking up, saw a dog-cart coming at a gallop down the road. It pulled up at our door, and our friend, the vicar, sprang from it and rushed up our garden path. Holmes was already dressed, and we hastened down to meet him.

Our visitor was so excited that he could hardly articulate, but at last in gasps and bursts his tragic story came out of him.

"We are devil-ridden, Mr. Holmes! My poor parish is devil-ridden!" he cried. "Satan himself is loose in it! We are given over into his hands!" He danced about in his agitation, a ludicrous object if it were not for his ashy face and startled eyes. Finally he shot out his terrible news.

"Mr. Mortimer Tregennis died during the night, and with exactly the same symptoms as the rest of his family."

Holmes sprang to his feet, all energy in an instant.

"Can you fit us both into your dog-cart?"

"Yes, I can."

"Then, Watson, we will postpone our breakfast. Mr. Roundhay, we are entirely at your disposal. Hurry—hurry, before things get disarranged."

The lodger occupied two rooms at the vicarage, which were in an angle by themselves, the one above the other. Below was a large sitting-room; above, his bedroom. They looked out upon a croquet lawn which came up to the windows. We had arrived before the doctor or the police, so that everything was absolutely undisturbed. Let me describe exactly the scene as we saw it upon that misty March morning. It has left an impression which can never be effaced from my mind.

The atmosphere of the room was of a horrible and depressing stuffiness. The servant who had first entered had thrown up the window, or it would have been even more intolerable. This might partly be due to the fact that a lamp stood flaring and smoking on the centre table. Beside it sat the dead man, leaning back in his chair, his thin beard projecting, his spectacles pushed up on to his forehead, and his lean dark face turned towards the window and twisted into the same distortion of terror which had marked the features of his dead sister. His limbs were convulsed and his fingers contorted as though he had died in a very paroxysm of fear. He was fully clothed, though there were signs that his dressing had been done in a hurry. We had already learned that his bed had been slept in, and that the tragic end had come to him in the early morning.

One realized the red-hot energy which underlay Holmes's phlegmatic exterior when one saw the sudden change which came over him from the moment that he entered the fatal apartment. In an instant he was tense and alert, his eyes shining, his face set, his limbs quivering with eager activity. He was out on the lawn, in through the window, round the room, and up into the bedroom, for all the world like a dashing foxhound drawing a cover. In the bedroom he made a rapid cast around and ended by throwing open the window, which appeared to give him some fresh cause for excitement, for he leaned out of it with loud ejaculations of interest and delight. Then he rushed down the stair, out through the open window, threw himself upon his face on the lawn, sprang up and into the room once more, all with the energy of the hunter who is at the very heels of his quarry. The lamp, which was an ordinary standard, he examined with minute care, making certain measurements upon its bowl. He carefully scrutinized with his lens the talc shield which covered the top of the chimney and scraped off some ashes which adhered to its upper surface, putting some of them into an envelope, which he placed in his pocketbook. Finally, just as the doctor and the official police put in an appearance, he beckoned to the vicar and we all three went out upon the lawn.

"I am glad to say that my investigation has not been entirely barren," he remarked. "I cannot remain to discuss the matter with the police, but I should be exceedingly obliged, Mr. Roundhay, if you would give the inspector my compliments and direct his attention to the bedroom window and to the sitting-room lamp. Each is suggestive, and together they are almost conclusive. If the police would desire further information I shall be happy to see any of them at the cottage. And now, Watson, I think that, perhaps, we shall be better employed elsewhere."

It may be that the police resented the intrusion of an amateur, or that they imagined themselves to be upon some hopeful line of investigation; but it is certain that we heard nothing from them for the next two days. During this time Holmes spent some of his time smoking and dreaming in the cottage; but a greater portion in country walks which he undertook alone, returning after many hours without remark as to where he had been. One experiment served to show me the line of his investigation. He had bought a lamp which was the duplicate of the one which had burned in the room of Mortimer Tregennis on the morning of the tragedy. This he filled with the same oil as that used at the vicarage, and he carefully timed the period which it would take to be exhausted. Another experiment which he made was of a more unpleasant nature, and one which I am not likely ever to forget.

"You will remember, Watson," he remarked one afternoon, "that there is a single common point of resemblance in the varying reports which have reached us. This concerns the effect of the atmosphere of the room in each case upon those who had first entered it. You will recollect that Mortimer Tregennis, in describing the episode of his last visit to his brother's house, remarked that the doctor on entering the room fell into a chair? You had forgotten? Well I can answer for it that it was so. Now, you will remember also that Mrs. Porter, the housekeeper, told us that she herself fainted upon entering the room and had afterwards opened the window. In the second case—that of Mortimer Tregennis himself—you cannot have forgotten the horrible stuffiness of the room when we arrived, though the servant had thrown open the window. That servant, I found upon inquiry, was so ill that she had gone to her bed. You will admit, Watson, that these facts are very suggestive. In each case there is evidence of a poisonous atmosphere. In each case, also, there is combustion going on in the room—in the one case a fire, in the other a lamp. The fire was needed, but the lamp was lit—as a comparison of the oil consumed will show—long after it was broad daylight. Why? Surely because there is some connection between three things—the burning, the stuffy atmosphere, and, finally, the madness or death of those unfortunate people. That is clear, is it not?"

"It would appear so."

"At least we may accept it as a working hypothesis. We will suppose, then, that something was burned in each case which produced an atmosphere causing strange toxic effects. Very good. In the first instance—that of the Tregennis family—this substance was placed in the fire. Now the window was shut, but the fire would naturally carry fumes to some extent up the chimney. Hence one would expect the effects of the poison to be less than in the second case, where there was less escape for the vapour. The result seems to indicate that it was so, since in the first case only the woman, who had presumably the more sensitive organism, was killed, the others exhibiting that temporary or permanent lunacy which is evidently the first effect of the drug. In the second case the result was complete. The facts, therefore, seem to bear out the theory of a poison which worked by combustion.

"With this train of reasoning in my head I naturally looked about in Mortimer Tregennis's room to find some remains of this substance. The obvious place to look was the talc shelf or smoke-guard of the lamp. There, sure enough, I perceived a number of flaky ashes, and round the edges a fringe of brownish powder, which had not yet been consumed. Half of this I took, as you saw, and I placed it in an envelope."

"Why half, Holmes?"

"It is not for me, my dear Watson, to stand in the way of the official police force. I leave them all the evidence which I found. The poison still remained upon the talc had they the wit to find it. Now, Watson, we will light our lamp; we will, however, take the precaution to open our window to avoid the premature decease of two deserving members of society, and you will seat yourself near that open window in an armchair unless, like a sensible man, you determine to have nothing to do with the affair. Oh, you will see it out, will you? I thought I knew my Watson. This chair I will place opposite yours, so that we may be the same distance from the poison and face to face. The door we will leave ajar. Each is now in a position to watch the other and to bring the experiment to an end should the symptoms seem alarming. Is that all clear? Well, then, I take our powder—or what remains of it—from the envelope, and I lay it above the burning lamp. So! Now, Watson, let us sit down and await developments."

They were not long in coming. I had hardly settled in my chair before I was conscious of a thick, musky odour, subtle and nauseous. At the very first whiff of it my brain and my imagination were beyond all control. A thick, black cloud swirled before my eyes, and my mind told me that in this cloud, unseen as yet, but about to spring out upon my appalled senses, lurked all that was vaguely horrible, all that was monstrous and inconceivably wicked in the universe. Vague shapes swirled and swam amid the dark cloud-bank, each a menace and a warning of something coming, the advent of some unspeakable dweller upon the threshold, whose very shadow would blast my soul. A freezing horror took possession of me. I felt that my hair was rising, that my eyes were protruding, that my mouth was opened, and my tongue like leather. The turmoil within my brain was such that something must surely snap. I tried to scream and was vaguely aware of some hoarse croak which was my own voice, but distant and detached from myself. At the same moment, in some effort of escape, I broke through that cloud of despair and had a glimpse of Holmes's face, white, rigid, and drawn with horror—the very look which I had seen upon the features of the dead. It was that vision which gave me an instant of sanity and of strength. I dashed from my chair, threw my arms round Holmes, and together we lurched through the door, and an instant afterwards had thrown ourselves down upon the grass plot and were lying side by side, conscious only of the glorious sunshine which was bursting its way through the hellish cloud of terror which had girt us in. Slowly it rose from our souls like the mists from a landscape until peace and reason had returned, and we were sitting upon the grass, wiping our clammy foreheads, and looking with apprehension at each other to mark the last traces of that terrific experience which we had undergone.

"Upon my word, Watson!" said Holmes at last with an unsteady voice, "I owe you both my thanks and an apology. It was an unjustifiable experiment even for one's self, and doubly so for a friend. I am really very sorry."

"You know," I answered with some emotion, for I have never seen so much of Holmes's heart before, "that it is my greatest joy and privilege to help you."

He relapsed at once into the half-humorous, half-cynical vein which was his habitual attitude to those about him. "It would be superfluous to drive us mad, my dear Watson," said he. "A candid observer would certainly declare that we were so already before we embarked upon so wild an experiment. I confess that I never imagined that the effect could be so sudden and so severe." He dashed into the cottage, and, reappearing with the burning lamp held at full arm's length, he threw it among a bank of brambles. "We must give the room a little time to clear. I take it, Watson, that you have no longer a shadow of a doubt as to how these tragedies were produced?"

"None whatever."

"But the cause remains as obscure as before. Come into the arbour here and let us discuss it together. That villainous stuff seems still to linger round my throat. I think we must admit that all the evidence points to this man, Mortimer Tregennis, having been the criminal in the first tragedy, though he was the victim in the second one. We must remember, in the first place, that there is some story of a family quarrel, followed by a reconciliation.

How bitter that quarrel may have been, or how hollow the reconciliation we cannot tell. When I think of Mortimer Tregennis, with the foxy face and the small shrewd, beady eyes behind the spectacles, he is not a man whom I should judge to be of a particularly forgiving disposition. Well, in the next place, you will remember that this idea of someone moving in the garden, which took our attention for a moment from the real cause of the tragedy, emanated from him. He had a motive in misleading us. Finally, if he did not throw the substance into the fire at the moment of leaving the room, who did do so? The affair happened immediately after his departure. Had anyone else come in, the family would certainly have risen from the table. Besides, in peaceful Cornwall, visitors did not arrive after ten o'clock at night. We may take it, then, that all the evidence points to Mortimer Tregennis as the culprit."

"Then his own death was suicide!"

"Well, Watson, it is on the face of it a not impossible supposition. The man who had the guilt upon his soul of having brought such a fate upon his own family might well be driven by remorse to inflict it upon himself. There are, however, some cogent reasons against it. Fortunately, there is one man in England who knows all about it, and I have made arrangements by which we shall hear the facts this afternoon from his own lips. Ah! he is a little before his time. Perhaps you would kindly step this way, Dr. Leon Sterndale. We have been conducing a chemical experiment indoors which has left our little room hardly fit for the reception of so distinguished a visitor."

I had heard the click of the garden gate, and now the majestic figure of the great African explorer appeared upon the path. He turned in some surprise towards the rustic arbour in which we sat.

"You sent for me, Mr. Holmes. I had your note about an hour ago, and I have come, though I really do not know why I should obey your summons."

"Perhaps we can clear the point up before we separate," said Holmes. "Meanwhile, I am much obliged to you for your courteous acquiescence. You will excuse this informal reception in the open air, but my friend Watson and I have nearly furnished an additional chapter to what the papers call the Cornish Horror, and we prefer a clear atmosphere for the present. Perhaps, since the matters which we have to discuss will affect you personally in a very intimate fashion, it is as well that we should talk where there can be no eavesdropping."

The explorer took his cigar from his lips and gazed sternly at my companion.

"I am at a loss to know, sir," he said, "what you can have to speak about which affects me personally in a very intimate fashion."

"The killing of Mortimer Tregennis," said Holmes.

For a moment I wished that I were armed. Sterndale's fierce face turned to a dusky red, his eyes glared, and the knotted, passionate veins started out in his forehead, while he sprang forward with clenched hands towards my companion. Then he stopped, and with a violent effort he resumed a cold, rigid calmness, which was, perhaps, more suggestive of danger than his hot-headed outburst.

"I have lived so long among savages and beyond the law," said he, "that I have got into the way of being a law to myself. You would do well, Mr. Holmes, not to forget it, for I have no desire to do you an injury."

"Nor have I any desire to do you an injury, Dr. Sterndale. Surely the clearest proof of it is that, knowing what I know, I have sent for you and not for the police."

Sterndale sat down with a gasp, overawed for, perhaps, the first time in his adventurous life. There was a calm assurance of power in Holmes's manner which could not be withstood. Our visitor stammered for a moment, his great hands opening and shutting in his agitation.

"What do you mean?" he asked at last. "If this is bluff upon your part, Mr. Holmes, you have chosen a bad man for your experiment. Let us have no more beating about the bush. What *do* you mean?"

"I will tell you," said Holmes, "and the reason why I tell you is that I hope frankness may beget frankness. What my next step may be will depend entirely upon the nature of your own defence."

"My defence?"

"Yes, sir."

"My defence against what?"

"Against the charge of killing Mortimer Tregennis."

Sterndale mopped his forehead with his handkerchief. "Upon my word, you are getting on," said he. "Do all your successes depend upon this prodigious power of bluff?"

"The bluff," said Holmes sternly, "is upon your side, Dr. Leon Sterndale, and not upon mine. As a proof I will tell you some of the facts upon which my conclusions are based. Of your return from Plymouth, allowing much of your property to go on to Africa, I will say nothing save that it first informed me that you were one of the factors which had to be taken into account in reconstructing this drama—"

"I came back—"

"I have heard your reasons and regard them as unconvincing and inadequate. We will pass that. You came down here to ask me whom I suspected. I refused to answer you. You then went to the vicarage, waited outside it for some time, and finally returned to your cottage."

"How do you know that?"

"I followed you."

"I saw no one."

"That is what you may expect to see when I follow you. You spent a restless night at your cottage, and you formed certain plans, which in the early morning you proceeded to put into execution. Leaving your door just as day was breaking, you filled your pocket with some reddish gravel that was lying heaped beside your gate."

Sterndale gave a violent start and looked at Holmes in amazement.

"You then walked swiftly for the mile which separated you from the vicarage. You were wearing, I may remark, the same pair of ribbed tennis shoes which are at the present moment upon your feet. At the vicarage you passed through the orchard and the side hedge, coming out under the window of the lodger Tregennis. It was now daylight, but the household was not yet stirring. You drew some of the gravel from your pocket, and you threw it up at the window above you."

Sterndale sprang to his feet.

"I believe that you are the devil himself!" he cried.

Holmes smiled at the compliment. "It took two, or possibly three, handfuls before the lodger came to the window. You beckoned him to come down. He dressed hurriedly and descended to his sitting-room. You entered by the window. There was an interview—a short one—during which you walked up and down the room. Then you passed out and closed the window, standing on the lawn outside smoking a cigar and watching what occurred. Finally, after the death of Tregennis, you withdrew as you had come. Now, Dr. Sterndale, how do you justify such conduct, and what were the motives for your actions? If you prevaricate or trifle with me, I give you my assurance that the matter will pass out of my hands forever."

Our visitor's face had turned ashen gray as he listened to the words of his accuser. Now he sat for some time in thought with his face sunk in his hands. Then with a sudden impulsive gesture he plucked a photograph from his breast-pocket and threw it on the rustic table before us.

"That is why I have done it," said he.

It showed the bust and face of a very beautiful woman. Holmes stooped over it.

"Brenda Tregennis," said he.

"Yes, Brenda Tregennis," repeated our visitor. "For years I have loved her. For years she has loved me. There is the secret of that Cornish seclusion which people have marvelled at. It has brought me close to the one thing on earth that was dear to me. I could not marry her, for I have a wife who has left me for years and yet whom, by the deplorable laws of England, I could not divorce. For years Brenda waited. For years I waited. And this is what we have waited for." A terrible sob shook his great frame, and he clutched his throat under his brindled beard. Then with an effort he mastered himself and spoke on:

"The vicar knew. He was in our confidence. He would tell you that she was an angel upon earth. That was why he telegraphed to me and I returned. What was my baggage or Africa to me when I learned that such a fate had come upon my darling? There you have the missing clue to my action, Mr. Holmes."

"Proceed," said my friend.

Dr. Sterndale drew from his pocket a paper packet and laid it upon the table. On the outside was written "Radix pedis diaboli" with a red poison label beneath it. He pushed it towards me. "I understand that you are a doctor, sir. Have you ever heard of this preparation?"

"Devil's-foot root! No, I have never heard of it."

"It is no reflection upon your professional knowledge," said he, "for I believe that, save for one sample in a laboratory at Buda, there is no other specimen in Europe. It has not yet found its way either into the pharmacopoeia or into the literature of toxicology. The root is shaped like a foot, half human, half goatlike; hence the fanciful name given by a botanical missionary. It is used as an ordeal poison by the medicine-men in certain districts of West Africa and is kept as a secret among them. This particular specimen I obtained under very extraordinary circumstances in the Ubangi country." He opened the paper as he spoke and disclosed a heap of reddish-brown, snuff-like powder.

"Well, sir?" asked Holmes sternly.

"I am about to tell you, Mr. Holmes, all that actually occurred, for you already know so much that it is clearly to my interest that you should know all. I have already explained the relationship in which I stood to the Tregennis family. For the sake of the sister I was friendly with the brothers. There was a family quarrel about money which estranged this man Mortimer, but it was supposed to be made up, and I afterwards met him as I did the others. He was a sly, subtle, scheming man, and several things arose which gave me a suspicion of him, but I had no cause for any positive quarrel.

"One day, only a couple of weeks ago, he came down to my cottage and I showed him some of my African curiosities. Among other things I exhibited this powder, and I told him of its strange properties, how it stimulates those brain centres which control the emotion of fear, and how either madness or death is the fate of the unhappy native who is subjected to the ordeal by the priest of his tribe. I told him also how powerless European science would be to detect it. How he took it I cannot say, for I never left the room, but there is no doubt that it was then, while I was opening cabinets and stooping to boxes, that he managed to abstract some of the devil's-foot root. I well remember how he plied me with questions as to the amount and the time that was needed for its effect, but I little dreamed that he could have a personal reason for asking.

"I thought no more of the matter until the vicar's telegram reached me at Plymouth. This villain had thought that I would be at sea before the news could reach me, and that I should be lost for years in Africa. But I returned at once. Of course, I could not listen to the details without feeling assured that my poison had been used. I came round to see you on the chance that some other explanation had suggested itself to you. But there could be none. I was convinced that Mortimer Tregennis was the murderer; that for the sake of money, and with the idea, perhaps, that if the other members of his family were all insane he would be the sole guardian of their joint property, he had used the devil's-foot powder upon them, driven two of them out of their senses, and killed his sister Brenda, the one human being whom I have ever loved or who has ever loved me. There was his crime; what was to be his punishment?

"Should I appeal to the law? Where were my proofs? I knew that the facts were true, but could I help to make a jury of countrymen believe so fantastic a story? I might or I might not. But I could not afford to fail. My soul cried out for revenge. I have said to you once before, Mr. Holmes, that I have spent much of my life outside the law, and that I have come at last to be a law to myself. So it was even now. I determined that the fate which he had given to others should be shared by himself. Either that or I would do justice upon him with my own hand. In all England there can be no man who sets less value upon his own life than I do at the present moment.

"Now I have told you all. You have yourself supplied the rest. I did, as you say, after a restless night, set off early from my cottage. I foresaw the difficulty of arousing him, so I gathered some gravel from the pile which you have mentioned, and I used it to throw up to his window. He came down and admitted me through the window of the sitting-room. I laid his offence before him. I told him that I had come both as judge and executioner. The wretch sank into a chair, paralyzed at the sight of my revolver. I lit the lamp, put the powder above it, and stood outside the window, ready to carry out my threat to shoot him should he try to leave the room. In five minutes he died. My God! how he died! But my heart was flint, for he endured nothing which my innocent darling had not felt before him. There is my story, Mr. Holmes. Perhaps, if you loved a woman, you would have done as much yourself. At any rate, I am in your hands. You can take what steps you like. As I have already said, there is no man living who can fear death less than I do."

Holmes sat for some little time in silence.

"What were your plans?" he asked at last.

"I had intended to bury myself in central Africa. My work there is but half finished."

"Go and do the other half," said Holmes. "I, at least, am not prepared to prevent you."

Dr. Sterndale raised his giant figure, bowed gravely, and walked from the arbour. Holmes lit his pipe and handed me his pouch.

"Some fumes which are not poisonous would be a welcome change," said he. "I think you must agree, Watson, that it is not a case in which we are called upon to interfere. Our investigation has been independent, and our action shall be so also. You would not denounce the man?"

"Certainly not," I answered.

"I have never loved, Watson, but if I did and if the woman I loved had met such an end, I might act even as our lawless lion-hunter has done. Who knows? Well, Watson, I will not offend your intelligence by explaining what is obvious. The gravel upon the window-sill was, of course, the starting-point of my research. It was unlike anything in the vicarage garden. Only when my attention had been drawn to Dr. Sterndale and his cottage did I find its counterpart. The lamp shining in broad daylight and the remains of powder upon the shield were successive links in a fairly obvious chain. And now, my dear Watson, I think we may dismiss the matter from our mind and go back with a clear conscience to the study of those Chaldean roots which are surely to be traced in the Cornish branch of the great Celtic speech."

THERE is no such vegetable as the devil's foot root, although that hasn't prevented Holmesian science buffs from offering possible real-life suspects (among them, the toxic Calabar bean, a primitive form of P.C.P., or the harmless devil's claw root infected with a hallucinogenic ergot fungus), but the horrors it sews are hardly fictional. The Granada TV adaptation of this story depicts Holmes' brush with this drug as a nightmarish bad trip, juxtaposing it with his habitual use of cocaine. While the horror is purely neurological and psychological, there is something very dark and dreamy about Watson's description: "[Behind the smoke] lurked all that was vaguely horrible, all that was monstrous and inconceivably wicked in the universe. Vague shapes swirled and swam amid the dark cloud-bank, each a menace and a warning of something coming, the advent of some unspeakable dweller upon the threshold, whose very shadow would blast my soul." It is a description worthy of Lovecraft (does "The Dweller Upon the Threshold" not just sound like a perfect title for one of his Weird Tales submissions?), which leads us to question whether the invisible dwellers of this hideous world were the personified phantoms of mental disease, a philosophical metaphor, or whether the good doctor is suggesting that exposure to this mind-peeling drug nearly opened his eyes to an unseen realm. In any case, the lunging specter of madness stalks throughout the tale, darkening the Cornish landscape with presentiments of horror and misery. The Great Detective represents all that is intellectual, rational, and cool, so it is no stretch of the imagination to say that he faced a far grislier fate – the blowing apart of his mind in an explosion of devolved madness – in this adventure than in any other, including the crashing waters of Reichenbach.

MARITIME fiction was a perennial favorite of most British authors of the Late Victorian era: Stevenson, Wells, Kipling, Conrad, Crane, London, Jacobs, and Twain all made notable contributions to nautical literature – some prolifically. Doyle's service as a surgeon on an Arctic whaling ship prepared him for more stories than just "The Captain of the Pole-Star," for he produced a truly respectable amount of seagoing tales, among which were several episodes of horror and the macabre. Most famously, of course, is his controversial interpretation of the Mary Celeste mystery – "J. Habakuk Jephson's Statement" – which launched an otherwise little-known shipping puzzle into an immortal enigma that has become a staple of the "unsolved mysteries" canon. Despite its popularity in anthologies of Doyle's speculative fiction, we omit it for a variety of reasons: namely, because it begins as a fine, suspenseful murder story that suddenly devolves into an outlandish and farfetched story of African supremacists who kill whites indiscriminately and hijack a Portugal-bound vessel in order to return in Africa. The story is sadly unworthy of its legacy, with its use of deus ex machina, conspiratorial racial politics, and one of the most extreme examples I have read of stretching the suspension of disbelief. It is a truly disappointing tale, but the following one – a clear descendent of its predecessor – is a far worthier seagoing mystery. Without enlisting aid from the supernatural, Doyle nimbly weaves a sinister and nefarious atmosphere into a tale about a derelict vessel with one very unusual piece of cargo...

The Striped Chest
{1897}

"WHAT do you make of her, Allardyce?" I asked.

My second mate was standing beside me upon the poop, with his short, thick legs astretch, for the gale had left a considerable swell behind it, and our two quarter-boats nearly touched the water with every roll. He steadied his glass against the mizzen-shrouds, and he looked long and hard at this disconsolate stranger every time she came reeling up on to the crest of a roller and hung balanced for a few seconds before swooping down upon the other side. She lay so low in the water that I could only catch an occasional glimpse of a pea-green line of bulwark. She was a brig, but her mainmast had been snapped short off some 10ft. above the deck, and no effort seemed to have been made to cut away the wreckage, which floated, sails and yards, like the broken wing of a wounded gull upon the water beside her. The foremast was still standing, but the foretopsail was flying loose, and the headsails were streaming out in long, white pennons in front of her. Never have I seen a vessel which appeared to have gone through rougher handling. But we could not be surprised at that, for there had been times during the last three days when it was a question whether our own barque would ever see land again. For thirty-six hours we had kept her nose to it, and if the *Mary Sinclair* had not been as good a seaboat as ever left the Clyde, we could not have gone through. And yet here we were at the end of it with the loss only of our gig and of part of the starboard bulwark. It did not astonish us, however, when the smother had cleared away, to find that others had been less lucky, and that this mutilated brig staggering about upon a blue sea and under a cloudless sky, had been left, like a blinded man after a lightning flash, to tell of the terror which is past. Allardyce, who was a slow and methodical Scotchman, stared long and hard at the little craft, while our seamen lined the bulwark or clustered upon the fore shrouds to have a view of the stranger. In latitude 20 degrees and longitude 10 degrees, which were about our bearings, one becomes a little curious as to whom one meets, for one has left the main lines of Atlantic commerce to the north. For ten days we had been sailing over a solitary sea.

"She's derelict, I'm thinking," said the second mate.

I had come to the same conclusion, for I could see no signs of life upon her deck, and there was no answer to the friendly wavings from our seamen. The crew had probably deserted her under the impression that she was about to founder.

"She can't last long," continued Allardyce, in his measured way. "She may put her nose down and her tail up any minute. The water's lipping up to the edge of her rail."

"What's her flag?" I asked.

"I'm trying to make out. It's got all twisted and tangled with the halyards. Yes, I've got it now, clear enough. It's the Brazilian flag, but it's wrong side up."

She had hoisted a signal of distress, then, before her people had abandoned her. Perhaps they had only just gone. I took the mate's glass and looked round over the tumultuous face of the deep blue Atlantic, still veined and starred with white lines and spoutings of foam. But nowhere could I see anything human beyond ourselves.

"There may be living men aboard," said I.

"There may be salvage," muttered the second mate.

"Then we will run down upon her lee side, and lie to." We were not more than a hundred yards from her when we swung our foreyard aback, and there we were, the barque and the brig, ducking and bowing like two clowns in a dance.

"Drop one of the quarter-boats," said I. "Take four men, Mr. Allardyce, and see what you can learn of her."

But just at that moment my first officer, Mr. Armstrong, came on deck, for seven bells had struck, and it was but a few minutes off his watch. It would interest me to go myself to this abandoned vessel and to see what there might be aboard of her. So, with a word to Armstrong, I swung myself over the side, slipped down the falls, and took my place in the sheets of the boat.

It was but a little distance, but it took some time to traverse, and so heavy was the roll that often when we were in the trough of the sea, we could not see either the barque which we had left or the brig which we were approaching. The sinking sun did not penetrate down there, and it was cold and dark in the hollows of the waves, but each passing billow heaved us up into the warmth and the sunshine once more. At each of these moments, as we hung upon a white-capped ridge between the two dark valleys, I caught a glimpse of the long, pea-green line, and the nodding foremast of the brig, and I steered so as to come round by her stern, so that we might determine which was the best way of boarding her. As we passed her we saw the name *Nossa Sehnora da Vittoria* painted across her dripping counter.

"The weather side, sir," said the second mate. "Stand by with the boat-hook, carpenter!" An instant later we had jumped over the bulwarks, which were hardly higher than our boat, and found ourselves upon the deck of the abandoned vessel. Our first thought was to provide for our own safety in case — as seemed very probable — the vessel should settle down beneath our feet. With this object two of our men held on to the painter of the boat, and fended her off from the vessel's side, so that she might be ready in case we had to make a hurried retreat. The carpenter was sent to find out how much water there was, and whether it was still gaming, while the other seaman, Allardyce and myself, made a rapid inspection of the vessel and her cargo.

The deck was littered with wreckage and with hen-coops, in which the dead birds were washing about. The boats were gone, with the exception of one, the bottom of which had been stove, and it was certain that the crew had abandoned the vessel. The cabin was in a deck-house, one side of which had been beaten in by a heavy sea. Allardyce and I entered it, and found the captain's table as he had left it, his books and papers — all Spanish or Portuguese — scattered over it, with piles of cigarette ash everywhere. I looked about for the log, but could not find it.

"As likely as not he never kept one," said Allardyce. "Things are pretty slack aboard a South American trader, and they don't do more than they can help. If there was one it must have been taken away with him in the boat."

"I should like to take all these books and papers," said I. "Ask the carpenter how much time we have."

His report was reassuring. The vessel was full of water, but some of the cargo was buoyant, and there was no immediate danger of her sinking. Probably she would never sink, but would drift about as one of those terrible unmarked reefs which have sent so many stout vessels to the bottom.

"In that case there is no danger in your going below, Mr. Allardyce," said I. "See what you can make of her and find out how much of her cargo may be saved. I'll look through these papers while you are gone."

The bills of lading, and some notes and letters which lay upon the desk, sufficed to inform me that the Brazilian brig *Nossa Sehnora da Vittoria* had cleared from Bahia a month before. The name of the captain was Texeira, but there was no record as to the number of the crew. She was bound for London, and a glance at the bills of lading was sufficient to show me that we were not likely to profit much in the way of salvage. Her cargo consisted of nuts, ginger, and wood, the latter in the shape of great logs of valuable tropical growths. It was these, no doubt, which had prevented the ill-fated vessel from going to the bottom, but they were of such a size as to make it impossible for us to extract them. Besides these, there were a few fancy goods, such as a number of ornamental birds for millinery purposes, and a hundred cases of preserved fruits. And then, as I turned over the papers, I came upon a short note in English, which arrested my attention.

It is requested (said the note) that the various old Spanish and Indian curiosities, which came out of the Santarem collection, and which are consigned to Prontfoot & Neuman of Oxford Street, London, should be put in some place where there may be no danger of these very valuable and unique articles being injured or tampered with. This applies most particularly to the treasure-chest of Don Ramirez di Leyra, which must on no account be placed where anyone can get at it.

The treasure-chest of Don Ramirez! Unique and valuable articles! Here was a chance of salvage after all. I had risen to my feet with the paper in my hand when my Scotch mate appeared in the doorway.

"I'm thinking all isn't quite as it should be aboard of this ship, sir," said he. He was a hard-faced man, and yet I could see that he had been startled.

"What's the matter?"

"Murder's the matter, sir. There's a man here with his brains beaten out."

"Killed in the storm?" said I.

"May be so, sir, but I'll be surprised if you think so after you have seen him."

"Where is he, then?"

"This way, sir; here in the maindeck house."

There appeared to have been no accommodation below in the brig, for there was the after-house for the captain, another by the main hatchway, with the cook's galley attached to it, and a third in the forecastle for the men. It was to this middle one that the mate led me. As you entered, the galley, with its litter of tumbled pots and dishes, was upon the right, and upon the left was a small room with two bunks for the officers. Then beyond there was a place about 12ft. square, which was littered with flags and spare canvas. All round the walls were a number of packets done up in coarse cloth and carefully lashed to the woodwork. At the other end was a great box, striped red and white, though the red was so faded and the white so dirty that it was only where the light fell directly upon it that one could see the colouring. The box was, by subsequent measurement, 4ft. 3ins. in

length, 3ft. 2ins. in height, and 3ft. across — considerably larger than a seaman's chest. But it was not to the box that my eyes or my thoughts were turned as I entered the store-room. On the floor, lying across the litter of bunting, there was stretched a small, dark man with a short, curling beard. He lay as far as it was possible from the box, with his feet towards it and his head away. A crimson patch was printed upon the white canvas on which his head was resting, and little red ribbons wreathed themselves round his swarthy neck and trailed away on to the floor, but there was no sign of a wound that I could see, and his face was as placid as that of a sleeping child. It was only when I stooped that I could perceive his injury, and then I turned away with an exclamation of horror. He had been pole-axed; apparently by some person standing behind him. A frightful blow had smashed in the top of his head and penetrated deeply into his brains. His face might well be placid, for death must have been absolutely instantaneous, and the position of the wound showed that he could never have seen the person who had inflicted it.

"Is that foul play or accident, Captain Barclay?" asked my second mate, demurely.

"You are quite right, Mr. Allardyce. The man has been murdered — struck down from above by a sharp and heavy weapon. But who was he, and why did they murder him?"

"He was a common seaman, sir," said the mate. "You can see that if you look at his fingers." He turned out his pockets as he spoke and brought to light a pack of cards, some tarred string, and a bundle of Brazilian tobacco.

"Hello, look at this!" said he.

It was a large, open knife with a stiff spring blade which he had picked up from the floor. The steel was shining and bright, so that we could not associate it with the crime, and yet the dead man had apparently held it in his hand when he was struck down, for it still lay within his grasp.

"It looks to me, sir, as if he knew he was in danger and kept his knife handy," said the mate. "However, we can't help the poor beggar now. I can't make out these things that are lashed to the wall. They seem to be idols and weapons and curios of all sorts done up in old sacking."

"That's right," said I. "They are the only things of value that we are likely to get from the cargo. Hail the barque and tell them to send the other quarter-boat to help us to get the stuff aboard."

While he was away I examined this curious plunder which had come into our possession. The curiosities were so wrapped up that I could only form a general idea as to their nature, but the striped box stood in a good light where I could thoroughly examine it. On the lid, which was clamped and cornered with metal-work, there was engraved a complex coat of arms, and beneath it was a line of Spanish which I was able to decipher as meaning, "The treasure-chest of Don Ramirez di Leyra, Knight of the Order of Saint James, Governor and Captain-General of Terra Firma and of the Province of Veraquas." In one corner was the date, 1606, and on the other a large white label, upon which was written in English, "You are earnestly requested, upon no account, to open this box." The same warning was repeated underneath in Spanish. As to the lock, it was a very complex and heavy one of engraved steel, with a Latin motto, which was above a seaman's comprehension. By the time I had finished this examination of the peculiar box, the other quarter-boat with Mr. Armstrong, the first officer, had come alongside, and we began to carry out and place in her the various curiosities which appeared to be the only objects worth moving from the derelict ship. When she was full I sent her back to the barque, and then Allardyce and I, with the carpenter and one seaman, shifted the striped box, which was the only thing left, to our boat, and lowered it over, balancing it upon the two middle thwarts, for it was so heavy that it would have given the boat a dangerous tilt had we placed it at either end. As to the dead man, we left him where we had found him. The mate had a theory that, at the moment of the desertion of the ship, this fellow had started plundering, and that the captain, in an attempt to preserve discipline, had struck him down with a hatchet or some other heavy weapon. It seemed more probable than any other explanation, and yet it did not entirely satisfy me either. But the ocean is full of mysteries, and we were content to leave the fate of the dead seaman of the Brazilian brig to be added to that long list which every sailor can recall.

The heavy box was slung up by ropes on to the deck of the *Mary Sinclair*, and was carried by four seamen into the cabin, where, between the table and the after-lockers, there was just space for it to stand. There it remained during supper, and after that meal the mates remained with me, and discussed over a glass of grog the event of the day. Mr. Armstrong was a long, thin, vulture-like man, an excellent seaman, but famous for his nearness and cupidity. Our treasure-trove had excited him greatly, and already he had begun with glistening eyes to reckon up how much it might be worth to each of us when the shares of the salvage came to be divided.

"If the paper said that they were unique, Mr. Barclay, then they may be worth anything that you like to name. You wouldn't believe the sums that the rich collectors give. A thousand pounds is nothing to them. We'll have something to show for our voyage, or I am mistaken."

"I don't think that," said I. "As far as I can see, they are not very different from any other South American curios."

"Well, sir, I've traded there for fourteen voyages, and I have never seen anything like that chest before. That's worth a pile of money, just as it stands. But it's so heavy that surely there must be something valuable inside it. Don't you think that we ought to open it and see?"

"If you break it open you will spoil it, as likely as not," said the second mate.

Armstrong squatted down in front of it, with his head on one side, and his long, thin nose within a few inches of the lock.

"The wood is oak," said he, "and it has shrunk a little with age. If I had a chisel or a strong-bladed knife I could force the lock back without doing any damage at all."

The mention of a strong-bladed knife made me think of the dead seaman upon the brig.

"I wonder if he could have been on the job when someone came to interfere with him," said I.

"I don't know about that, sir, but I am perfectly certain that I could open the box. There's a screwdriver here in the locker. Just hold the lamp, Allardyce, and I'll have it done in a brace of shakes."

"Wait a bit," said I, for already, with eyes which gleamed with curiosity and with avarice, he was stooping over the lid. "I don't see that there is any hurry over this matter. You've read that card which warns us not to open it. It may mean anything or it may mean nothing, but somehow I feel inclined to obey it. After all, whatever is in it will keep, and if it is valuable it will be worth as much if it is opened in the owner's offices as in the cabin of the *Mary Sinclair*."

The first officer seemed bitterly disappointed at my decision.

"Surely, sir, you are not superstitious about it," said he, with a slight sneer upon his thin lips. "If it gets out of our own hands, and we don't see for ourselves what is inside it, we may be done out of our rights; besides —"

"That's enough, Mr. Armstrong," said I, abruptly. "You may have every confidence that you will get your rights, but I will not have that box opened to-night."

"Why, the label itself shows that the box has been examined by Europeans," Allardyce added. "Because a box is a treasure-box is no reason that it has treasures inside it now. A good many folk have had a peep into it since the days of the old Governor of Terra Firma."

Armstrong threw the screwdriver down upon the table and shrugged his shoulders.

"Just as you like," said he; but for the rest of the evening, although we spoke upon many subjects, I noticed that his eyes were continually coming round, with the same expression of curiosity and greed, to the old striped box.

And now I come to that portion of my story which fills me even now with a shuddering horror when I think of it. The main cabin had the rooms of the officers round it, but mine was the farthest away from it at the end of the little passage which led to the companion. No regular watch was kept by me, except in cases of emergency, and the three mates divided the watches among them. Armstrong had the middle watch, which ends at four in the morning, and he was relieved by Allardyce. For my part I have always been one of the soundest of sleepers, and it is rare for anything less than a hand upon my shoulder to arouse me.

And yet I was aroused that night, or rather in the early grey of the morning. It was just half-past four by my chronometer when something caused me to sit up in my berth wide awake and with every nerve tingling. It was a sound of some sort, a crash with a human cry at the end of it, which still jarred on my ears. I sat listening, but all was now silent. And yet it could not have been imagination, that hideous cry, for the echo of it still rang in my head, and it seemed to have come from some place quite close to me. I sprang from my bunk, and, pulling on some clothes, I made my way into the cabin. At first I saw nothing unusual there. In the cold, grey light I made out the red-clothed table, the six rotating chairs, the walnut lockers, the swinging barometer, and there, at the end, the big striped chest. I was turning away, with the intention of going upon deck and asking the second mate if he had heard anything, when my eyes fell suddenly upon something which projected from under the table. It was the leg of a man — a leg with a long sea-boot upon it. I stooped, and there was a figure sprawling upon his face, his arms thrown forward and his body twisted. One glance told me that it was Armstrong, the first officer, and a second that he was a dead man. For a few moments I stood gasping. Then I rushed on to the deck, called Allardyce to my assistance, and came back with him into the cabin.

Together we pulled the unfortunate fellow from under the table, and as we looked at his dripping head we exchanged glances, and I do not know which was the paler of the two.

"The same as the Spanish sailor," said I.

"The very same. God preserve us! It's that infernal chest! Look at Armstrong's hand!"

He held up the mate's right hand, and there was the screwdriver which he had wished to use the night before.

"He's been at the chest, sir. He knew that I was on deck and you were asleep. He knelt down in front of it, and he pushed the lock back with that tool. Then something happened to him, and he cried out so that you heard him."

"Allardyce," I whispered, "what *could* have happened to him?"

The second mate put his hand upon my sleeve and drew me into his cabin.

"We can talk here, sir, and we don't know who may be listening to us in there. What do you suppose is in that box, Captain Barclay?"

"I give you my word, Allardyce, that I have no idea."

"Well, I can only find one theory which will fit all the facts. Look at the size of the box. Look at all the carving and metal-work which may conceal any number of holes. Look at the weight of it; it took four men to carry it. On top of that, remember that two men have tried to open it, and both have come to their end through it. Now, sir, what can it mean except one thing?"

"You mean there is a man in it?"

"Of course there is a man in it. You know how it is in these South American States, sir. A man may be president one week and hunted like a dog the next — they are for ever flying for their lives. My idea is that there is some fellow in hiding there, who is armed and desperate, and who will fight to the death before he is taken."

"But his food and drink?"

"It's a roomy chest, sir, and he may have some provisions stowed away. As to his drink, he had a friend among the crew upon the brig who saw that he had what he needed."

"You think, then, that the label asking people not to open the box was simply written in his interest?"

"Yes, sir, that is my idea. Have you any other way of explaining the facts?"

I had to confess that I had not.

"The question is what we are to do?" I asked.

"The man's a dangerous ruffian, who sticks at nothing. I'm thinking it wouldn't be a bad thing to put a rope round the chest and tow it alongside for half an hour; then we could open it at our ease. Or if we just tied the box up and kept him from getting any water maybe that would do as well. Or the carpenter could put a coat of varnish over it and stop all the blow-holes."

"Come, Allardyce," said I, angrily. "You don't seriously mean to say that a whole ship's company are going to be terrorised by a single man in a box. If he's there, I'll engage to fetch him out!" I went to my room and came back with my revolver in my hand. "Now, Allardyce," said I, "do you open the lock, and I'll stand on guard."

"For God's sake, think what you are doing, sir!" cried the mate. "Two men have lost their lives over it, and the blood of one not yet dry upon the carpet."

"The more reason why we should revenge him."

"Well, sir, at least let me call the carpenter. Three are better than two, and he is a good stout man."

He went off in search of him, and I was left alone with the striped chest in the cabin. I don't think that I'm a nervous man, but I kept the table between me and this solid old relic of the Spanish Main. In the growing light of morning the red and white striping was beginning to appear, and the curious scrolls and wreaths of metal and carving which showed the loving pains which cunning craftsmen had expended upon it. Presently the carpenter and the mate came back together, the former with a hammer in his hand.

"It's a bad business, this, sir," said he, shaking his head, as he looked at the body of the mate. "And you think there's someone hiding in the box?"

"There's no doubt about it," said Allardyce, picking up the screwdriver and setting his jaw like a man who needs to brace his courage. "I'll drive the lock back if you will both stand by. If he rises let him have it on the head with your hammer, carpenter. Shoot at once, sir, if he raises his hand. Now!"

He had knelt down in front of the striped chest, and passed the blade of the tool under the lid. With a sharp snick the lock flew back. "Stand by!"

yelled the mate, and with a heave he threw open the massive top of the box. As it swung up we all three sprang back, I with my pistol levelled, and the carpenter with the hammer above his head. Then, as nothing happened, we each took a step forward and peeped in. The box was empty.

Not quite empty either, for in one corner was lying an old yellow candlestick, elaborately engraved, which appeared to be as old as the box itself. Its rich yellow tone and artistic shape suggested that it was an object of value. For the rest there was nothing more weighty or valuable than dust in the old striped treasure-chest.

"Well, I'm blessed!" cried Allardyce, staring blankly into it. "Where does the weight come in, then?"

"Look at the thickness of the sides, and look at the lid. Why, it's five inches through. And see that great metal spring across it."

"That's for holding the lid up," said the mate. "You see, it won't lean back. What's that German printing on the inside?"

"It means that it was made by Johann Rothstein of Augsburg, in 1606."

"And a solid bit of work, too. But it doesn't throw much light on what has passed, does it, Captain Barclay? That candlestick looks like gold. We shall have something for our trouble after all."

He leant forward to grasp it, and from that moment I have never doubted as to the reality of inspiration, for on the instant I caught him by the collar and pulled him straight again. It may have been some story of the Middle Ages which had come back to my mind, or it may have been that my eye had caught some red which was not that of rust upon the upper part of the lock, but to him and to me it will always seem an inspiration, so prompt and sudden was my action.

"There's devilry here," said I. "Give me the crooked stick from the corner."

It was an ordinary walking-cane with a hooked top. I passed it over the candlestick and gave it a pull. With a flash a row of polished steel fangs shot out from below the upper lip, and the great striped chest snapped at us like a wild animal. Clang came the huge lid into its place, and the glasses on the swinging rack sang and tinkled with the shock. The mate sat down on the edge of the table and shivered like a frightened horse.

"You've saved my life, Captain Barclay!" said he.

So this was the secret of the striped treasure-chest of old Don Ramirez di Leyra, and this was how he preserved his ill-gotten gains from the Terra Firma and the Province of Veraquas. Be the thief ever so cunning he could not tell that golden candlestick from the other articles of value, and the instant that he laid hand upon it the terrible spring was unloosed and the murderous steel pikes were driven into his brain, while the shock of the blow sent the victim backward and enabled the chest to automatically close itself. How many, I wondered, had fallen victims to the ingenuity of the mechanic of Ausgburg? And as I thought of the possible history of that grim striped chest my resolution was very quickly taken.

"Carpenter, bring three men, and carry this on deck."

"Going to throw it overboard, sir?"

"Yes, Mr. Allardyce. I'm not superstitious as a rule, but there are some things which are more than a sailor can be called upon to stand."

"No wonder that brig made heavy weather, Captain Barclay, with such a thing on board. The glass is dropping fast, sir, and we are only just in time."

So we did not even wait for the three sailors, but we carried it out, the mate, the carpenter, and I, and we pushed it with our own hands over the bulwarks. There was a white spout of water, and it was gone. There it lies, the striped chest, a thousand fathoms deep, and if, as they say, the sea will some day be dry land, I grieve for the man who finds that old box and tries to penetrate into its secret.

DOYLE'S nautical fiction, *in toto*, left an even more notable legacy than "Jephson's" contributions to the mystery of the *Mary Celeste*. The single greatest writer of nautical horror was a mere eight years from launching his first entry of his horrific, parasitic vision of the greedy seas – a series which came to be known as the Sargasso Sea Mythos. William Hope Hodgson's stories were riddled with cursed derelict ships, primordial predators, hideous mutations, sea raiders, fungoid monstrosities, mind-melting storms, and – of course – were-sharks. One extremely common trope in his tales runs thus: the carefree crew of a middle-sized cargo vessel sail into becalmed waters where they notice a derelict floating nearby in disrepair. They hail her without response and decide to board her out of curiosity and greed for her cargo. Upon exploring the empty vessel, they discover a horrible, malignant presence – sometimes inadvertently carrying it over to their own ship, other times successfully fleeing it hulk, leaving it to float across the seas, preying on other, less fortunate victims. Stories which follow this model (e.g., "The Stone Ship," "The Albatross," "The Mystery of the Water-Logged Ship," "The Ghosts of the *Glen Doon*," and "The Ghost Pirates") clearly display Doyle's influence – especially through "The Striped Chest." Throughout his life Doyle continued to be fascinated with nautical fiction, and his stories often employed sailors as characters and ships as plot devices and settings. "The Striped Chest" certainly seems to take a more realistic (yet no less romantic) approach to the *Mary Celeste* case than "Jephson's Statement," arguing – it would seem – that the similarly abandoned Brazilian brig was left fend for itself in the Atlantic squalls, not due to black supremacists' bizarre machinations, but from a misunderstanding of what the chest was: not haunted but engineered. In some ways the derelict in this tale is far more like the real *Mary Celeste* than to Doyle's earlier treatment: the likeliest scenarios of the historical ship's abandonment involve an undersea earthquake which upset the *Celeste's* explosive cargo of alcohol, leading the crew to panic, abandon ship, and become swallowed by the seas – all due to confusion and misunderstanding.

"OUT *of the depths...*" The phrase "De Profundis" comes from the first line of Psalm 130's Latin translation – "out of the depths have I cried unto Thee, O LORD" – a plaintive cry to God for mercy and salvation. The following tale is a dark but poetic episode blending Doyle's desperate hope in Spiritualism with the cynical, rationalistic logic that defined his greatest character. One of his most Poe-esque stories (it bears strong similarities to "The Oblong Box," "The Premature Burial," *Arthur Gordon Pym*, and "The Sphinx"), the tale copies Poe's tendency to use his tales as existential dialectics – probing the relationships between the physical and the psychical, the material and the mental. In this manner it is a more profound exploration of the supernatural than many of Doyle's spiritualist tales, calling into question both the reality of spiritualism and the determinism of ordinary life.

De Profundis

{1892}

SO long as the oceans are the ligaments which bind together the great broad-cast British Empire, so long will there be a dash of romance in our minds. For the soul is swayed by the waters, as the waters are by the moon, and when the great highways of an empire are along such roads as these, so full of strange sights and sounds, with danger ever running like a hedge on either side of the course, it is a dull mind indeed which does not bear away with it some trace of such a passage. And now, Britain lies far beyond herself, for the three-mile limit of every seaboard is her frontier, which has been won by hammer and loom and pick rather than by arts of war. For it is written in history that neither king nor army can bar the path to the man who having twopence in his strong box, and knowing well where he can turn it to threepence, sets his mind to that one end. And as the frontier has broadened, the mind of Britain has broadened too, spreading out until all men can see that the ways of the island are continental, even as those of the Continent are insular.

But for this a price must be paid, and the price is a grievous one. As the beast of old must have one young human life as a tribute every year, so to our Empire we throw from day to day the pick and flower of our youth. The engine is world-wide and strong, but the only fuel that will drive it is the lives of British men. Thus it is that in the grey old cathedrals, as we look round upon the brasses on the walls, we see strange names, such names as they who reared those walls had never heard, for it is in Peshawar, and Umballah, and Korti and Fort Pearson that the youngsters die, leaving only a precedent and a brass behind them. But if every man had his obelisk, even where he lay, then no frontier line need be drawn, for a cordon of British graves would ever show how high the Anglo-Celtic tide had lapped.

This, then, as well as the waters which join us to the world, has done something to tinge us with romance. For when so many have their loved ones over the seas, walking amid hillmen's bullets, or swamp malaria, where death is sudden and distance great, then mind communes with mind, and strange stories arise of dream, presentiment or vision, where the mother sees her dying son, and is past the first bitterness of her grief ere the message comes which should have broken the news. The learned have of late looked into the matter and have even labelled it with a name; but what can we know more of it save that a poor stricken soul, when hard-pressed and driven, can shoot across the earth some ten-thousand-mile-distant picture of its trouble to the mind which is most akin to it. Far be it from me to say that there lies no such power within us, for of all things which the brain will grasp the last will be itself; but yet it is well to be very cautious over such matters, for once at least I have known that which was within the laws of nature seem to be far upon the further side of them.

John Vansittart was the younger partner of the firm of Hudson and Vansittart, coffee exporters of the Island of Ceylon, three-quarters Dutchman by descent, but wholly English in his sympathies. For years I had been his agent in London, and when in '72 he came over to England for a three months' holiday, he turned to me for the introductions which would enable him to see something of town and country life. Armed with seven letters he left my offices, and for many weeks scrappy notes from different parts of the country let me know that he had found favour in the eyes of my friends. Then came word of his engagement to Emily Lawson, of a cadet branch of the Hereford Lawsons, and at the very tail of the first flying rumour the news of his absolute marriage, for the wooing of a wanderer must be short, and the days were already crowding on towards the date when he must be upon his homeward journey. They were to return together to Colombo in one of the firm's own thousand-ton barque-rigged sailing ships, and this was to be their princely honeymoon, at once a necessity and a delight.

Those were the royal days of coffee-planting in Ceylon, before a single season and a rotten fungus drove a whole community through years of despair to one of the greatest commercial victories which pluck and ingenuity ever won. Not often is it that men have the heart when their one great industry is withered to rear up in a few years another as rich to take its place, and the tea-fields of Ceylon are as true a monument to courage as is the lion at Waterloo. But in '72 there was no cloud yet above the skyline, and the hopes of the planters were as high and as bright as the hillsides on which they reared their crops. Vansittart came down to London with his young and beautiful wife. I was introduced, dined with them, and it was finally arranged that I, since business called me also to Ceylon, should be a fellow-passenger with them on the *Eastern Star*, which was timed to sail on the following Monday.

It was on the Sunday evening that I saw him again. He was shown up into my rooms about nine o'clock at night, with the air of a man who is bothered and out of sorts. His hand, as I shook it, was hot and dry.

"I wish, Atkinson," said he, "that you could give me a little lime juice and water. I have a beastly thirst upon me, and the more I take the more I seem to want."

I rang and ordered a carafe and glasses. "You are flushed," said I. "You don't look the thing."

"No, I'm clean off colour. Got a touch of rheumatism in my back, and don't seem to taste my food. It is this vile London that is choking me. I'm not used to breathing air which has been used up by four million lungs all sucking away on every side of you." He flapped his crooked hands before his face, like a man who really struggles for his breath.

"A touch of the sea will soon set you right."

"Yes, I'm of one mind with you there. That's the thing for me. I want no other doctor. If I don't get to sea to-morrow I'll have an illness. There are no two ways about it." He drank off a tumbler of lime juice, and clapped his two hands with his knuckles doubled up into the small of his back.

"That seems to ease me," said he, looking at me with a filmy eye. "Now I want your help, Atkinson, for I am rather awkwardly placed."

"As how?"

"This way. My wife's mother got ill and wired for her. I couldn't go--you know best yourself how tied I have been--so she had to go alone. Now I've had another wire to say that she can't come to-morrow, but that she will pick up the ship at Falmouth on Wednesday. We put in there, you know, and in, though I count it hard, Atkinson, that a man should be asked to believe in a mystery, and cursed if he can't do it. Cursed, mind you, no less." He leaned forward and began to draw a catchy breath like a man who is poised on the very edge of a sob.

Then first it came to my mind that I had heard much of the hard-drinking life of the island, and that from brandy came those wild words and fevered hands. The flushed cheek and the glazing eye were those of one whose drink is strong upon him. Sad it was to see so noble a young man in the grip of that most bestial of all the devils.

"You should lie down," I said, with some severity.

He screwed up his eyes like a man who is striving to wake himself, and looked up with an air of surprise.

"So I shall presently," said he, quite rationally. "I felt quite swimmy just now, but I am my own man again now. Let me see, what was I talking about? Oh ah, of course, about the wife. She joins the ship at Falmouth. Now I want to go round by water. I believe my health depends upon it. I just want a little clean first-lung air to set me on my feet again. I ask you, like a good fellow, to go to Falmouth by rail, so that in case we should be late you may be there to look after the wife. Put up at the Royal Hotel, and I will wire her that you are there. Her sister will bring her down, so that it will be all plain sailing."

"I'll do it with pleasure," said I. "In fact, I would rather go by rail, for we shall have enough and to spare of the sea before we reach Colombo. I believe too that you badly need a change. Now, I should go and turn in, if I were you."

"Yes, I will. I sleep aboard tonight. You know," he continued, as the film settled down again over his eyes, "I've not slept well the last few nights. I've been troubled with theolololog--that is to say, theolological--hang it," with a desperate effort, "with the doubts of theolologicians. Wondering why the Almighty made us, you know, and why He made our heads swimmy, and fixed little pains into the small of our backs. Maybe I'll do better tonight." He rose and steadied himself with an effort against the corner of the chair back.

"Look here, Vansittart," said I, gravely, stepping up to him, and laying my hand upon his sleeve, "I can give you a shakedown here. You are not fit to go out. You are all over the place. You've been mixing your drinks."

"Drinks!" He stared at me stupidly.

"You used to carry your liquor better than this."

"I give you my word, Atkinson, that I have not had a drain for two days. It's not drink. I don't know what it is. I suppose you think this is drink." He took up my hand in his burning grasp, and passed it over his own forehead.

"Great Lord!" said I.

His skin felt like a thin sheet of velvet beneath which lies a close-packed layer of small shot. It was smooth to the touch at any one place, but to a finger passed along it, rough as a nutmeg grater.

"It's all right," said he, smiling at my startled face. "I've had the prickly heat nearly as bad."

"But this is never prickly heat."

"No, it's London. It's breathing bad air. But tomorrow it'll be all right. There's a surgeon aboard, so I shall be in safe hands. I must be off now."

"Not you," said I, pushing him back into a chair. "This is past a joke. You don't move from here until a doctor sees you. Just stay where you are."

I caught up my hat, and rushing round to the house of a neighbouring physician, I brought him back with me. The room was empty and Vansittart gone. I rang the bell. The servant said that the gentleman had ordered a cab the instant that I had left, and had gone off in it. He had told the cabman to drive to the docks.

"Did the gentleman seem ill?" I asked.

"Ill!" The man smiled. "No, sir, he was singin' his 'ardest all the time."

The information was not as reassuring as my servant seemed to think, but I reflected that he was going straight back to the *Eastern Star*, and that there was a doctor aboard of her, so that there was nothing which I could do in the matter. None the less, when I thought of his thirst, his burning hands, his heavy eye, his tripping speech, and lastly, of that leprous forehead, I carried with me to bed an unpleasant memory of my visitor and his visit.

At eleven o'clock next day I was at the docks, but the *Eastern Star* had already moved down the river, and was nearly at Gravesend. To Gravesend I went by train, but only to see her topmasts far off, with a plume of smoke from a tug in front of her. I would hear no more of my friend until I rejoined him at Falmouth. When I got back to my offices, a telegram was awaiting me from Mrs. Vansittart, asking me to meet her; and next evening found us both at the Royal Hotel, Falmouth, where we were to wait for the *Eastern Star*. Ten days passed, and there came no news of her.

They were ten days which I am not likely to forget. On the very day that the *Eastern Star* had cleared from the Thames, a furious easterly gale had sprung up, and blew on from day to day for the greater part of a week without the sign of a lull. Such a screaming, raving, long-drawn storm has never been known on the southern coast. From our hotel windows the sea view was all banked in haze, with a little rain-swept half-circle under our very eyes, churned and lashed into one tossing stretch of foam. So heavy was the wind upon the waves that little sea could rise, for the crest of each billow was torn shrieking from it, and lashed broadcast over the bay. Clouds, wind, sea, all were rushing to the west, and there, looking down at this mad jumble of elements, I waited on day after day, my sole companion a white, silent woman, with terror in her eyes, her forehead pressed ever against the window, her gaze from early morning to the fall of night fixed upon that wall of grey haze through which the loom of a vessel might come. She said nothing, but that face of hers was one long wail of fear.

On the fifth day I took counsel with an old seaman. I should have preferred to have done so alone, but she saw me speak with him, and was at our side in an instant, with parted lips and a prayer in her eyes.

"Seven days out from London," said he, "and five in the gale. Well, the Channel's swept clear by this wind. There's three things for it. She may have popped into port on the French side. That's like enough."

"No, no; he knew we were here. He would have telegraphed."

"Ah, yes, so he would. Well, then, he might have run for it, and if he did that he won't be very far from Madeira by now. That'll be it, marm, you may depend."

"Or else? You said there was a third chance."

"Did I, marm? No, only two, I think. I don't think I said anything of a third. Your ship's out there, depend upon it, away out in the Atlantic, and you'll hear of it time enough, for the weather is breaking. Now don't you fret, marm, and wait quiet, and you'll find a real blue Cornish sky tomorrow."

The old seaman was right in his surmise, for the next day broke calm and bright, with only a low dwindling cloud in the west to mark the last trailing wreaths of the storm-wrack. But still there came no word from the sea, and no sign of the ship. Three more weary days had passed, the weariest that I have ever spent, when there came a seafaring man to the hotel with a letter. I gave a shout of joy. It was from the captain of the *Eastern Star*. As I read the first lines of it I whisked my hand over it, but she laid her own upon it and drew it away. "I have seen it," said she, in a cold, quiet voice. "I may as well see the rest, too."

"DEAR SIR," said the letter, *"Mr. Vansittart is down with the small-pox, and we are blown so far on our course that we don't know what to do, he being off his head and unfit to tell us. By dead reckoning we are but three hundred miles from Funchal, so I take it that it is best that we should push on there, get Mr. V. into hospital, and wait in the Bay until you come. There's a sailing-ship due from Falmouth to Funchal in a few days' time, as I understand. This goes by the brig _Marian_ of Falmouth, and five pounds is due to the master, Yours respectfully,*

"JNO. HINES."

She was a wonderful woman that, only a chit of a girl fresh from school, but as quiet and strong as a man. She said nothing--only pressed her lips together tight, and put on her bonnet.

"You are going out?" I asked.

"Yes."

"Can I be of use?"

"No; I am going to the doctor's."

"To the doctor's?"

"Yes. To learn how to nurse a small-pox case."

She was busy at that all the evening, and next morning we were off with a fine ten-knot breeze in the barque _Rose of Sharon_ for Madeira. For five days we made good time, and were no great way from the island; but on the sixth there fell a calm, and we lay without motion on a sea of oil, heaving slowly, but making not a foot of way.

At ten o'clock that night Emily Vansittart and I stood leaning on the starboard railing of the poop, with a full moon shining at our backs, and casting a black shadow of the barque, and of our own two heads upon the shining water. From the shadow a broadening path of moonshine stretched away to the lonely sky-line, flickering and shimmering in the gentle heave of the swell. We were talking with bent heads, chatting of the calm, of the chances of wind, of the look of the sky, when there came a sudden plop, like a rising salmon, and there, in the clear light, John Vansittart sprang out of the water and looked up at us.

I never saw anything clearer in my life than I saw that man. The moon shone full upon him, and he was but three oars' lengths away. His face was more puffed than when I had seen him last, mottled here and there with dark scabs, his mouth and eyes open as one who is struck with some overpowering surprise. He had some white stuff streaming from his shoulders, and one hand was raised to his ear, the other crooked across his

breast. I saw him leap from the water into the air, and in the dead calm the waves of his coming lapped up against the sides of the vessel. Then his figure sank back into the water again, and I heard a rending, crackling sound like a bundle of brushwood snapping in the fire on a frosty night. There were no signs of him when I looked again, but a swift swirl and eddy on the still sea still marked the spot where he had been. How long I stood there, tingling to my finger-tips, holding up an unconscious woman with one hand, clutching at the rail of the vessel with the other, was more than I could afterwards tell. I had been noted as a man of-slow and unresponsive emotions, but this time at least I was shaken to the core. Once and twice I struck my foot upon the deck to be certain that I was indeed the master of my own senses, and that this was not some mad prank of an unruly brain. As I stood, still marvelling, the woman shivered, opened her eyes, gasped, and then standing erect with her hands upon the rail, looked out over the moonlit sea with a face which had aged ten years in a summer night.

"You saw his vision?" she murmured.

"I saw something."

"It was he! It was John! He is dead!"

I muttered some lame words of doubt.

"Doubtless he died at this hour," she whispered. "In hospital at Madeira. I have read of such things. His thoughts were with me. His vision came to me. Oh, my John, my dear, dear, lost John!"

She broke out suddenly into a storm of weeping, and I led her down into her cabin, where I left her with her sorrow. That night a brisk breeze blew up from the east, and in the evening of the next day we passed the two islets of Los Desertos, and dropped anchor at sundown in the Bay of Funchal. The *Eastern Star* lay no great distance from us, with the quarantine flag flying from her main, and her Jack half-way up her peak.

"You see," said Mrs. Vansittart, quickly. She was dry-eyed now, for she had known how it would be.

That night we received permission from the authorities to move on board the *Eastern Star*. The captain, Hines, was waiting upon deck with confusion and grief contending upon his bluff face as he sought for words with which to break this heavy tidings, but she took the story from his lips.

"I know that my husband is dead," she said. "He died yesterday night, about ten o'clock, in hospital at Madeira, did he not?"

The seaman stared aghast. "No, marm, he died eight days ago at sea, and we had to bury him out there, for we lay in a belt of calm, and could not say when we might make the land."

Well, those are the main facts about the death of John Vansittart, and his appearance to his wife somewhere about lat. 35 N. and long. 15 W. A clearer case of a wraith has seldom been made out, and since then it has been told as such, and put into print as such, and endorsed by a learned society as such, and so floated off with many others to support the recent theory of telepathy. For myself, I hold telepathy to be proved, but I would snatch this one case from amid the evidence, and say that I do not think that it was the wraith of John Vansittart, but John Vansittart himself whom we saw that night leaping into the moonlight out of the depths of the Atlantic. It has ever been my belief that some strange chance--one of those chances which seem so improbable and yet so constantly occur--had becalmed us over the very spot where the man had been buried a week before. For the rest, the surgeon tells me that the leaden weight was not too firmly fixed, and that seven days bring about changes which fetch a body to the surface. Coming from the depth to which the weight would have sunk it, he explains that it might well attain such a velocity as to carry it clear of the water. Such is my own explanation of the matter, and if you ask me what then became of the body, I must recall to you that snapping, crackling sound, with the swirl in the water. The shark is a surface feeder and is plentiful in those parts.

LIKE Poe, Doyle saw life as a struggle to find a balance between corporeal and incorporeal realities – between imagination and actuality, insanity and logic, the spiritual and the physical, life and death, the body and the soul. Poe's tales often warned against coming too close to the immaterial world: here lurks madness, neuroses, murder, and schizoid delusions. His characters commonly staved off insanity by choosing to focus on facts and logic in the face of mind-searing natural sublimity (cf. "Pit and the Pendulum," "Descent into the Maelstrom," "MS Found in a Bottle"). Nonetheless, both writers saw the relationship between the two extremes as fluid and viscous, often intertwining with one another, blurring their borders, and encroaching on one another's territory. The apparent resurrections of the female characters in "Berenice," "Ligeia," "Morella," "The Black Cat," and "House of Usher" are both somewhat spiritual and somewhat physical – an effect of madness and an effect of reality, never thoroughly explained or even verified. Likewise Doyle's Poesque maritime tale features an unexpected resurrection. The wife believes it to be wholly spiritual – a telepathic vision – while the protagonist suggests that it may be thoroughly explained with logic, but the result is a collusion between fatefulness and happenstance, design and coincidence. That the appearance occurred *when* it did and *how* it did leads the reader to be unsure of its direct cause (whether natural, supernatural, or both), and whether you lean towards ghostly vision, extraordinary coincidence, or some combination of the two, Doyle's purpose has been achieved if you walk away from it a little less sure of the boundaries between free will and determinism.

BEFORE Arthur Conan Doyle, mummy literature tended to run in one of two directions: cynical sociological humor or optimistic science fiction. Edgar Allan Poe's "Some Words With a Mummy" is a bone-dry social satire, and has – as a result – unwittingly disappointed countless horror fans who first picked it up expecting the mood of "The Fall of the House of Usher" (it is truly hilarious but lacks a single moment of dread). Other stories used mummies as time travelers, star-crossed lovers, or midnight entertainers. As Egyptological studies began to boom in the early 19th century and continued on into the 20th, there was something unquestionably philosophical about the mummies that were being pulled out of the sand and exhibited in museums: many of them were older than Moses himself, yet modern audiences could stare them in the face. Victorian authors often tried to use these well-preserved corpses as plot devices to allow a meeting between the past and present without requiring a great deal of scientific explanation. These stories tended to be silly or hopelessly dated adventure novels and have all been forgotten, but Arthur Conan Doyle completely changed the genre with two brilliant stories, both of which are almost single-handedly responsible for every mummy film ever made – none exist without his fingerprints on them. The first develops the romantic layer of Boris Karloff's tragic Imhotep: a desperate lover who employs the dark rites of Memphis to resurrect his lover in a hopeless but fantastical gambol against death. It is a beautiful tale of the supernatural. In the next tale, however, we will meet the second layer – the monster – and he is not a pleasant flat-mate.

The Ring of Thoth
{1890}

MR. John Vansittart Smith, F.R.S., of 147-A Gower Street, was a man whose energy of purpose and clearness of thought might have placed him in the very first rank of scientific observers. He was the victim, however, of a universal ambition which prompted him to aim at distinction in many subjects rather than preeminence in one.

In his early days he had shown an aptitude for zoology and for botany which caused his friends to look upon him as a second Darwin, but when a professorship was almost within his reach he had suddenly discontinued his studies and turned his whole attention to chemistry. Here his researches upon the spectra of the metals had won him his fellowship in the Royal Society; but again he played the coquette with his subject, and after a year's absence from the laboratory he joined the Oriental Society, and delivered a paper on the Hieroglyphic and Demotic inscriptions of El Kab, thus giving a crowning example both of the versatility and of the inconstancy of his talents.

The most fickle of wooers, however, is apt to be caught at last, and so it was with John Vansittart Smith. The more he burrowed his way into Egyptology the more impressed he became by the vast field which it opened to the inquirer, and by the extreme importance of a subject which promised to throw a light upon the first germs of human civilisation and the origin of the greater part of our arts and sciences. So struck was Mr. Smith that he straightway married an Egyptological young lady who had written upon the sixth dynasty, and having thus secured a sound base of operations he set himself to collect materials for a work which should unite the research of Lepsius and the ingenuity of Champollion. The preparation of this magnum opus entailed many hurried visits to the magnificent Egyptian collections of the Louvre, upon the last of which, no longer ago than the middle of last October, he became involved in a most strange and noteworthy adventure.

The trains had been slow and the Channel had been rough, so that the student arrived in Paris in a somewhat befogged and feverish condition. On reaching the Hotel de France, in the Rue Laffitte, he had thrown himself upon a sofa for a couple of hours, but finding that he was unable to sleep, he determined, in spite of his fatigue, to make his way to the Louvre, settle the point which he had come to decide, and take the evening train back to Dieppe. Having come to this conclusion, he donned his greatcoat, for it was a raw rainy day, and made his way across the Boulevard des Italiens and down the Avenue de l'Opera. Once in the Louvre he was on familiar ground, and he speedily made his way to the collection of papyri which it was his intention to consult.

The warmest admirers of John Vansittart Smith could hardly claim for him that he was a handsome man. His high-beaked nose and prominent chin had something of the same acute and incisive character which distinguished his intellect. He held his head in a birdlike fashion, and birdlike, too, was the pecking motion with which, in conversation, he threw out his objections and retorts. As he stood, with the high collar of his greatcoat raised to his ears, he might have seen from the reflection in the glass-case before him that his appearance was a singular one. Yet it came upon him as a sudden jar when an English voice behind him exclaimed in very audible tones, "What a queer-looking mortal!"

The student had a large amount of petty vanity in his composition which manifested itself by an ostentatious and overdone disregard of all personal considerations. He straightened his lips and looked rigidly at the roll of papyrus, while his heart filled with bitterness against the whole race of travelling Britons.

"Yes," said another voice, "he really is an extraordinary fellow."

"Do you know," said the first speaker, "one could almost believe that by the continual contemplation of mummies the chap has become half a mummy himself?"

"He has certainly an Egyptian cast of countenance," said the other.

John Vansittart Smith spun round upon his heel with the intention of shaming his countrymen by a corrosive remark or two. To his surprise and relief, the two young fellows who had been conversing had their shoulders turned towards him, and were gazing at one of the Louvre attendants who was polishing some brass-work at the other side of the room.

"Carter will be waiting for us at the Palais Royal," said one tourist to the other, glancing at his watch, and they clattered away, leaving the student to his labours.

"I wonder what these chatterers call an Egyptian cast of countenance," thought John Vansittart Smith, and he moved his position slightly in order to catch a glimpse of the man's face. He started as his eyes fell upon it. It was indeed the very face with which his studies had made him familiar. The regular statuesque features, broad brow, well-rounded chin, and dusky complexion were the exact counterpart of the innumerable statues, mummy-cases, and pictures which adorned the walls of the apartment.

The thing was beyond all coincidence. The man must be an Egyptian.

The national angularity of the shoulders and narrowness of the hips were alone sufficient to identify him.

John Vansittart Smith shuffled towards the attendant with some intention of addressing him. He was not light of touch in conversation, and found it difficult to strike the happy mean between the brusqueness of the superior and the geniality of the equal. As he came nearer, the man presented his side face to him, but kept his gaze still bent upon his work. Vansittart Smith, fixing his eyes upon the fellow's skin, was conscious of a sudden impression that there was something inhuman and preternatural about its appearance. Over the temple and cheek-bone it was as glazed and as shiny as varnished parchment. There was no suggestion of pores. One could not fancy a drop of moisture upon that arid surface. From brow to chin, however, it was cross- hatched by a million delicate wrinkles, which shot and interlaced as though Nature in some Maori mood had tried how wild and intricate a pattern she could devise.

"Ou est la collection de Memphis?" asked the student, with the awkward air of a man who is devising a question merely for the purpose of opening a conversation.

"C'est la," replied the man brusquely, nodding his head at the other side of the room.

"Vous etes un Egyptien, n'est-ce pas?" asked the Englishman.

The attendant looked up and turned his strange dark eyes upon his questioner. They were vitreous, with a misty dry shininess, such as Smith had never seen in a human head before. As he gazed into them he saw some strong emotion gather in their depths, which rose and deepened until it broke into a look of something akin both to horror and to hatred.

"Non, monsieur; je suis Fransais." The man turned abruptly and bent low over his polishing. The student gazed at him for a moment in astonishment, and then turning to a chair in a retired corner behind one of the doors he proceeded to make notes of his researches among the papyri. His thoughts, however refused to return into their natural groove. They would run upon the enigmatical attendant with the sphinx-like face and the parchment skin.

"Where have I seen such eyes?" said Vansittart Smith to himself. "There is something saurian about them, something reptilian. There's the membrana nictitans of the snakes," he mused, bethinking himself of his zoological studies. "It gives a shiny effect. But there was something more here. There was a sense of power, of wisdom--so I read them--and of weariness, utter weariness, and ineffable despair. It may be all imagination, but I never had so strong an impression. By Jove, I must have another look at them!" He rose and paced round the Egyptian rooms, but the man who had excited his curiosity had disappeared.

ൻ

The student sat down again in his quiet corner, and continued to work at his notes. He had gained the information which he required from the papyri, and it only remained to write it down while it was still fresh in his memory. For a time his pencil travelled rapidiy over the paper, but soon the lines became less level, the words more blurred, and finally the pencil tinkled down upon the floor, and the head of the student dropped heavily forward upon his chest.

Tired out by his journey, he slept so soundly in his lonely post behind the door that neither the clanking civil guard, nor the footsteps of sightseers, nor even the loud hoarse bell which gives the signal for closing, were sufficient to arouse him.

Twilight deepened into darkness, the bustle from the Rue de Rivoli waxed and then waned, distant Notre Dame clanged out the hour of midnight, and still the dark and lonely figure sat silently in the shadow. It was not until close upon one in the morning that, with a sudden gasp and an intaking of the breath, Vansittart Smith returned to consciousness. For a moment it flashed upon him that he had dropped asleep in his study-chair at home. The moon was shining fitfully through the unshuttered window, however, and, as his eye ran along the lines of mummies and the endless array of polished cases, he remembered clearly where he was and how he came there. The student was not a nervous man. He possessed that love of a novel situation which is peculiar to his race. Stretching out his cramped limbs, he looked at his watch, and burst into a chuckle as he observed the hour. The episode would make an admirable anecdote to be introduced into his next paper as a relief to the graver and heavier speculations. He was a little cold, but wide awake and much refreshed. It was no wonder that the guardians had overlooked him, for the door threw its heavy black shadow right across him.

The complete silence was impressive. Neither outside nor inside was there a creak or a murmur. He was alone with the dead men of a dead civilisation. What though the outer city reeked of the garish nineteenth century! In all this chamber there was scarce an article, from the shrivelled ear of wheat to the pigment-box of the painter, which had not held its own against four thousand years. Here was the flotsam and jetsam washed up by the great ocean of time from that far-off empire. From stately Thebes, from lordly Luxor, from the great temples of Heliopolis, from a hundred rifled tombs, these relics had been brought. The student glanced round at the long silent figures who flickered vaguely up through the gloom, at the busy toilers who were now so restful, and he fell into a reverent and thoughtful mood. An unwonted sense of his own youth and insignificance came over him. Leaning back in his chair, he gazed dreamily down the long vista of rooms, all silvery with the moonshine, which extend through the whole wing of the widespread building. His eyes fell upon the yellow glare of a distant lamp.

John Vansittart Smith sat up on his chair with his nerves all on edge. The light was advancing slowly towards him, pausing from time to time, and then coming jerkily onwards. The bearer moved noiselessly. In the utter silence there was no suspicion of the pat of a footfall. An idea of robbers entered the Englishman's head. He snuggled up further into the corner. The light was two rooms off. Now it was in the next chamber, and still there was no sound. With something approaching to a thrill of fear the student observed a face, floating in the air as it were, behind the flare of the lamp. The figure was wrapped in shadow, but the light fell full upon the strange eager face. There was no mistaking the metallic glistening eyes and the cadaverous skin. It was the attendant with whom he had conversed.

Vansittart Smith's first impulse was to come forward and address him. A few words of explanation would set the matter clear, and lead doubtless to his being conducted to some side door from which he might make his way to his hotel. As the man entered the chamber, however, there was something so stealthy in his movements, and so furtive in his expression, that the Englishman altered his intention. This was clearly no ordinary official walking the rounds. The fellow wore felt-soled slippers, stepped with a rising chest, and glanced quickly from left to right, while his hurried gasping breathing thrilled the flame of his lamp. Vansittart Smith crouched silently back into the corner and watched him keenly, convinced that his errand was one of secret and probably sinister import.

There was no hesitation in the other's movements. He stepped lightly and swiftly across to one of the great cases, and, drawing a key from his pocket, he unlocked it. From the upper shelf he pulled down a mummy, which he bore away with him, and laid it with much care and solicitude upon the ground. By it he placed his lamp, and then squatting down beside it in Eastern fashion he began with long quivering fingers to undo the cerecloths and bandages which girt it round. As the crackling rolls of linen peeled off one after the other, a strong aromatic odour filled the chamber, and fragments of scented wood and of spices pattered down upon the marble floor.

It was clear to John Vansittart Smith that this mummy had never been unswathed before. The operation interested him keenly. He thrilled all over with curiosity, and his birdlike head protruded further and further from behind the door. When, however, the last roll had been removed from the four-thousand-year-old head, it was all that he could do to stifle an outcry of amazement. First, a cascade of long, black, glossy tresses poured over the workman's hands and arms. A second turn of the bandage revealed a low, white forehead, with a pair of delicately arched eyebrows. A third uncovered a pair of bright, deeply fringed eyes, and a straight, well-cut nose, while a fourth and last showed a sweet, full, sensitive mouth, and a beautifully curved chin. The whole face was one of extraordinary loveliness, save for the one blemish that in the centre of the forehead there was a single irregular, coffee- coloured splotch. It was a triumph of the embalmer's art. Vansittart Smith's eyes grew larger and larger as he gazed upon it, and he chirruped in his throat with satisfaction.

Its effect upon the Egyptologist was as nothing, however, compared with that which it produced upon the strange attendant. He threw his hands up into the air, burst into a harsh clatter of words, and then, hurling himself down upon the ground beside the mummy, he threw his arms round her, and kissed her repeatedly upon the lips and brow. "Ma petite!" he groaned in French. "Ma pauvre petite!" His voice broke with emotion, and his innumerable wrinkles quivered and writhed, but the student observed in the lamplight that his shining eyes were still as dry and tearless as two beads of steel. For some minutes he lay, with a twitching face, crooning and moaning over the beautiful head. Then he broke into a sudden smile, said some words in an unknown tongue, and sprang to his feet with the vigorous air of one who has braced himself for an effort.

In the centre of the room there was a large circular case which contained, as the student had frequently remarked, a magnificent collection of early Egyptian rings and precious stones. To this the attendant strode, and, unlocking it, he threw it open. On the ledge at the side he placed his lamp, and beside it a small earthenware jar which he had drawn from his pocket. He then took a handful of rings from the case, and with a most serious and anxious face he proceeded to smear each in turn with some liquid substance from the earthen pot, holding them to the light as he did so. He was clearly disappointed with the first lot, for he threw them petulantly back into the case, and drew out some more. One of these, a massive ring with a large crystal set in it, he seized and eagerly tested with the contents of the jar. Instantly he uttered a cry of joy, and threw out his arms in a wild gesture which upset the pot and sent the liquid streaming across the floor to the very feet of the Englishman. The attendant drew a red handkerchief from his bosom, and, mopping up the mess, he followed it into the corner, where in a moment he found himself face to face with his observer.

"Excuse me," said John Vansittart Smith, with all imaginable politeness; "I have been unfortunate enough to fall asleep behind this door."

"And you have been watching me?" the other asked in English, with a most venomous look on his corpse-like face.

The student was a man of veracity. "I confess," said he, "that I have noticed your movements, and that they have aroused my curiosity and interest in the highest degree."

The man drew a long flamboyant-bladed knife from his bosom. "You have had a very narrow escape," he said; "had I seen you ten minutes ago, I should have driven this through your heart. As it is, if you touch me or interfere with me in any way you are a dead man."

"I have no wish to interfere with you," the student answered. "My presence here is entirely accidental. All I ask is that you will have the extreme kindness to show me out through some side door." He spoke with great suavity, for the man was still pressing the tip of his dagger against the palm of his left hand, as though to assure himself of its sharpness, while his face preserved its malignant expression.

"If I thought----" said he. "But no, perhaps it is as well. What is your name?"

The Englishman gave it.

"Vansittart Smith," the other repeated. "Are you the same Vansittart Smith who gave a paper in London upon El Kab? I saw a report of it. Your knowledge of the subject is contemptible."

"Sir!" cried the Egyptologist.

"Yet it is superior to that of many who make even greater pretensions. The whole keystone of our old life in Egypt was not the inscriptions or monuments of which you make so much, but was our hermetic philosophy and mystic knowledge, of which you say little or nothing."

"Our old life!" repeated the scholar, wide-eyed; and then suddenly, "Good God, look at the mummy's face!"

The strange man turned and flashed his light upon the dead woman, uttering a long doleful cry as he did so. The action of the air had already undone all the art of the embalmer. The skin had fallen away, the eyes had sunk inwards, the discoloured lips had writhed away from the yellow teeth, and the brown mark upon the forehead alone showed that it was indeed the same face which had shown such youth and beauty a few short minutes before.

The man flapped his hands together in grief and horror. Then mastering himself by a strong effort he turned his hard eyes once more upon the Englishman.

"It does not matter," he said, in a shaking voice. "It does not really matter. I came here to-night with the fixed determination to do something. It is now done. All else is as nothing. I have found my quest. The old curse is broken. I can rejoin her. What matter about her inanimate shell so long as her spirit is awaiting me at the other side of the veil!"

"These are wild words," said Vansittart Smith. He was becoming more and more convinced that he had to do with a madman.

"Time presses, and I must go," continued the other. "The moment is at hand for which I have waited this weary time. But I must show you out first. Come with me."

Taking up the lamp, he turned from the disordered chamber, and led the student swiftly through the long series of the Egyptian, Assyrian, and Persian apartments. At the end of the latter he pushed open a small door let into the wall and descended a winding stone stair. The Englishman felt the cold fresh air of the night upon his brow. There was a door opposite him which appeared to communicate with the street. To the right of this another door stood ajar, throwing a spurt of yellow light across the passage. "Come in here!" said the attendant shortly.

Vansittart Smith hesitated. He had hoped that he had come to the end of his adventure. Yet his curiosity was strong within him. He could not leave the matter unsolved, so he followed his strange companion into the lighted chamber.

It was a small room, such as is devoted to a concierge. A wood fire sparkled in the grate. At one side stood a truckle bed, and at the other a coarse wooden chair, with a round table in the centre, which bore the remains of a meal. As the visitor's eye glanced round he could not but remark with an ever-recurring thrill that all the small details of the room were of the most quaint design and antique workmanship. The candlesticks, the vases upon the chimney-piece, the fire-irons, the ornaments upon the walls, were all such as he had been wont to associate with the remote past. The gnarled heavy-eyed man sat himself down upon the edge of the bed, and motioned his guest into the chair.

"There may be design in this," he said, still speaking excellent English. "It may be decreed that I should leave some account behind as a warning to all rash mortals who would set their wits up against workings of Nature. I leave it with you. Make such use as you will of it. I speak to you now with my feet upon the threshold of the other world.

"I am, as you surmised, an Egyptian--not one of the down-trodden race of slaves who now inhabit the Delta of the Nile, but a survivor of that fiercer and harder people who tamed the Hebrew, drove the Ethiopian back into the southern deserts, and built those mighty works which have been the envy and the wonder of all after generations. It was in the reign of Tuthmosis, sixteen hundred years before the birth of Christ, that I first saw the light. You shrink away from me. Wait, and you will see that I am more to be pitied than to be feared.

"My name was Sosra. My father had been the chief priest of Osiris in the great temple of Abaris, which stood in those days upon the Bubastic branch of the Nile. I was brought up in the temple and was trained in all those mystic arts which are spoken of in your own Bible. I was an apt pupil. Before I was sixteen I had learned all which the wisest priest could teach me. From that time on I studied Nature's secrets for myself, and shared my knowledge with no man.

"Of all the questions which attracted me there were none over which I laboured so long as over those which concern themselves with the nature of life. I probed deeply into the vital principle. The aim of medicine had been to drive away disease when it appeared. It seemed to me that a method might be devised which should so fortify the body as to prevent weakness or death from ever taking hold of it. It is useless that I should recount my researches. You would scarce comprehend them if I did. They were carried out partly upon animals, partly upon slaves, and partly on myself. Suffice it that their result was to furnish me with a substance which, when injected into the blood, would endow the body with strength to resist the effects of time, of violence, or of disease. It would not indeed confer immortality, but its potency would endure for many thousands of years. I used it upon a cat, and afterwards drugged the creature with the most deadly poisons. That cat is alive in Lower Egypt at the present moment. There was nothing of mystery or magic in the matter. It was simply a chemical discovery, which may well be made again.

"Love of life runs high in the young. It seemed to me that I had broken away from all human care now that I had abolished pain and driven death to such a distance. With a light heart I poured the accursed stuff into my veins. Then I looked round for some one whom I could benefit. There was a young priest of Thoth, Parmes by name, who had won my goodwill by his earnest nature and his devotion to his studies. To him I whispered my secret, and at his request I injected him with my elixir. I should now, I reflected, never be without a companion of the same age as myself.

"After this grand discovery I relaxed my studies to some extent, but Parmes continued his with redoubled energy. Every day I could see him working with his flasks and his distiller in the Temple of Thoth, but he said little to me as to the result of his labours. For my own part, I used to walk through the city and look around me with exultation as I reflected that all this was destined to pass away, and that only I should remain. The people would bow to me as they passed me, for the fame of my knowledge had gone abroad.

"There was war at this time, and the Great King had sent down his soldiers to the eastern boundary to drive away the Hyksos. A Governor, too, was sent to Abaris, that he might hold it for the King. I had heard much of the beauty of the daughter of this Governor, but one day as I walked out with Parmes we met her, borne upon the shoulders of her slaves. I was struck with love as with lightning. My heart went out from me. I could have thrown myself beneath the feet of her bearers. This was my woman. Life without her was impossible. I swore by the head of Horus that she should be mine. I swore it to the Priest of Thoth. He turned away from me with a brow which was as black as midnight.

"There is no need to tell you of our wooing. She came to love me even as I loved her. I learned that Parmes had seen her before I did, and had shown her that he too loved her, but I could smile at his passion, for I knew that her heart was mine. The white plague had come upon the city and many were stricken, but I laid my hands upon the sick and nursed them without fear or scathe. She marvelled at my daring. Then I told her my secret, and begged her that she would let me use my art upon her.

"`Your flower shall then be unwithered, Atma,' I said. `Other things may pass away, but you and I, and our great love for each other, shall outlive the tomb of King Chefru.'

"But she was full of timid, maidenly objections. `Was it right?' she asked, `was it not a thwarting of the will of the gods? If the great Osiris had wished that our years should be so long, would he not himself have brought it about?'

"With fond and loving words I overcame her doubts, and yet she hesitated. It was a great question, she said. She would think it over for this one night. In the morning I should know her resolution. Surely one night was not too much to ask. She wished to pray to Isis for help in her decision.

"With a sinking heart and a sad foreboding of evil I left her with her tirewomen. In the morning, when the early sacrifice was over, I hurried to her house. A frightened slave met me upon the steps. Her mistress was ill, she said, very ill. In a frenzy I broke my way through the attendants, and rushed through hall and corridor to my Atma's chamber. She lay upon her couch, her head high upon the pillow, with a pallid face and a glazed eye. On her forehead there blazed a single angry purple patch. I knew that hell-mark of old. It was the scar of the white plague, the sign- manual of death.

"Why should I speak of that terrible time? For months I was mad, fevered, delirious, and yet I could not die. Never did an Arab thirst after the sweet wells as I longed after death. Could poison or steel have shortened the thread of my existence, I should soon have rejoined my love in the land with the narrow portal. I tried, but it was of no avail. The accursed influence was too strong upon me. One night as I lay upon my couch, weak and weary, Parmes, the priest of Thoth, came to my chamber. He stood in the circle of the lamplight, and he looked down upon me with eyes which were bright with a mad joy.

"`Why did you let the maiden die?' he asked; `why did you not strengthen her as you strengthened me?'

"`I was too late,' I answered. `But I had forgot. You also loved her. You are my fellow in misfortune. Is it not terrible to think of the centuries which must pass ere we look upon her again? Fools, fools, that we were to take death to be our enemy!'

"`You may say that,' he cried with a wild laugh; `the words come well from your lips. For me they have no meaning.'

"`What mean you?' I cried, raising myself upon my elbow. `Surely, friend, this grief has turned your brain.' His face was aflame with joy, and he writhed and shook like one who hath a devil.

"`Do you know whither I go?' he asked.

"`Nay,' I answered, `I cannot tell.'

"`I go to her,' said he. `She lies embalmed in the further tomb by the double palm-tree beyond the city wall.'

"`Why do you go there?' I asked.

"`To die!' he shrieked, `to die! I am not bound by earthen fetters.'

"`But the elixir is in your blood,' I cried.

"`I can defy it,' said he; `I have found a stronger principle which will destroy it. It is working in my veins at this moment, and in an hour I shall be a dead man. I shall join her, and you shall remain behind.'

"As I looked upon him I could see that he spoke words of truth. The light in his eye told me that he was indeed beyond the power of the elixir.

"`You will teach me!' I cried.

"`Never!' he answered.

"`I implore you, by the wisdom of Thoth, by the majesty of Anubis!'

"`It is useless,' he said coldly.

"`Then I will find it out,' I cried.

"`You cannot,' he answered; `it came to me by chance. There is one ingredient which you can never get. Save that which is in the ring of Thoth, none will ever more be made.

"`In the ring of Thoth!' I repeated; `where then is the ring of Thoth?'

"`That also you shall never know,' he answered. `You won her love.

Who has won in the end? I leave you to your sordid earth life. My chains are broken. I must go!' He turned upon his heel and fled from the chamber. In the morning came the news that the Priest of Thoth was dead.

"My days after that were spent in study. I must find this subtle poison which was strong enough to undo the elixir. From early dawn to midnight I bent over the test-tube and the furnace. Above all, I collected the papyri and the chemical flasks of the Priest of Thoth. Alas! they taught me little. Here and there some hint or stray expression would raise hope in my bosom, but no good ever came of it. Still, month after month, I struggled on. When my heart grew faint I would make my way to the tomb by the palm-trees.

There, standing by the dead casket from which the jewel had been rifled, I would feel her sweet presence, and would whisper to her that I would rejoin her if mortal wit could solve the riddle.

"Parmes had said that his discovery was connected with the ring of Thoth. I had some remembrance of the trinket. It was a large and weighty circlet, made, not of gold, but of a rarer and heavier metal brought from the mines of Mount Harbal. Platinum, you call it. The ring had, I remembered, a hollow crystal set in it, in which some few drops of liquid might be stored. Now, the secret of Parmes could not have to do with the metal alone, for there were many rings of that metal in the Temple. Was it not more likely that he had stored his precious poison within the cavity of the crystal? I had scarce come to this conclusion before, in hunting through his papers, I came upon one which told me that it was indeed so, and that there was still some of the liquid unused.

"But how to find the ring? It was not upon him when he was stripped for the embalmer. Of that I made sure. Neither was it among his private effects. In vain I searched every room that he had entered, every box, and vase, and chattel that he had owned. I sifted the very sand of the desert in the places where he had been wont to walk; but, do what I would, I could come upon no traces of the ring of Thoth. Yet it may be that my labours would have overcome all obstacles had it not been for a new and unlooked- for misfortune.

"A great war had been waged against the Hyksos, and the Captains of the Great King had been cut off in the desert, with all their bowmen and horsemen. The shepherd tribes were upon us like the locusts in a dry year. From the wilderness of Shur to the great bitter lake there was blood by day and fire by night. Abaris was the bulwark of Egypt, but we could not keep the savages back. The city fell. The Governor and the soldiers were put to the sword, and I, with many more, was led away into captivity.

"For years and years I tended cattle in the great plains by the Euphrates. My master died, and his son grew old, but I was still as far from death as ever. At last I escaped upon a swift camel, and made my way back to Egypt. The Hyksos had settled in the land which they had conquered, and their own King ruled over the country Abaris had been torn down, the city had been burned, and of the great Temple there was nothing left save an unsightly mound. Everywhere the tombs had been rifled and the monuments destroyed. Of my Atma's grave no sign was left. It was buried in the sands of the desert, and the palm-trees which marked the spot had long disappeared. The papers of Parmes and the remains of the Temple of Thoth were either destroyed or scattered far and wide over the deserts of Syria. All search after them was vain.

"From that time I gave up all hope of ever finding the ring or discovering the subtle drug. I set myself to live as patiently as might be until the effect of the elixir should wear away. How can you understand how terrible a thing time is, you who have experience only of the narrow course which lies between the cradle and the grave! I know it to my cost, I who have floated down the whole stream of history. I was old when Ilium fell. I was very old when Herodotus came to Memphis. I was bowed down with years when the new gospel came upon earth. Yet you see me much as other men are, with the cursed elixir still sweetening my blood, and guarding me against that which I would court. Now at last, at last I have come to the end of it!

"I have travelled in all lands and I have dwelt with all nations. Every tongue is the same to me. I learned them all to help pass the weary time. I need not tell you how slowly they drifted by, the long dawn of modern civilisation, the dreary middle years, the dark times of barbarism. They are all behind me now, I have never looked with the eyes of love upon another woman. Atma knows that I have been constant to her.

"It was my custom to read all that the scholars had to say upon Ancient Egypt. I have been in many positions, sometimes affluent, sometimes poor, but I have always found enough to enable me to buy the journals which deal with such matters. Some nine months ago I was in San Francisco, when I read an account of some discoveries made in the neighbourhood of Abaris. My heart leapt into my mouth as I read it. It said that the excavator had busied himself in exploring some tombs recently unearthed. In one there had been found an unopened mummy with an inscription upon the outer case setting forth that it contained the body of the daughter of the Governor of the city in the days of Tuthmosis. It added that on removing the outer case there had been exposed a large platinum ring set with a crystal, which had been laid upon the breast of the embalmed woman. This, then was where Parmes had hid the ring of Thoth. He might well say that it was safe, for no Egyptian would ever stain his soul by moving even the outer case of a buried friend.

"That very night I set off from San Francisco, and in a few weeks I found myself once more at Abaris, if a few sand-heaps and crumbling walls may retain the name of the great city. I hurried to the Frenchmen who were digging there and asked them for the ring. They replied that both the ring and the mummy had been sent to the Boulak Museum at Cairo. To Boulak I went, but only to be told that Mariette Bey had claimed them and had shipped them to the Louvre. I followed them, and there at last, in the Egyptian chamber, I came, after close upon four thousand years, upon the remains of my Atma, and upon the ring for which I had sought so long.

"But how was I to lay hands upon them? How was I to have them for my very own? It chanced that the office of attendant was vacant. I went to the Director. I convinced him that I knew much about Egypt. In my eagerness I said too much. He remarked that a Professor's chair would suit me better than a seat in the Conciergerie. I knew more, he said, than he did. It was only by blundering, and letting him think that he had over-estimated my knowledge, that I prevailed upon him to let me move the few effects which I have retained into this chamber. It is my first and my last night here.

"Such is my story, Mr. Vansittart Smith. I need not say more to a man of your perception. By a strange chance you have this night looked upon the face of the woman whom I loved in those far- off days. There were many rings with crystals in the case, and I had to test for the platinum to be sure of the one which I wanted. A glance at the crystal has shown me that the liquid is indeed within it, and that I shall at last be able to shake off that accursed health which has been worse to me than the foulest disease. I have nothing more to say to you. I have unburdened myself. You may tell my story or you may withhold it at your pleasure. The choice rests with you. I owe you some amends, for you have had a narrow escape of your life this night. I was a desperate man, and not to be baulked in my purpose. Had I seen you before the thing was done, I might have put it beyond your power to oppose me or to raise an alarm. This is the door. It leads into the Rue de Rivoli. Good night!"

The Englishman glanced back. For a moment the lean figure of Sosra the Egyptian stood framed in the narrow doorway. The next the door had slammed, and the heavy rasping of a bolt broke on the silent night.

It was on the second day after his return to London that Mr. John Vansittart Smith saw the following concise narrative in the Paris correspondence of the Times:--

"Curious Occurrence in the Louvre.--Yesterday morning a strange discovery was made in the principal Egyptian Chamber. The ouvriers who are employed to clean out the rooms in the morning found one of the attendants lying dead upon the floor with his arms round one of the mummies. So close was his embrace that it was only with the utmost difficulty that they were separated. One of the cases containing valuable rings had been opened and rifled. The authorities are of opinion that the man was bearing away the mummy with some idea of selling it to a private collector, but that he was struck down in the very act by long-standing disease of the heart. It is said that he was a man of uncertain age and eccentric habits, without any living relations to mourn over his dramatic and untimely end."

THOSE who have watched Karl Freund's 1932 masterpiece of horror, *The Mummy*, will immediately note the debt owed to this story. Karloff's chilling portrayal of Imhotep as a tragic villain draws both from Sosra and from the hellish zombie in "Lot No. 249," but the greater portion of the supernatural classic resembles the plot of the former tale: from the hopeless pining of the immortal Egyptian mystic, to his overqualified status as a humble donor to a European museum, to his grotesquely dry and wrinkled face pierced by two chilling eyes. Further boosted with the overt horror of "Lot No. 249," *The Mummy* unquestionably affords Doyle a place in the great canon of classic monster-makers alongside Stoker, Stevenson, and Shelley: what they are to stories of vampires, werewolves, and monsters, respectively, Doyle is to the supernatural mummy. The tale takes off where popular culture had left it: it is romantic, sentimental, and imbued with elements of science fiction and social perspective (much like Poe's mummy, this one dismisses the "advances" of modernity and serves as an authority on comparative culture and history), but Doyle progresses the trope from that of a plot element to a fully formed protagonist, investing Sosra with the same devastating pathos of Shelley's creature, the arresting nobility of Stoker's Dracula, and the troubling philosophy of Stevenson's Jekyll and Hyde. It is no wonder that Hollywood finally pounced on Doyle's Egyptological stories and fused his two great mummy tales into one of the most enduring supernatural beings in cinematic history.

EDWARDIAN writers of speculative fiction found a pet topic in reincarnation. Whether through traditional linear rebirth, possession, or visions of the past, the concept of a long dead personality taking hold of the present and voicing his passions was a recurring theme of the age. It haunted the oeuvre of almost every notable member of that class: Oliver Onions ("Io," "The Rosewood Door," "Phantas," "The Painted Face," and many others), M. R. James ("The Rose Garden," "The Ash Tree"), E. F. Benson ("Between the Lights," "The Temple," "The Outcast," and many others), H. P. Lovecraft ("The Tomb," Charles Dexter Ward, "Rats in the Wall," and many others), Algernon Blackwood ("The Insanity of Jones," "Ancient Sorceries," The Wave, and many others) to mention a few notables. The genre addressed several universal anxieties which were particular to that period – a feeling of disconnection with their fading Victorian past and its outdated values, a loss of moral idealism, the progress of science and the subsequent relativism of morality, the romanticizing of primal cultures, and the simultaneous tiresomeness of what seemed to be a dull, overly-simplified, unchallenging modern society. In the 2010s and 2020s we find ourselves at a similar crossroads, and historical dramas have been tremendously popular as a result, especially those with a romantic bent which focus on the brutal sexuality of "simpler times." The ravenous appetites of the Tudors, the Borgias, the Jacobite Highlanders, the Spartans, the Romans, and even – ironically – the Victorians have consumed our imagination and given an odd comfort to our seemingly undersexed, overworked spirits. Somehow it seems that it would be grand to be a wife of Henry VIII, a slave to a Roman libertine, or a prostitute in a Whitechapel brothel. These are ludicrous fantasies, of course, but to Doyle's Mr. and Mrs. Brown there is no fantasy in the centuries' old trauma they are about to relive.

Through the Veil

{1910}

HE was a great shock-headed, freckle-faced Borderer, the lineal descendant of a cattle-thieving clan in Liddesdale. In spite of his ancestry he was as solid and sober a citizen as one would wish to see, a town councillor of Melrose, an elder of the Church, and the chairman of the local branch of the Young Men's Christian Association. Brown was his name—and you saw it printed up as "Brown and Handiside" over the great grocery stores in the High Street. His wife, Maggie Brown, was an Armstrong before her marriage, and came from an old farming stock in the wilds of Teviothead. She was small, swarthy, and dark-eyed, with a strangely nervous temperament for a Scotch woman. No greater contrast could be found than the big tawny man and the dark little woman; but both were of the soil as far back as any memory could extend.

One day—it was the first anniversary of their wedding—they had driven over together to see the excavations of the Roman Fort at Newstead. It was not a particularly picturesque spot. From the northern bank of the Tweed, just where the river forms a loop, there extends a gentle slope of arable land. Across it run the trenches of the excavators, with here and there an exposure of old stonework to show the foundations of the ancient walls. It had been a huge place, for the camp was fifty acres in extent, and the fort fifteen. However, it was all made easy for them since Mr. Brown knew the farmer to whom the land belonged. Under his guidance they spent a long summer evening inspecting the trenches, the pits, the ramparts, and all the strange variety of objects which were waiting to be transported to the Edinburgh Museum of Antiquities. The buckle of a woman's belt had been dug up that very day, and the farmer was discoursing upon it when his eyes fell upon Mrs. Brown's face.

"Your good leddy's tired," said he. "Maybe you'd best rest a wee before we gang further."

Brown looked at his wife. She was certainly very pale, and her dark eyes were bright and wild.

"What is it, Maggie? I've wearied you. I'm thinkin' it's time we went back."

"No, no, John, let us go on. It's wonderful! It's like a dreamland place. It all seems so close and so near to me. How long were the Romans here, Mr. Cunningham?"

"A fair time, mam. If you saw the kitchen midden-pits you would guess it took a long time to fill them."

"And why did they leave?"

"Well, mam, by all accounts they left because they had to. The folk round could thole them no longer, so they just up and burned the fort aboot their lugs. You can see the fire marks on the stanes."

The woman gave a quick little shudder. "A wild night—a fearsome night," said she. "The sky must have been red that night—and these grey stones, they may have been red also."

"Aye, I think they were red," said her husband. "It's a queer thing, Maggie, and it may be your words that have done it; but I seem to see that business aboot as clear as ever I saw anything in my life. The light shone on the water."

"Aye, the light shone on the water. And the smoke gripped you by the throat. And all the savages were yelling."

The old farmer began to laugh. "The leddy will be writin' a story aboot the old fort," said he. "I've shown many a one over it, but I never heard it put so clear afore. Some folk have the gift."

They had strolled along the edge of the foss, and a pit yawned upon the right of them.

"That pit was fourteen foot deep," said the farmer. "What d'ye think we dug oot from the bottom o't? Weel, it was just the skeleton of a man wi' a spear by his side. I'm thinkin' he was grippin' it when he died. Now, how cam' a man wi' a spear doon a hole fourteen foot deep? He wasna' buried there, for they aye burned their dead. What make ye o' that, mam?"

"He sprang doon to get clear of the savages," said the woman.

"Weel, it's likely enough, and a' the professors from Edinburgh couldna gie a better reason. I wish you were aye here, mam, to answer a' oor difficulties sae readily. Now, here's the altar that we foond last week. There's an inscreeption. They tell me it's Latin, and it means that the men o' this fort give thanks to God for their safety."

They examined the old worn stone. There was a large deeply-cut "VV" upon the top of it. "What does 'VV' stand for?" asked Brown.

"Naebody kens," the guide answered.

"Valeria Victrix," said the lady softly. Her face was paler than ever, her eyes far away, as one who peers down the dim aisles of overarching centuries.

"What's that?" asked her husband sharply.

She started as one who wakes from sleep. "What were we talking about?" she asked.

"About this 'VV' upon the stone."

"No doubt it was just the name of the Legion which put the altar up."

"Aye, but you gave some special name."

"Did I? How absurd! How should I ken what the name was?"

"You said something—'Victrix,' I think."

"I suppose I was guessing. It gives me the queerest feeling, this place, as if I were not myself, but someone else."

"Aye, it's an uncanny place," said her husband, looking round with an expression almost of fear in his bold grey eyes. "I feel it mysel'. I think we'll just be wishin' you good evenin', Mr. Cunningham, and get back to Melrose before the dark sets in."

Neither of them could shake off the strange impression which had been left upon them by their visit to the excavations. It was as if some miasma had risen from those damp trenches and passed into their blood. All the evening they were silent and thoughtful, but such remarks as they did make showed that the same subject was in the minds of each. Brown had a restless night, in which he dreamed a strange connected dream, so vivid that he woke sweating and shivering like a frightened horse. He tried to convey it all to his wife as they sat together at breakfast in the morning.

"It was the clearest thing, Maggie," said he. "Nothing that has ever come to me in my waking life has been more clear than that. I feel as if these hands were sticky with blood."

"Tell me of it—tell me slow," said she.

"When it began, I was oot on a braeside. I was laying flat on the ground. It was rough, and there were clumps of heather. All round me was just darkness, but I could hear the rustle and the breathin' of men. There seemed a great multitude on every side of me, but I could see no one. There was a low chink of steel sometimes, and then a number of voices would whisper 'Hush!' I had a ragged club in my hand, and it had spikes o' iron near the end of it. My heart was beatin' quickly, and I felt that a moment of great danger and excitement was at hand. Once I dropped my club, and again from all round me the voices in the darkness cried, 'Hush!' I put oot my hand, and it touched the foot of another man lying in front of me. There was some one at my very elbow on either side. But they said nothin'.

"Then we all began to move. The whole braeside seemed to be crawlin' downwards. There was a river at the bottom and a high-arched wooden bridge. Beyond the bridge were many lights—torches on a wall. The creepin' men all flowed towards the bridge. There had been no sound of any kind, just a velvet stillness. And then there was a cry in the darkness, the cry of a man who has been stabbed suddenly to the hairt. That one cry swelled out for a moment, and then the roar of a thoosand furious voices. I was runnin'. Every one was runnin'. A bright red light shone out, and the river was a scarlet streak. I could see my companions now. They were more like devils than men, wild figures clad in skins, with their hair and beards streamin'. They were all mad with rage, jumpin' as they ran, their mouths open, their arms wavin', the red light beatin' on their faces. I ran, too, and yelled out curses like the rest. Then I heard a great cracklin' of wood, and I knew that the palisades were doon. There was a loud whistlin' in my ears, and I was aware that arrows were flyin' past me. I got to the bottom of a dyke, and I saw a hand stretched doon from above. I took it, and was dragged to the top. We looked doon, and there were silver men beneath us holdin' up their spears. Some of our folk sprang on to the spears. Then we others followed, and we killed the soldiers before they could draw the spears oot again. They shouted loud in some foreign tongue, but no mercy was shown them. We went ower them like a wave, and trampled them doon into the mud, for they were few, and there was no end to our numbers.

"I found myself among buildings, and one of them was on fire. I saw the flames spoutin' through the roof. I ran on, and then I was alone among the buildings. Some one ran across in front o' me. It was a woman. I caught her by the arm, and I took her chin and turned her face so as the light of the fire would strike it. Whom think you that it was, Maggie?"

His wife moistened her dry lips. "It was I," she said.

He looked at her in surprise. "That's a good guess," said he. "Yes, it was just you. Not merely like you, you understand. It was you—you yourself. I saw the same soul in your frightened eyes. You looked white and bonny and wonderful in the firelight. I had just one thought in my head —to get you awa' with me; to keep you all to mysel' in my own home somewhere beyond

the hills. You clawed at my face with your nails. I heaved you over my shoulder, and I tried to find a way oot of the light of the burning hoose and back into the darkness.

"Then came the thing that I mind best of all. You're ill, Maggie. Shall I stop? My God! You nave the very look on your face that you had last night in my dream. You screamed. He came runnin' in the firelight. His head was bare; his hair was black and curled; he had a naked sword in his hand, short and broad, little more than a dagger. He stabbed at me, but he tripped and fell. I held you with one hand, and with the other—"

His wife had sprung to her feet with writhing features.

"Marcus!" she cried. "My beautiful Marcus! Oh, you brute! you brute! you brute!" There was a clatter of tea-cups as she fell forward senseless upon the table.

They never talk about that strange isolated incident in their married life. For an instant the curtain of the past had swung aside, and some strange glimpse of a forgotten life had come to them. But it closed down, never to open again. They live their narrow round—he in his shop, she in her household—and yet new and wider horizons have vaguely formed themselves around them since that summer evening by the crumbling Roman fort.

E. F. Benson, Algernon Blackwood, Oliver Onions, H. P. Lovecraft, and many other writers who flourished during the Edwardian Era (1901 – 1918) dabbled liberally in reincarnation literature. Blackwood genuinely believed in the philosophy, claiming to be the reborn spirit of a Native American medicine man. The concept spoke comfort to a dark and vulnerable part of the souls of those who had lived through the vainglorious years of the Victorian empire and had watched the self-assuredness of their grandfathers melt into squishy relativism. Perhaps simply being British *wasn't* the end all be all. Perhaps the 19th century *wasn't* the grandest era in history. Perhaps sexual self-control and self-discipline *weren't* the only means of becoming a great person. The Decadence Movement had been squelched during the fallout of the Oscar Wilde trial, but it was a pyrrhic victory for puritanical Victorians, and an era of self-indulgence, romanticism, and libertinism followed, questioning everything from Christian theology to gender roles and the heretofore unquestioned status of Anglo-Saxon supremacy. Doyle rejects the trend of so many of the Edwardian reincarnation writers, who typically imagined their characters (mostly bourgeois-yet-strangely-noble members of the British middle and working classes) as being the reborn souls of passionate lovers, brave warriors, exalted royals, and the like. In his version of the trope, a polite, Christian couple are revealed to be the reincarnations of a barbaric rapist and the Roman victim whose husband he slew. More grim than grand, his story speaks to a truth that the Victorians knew well but refrained from voicing: within us all there lurk ancient evils and unspoken appetites for sin. However artless and melodramatic his tale is, it remains an astute parable for the dark corners that exist in every human soul – regardless of how prim, dull, and put together they may seem on the outside.

ARTHUR Conan Doyle's obsession with spiritualism didn't reach its full fervor until after World War One. He lost his first wife in 1906 to tuberculosis, and both his son and brother died in the 1918 Spanish flu pandemic, drowning him in a tremendous depression. But his interest in the supernatural predated these deaths which would ultimately lead him to convert to Spiritualism – as does this "mediumistic" tale. Before these tragedies, Doyle had been a member of the Society for Psychical Research – a renowned paranormal club whose members included Carl Jung, Sigmund Freud, W.B. Yates, and the great ghost story writer Algernon Blackwood. The SPR typically investigated reported hauntings, ghost photographs, medium claims, and other purportedly supernatural events. Séances were the bread and butter of these investigations and were consequentially some of the most infamous episodes of exposed fakery. Disembodied raps, ghostly voices, levitating tables, and phantom hands were consistently proven to be the result of elaborate chicanery, sleight of hand work, hypnotism, and ventriloquism. The following story may be seen as wish fulfilment in part, but also as a self-addressed warning: as much as he might desire to see the spirit world accessed and proven, Doyle understood that such a break-through could be more of a curse than a blessing. Despite all his passionate research into the afterlife, Doyle surely wondered from time to time if his investigations were little more than playing with fire.

Playing with Fire
{1900}

I cannot pretend to say what occurred on the 14th of April last at No. 17, Badderly Gardens. Put down in black and white, my surmise might seem too crude, too grotesque, for serious consideration. And yet that something did occur, and that it was of a nature which will leave its mark upon every one of us for the rest of our lives, is as certain as the unanimous testimony of five witnesses can make it. I will not enter into any argument or speculation. I will only give a plain statement, which will be submitted to John Moir, Harvey Deacon, and Mrs. Delamere, and withheld from publication unless they are prepared to corroborate every detail. I cannot obtain the sanction of Paul Le Duc, for he appears to have left the country.

It was John Moir (the well-known senior partner of Moir, Moir, and Sanderson) who had originally turned our attention to occult subjects. He had, like many very hard and practical men of business, a mystic side to his nature, which had led him to the examination, and eventually to the acceptance, of those elusive phenomena which are grouped together with much that is foolish, and much that is fraudulent, under the common heading of spiritualism. His researches, which had begun with an open mind, ended unhappily in dogma, and he became as positive and fanatical as any other bigot. He represented in our little group the body of men who have turned these singular phenomena into a new religion.

Mrs. Delamere, our medium, was his sister, the wife of Delamere, the rising sculptor. Our experience had shown us that to work on these subjects without a medium was as futile as for an astronomer to make observations without a telescope. On the other hand, the introduction of a paid medium was hateful to all of us. Was it not obvious that he or she would feel bound to return some result for money received, and that the temptation to fraud would be an overpowering one? No phenomena could be relied upon which were produced at a guinea an hour. But, fortunately, Moir had discovered that his sister was mediumistic--in other words, that she was a battery of that animal magnetic force which is the only form of energy which is subtle enough to be acted upon from the spiritual plane as well as from our own material one. Of course, when I say this, I do not mean to beg the question; but I am simply indicating the theories upon which we were ourselves, rightly or wrongly, explaining what we saw. The lady came, not altogether with the approval of her husband, and though she never gave indications of any very great psychic force, we were able, at least, to obtain those usual phenomena of message-tilting which are at the same time so puerile and so inexplicable. Every Sunday evening we met in Harvey Deacon's studio at Badderly Gardens, the next house to the corner of Merton Park Road.

Harvey Deacon's imaginative work in art would prepare any one to find that he was an ardent lover of everything which was *outre* and sensational. A certain picturesqueness in the study of the occult had been the quality which had originally attracted him to it, but his attention was speedily arrested by some of those phenomena to which I have referred, and he was coming rapidly to the conclusion that what he had looked upon as an amusing romance and an after-dinner entertainment was really a very formidable reality. He is a man with a remarkably clear and logical brain--a true descendant of his ancestor, the well-known Scotch professor--and he represented in our small circle the critical element, the man who has no prejudices, is prepared to follow facts as far as he can see them, and refuses to theorise in advance of his data. His caution annoyed Moir as much as the latter's robust faith amused Deacon, but each in his own way was equally keen upon the matter.

And I? What am I to say that I represented? I was not the devotee. I was not the scientific critic. Perhaps the best that I can claim for myself is that I was the dilettante man about town, anxious to be in the swim of every fresh movement, thankful for any new sensation which would take me out of myself and open up fresh possibilities of existence. I am not an enthusiast myself, but I like the company of those who are. Moir's talk, which made me feel as if we had a private pass-key through the door of death, filled me with a vague contentment. The soothing atmosphere of the seance with the darkened lights was delightful to me. In a word, the thing amused me, and so I was there.

It was, as I have said, upon the 14th of April last that the very singular event which I am about to put upon record took place. I was the first of the men to arrive at the studio, but Mrs. Delamere was already there, having had afternoon tea with Mrs. Harvey Deacon. The two ladies and Deacon himself were standing in front of an unfinished picture of his upon the easel. I am not an expert in art, and I have never professed to understand what Harvey Deacon meant by his pictures; but I could see in this instance that it was all very clever and imaginative, fairies and animals and allegorical figures of all sorts. The ladies were loud in their praises, and indeed the colour effect was a remarkable one.

"What do you think of it, Markham?" he asked.

"Well, it's above me," said I. "These beasts--what are they?"

"Mythical monsters, imaginary creatures, heraldic emblems--a sort of weird, bizarre procession of them."

"With a white horse in front!"

"It's not a horse," said he, rather testily--which was surprising, for he was a very good-humoured fellow as a rule, and hardly ever took himself seriously.

"What is it, then?"

"Can't you see the horn in front? It's a unicorn. I told you they were heraldic beasts. Can't you recognise one?"

"Very sorry, Deacon," said I, for he really seemed to be annoyed.

He laughed at his own irritation.

"Excuse me, Markham!" said he; "the fact is that I have had an awful job over the beast. All day I have been painting him in and painting him out, and trying to imagine what a real live, ramping unicorn would look like. At last I got him, as I hoped; so when you failed to recognise it, it took me on the raw."

"Why, of course it's a unicorn," said I, for he was evidently depressed at my obtuseness. "I can see the horn quite plainly, but I never saw a unicorn except beside the Royal Arms, and so I never thought of the creature. And these others are griffins and cockatrices, and dragons of sorts?"

"Yes, I had no difficulty with them. It was the unicorn which bothered me. However, there's an end of it until to-morrow." He turned the picture round upon the easel, and we all chatted about other subjects.

Moir was late that evening, and when he did arrive he brought with him, rather to our surprise, a small, stout Frenchman, whom he introduced as Monsieur Paul Le Duc. I say to our surprise, for we held a theory that any intrusion into our spiritual circle deranged the conditions, and introduced an element of suspicion. We knew that we could trust each other, but all our results were vitiated by the presence of an outsider. However, Moir soon reconciled us to the innovation. Monsieur Paul Le Duc was a famous student of occultism, a seer, a medium, and a mystic. He was travelling in England with a letter of introduction to Moir from the President of the Parisian brothers of the Rosy Cross. What more natural than that he should bring him to our little seance, or that we should feel honoured by his presence?

He was, as I have said, a small, stout man, undistinguished in appearance, with a broad, smooth, clean-shaven face, remarkable only for a pair of large, brown, velvety eyes, staring vaguely out in front of him. He was well dressed, with the manners of a gentleman, and his curious little turns of English speech set the ladies smiling. Mrs. Deacon had a prejudice against our researches and left the room, upon which we lowered the lights, as was our custom, and drew up our chairs to the square mahogany table which stood in the centre of the studio. The light was subdued, but sufficient to allow us to see each other quite plainly. I remember that I could even observe the curious, podgy little square-topped hands which the Frenchman laid upon the table.

"What a fun!" said he. "It is many years since I have sat in this fashion, and it is to me amusing. Madame is medium. Does madame make the trance?"

"Well, hardly that," said Mrs. Delamere. "But I am always conscious of extreme sleepiness."

"It is the first stage. Then you encourage it, and there comes the trance. When the trance comes, then out jumps your little spirit and in jumps another little spirit, and so you have direct talking or writing. You leave your machine to be worked by another. *Hein?* But what have unicorns to do with it?"

Harvey Deacon started in his chair. The Frenchman was moving his head slowly round and staring into the shadows which draped the walls.

"What a fun!" said he. "Always unicorns. Who has been thinking so hard upon a subject so bizarre?"

"This is wonderful!" cried Deacon. "I have been trying to paint one all day. But how could you know it?"

"You have been thinking of them in this room."

"Certainly."

"But thoughts are things, my friend. When you imagine a thing you make a thing. You did not know it, *hein*? But I can see your unicorns because it is not only with my eye that I can see."

"Do you mean to say that I create a thing which has never existed by merely thinking of it?"

"But certainly. It is the fact which lies under all other facts. That is why an evil thought is also a danger."

"They are, I suppose, upon the astral plane?" said Moir.

"Ah, well, these are but words, my friends. They are there--somewhere--everywhere--I cannot tell myself. I see them. I could touch them."

"You could not make *us* see them."

"It is to materialise them. Hold! It is an experiment. But the power is wanting. Let us see what power we have, and then arrange what we shall do. May I place you as I wish?"

"You evidently know a great deal more about it than we do," said Harvey Deacon; "I wish that you would take complete control."

"It may be that the conditions are not good. But we will try what we can do. Madame will sit where she is, I next, and this gentleman beside me. Meester Moir will sit next to madame, because it is well to have blacks and blondes in turn. So! And now with your permission I will turn the lights all out."

"What is the advantage of the dark?" I asked.

"Because the force with which we deal is a vibration of ether and so also is light. We have the wires all for ourselves now--*hein*? You will not be frightened in the darkness, madame? What a fun is such a seance!"

At first the darkness appeared to be absolutely pitchy, but in a few minutes our eyes became so far accustomed to it that we could just make out each other's presence--very dimly and vaguely, it is true. I could see nothing else in the room--only the black loom of the motionless figures. We were all taking the matter much more seriously than we had ever done before.

"You will place your hands in front. It is hopeless that we touch, since we are so few round so large a table. You will compose yourself, madame, and if sleep should come to you you will not fight against it. And now we sit in silence and we expect--*hein*?"

So we sat in silence and expected, staring out into the blackness in front of us. A clock ticked in the passage. A dog barked intermittently far away. Once or twice a cab rattled past in the street, and the gleam of its lamps through the chink in the curtains was a cheerful break in that gloomy vigil. I felt those physical symptoms with which previous seances had made me familiar--the coldness of the feet, the tingling in the hands, the glow of the palms, the feeling of a cold wind upon the back. Strange little shooting pains came in my forearms, especially as it seemed to me in my left one, which was nearest to our visitor--due no doubt to disturbance of the vascular system, but worthy of some attention all the same. At the same time I was conscious of a strained feeling of expectancy which was almost painful. From the rigid, absolute silence of my companions I gathered that their nerves were as tense as my own.

And then suddenly a sound came out of the darkness--a low, sibilant sound, the quick, thin breathing of a woman. Quicker and thinner yet it came, as between clenched teeth, to end in a loud gasp with a dull rustle of cloth.

"What's that? Is all right?" some one asked in the darkness.

"Yes, all is right," said the Frenchman. "It is madame. She is in her trance. Now, gentlemen, if you will wait quiet you will see something, I think, which will interest you much."

Still the ticking in the hall. Still the breathing, deeper and fuller now, from the medium. Still the occasional flash, more welcome than ever, of the passing lights of the hansoms. What a gap we were bridging, the half-raised veil of the eternal on the one side and the cabs of London on the other. The table was throbbing with a mighty pulse. It swayed steadily, rhythmically, with an easy swooping, scooping motion under our fingers. Sharp little raps and cracks came from its substance, file-firing, volley-firing, the sounds of a fagot burning briskly on a frosty night.

"There is much power," said the Frenchman. "See it on the table!"

I had thought it was some delusion of my own, but all could see it now. There was a greenish-yellow phosphorescent light--or I should say a luminous vapour rather than a light--which lay over the surface of the table. It rolled and wreathed and undulated in dim glimmering folds, turning and swirling like clouds of smoke. I could see the white, square-ended hands of the French medium in this baleful light.

"What a fun!" he cried. "It is splendid!"

"Shall we call the alphabet?" asked Moir.

"But no--for we can do much better," said our visitor. "It is but a clumsy thing to tilt the table for every letter of the alphabet, and with such a medium as madame we should do better than that."

"Yes, you will do better," said a voice.

"Who was that? Who spoke? Was that you, Markham?"

"No, I did not speak."

"It was madame who spoke."

"But it was not her voice."

"Is that you, Mrs. Delamere?"

"It is not the medium, but it is the power which uses the organs of the medium," said the strange, deep voice.

"Where is Mrs. Delamere? It will not hurt her, I trust."

"The medium is happy in another plane of existence. She has taken my place, as I have taken hers."

"Who are you?"

"It cannot matter to you who I am. I am one who has lived as you are living, and who has died as you will die."

We heard the creak and grate of a cab pulling up next door. There was an argument about the fare, and the cabman grumbled hoarsely down the street. The green-yellow cloud still swirled faintly over the table, dull elsewhere, but glowing into a dim luminosity in the direction of the medium. It seemed to be piling itself up in front of her. A sense of fear and cold struck into my heart. It seemed to me that lightly and flippantly we had

approached the most real and august of sacraments, that communion with the dead of which the fathers of the Church had spoken.

"Don't you think we are going too far? Should we not break up this seance?" I cried.

But the others were all earnest to see the end of it. They laughed at my scruples.

"All the powers are made for use," said Harvey Deacon. "If we *can* do this, we *should* do this. Every new departure of knowledge has been called unlawful in its inception. It is right and proper that we should inquire into the nature of death."

"It is right and proper," said the voice.

"There, what more could you ask?" cried Moir, who was much excited. "Let us have a test. Will you give us a test that you are really there?"

"What test do you demand?"

"Well, now--I have some coins in my pocket. Will you tell me how many?"

"We come back in the hope of teaching and of elevating, and not to guess childish riddles."

"Ha, ha, Meester Moir, you catch it that time," cried the Frenchman. "But surely this is very good sense what the Control is saying."

"It is a religion, not a game," said the cold, hard voice.

"Exactly--the very view I take of it," cried Moir. "I am sure I am very sorry if I have asked a foolish question. You will not tell me who you are?"

"What does it matter?"

"Have you been a spirit long?"

"Yes."

"How long?"

"We cannot reckon time as you do. Our conditions are different."

"Are you happy?"

"Yes."

"You would not wish to come back to life?"

"No--certainly not."

"Are you busy?"

"We could not be happy if we were not busy."

"What do you do?"

"I have said that the conditions are entirely different."

"Can you give us no idea of your work?"

"We labour for our own improvement and for the advancement of others."

"Do you like coming here to-night?"

"I am glad to come if I can do any good by coming."

"Then to do good is your object?"

"It is the object of all life on every plane."

"You see, Markham, that should answer your scruples."

It did, for my doubts had passed and only interest remained.

"Have you pain in your life?" I asked.
"No; pain is a thing of the body."
"Have you mental pain?"
"Yes; one may always be sad or anxious."
"Do you meet the friends whom you have known on earth?"
"Some of them."
"Why only some of them?"
"Only those who are sympathetic."
"Do husbands meet wives?"
"Those who have truly loved."
"And the others?"
"They are nothing to each other."
"There must be a spiritual connection?"
"Of course."
"Is what we are doing right?"
"If done in the right spirit."
"What is the wrong spirit?"
"Curiosity and levity."
"May harm come of that?"
"Very serious harm."
"What sort of harm?"
"You may call up forces over which you have no control."
"Evil forces?"
"Undeveloped forces."
"You say they are dangerous. Dangerous to body or mind?"
"Sometimes to both."

There was a pause, and the blackness seemed to grow blacker still, while the yellow-green fog swirled and smoked upon the table.

"Any questions you would like to ask, Moir?" said Harvey Deacon.
"Only this--do you pray in your world?"
"One should pray in every world."
"Why?"
"Because it is the acknowledgment of forces outside ourselves."
"What religion do you hold over there?"
"We differ exactly as you do."
"You have no certain knowledge?"
"We have only faith."

"These questions of religion," said the Frenchman, "they are of interest to you serious English people, but they are not so much fun. It seems to me that with this power here we might be able to have some great experience--*hein*? Something of which we could talk."

"But nothing could be more interesting than this," said Moir.

"Well, if you think so, that is very well," the Frenchman answered, peevishly. "For my part, it seems to me that I have heard all this before, and that to-night I should weesh to try some experiment with all this force which is given to us. But if you have other questions, then ask them, and when you are finish we can try something more."

But the spell was broken. We asked and asked, but the medium sat silent in her chair. Only her deep, regular breathing showed that she was there. The mist still whirled upon the table.

"You have disturbed the harmony. She will not answer."

"But we have learned already all that she can tell--*hein*? For my part I wish to see something I have never seen before."

"What then?"

"You will let me try?"

"What would you do?"

"I have said to you that thoughts are things. Now I wish to *prove* it to you, and to show you that which is only a thought. Yes, yes, I can do it and you will see. Now I ask you only to sit still and say nothing, and keep ever your hands quiet upon the table."

The room was blacker and more silent than ever. The same feeling of apprehension which had lain heavily upon me at the beginning of the seance was back at my heart once more. The roots of my hair were tingling.

"It is working! It is working!" cried the Frenchman, and there was a crack in his voice as he spoke which told me that he also was strung to his tightest.

The luminous fog drifted slowly off the table, and wavered and flickered across the room. There in the farther and darkest corner it gathered and glowed, hardening down into a shining core--a strange, shifty, luminous, and yet non-illuminating patch of radiance, bright itself, but throwing no rays into the darkness. It had changed from a greenish-yellow to a dusky sullen red. Then round this centre there coiled a dark, smoky substance, thickening, hardening, growing denser and blacker. And then the light went out, smothered in that which had grown round it.

"It has gone."

"Hush--there's something in the room."

We heard it in the corner where the light had been, something which breathed deeply and fidgeted in the darkness.

"What is it? Le Duc, what have you done?"

"It is all right. No harm will come." The Frenchman's voice was treble with agitation.

"Good heavens, Moir, there's a large animal in the room. Here it is, close by my chair! Go away! Go away!"

It was Harvey Deacon's voice, and then came the sound of a blow upon some hard object. And then ... And then ... how can I tell you what happened then?

Some huge thing hurtled against us in the darkness, rearing, stamping, smashing, springing, snorting. The table was splintered. We were scattered in every direction. It clattered and scrambled amongst us, rushing with horrible energy from one corner of the room to another. We were all screaming with fear, grovelling upon our hands and knees to get away from it. Something trod upon my left hand, and I felt the bones splinter under the weight.

"A light! A light!" some one yelled.

"Moir, you have matches, matches!"

"No, I have none. Deacon, where are the matches? For God's sake, the matches!"

"I can't find them. Here, you Frenchman, stop it!"

"It is beyond me. Oh, *mon Dieu*, I cannot stop it. The door! Where is the door?"

My hand, by good luck, lit upon the handle as I groped about in the darkness. The hard-breathing, snorting, rushing creature tore past me and butted with a fearful crash against the oaken partition. The instant that it had passed I turned the handle, and next moment we were all outside, and the door shut behind us. From within came a horrible crashing and rending and stamping.

"What is it? In Heaven's name, what is it?"

"A horse. I saw it when the door opened. But Mrs. Delamere----?"

"We must fetch her out. Come on, Markham; the longer we wait the less we shall like it."

He flung open the door and we rushed in. She was there on the ground amidst the splinters of her chair. We seized her and dragged her swiftly out, and as we gained the door I looked over my shoulder into the darkness. There were two strange eyes glowing at us, a rattle of hoofs, and I had just time to slam the door when there came a crash upon it which split it from top to bottom.

"It's coming through! It's coming!"

"Run, run for your lives!" cried the Frenchman.

Another crash, and something shot through the riven door. It was a long white spike, gleaming in the lamplight. For a moment it shone before us, and then with a snap it disappeared again.

"Quick! Quick! This way!" Harvey Deacon shouted. "Carry her in! Here! Quick!"

We had taken refuge in the dining-room, and shut the heavy oak door. We laid the senseless woman upon the sofa, and as we did so, Moir, the hard man of business, drooped and fainted across the hearth-rug. Harvey Deacon was as white as a corpse, jerking and twitching like an epileptic. With a crash we heard the studio door fly to pieces, and the snorting and stamping were in the passage, up and down, shaking the house with their fury. The Frenchman had sunk his face on his hands, and sobbed like a frightened child.

"What shall we do?" I shook him roughly by the shoulder. "Is a gun any use?"

"No, no. The power will pass. Then it will end."

"You might have killed us all--you unspeakable fool--with your infernal experiments."

"I did not know. How could I tell that it would be frightened? It is mad with terror. It was his fault. He struck it."

Harvey Deacon sprang up. "Good heavens!" he cried.

A terrible scream sounded through the house.

"It's my wife! Here, I'm going out. If it's the Evil One himself I am going out!"

He had thrown open the door and rushed out into the passage. At the end of it, at the foot of the stairs, Mrs. Deacon was lying senseless, struck down by the sight which she had seen. But there was nothing else.

With eyes of horror we looked about us, but all was perfectly quiet and still. I approached the black square of the studio door, expecting with every slow step that some atrocious shape would hurl itself out of it. But nothing came, and all was silent inside the room. Peeping and peering, our hearts in our mouths, we came to the very threshold, and stared into the darkness. There was still no sound, but in one direction there was also no darkness. A luminous, glowing cloud, with an incandescent centre, hovered in the corner of the room. Slowly it dimmed and faded, growing thinner and fainter, until at last the same dense, velvety blackness filled the whole studio. And with the last flickering gleam of that baleful light the Frenchman broke into a shout of joy.

"What a fun!" he cried. "No one is hurt, and only the door broken, and the ladies frightened. But, my friends, we have done what has never been done before."

"And as far as I can help," said Harvey Deacon, "it will certainly never be done again."

And that was what befell on the 14th of April last at No. 17 Badderly Gardens. I began by saying that it would seem too grotesque to dogmatise as to what it was which actually did occur; but I give my impressions, *our* impressions (since they are corroborated by Harvey Deacon and John Moir), for what they are worth. You may, if it pleases you, imagine that we were the victims of an elaborate and extraordinary hoax. Or you may think with us that we underwent a very real and a very terrible experience. Or perhaps you may know more than we do of such occult matters, and can inform us of some similar occurrence. In this latter case a letter to William Markham, 146M, the Albany, would help to throw a light upon that which is very dark to us.

A unicorn is certainly a bizarre phantom to conjure, and Doyle avoids a ludicrous scene by using discretion in the creature's appearance. Like in "The Leather Funnel" where he pulls away from the torture scene just as it's about to get grisly, he demonstrates self-control by revealing nothing more than a thrusting spike and two glowing, maddened eyes. Despite its somewhat ludicrous plot, the message of the tale was an important one to Doyle, and one which he should have taken heed of later in his life. It was one of warning and caution, urging its readers to wonder and be amazed at the vast universe with its mysteries and secrets, but to do so like a man watching lightning from behind a window, *not* the man who races to the top of a hill for a better view. This was even a problem for the members of the SPR, whose evolving culture increasingly seemed to be abandoning spiritual humility in favor of what Doyle considered scientific hubris, causing him to resign his membership the year of his death. He felt that they were too enamored with science and had lost the soul of their mission. Perhaps it was his own movement away from wondrous ignorance to arrogant dogmatism that later made his name a laughingstock in households across the world. Doyle's stubborn and thoroughly ludicrous decisions to support the obviously fraudulent "fairy photos," to feud with Harry Houdini, to try to employ psychics in police work, to promote "scientific" arguments for the existence of fairies, champion the veracity of mediums, and defend the reputations of confessed charlatans all piled against him in his last years, and although he was never convinced of his mistakes, it caused his life fade away into bitterness and depression. He had indeed called forth a unicorn of his own making, and it came to him, only to trample his reputation into a shambles.

AUTOMOBILES were a favorite hobby of Doyle's, and in 1911 he was celebrated for his participation in an international car race wherein he and his wife piloted one of the cars to lead the British team in victory against the Germans (led by a Prussian crown prince, no less). But his enthusiasm was not without a healthy dose of caution – one year after buying his first automobile he narrowly escaped death. It was a brisk winter morning in 1904, and Doyle was steering his Wolseley Motoring Machine through the gates of his Surrey residence for a day of joy riding with his brother Innes. The car was clumsily handled as it passed through the gates and onto the road when it smote the gatepost, causing the vehicle to charge up a steep grade and fall backwards on top of its driver. Innes was thrown clear and survived, but his famous brother was caught beneath the machine, only saved by the steering column which propped it up... momentarily: a few seconds later it was bent under the weight, and the car settled on top of Doyle, pinning his face to the earth. Dazed and horrified, Doyle was rescued by a crowd of onlookers who pulled it off in time. "The secret of safe brakes had not yet been discovered," he said on the event, "and my pair used to break as if they were glass. More than once I have known what it is to steer a car when it is flying backwards under no control down a winding hill." It is hardly conceivable that this terribly brush with death had no influence on the following cataclysmic episode.

How it Happened
{1913}

SHE *was a writing medium. This is what she wrote: —*

I can remember some things upon that evening most distinctly, and others are like some vague, broken dreams. That is what makes it so difficult to tell a connected story. I have no idea now what it was that had taken me to London and brought me back so late. It just merges into all my other visits to London. But from the time that I got out at the little country station everything is extraordinarily clear. I can live it again--every instant of it.

I remember so well walking down the platform and looking at the illuminated clock at the end which told me that it was half-past eleven. I remember also my wondering whether I could get home before midnight. Then I remember the big motor, with its glaring head-lights and glitter of polished brass, waiting for me outside. It was my new thirty-horse- power Robur, which had only been delivered that day. I remember also asking Perkins, my chauffeur, how she had gone, and his saying that he thought she was excellent.

"I'll try her myself," said I, and I climbed into the driver's seat.

"The gears are not the same," said he. "Perhaps, sir, I had better drive."

"No; I should like to try her," said I.

And so we started on the five-mile drive for home.

My old car had the gears as they used always to be in notches on a bar. In this car you passed the gear-lever through a gate to get on the higher ones. It was not difficult to master, and soon I thought that I understood it. It was foolish, no doubt, to begin to learn a new system in the dark, but one often does foolish things, and one has not always to pay the full price for them. I got along very well until I came to Claystall Hill. It is one of the worst hills in England, a mile and a half long and one in six in places, with three fairly sharp curves. My park gates stand at the very foot of it upon the main London road.

We were just over the brow of this hill, where the grade is steepest, when the trouble began. I had been on the top speed, and wanted to get her on the free; but she stuck between gears, and I had to get her back on the top again. By this time she was going at a great rate, so I clapped on both brakes, and one after the other they gave way. I didn't mind so much when I felt my footbrake snap, but when I put all my weight on my side-brake, and the lever clanged to its full limit without a catch, it brought a cold sweat out of me. By this time we were fairly tearing down the slope. The lights were brilliant, and I brought her round the first curve all right. Then we did the second one, though it was a close shave for the ditch. There was a mile of straight then with the third curve beneath it, and after that the gate of the park. If I could shoot into that harbour all would be well, for the slope up to the house would bring her to a stand.

Perkins behaved splendidly. I should like that to be known. He was perfectly cool and alert. I had thought at the very beginning of taking the bank, and he read my intention.

"I wouldn't do it, sir," said he. "At this pace it must go over and we should have it on the top of us."

Of course he was right. He got to the electric switch and had it off, so we were in the free; but we were still running at a fearful pace. He laid his hands on the wheel.

"I'll keep her steady," said he, "if you care to jump and chance it. We can never get round that curve. Better jump, sir."

"No," said I; "I'll stick it out. You can jump if you like."

"I'll stick it with you, sir," said he.

If it had been the old car I should have jammed the gear-lever into the reverse, and seen what would happen. I expect she would have stripped her gears or smashed up somehow, but it would have been a chance. As it was, I was helpless. Perkins tried to climb across, but you couldn't do it going at that pace. The wheels were whirring like a high wind and the big body creaking and groaning with the strain. But the lights were brilliant, and one could steer to an inch. I remember thinking what an awful and yet majestic

sight we should appear to any one who met us. It was a narrow road, and we were just a great, roaring, golden death to any one who came in our path.

We got round the corner with one wheel three feet high upon the bank. I thought we were surely over, but after staggering for a moment she righted and darted onwards. That was the third corner and the last one. There was only the
park gate now. It was facing us, but, as luck would have it, not facing us directly. It was about twenty yards to the left up the main road into which we ran. Perhaps I could have done it, but I expect that the steering-gear had been jarred when we ran on the bank. The wheel did not turn easily. We shot out of the lane. I saw the open gate on the left. I whirled round my wheel with all the strength of my wrists. Perkins and I threw our bodies across, and then the next instant, going at fifty miles an hour, my right front wheel struck full on the right-hand pillar of my own gate. I heard the crash. I was conscious of flying through the air, and then--and then--!

ᘓ

When I became aware of my own existence once more I was among some brushwood in the shadow of the oaks upon the lodge side of the drive. A man was standing beside me. I imagined at first that it was Perkins, but when I looked again I saw that it was Stanley, a man whom I had known at college some years before, and for whom I had a really genuine affection. There was always something peculiarly sympathetic to me in Stanley's personality; and I was proud to think that I had some similar influence upon him. At the present moment I was surprised to see him, but I was like a man in a dream, giddy and shaken and quite prepared to take things as I found them without questioning them.

"What a smash!" I said. "Good Lord, what an awful smash!"

He nodded his head, and even in the gloom I could see that he was smiling the gentle, wistful smile which I connected with him.

I was quite unable to move. Indeed, I had not any desire to try to move. But my senses were exceedingly alert. I saw the wreck of the motor lit up by the moving lanterns. I saw the little group of people and heard the hushed voices. There were the lodge-keeper and his wife, and one or two more. They were taking no notice of me, but were very busy round the car. Then suddenly I heard a cry of pain.

"The weight is on him. Lift it easy," cried a voice.

"It's only my leg!" said another one, which I recognized as Perkins's. "Where's master?" he cried.

"Here I am," I answered, but they did not seem to hear me. They were all bending over something which lay in front of the car.

Stanley laid his hand upon my shoulder, and his touch was inexpressibly soothing. I felt light and happy, in spite of all.

"No pain, of course?" said he.

"None," said I.

"There never is," said he.

And then suddenly a wave of amazement passed over me. Stanley! Stanley! Why, Stanley had surely died of enteric at Bloemfontein in the Boer War!

"Stanley!" I cried, and the words seemed to choke my throat--"Stanley, you are dead."

He looked at me with the same old gentle, wistful smile.

"So are you," he answered.

A fine little piece of Halloween-ish fun, "How it Happened" is not great literature, or even terribly creative, but it never fails to generate a grisly chill in my spine when the spirit peels away from its mangled body, unaware of the critical transition which has taken place, and stumbles dumbly around its former domain. The impression that remains is a poignant sense of how quickly life can be exterminated, how sudden that extermination can be, and how hopelessly we avoid and deny the inevitability and permanence of that final destination. Even those of us who accept the fact of death without fear or delusion will likely be caught off guard and astonished when we are faced with it. Doyle's hapless adventurer is now cut adrift from his physical life without a chance to correct his mistakes, contact his friends, or set his affairs aright. It is over, finished, and done, and his only recourse is to speak through a "writing medium," although how effective this achievement has been is open to question. Ultimately, the star of the story is the title's subject: "*It*." "It" happens to us all. "It" happens all the time. "It" is commonplace and frequent, yet we avoid "It" and deny "It" until the day comes when "It" swallows us without courtesy or mercy. This simply happens to be the story of how It happened to one poor mortal, just as it is a story of how "It" nearly happened to Doyle himself, one bitter winter's day in 1904, before "It" came back to call – and successfully collected "Its" fare in the hallway of his manor house on a steamy July day in 1930.

THE supernatural femme fatale is a time-honored trope dating back to ancient mythology. Some of the earliest examples we have are Homer's alluring Sirens, Greece's Lamia and Empusa, Rome's strix, Babylon's Lamashtu, Judaism's Lilith, Egypt's Sekhmet, and (of course) Medusa herself – all of whom were renowned female maneaters. The Romantics borrowed from these traditions liberally: Goethe introduced the murderous "Bride of Corinth," Coleridge gave us his leprous "Life-in-Death," and his reptilian lesbian Geraldine, while Keats created the ambiguous but sinister "La Belle Dame Sans Merci," and among Poe's many Sirens are the indomitable Ligeia, Morella, and Madeline Usher. Not to be beat, Le Fanu generated the greatest female vampire in the English language: the Byronic seductress Carmilla. The following tale certainly owes a great deal to Keats, Poe, and Le Fanu in particular, as well as Arthur Machen (for it is an unmistakable cousin of "The Great God Pan" and its shapeshifting, suicide-inducing villain, Helen Vaughan). But – like most of the creatures mentioned so far – the antagonist is only loosely vampiric. She does not – so far as can be asserted – drink blood, and though she may be powerful, she is not unmistakably undead, or even immortal. She is a psychic vampire, a woman who generates her energy through the predatory application of her overwhelming will, the manner in which she overpowers her doomed suitors, and the hidden horrors which she can at any moment unveil to them – depriving them of sanity, life, and self-respect. While we will dwell in the conclusion on the psycho-social implications of this trope, let us enter the story – which features one of Doyle's most malevolent, understated, and underappreciated villains: a subtle sadist and a low-lit source of psychological horror – with no further commentary.

John Barrington Cowles
{1887}

IT might seem rash of me to say that I ascribe the death of my poor friend, John Barrington Cowles, to any preternatural agency. I am aware that in the present state of public feeling a chain of evidence would require to be strong indeed before the possibility of such a conclusion could be admitted.

I shall therefore merely state the circumstances which led up to this sad event as concisely and as plainly as I can, and leave every reader to draw his own deductions. Perhaps there may be some one who can throw light upon what is dark to me.

I first met Barrington Cowles when I went up to Edinburgh University to take out medical classes there. My landlady in Northumberland Street had a large house, and, being a widow without children, she gained a livelihood by providing accommodation for several students.

Barrington Cowles happened to have taken a bedroom upon the same floor as mine, and when we came to know each other better we shared a small sitting-room, in which we took our meals. In this manner we originated a friendship which was unmarred by the slightest disagreement up to the day of his death.

Cowles' father was the colonel of a Sikh regiment and had remained in India for many years. He allowed his son a handsome income, but seldom gave any other sign of parental affection--writing irregularly and briefly.

My friend, who had himself been born in India, and whose whole disposition was an ardent tropical one, was much hurt by this neglect. His mother was dead, and he had no other relation in the world to supply the blank.

Thus he came in time to concentrate all his affection upon me, and to confide in me in a manner which is rare among men. Even when a stronger and deeper passion came upon him, it never infringed upon the old tenderness between us.

Cowles was a tall, slim young fellow, with an olive, Velasquez-like face, and dark, tender eyes. I have seldom seen a man who was more likely to excite a woman's interest, or to captivate her imagination. His expression was, as a rule, dreamy, and even languid; but if in conversation a subject arose which interested him he would be all animation in a moment. On such occasions his colour would heighten, his eyes gleam, and he could speak with an eloquence which would carry his audience with him.

In spite of these natural advantages he led a solitary life, avoiding female society, and reading with great diligence. He was one of the foremost men of his year, taking the senior medal for anatomy, and the Neil Arnott prize for physics.

How well I can recollect the first time we met her! Often and often I have recalled the circumstances, and tried to remember what the exact impression was which she produced on my mind at the time.

After we came to know her my judgment was warped, so that I am curious to recollect what my unbiased instincts were. It is hard, however, to eliminate the feelings which reason or prejudice afterwards raised in me.

It was at the opening of the Royal Scottish Academy in the spring of 1879. My poor friend was passionately attached to art in every form, and a pleasing chord in music or a delicate effect upon canvas would give exquisite pleasure to his highly-strung nature. We had gone together to see the pictures, and were standing in the grand central salon, when I noticed an extremely beautiful woman standing at the other side of the room. In my whole life I have never seen such a classically perfect countenance. It was the real Greek type--the forehead broad, very low, and as white as marble, with a cloudlet of delicate locks wreathing round it, the nose straight and clean cut, the lips inclined to thinness, the chin and lower jaw beautifully rounded off, and yet sufficiently developed to promise unusual strength of character.

But those eyes--those wonderful eyes! If I could but give some faint idea of their varying moods, their steely hardness, their feminine softness, their power of command, their penetrating intensity suddenly melting away into an expression of womanly weakness--but I am speaking now of future impressions!

There was a tall, yellow-haired young man with this lady, whom I at once recognised as a law student with whom I had a slight acquaintance.

Archibald Reeves--for that was his name--was a dashing, handsome young fellow, and had at one time been a ringleader in every university escapade; but of late I had seen little of him, and the report was that he was engaged to be married. His companion was, then, I presumed, his fiancee. I seated myself upon the velvet settee in the centre of the room, and furtively watched the couple from behind my catalogue.

The more I looked at her the more her beauty grew upon me. She was somewhat short in stature, it is true; but her figure was perfection, and she bore herself in such a fashion that it was only by actual comparison that one would have known her to be under the medium height.

As I kept my eyes upon them, Reeves was called away for some reason, and the young lady was left alone. Turning her back to the pictures, she passed the time until the return of her escort in taking a deliberate survey of the company, without paying the least heed to the fact that a dozen pair of eyes, attracted by her elegance and beauty, were bent curiously upon her. With one of her hands holding the red silk cord which railed off the pictures, she stood languidly moving her eyes from face to face with as little self-consciousness as if she were looking at the canvas creatures behind her. Suddenly, as I watched her, I saw her gaze become fixed, and, as it were, intense. I followed the direction of her looks, wondering what could have attracted her so strongly.

John Barrington Cowles was standing before a picture--one, I think, by Noel Paton--I know that the subject was a noble and ethereal one. His profile was turned towards us, and never have I seen him to such advantage. I have said that he was a strikingly handsome man, but at that moment he looked absolutely magnificent. It was evident that he had momentarily forgotten his surroundings, and that his whole soul was in sympathy with the picture before him. His eyes sparkled, and a dusky pink shone through his clear olive cheeks. She continued to watch him fixedly, with a look of interest upon her face, until he came out of his reverie with a start, and turned abruptly round, so that his gaze met hers. She glanced away at once, but his eyes remained fixed upon her for some moments. The picture was forgotten already, and his soul had come down to earth once more.

We caught sight of her once or twice before we left, and each time I noticed my friend look after her. He made no remark, however, until we got out into the open air, and were walking arm-in-arm along Princes Street.

"Did you notice that beautiful woman, in the dark dress, with the white fur?" he asked.

"Yes, I saw her," I answered.

"Do you know her?" he asked eagerly. "Have you any idea who she is?"

"I don't know her personally," I replied. "But I have no doubt I could find out all about her, for I believe she is engaged to young Archie Reeves, and he and I have a lot of mutual friends."

"Engaged!" ejaculated Cowles.

"Why, my dear boy," I said, laughing, "you don't mean to say you are so susceptible that the fact that a girl to whom you never spoke in your life is engaged is enough to upset you?"

"Well, not exactly to upset me," he answered, forcing a laugh. "But I don't mind telling you, Armitage, that I never was so taken by any one in my life. It wasn't the mere beauty of the face-- though that was perfect enough-- but it was the character and the intellect upon it. I hope, if she is engaged, that it is to some man who will be worthy of her."

"Why," I remarked, "you speak quite feelingly. It is a clear case of love at first sight, Jack. However, to put your perturbed spirit at rest, I'll make a point of finding out all about her whenever I meet any fellow who is likely to know."

Barrington Cowles thanked me, and the conversation drifted off into other channels. For several days neither of us made any allusion to the subject, though my companion was perhaps a little more dreamy and distraught than usual. The incident had almost vanished from my remembrance, when one day young Brodie, who is a second cousin of mine, came up to me on the university steps with the face of a bearer of tidings.

"I say," he began, "you know Reeves, don't you?"

"Yes. What of him?"

"His engagement is off."

"Off!" I cried. "Why, I only learned the other day that it was on."

"Oh, yes--it's all off. His brother told me so. Deucedly mean of Reeves, you know, if he has backed out of it, for she was an uncommonly nice girl."

"I've seen her," I said; "but I don't know her name."

"She is a Miss Northcott, and lives with an old aunt of hers in Abercrombie Place. Nobody knows anything about her people, or where she comes from. Anyhow, she is about the most unlucky girl in the world, poor soul!"

"Why unlucky?"

"Well, you know, this was her second engagement," said young Brodie, who had a marvellous knack of knowing everything about everybody. "She was engaged to Prescott--William Prescott, who died. That was a very sad affair. The wedding day was fixed, and the whole thing looked as straight as a die when the smash came."

"What smash?" I asked, with some dim recollection of the circumstances.

"Why, Prescott's death. He came to Abercrombie Place one night, and stayed very late. No one knows exactly when he left, but about one in the morning a fellow who knew him met him walking rapidly in the direction of the Queen's Park. He bade him good night, but Prescott hurried on without heeding him, and that was the last time he was ever seen alive. Three days afterwards his body was found floating in St. Margaret's Loch, under St. Anthony's Chapel. No one could ever understand it, but of course the verdict brought it in as temporary insanity."

"It was very strange," I remarked.

"Yes, and deucedly rough on the poor girl," said Brodie. "Now that this other blow has come it will quite crush her. So gentle and ladylike she is too!"

"You know her personally, then!" I asked.

"Oh, yes, I know her. I have met her several times. I could easily manage that you should be introduced to her."

"Well," I answered, "it's not so much for my own sake as for a friend of mine. However, I don't suppose she will go out much for some little time after this. When she does I will take advantage of your offer."

We shook hands on this, and I thought no more of the matter for some time.

The next incident which I have to relate as bearing at all upon the question of Miss Northcott is an unpleasant one. Yet I must detail it as accurately as possible, since it may throw some light upon the sequel. One cold night, several months after the conversation with my second cousin which I have quoted above, I was walking down one of the lowest streets in the city on my way back from a case which I had been attending. It was very late, and I was picking my way among the dirty loungers who were clustering round the doors of a great gin-palace, when a man staggered out from among them, and held out his hand to me with a drunken leer. The gaslight fell full upon his face, and, to my intense astonishment, I recognised in the degraded creature before me my former acquaintance, young Archibald Reeves, who had once been famous as one of the most dressy and particular men in the whole college. I was so utterly surprised that for a moment I almost doubted the evidence of my own senses; but there was no mistaking those features, which, though bloated with drink, still retained something of their former comeliness. I was determined to rescue him, for one night at least, from the company into which he had fallen.

"Holloa, Reeves!" I said. "Come along with me. I'm going in your direction."

He muttered some incoherent apology for his condition, and took my arm. As I supported him towards his lodgings I could see that he was not only suffering from the effects of a recent debauch, but that a long course of intemperance had affected his nerves and his brain. His hand when I touched it was dry and feverish, and he started from every shadow which fell upon the pavement. He rambled in his speech, too, in a manner which suggested the delirium of disease rather than the talk of a drunkard.

When I got him to his lodgings I partially undressed him and laid him upon his bed. His pulse at this time was very high, and he was evidently extremely feverish. He seemed to have sunk into a doze; and I was about to steal out of the room to warn his landlady of his condition, when he started up and caught me by the sleeve of my coat.

"Don't go!" he cried. "I feel better when you are here. I am safe from her then."

"From her!" I said. "From whom?"

"Her! her!" he answered peevishly. "Ah! you don't know her. She is the devil! Beautiful--beautiful; but the devil!"

"You are feverish and excited," I said. "Try and get a little sleep. You will wake better."

"Sleep!" he groaned. "How am I to sleep when I see her sitting down yonder at the foot of the bed with her great eyes watching and watching hour after hour? I tell you it saps all the strength and manhood out of me. That's what makes me drink. God help me--I'm half drunk now!"

"You are very ill," I said, putting some vinegar to his temples; "and you are delirious. You don't know what you say."

"Yes, I do," he interrupted sharply, looking up at me. "I know very well what I say. I brought it upon myself. It is my own choice. But I couldn't--no, by heaven, I couldn't--accept the alternative. I couldn't keep my faith to her. It was more than man could do."

I sat by the side of the bed, holding one of his burning hands in mine, and wondering over his strange words. He lay still for some time, and then, raising his eyes to me, said in a most plaintive voice--

"Why did she not give me warning sooner? Why did she wait until I had learned to love her so?"

He repeated this question several times, rolling his feverish head from side to side, and then he dropped into a troubled sleep. I crept out of the room, and, having seen that he would be properly cared for, left the house. His words, however, rang in my ears for days afterwards, and assumed a deeper significance when taken with what was to come.

My friend, Barrington Cowles, had been away for his summer holidays, and I had heard nothing of him for several months. When the winter session came on, however, I received a telegram from him, asking me to secure the old rooms in Northumberland Street for him, and telling me the train by which he would arrive. I went down to meet him, and was delighted to find him looking wonderfully hearty and well.

"By the way," he said suddenly, that night, as we sat in our chairs by the fire, talking over the events of the holidays, "you have never congratulated me yet!"

"On what, my boy?" I asked.

"What! Do you mean to say you have not heard of my engagement?"

"Engagement! No!" I answered. "However, I am delighted to hear it, and congratulate you with all my heart."

"I wonder it didn't come to your ears," he said. "It was the queerest thing. You remember that girl whom we both admired so much at the Academy?"

"What!" I cried, with a vague feeling of apprehension at my heart. "You don't mean to say that you are engaged to her?"

"I thought you would be surprised," he answered. "When I was staying with an old aunt of mine in Peterhead, in Aberdeenshire, the Northcotts happened to come there on a visit, and as we had mutual friends we soon met. I found out that it was a false alarm about her being engaged, and then--well, you know what it is when you are thrown into the society of such a girl in a place like Peterhead. Not, mind you," he added, "that I consider I did a foolish or hasty thing. I have never regretted it for a moment. The more I know Kate the more I admire her and love her. However, you must be introduced to her, and then you will form your own opinion."

I expressed my pleasure at the prospect, and endeavoured to speak as lightly as I could to Cowles upon the subject, but I felt depressed and anxious at heart. The words of Reeves and the unhappy fate of young Prescott recurred to my recollection, and though I could assign no tangible reason for it, a vague, dim fear and distrust of the woman took possession of me. It may be that this was foolish prejudice and superstition upon my part, and that I involuntarily contorted her future doings and sayings to fit into some half-formed wild theory of my own. This has been suggested to me by others as an explanation of my narrative. They are welcome to their opinion if they can reconcile it with the facts which I have to tell.

I went round with my friend a few days afterwards to call upon Miss Northcott. I remember that, as we went down Abercrombie Place, our attention was attracted by the shrill yelping of a dog--which noise proved eventually to come from the house to which we were bound. We were shown upstairs, where I was introduced to old Mrs. Merton, Miss Northcott's aunt, and to the young lady herself. She looked as beautiful as ever, and I could not wonder at my friend's infatuation. Her face was a little more flushed than usual, and she held in her hand a heavy dog-whip, with which she had been chastising a small Scotch terrier, whose cries we had heard in the street. The poor brute was cringing up against the wall, whining piteously, and evidently completely cowed.

"So Kate," said my friend, after we had taken our seats, "you have been falling out with Carlo again."

"Only a very little quarrel this time," she said, smiling charmingly. "He is a dear, good old fellow, but he needs correction now and then." Then, turning to me, "We all do that, Mr. Armitage, don't we? What a capital thing if, instead of receiving a collective punishment at the end of our lives, we were to have one at once, as the dogs do, when we did anything wicked. It would make us more careful, wouldn't it?"

I acknowledged that it would.

"Supposing that every time a man misbehaved himself a gigantic hand were to seize him, and he were lashed with a whip until he fainted"--she clenched her white fingers as she spoke, and cut out viciously with the dog-whip--"it would do more to keep him good than any number of high-minded theories of morality."

"Why, Kate," said my friend, "you are quite savage to-day."

"No, Jack," she laughed. "I'm only propounding a theory for Mr. Armitage's consideration."

The two began to chat together about some Aberdeenshire reminiscence, and I had time to observe Mrs. Merton, who had remained silent during our short conversation. She was a very strange-looking old lady. What attracted attention most in her appearance was the utter want of colour which she exhibited. Her hair was snow-white, and her face extremely pale. Her lips were bloodless, and even her eyes were of such a light tinge of blue that they hardly relieved the general pallor. Her dress was a grey silk, which harmonised with her general appearance. She had a peculiar expression of countenance, which I was unable at the moment to refer to its proper cause.

She was working at some old-fashioned piece of ornamental needlework, and as she moved her arms her dress gave forth a dry, melancholy rustling, like the sound of leaves in the autumn. There was something mournful and depressing in the sight of her. I moved my chair a little nearer, and asked her how she liked Edinburgh, and whether she had been there long.

When I spoke to her she started and looked up at me with a scared look on her face. Then I saw in a moment what the expression was which I had observed there. It was one of fear--intense and overpowering fear. It was so marked that I could have staked my life on the woman before me having at some period of her life been subjected to some terrible experience or dreadful misfortune.

"Oh, yes, I like it," she said, in a soft, timid voice; "and we have been here long--that is, not very long. We move about a great deal." She spoke with hesitation, as if afraid of committing herself.

"You are a native of Scotland, I presume?" I said.

"No--that is, not entirely. We are not natives of any place. We are cosmopolitan, you know." She glanced round in the direction of Miss Northcott as she spoke, but the two were still chatting together near the window. Then she suddenly bent forward to me, with a look of intense earnestness upon her face, and said--

"Don't talk to me any more, please. She does not like it, and I shall suffer for it afterwards. Please, don't do it."

I was about to ask her the reason for this strange request, but when she saw I was going to address her, she rose and walked slowly out of the room. As she did so I perceived that the lovers had ceased to talk and that Miss Northcott was looking at me with her keen, grey eyes.

"You must excuse my aunt, Mr. Armitage," she said; "she is odd, and easily fatigued. Come over and look at my album."

We spent some time examining the portraits. Miss Northcott's father and mother were apparently ordinary mortals enough, and I could not detect in either of them any traces of the character which showed itself in their daughter's face. There was one old daguerreotype, however, which arrested my attention. It represented a man of about the age of forty, and strikingly handsome. He was clean shaven, and extraordinary power was expressed upon his prominent lower jaw and firm, straight mouth. His eyes were somewhat deeply set in his head, however, and there was a snake-like flattening at the upper part of his forehead, which detracted from his appearance. I almost involuntarily, when I saw the head, pointed to it, and exclaimed--

"There is your prototype in your family, Miss Northcott."

"Do you think so?" she said. "I am afraid you are paying me a very bad compliment. Uncle Anthony was always considered the black sheep of the family."

"Indeed," I answered; "my remark was an unfortunate one, then."

"Oh, don't mind that," she said; "I always thought myself that he was worth all of them put together. He was an officer in the Forty-first Regiment, and he was killed in action during the Persian War--so he died nobly, at any rate."

"That's the sort of death I should like to die," said Cowles, his dark eyes flashing, as they would when he was excited; "I often wish I had taken to my father's profession instead of this vile pill-compounding drudgery."

"Come, Jack, you are not going to die any sort of death yet," she said, tenderly taking his hand in hers.

I could not understand the woman. There was such an extraordinary mixture of masculine decision and womanly tenderness about her, with the consciousness of something all her own in the background, that she fairly puzzled me. I hardly knew, therefore, how to answer Cowles when, as we walked down the street together, he asked the comprehensive question--

"Well, what do you think of her?"

"I think she is wonderfully beautiful," I answered guardedly.

"That, of course," he replied irritably. "You knew that before you came!"

"I think she is very clever too," I remarked.

Barrington Cowles walked on for some time, and then he suddenly turned on me with the strange question--

"Do you think she is cruel? Do you think she is the sort of girl who would take a pleasure in inflicting pain?"

"Well, really," I answered, "I have hardly had time to form an opinion."

We then walked on for some time in silence.

"She is an old fool," at length muttered Cowles. "She is mad."

"Who is?" I asked.

"Why, that old woman--that aunt of Kate's--Mrs. Merton, or whatever her name is."

Then I knew that my poor colourless friend had been speaking to Cowles, but he never said anything more as to the nature of her communication.

My companion went to bed early that night, and I sat up a long time by the fire, thinking over all that I had seen and heard. I felt that there was some mystery about the girl--some dark fatality so strange as to defy conjecture. I thought of Prescott's interview with her before their marriage, and the fatal termination of it. I coupled it with poor drunken Reeves' plaintive cry, "Why did she not tell me sooner?" and with the other words he had spoken. Then my mind ran over Mrs. Merton's warning to me, Cowles' reference to her, and even the episode of the whip and the cringing dog.

The whole effect of my recollections was unpleasant to a degree, and yet there was no tangible charge which I could bring against the woman. It would be worse than useless to attempt to warn my friend until I had definitely made up my mind what I was to warn him against. He would treat any charge against her with scorn. What could I do? How could I get at some tangible conclusion as to her character and antecedents? No one in Edinburgh knew them except as recent acquaintances. She was an orphan, and as far as I knew she had never disclosed where her former home had been. Suddenly an idea struck me. Among my father's friends there was a Colonel Joyce, who had served a long time in India upon the staff, and who would be likely to know most of the officers who had been out there since the Mutiny. I sat down at once, and, having trimmed the lamp, proceeded to write a letter to the Colonel. I told him that I was very curious to gain some particulars about a certain Captain Northcott, who had served in the Forty-first Foot, and who had fallen in the Persian War. I described the man as well as I could from my recollection of the daguerreotype, and then, having directed the letter, posted it that very night, after which, feeling that I had done all that could be done, I retired to bed, with a mind too anxious to allow me to sleep.

Part II.

I got an answer from Leicester, where the Colonel resided, within two days. I have it before me as I write, and copy it verbatim.

"DEAR BOB," it said,

"I remember the man well. I was with him at Calcutta, and afterwards at Hyderabad. He was a curious, solitary sort of mortal; but a gallant soldier enough, for he distinguished himself at Sobraon, and was wounded, if I remember right. He was not popular in his corps--they said he was a pitiless, cold-blooded fellow, with no geniality in him. There was a rumour, too, that he was a devil-worshipper, or something of that sort, and also that he had the evil eye, which, of course, was all nonsense. He had some strange theories, I remember, about the power of the human will and the effects of mind upon matter.

"How are you getting on with your medical studies? Never forget, my boy, that your father's son has every claim upon me, and that if I can serve you in any way I am always at your command.
--Ever affectionately yours, EDWARD JOYCE.

"P.S.--By the way, Northcott did not fall in action. He was killed after peace was declared in a crazy attempt to get some of the eternal fire from the sun-worshippers' temple. There was considerable mystery about his death."

I read this epistle over several times--at first with a feeling of satisfaction, and then with one of disappointment. I had come on some curious information, and yet hardly what I wanted. He was an eccentric man, a devil-worshipper, and rumoured to have the power of the evil eye. I could believe the young lady's eyes, when endowed with that cold, grey shimmer which I had noticed in them once or twice, to be capable of any evil which human eye ever wrought; but still the superstition was an effete one. Was there not more meaning in that sentence which followed--"He had theories of the power of the human will and of the effect of mind upon matter"? I remember having once read a quaint treatise, which I had imagined to be mere charlatanism at the time, of the power of certain human minds, and of effects produced by them at a distance.

Was Miss Northcott endowed with some exceptional power of the sort?

The idea grew upon me, and very shortly I had evidence which convinced me of the truth of the supposition.

It happened that at the very time when my mind was dwelling upon this subject, I saw a notice in the paper that our town was to be visited by Dr. Messinger, the well-known medium and mesmerist. Messinger was a man whose performance, such as it was, had been again and again pronounced to be genuine by competent judges. He was far above trickery, and had the reputation of being the soundest living authority upon the strange pseudo-sciences of animal magnetism and electro-biology. Determined, therefore, to see what the human will could do, even against all the disadvantages of glaring footlights and a public platform, I took a ticket for the first night of the performance, and went with several student friends.

We had secured one of the side boxes, and did not arrive until after the performance had begun. I had hardly taken my seat before I recognised Barrington Cowles, with his fiancee and old Mrs. Merton, sitting in the third or fourth row of the stalls. They caught sight of me at almost the same moment, and we bowed to each other. The first portion of the lecture was somewhat commonplace, the lecturer giving tricks of pure legerdemain, with one or two manifestations of mesmerism, performed upon a subject whom he had brought with him. He gave us an exhibition of clairvoyance too, throwing his subject into a trance, and then demanding particulars as to the movements of absent friends, and the whereabouts of hidden objects all of which appeared to be answered satisfactorily. I had seen all this before, however. What I wanted to see now was the effect of the lecturer's will when exerted upon some independent member of the audience.

He came round to that as the concluding exhibition in his performance. "I have shown you," he said, "that a mesmerised subject is entirely dominated by the will of the mesmeriser. He loses all power of volition, and his very thoughts are such as are suggested to him by the master-mind. The same end may be attained without any preliminary process. A strong will can, simply by virtue of its strength, take possession of a weaker one, even at a distance, and can regulate the impulses and the actions of the owner of it. If there was one man in the world who had a very much more highly-developed will than any of the rest of the human family, there is no reason why he should not be able to rule over them all, and to reduce his fellow-creatures to the condition of automatons. Happily there is such a dead level of mental power, or rather of mental weakness, among us that such a catastrophe is not likely to occur; but still within our small compass there are variations which produce surprising effects. I shall now single out one of the audience, and endeavour `by the mere power of will' to compel him to come upon the platform, and do and say what I wish. Let me assure you that there is no collusion, and that the subject whom I may select is at perfect liberty to resent to the uttermost any impulse which I may communicate to him."

With these words the lecturer came to the front of the platform, and glanced over the first few rows of the stalls. No doubt Cowles' dark skin and bright eyes marked him out as a man of a highly nervous temperament, for the mesmerist picked him out in a moment, and fixed his eyes upon him. I saw my friend give a start of surprise, and then settle down in his chair, as if to express his determination not to yield to the influence of the operator. Messinger was not a man whose head denoted any great brain-power, but his gaze was singularly intense and penetrating. Under the influence of it Cowles made one or two spasmodic motions of his hands, as if to grasp the sides of his seat, and then half rose, but only to sink down again, though with an evident effort. I was watching the scene with intense interest, when I happened to catch a glimpse of Miss Northcott's face. She was sitting with her eyes fixed intently upon the mesmerist, and with such an expression of concentrated power upon her features as I have never seen on any other human countenance. Her jaw was firmly set, her lips compressed, and her face as hard as if it were a beautiful sculpture cut out of the whitest marble. Her eyebrows were drawn down, however, and from beneath them her grey eyes seemed to sparkle and gleam with a cold light.

I looked at Cowles again, expecting every moment to see him rise and obey the mesmerist's wishes, when there came from the platform a short, gasping cry as of a man utterly worn out and prostrated by a prolonged struggle. Messinger was leaning against the table, his hand to his forehead, and the perspiration pouring down his face. "I won't go on," he cried, addressing the audience. "There is a stronger will than mine acting against me. You must excuse me for to-night." The man was evidently ill, and utterly unable to proceed, so the curtain was lowered, and the audience dispersed, with many comments upon the lecturer's sudden indisposition.

I waited outside the hall until my friend and the ladies came out. Cowles was laughing over his recent experience.

"He didn't succeed with me, Bob," he cried triumphantly, as he shook my hand. "I think he caught a Tartar that time."

"Yes," said Miss Northcott, "I think that Jack ought to be very proud of his strength of mind; don't you! Mr. Armitage?"

"It took me all my time, though," my friend said seriously. "You can't conceive what a strange feeling I had once or twice. All the strength seemed to have gone out of me--especially just before he collapsed himself."

I walked round with Cowles in order to see the ladies home. He walked in front with Mrs. Merton, and I found myself behind with the young lady. For a minute or so I walked beside her without making any remark, and then I suddenly blurted out, in a manner which must have seemed somewhat brusque to her--

"You did that, Miss Northcott."

"Did what?" she asked sharply.

"Why, mesmerised the mesmeriser--I suppose that is the best way of describing the transaction."

"What a strange idea!" she said, laughing. "You give me credit for a strong will then?"

"Yes," I said. "For a dangerously strong one."

"Why dangerous?" she asked, in a tone of surprise.

"I think," I answered, "that any will which can exercise such power is dangerous--for there is always a chance of its being turned to bad uses."

"You would make me out a very dreadful individual, Mr. Armitage," she said; and then looking up suddenly in my face--"You have never liked me. You are suspicious of me and distrust me, though I have never given you cause."

The accusation was so sudden and so true that I was unable to find any reply to it. She paused for a moment, and then said in a voice which was hard and cold--

"Don't let your prejudice lead you to interfere with me, however, or say anything to your friend, Mr. Cowles, which might lead to a difference between us. You would find that to be very bad policy."

There was something in the way she spoke which gave an indescribable air of a threat to these few words.

"I have no power," I said, "to interfere with your plans for the future. I cannot help, however, from what I have seen and heard, having fears for my friend."

"Fears!" she repeated scornfully. "Pray what have you seen and heard. Something from Mr. Reeves, perhaps--I believe he is another of your friends?"

"He never mentioned your name to me," I answered, truthfully enough. "You will be sorry to hear that he is dying." As I said it we passed by a lighted window, and I glanced down to see what effect my words had upon her. She was laughing--there was no doubt of it; she was laughing quietly to herself. I could see merriment in every feature of her face. I feared and mistrusted the woman from that moment more than ever.

We said little more that night. When we parted she gave me a quick, warning glance, as if to remind me of what she had said about the danger of interference. Her cautions would have made little difference to me could I have seen my way to benefiting Barrington Cowles by anything which I might say. But what could I say? I might say that her former suitors had been unfortunate. I might say that I believed her to be a cruel-hearted woman. I might say that I considered her to possess wonderful, and almost preternatural powers. What impression would any of these accusations make upon an ardent lover--a man with my friend's enthusiastic temperament? I felt that it would be useless to advance them, so I was silent.

And now I come to the beginning of the end. Hitherto much has been surmise and inference and hearsay. It is my painful task to relate now, as dispassionately and as accurately as I can, what actually occurred under my own notice, and to reduce to writing the events which preceded the death of my friend.

Towards the end of the winter Cowles remarked to me that he intended to marry Miss Northcott as soon as possible--probably some time in the spring. He was, as I have already remarked, fairly well off, and the young lady had some money of her own, so that there was no pecuniary reason for a long engagement. "We are going to take a little house out at Corstorphine," he said, "and we hope to see your face at our table, Bob, as often as you can possibly come." I thanked him, and tried to shake off my apprehensions, and persuade myself that all would yet be well.

It was about three weeks before the time fixed for the marriage, that Cowles remarked to me one evening that he feared he would be late that night. "I have had a note from Kate," he said, "asking me to call about eleven o'clock to-night, which seems rather a late hour, but perhaps she wants to talk over something quietly after old Mrs. Merton retires."

It was not until after my friend's departure that I suddenly recollected the mysterious interview which I had been told of as preceding the suicide of young Prescott. Then I thought of the ravings of poor Reeves, rendered more tragic by the fact that I had heard that very day of his death. What was the meaning of it all? Had this woman some baleful secret to disclose which must be known before her marriage? Was it some reason which forbade her to marry? Or was it some reason which forbade others to marry her? I felt so uneasy that I would have followed Cowles, even at the risk of offending him, and endeavoured to dissuade him from keeping his appointment, but a glance at the clock showed me that I was too late.

I was determined to wait up for his return, so I piled some coals upon the fire and took down a novel from the shelf. My thoughts proved more interesting than the book, however, and I threw it on one side. An indefinable feeling of anxiety and depression weighed upon me. Twelve o'clock came, and then half-past, without any sign of my friend. It was nearly one when I heard a step in the street outside, and then a knocking at the door. I was surprised, as I knew that my friend always carried a key-- however, I hurried down and undid the latch. As the door flew open I knew in a moment that my worst apprehensions had been fulfilled. Barrington Cowles was leaning against the railings outside with his face sunk upon his breast, and his whole attitude expressive of the most intense despondency. As he passed in he gave a stagger, and would have fallen had I not thrown my left arm around him. Supporting him with this, and holding the lamp in my other hand, I led him slowly upstairs into our sitting-room. He sank down upon the sofa without a word. Now that I could get a good view of him, I was horrified to see the change which had come over him. His face was deadly pale, and his very lips were bloodless. His cheeks and forehead were clammy, his eyes glazed, and his whole expression altered. He looked like a man who had gone through some terrible ordeal, and was thoroughly unnerved.

"My dear fellow, what is the matter?" I asked, breaking the silence. "Nothing amiss, I trust? Are you unwell?"

"Brandy!" he gasped. "Give me some brandy!"

I took out the decanter, and was about to help him, when he snatched it from me with a trembling hand, and poured out nearly half a tumbler of the spirit. He was usually a most abstemious man, but he took this off at a gulp without adding any water to it.

It seemed to do him good, for the colour began to come back to his face, and he leaned upon his elbow.

"My engagement is off, Bob," he said, trying to speak calmly, but with a tremor in his voice which he could not conceal. "It is all over."

"Cheer up!" I answered, trying to encourage him.

Don't get down on your luck. How was it? What was it all about?"

"About?" he groaned, covering his face with his hands. "If I did tell you, Bob, you would not believe it. It is too dreadful-- too horrible--unutterably awful and incredible! O Kate, Kate!" and he rocked himself to and fro in his grief; "I pictured you an angel and I find you a----"

"A what?" I asked, for he had paused.

He looked at me with a vacant stare, and then suddenly burst out, waving his arms: "A fiend!" he cried. "A ghoul from the pit! A vampire soul behind a lovely face! Now, God forgive me!" he went on in a lower tone, turning his face to the wall; "I have said more than I should. I have loved her too much to speak of her as she is. I love her too much now."

He lay still for some time, and I had hoped that the brandy had had the effect of sending him to sleep, when he suddenly turned his face towards me.

"Did you ever read of wehr-wolves?" he asked.

I answered that I had.

"There is a story," he said thoughtfully, "in one of Marryat's books, about a beautiful woman who took the form of a wolf at night and devoured her own children. I wonder what put that idea into Marryat's head?"

He pondered for some minutes, and then he cried out for some more brandy. There was a small bottle of laudanum upon the table, and I managed, by insisting upon helping him myself, to mix about half a drachm with the spirits. He drank it off, and sank his head once more upon the pillow. "Anything better than that," he groaned. "Death is better than that. Crime and cruelty; cruelty and crime. Anything is better than that," and so on, with the monotonous refrain, until at last the words became indistinct, his eyelids closed over his weary eyes, and he sank into a profound slumber. I carried him into his bedroom without arousing him; and making a couch for myself out of the chairs, I remained by his side all night.

In the morning Barrington Cowles was in a high fever. For weeks he lingered between life and death. The highest medical skill of Edinburgh was called in, and his vigorous constitution slowly got the better of his disease. I nursed him during this anxious time; but through all his wild delirium and ravings he never let a word escape him which explained the mystery connected with Miss Northcott. Sometimes he spoke of her in the tenderest words and most loving voice. At others he screamed out that she was a fiend, and stretched out his arms, as if to keep her off. Several times he cried that he would not sell his soul for a beautiful face, and then he would moan in a most piteous voice, "But I love her--I love her for all that; I shall never cease to love her."

When he came to himself he was an altered man. His severe illness had emaciated him greatly, but his dark eyes had lost none of their brightness. They shone out with startling brilliancy from under his dark, overhanging brows. His manner was eccentric and variable--sometimes irritable, sometimes recklessly mirthful, but never natural. He would glance about him in a strange, suspicious manner, like one who feared something, and yet hardly knew what it was he dreaded. He never mentioned Miss Northcott's name-- never until that fatal evening of which I have now to speak.

In an endeavour to break the current of his thoughts by frequent change of scene, I travelled with him through the highlands of Scotland, and afterwards down the east coast. In one of these peregrinations of ours we visited the Isle of May, an island near the mouth of the Firth of Forth, which, except in the tourist season, is singularly barren and desolate. Beyond the keeper of the lighthouse there are only one or two families of poor fisher- folk, who sustain a precarious existence by their nets, and by the capture of cormorants and solan geese. This grim spot seemed to have such a fascination for Cowles that we engaged a room in one of the fishermen's huts, with the intention of passing a week or two there. I found it very dull, but the loneliness appeared to be a relief to my friend's mind. He lost the look of apprehension which had become habitual to him, and became something like his old self.

He would wander round the island all day, looking down from the summit of the great cliffs which gird it round, and watching the long green waves as they came booming in and burst in a shower of spray over the rocks beneath.

One night--I think it was our third or fourth on the island-- Barrington Cowles and I went outside the cottage before retiring to rest, to enjoy a little fresh air, for our room was small, and the rough lamp caused an unpleasant odour. How well I remember every little circumstance in connection with that night! It promised to be tempestuous, for the clouds were piling up in the north-west, and the dark wrack was drifting across the face of the moon, throwing alternate belts of light and shade upon the rugged surface of the island and the restless sea beyond.

We were standing talking close by the door of the cottage, and I was thinking to myself that my friend was more cheerful than he had been since his illness, when he gave a sudden, sharp cry, and looking round at him I saw, by the light of the moon, an expression of unutterable horror come over his features. His eyes became fixed and staring, as if riveted upon some approaching object, and he extended his long thin forefinger, which quivered as he pointed.

"Look there!" he cried. "It is she! It is she! You see her there coming down the side of the brae." He gripped me convulsively by the wrist as he spoke. "There she is, coming towards us!"

"Who?" I cried, straining my eyes into the darkness.

"She--Kate--Kate Northcott!" he screamed. "She has come for me. Hold me fast, old friend. Don't let me go!"

"Hold up, old man," I said, clapping him on the shoulder. "Pull yourself together; you are dreaming; there is nothing to fear."

"She is gone!" he cried, with a gasp of relief. "No, by heaven! there she is again, and nearer--coming nearer. She told me she would come for me, and she keeps her word."

"Come into the house," I said. His hand, as I grasped it, was as cold as ice.

"Ah, I knew it!" he shouted. "There she is, waving her arms. She is beckoning to me. It is the signal. I must go. I am coming, Kate; I am coming!"

I threw my arms around him, but he burst from me with superhuman strength, and dashed into the darkness of the night. I followed him, calling to him to stop, but he ran the more swiftly. When the moon shone out between the clouds I could catch a glimpse of his dark figure, running rapidly in a straight line, as if to reach some definite goal. It may have been imagination, but it seemed to me that in the flickering light I could distinguish a vague something in front of him--a shimmering form which eluded his grasp and led him onwards. I saw his outlines stand out hard against the sky behind him as he surmounted the brow of a little hill, then he disappeared, and that was the last ever seen by mortal eye of Barrington Cowles.

The fishermen and I walked round the island all that night with lanterns, and examined every nook and corner without seeing a trace of my poor lost friend. The direction in which he had been running terminated in a rugged line of jagged cliffs overhanging the sea. At one place here the edge was somewhat crumbled, and there appeared marks upon the turf which might have been left by human feet. We lay upon our faces at this spot, and peered with our lanterns over the edge, looking down on the boiling surge two hundred feet below. As we lay there, suddenly, above the beating of the waves and the howling of the wind, there rose a strange wild screech from the abyss below. The fishermen--a naturally superstitious race--averred that it was the sound of a woman's laughter, and I could hardly persuade them to continue the search. For my own part I think it may have been the cry of some sea-fowl startled from its nest by the flash of the lantern. However that may be, I never wish to hear such a sound again.

And now I have come to the end of the painful duty which I have undertaken. I have told as plainly and as accurately as I could the story of the death of John Barrington Cowles, and the train of events which preceded it. I am aware that to others the sad episode seemed commonplace enough. Here is the prosaic account which appeared in the Scotsman a couple of days afterwards:--

"Sad Occurrence on the Isle of May.--The Isle of May has been the scene of a sad disaster. Mr. John Barrington Cowles, a gentleman well known in University circles as a most distinguished student, and the present holder of the Neil Arnott prize for physics, has been recruiting his health in this quiet retreat. The night before last he suddenly left his friend, Mr. Robert Armitage, and he has not since been heard of. It is almost certain that he has met his death by falling over the cliffs which surround the island. Mr. Cowles' health has been failing for some time, partly from over study and partly from worry connected with family affairs. By his death the University loses one of her most promising alumni."

I have nothing more to add to my statement. I have unburdened my mind of all that I know. I can well conceive that many, after weighing all that I have said, will see no ground for an accusation against Miss Northcott. They will say that, because a man of a naturally excitable disposition says and does wild things, and even eventually commits self-murder after a sudden and heavy disappointment, there is no reason why vague charges should be advanced against a young lady. To this, I answer that they are welcome to their opinion. For my own part, I ascribe the death of William Prescott, of Archibald Reeves, and of John Barrington Cowles to this woman with as much confidence as if I had seen her drive a dagger into their hearts.

You ask me, no doubt, what my own theory is which will explain all these strange facts. I have none, or, at best, a dim and vague one. That Miss Northcott possessed extraordinary powers over the minds, and through the minds over the bodies, of others, I am convinced, as well as that her instincts were to use this power for base and cruel purposes. That some even more fiendish and terrible phase of character lay behind this--some horrible trait which it was necessary for her to reveal before marriage--is to be inferred from the experience of her three lovers, while the dreadful nature of the mystery thus revealed can only be surmised from the fact that the very mention of it drove from her those who had loved her so passionately. Their subsequent fate was, in my opinion, the result of her vindictive remembrance of their desertion of her, and that they were forewarned of it at the time was shown by the words of both Reeves and Cowles. Above this, I can say nothing. I lay the facts soberly before the public as they came under my notice. I have never seen Miss Northcott since, nor do I wish to do so. If by the words I have written I can save any one human being from the snare of those bright eyes and that beautiful face, then I can lay down my pen with the assurance that my poor friend has not died altogether in vain.

KATE is unquestionably wrought in the tradition of queered seductresses like Ligeia, Carmilla, and Geraldine, but she *most* closely follows the literary example of Machen's Helen Vaughan: another Victorian vampiress and seductive socialite, who lures, enslaves, and destroys men, collecting their souls as trophies of conquest. Both characters share one more, very important trait: their victims are *well-bred, socially powerful men*, whereas they are unattached women without guardians, fortunes, or high-born families. "John Barrington Cowles" is a study in lust and its power to break through all barriers, even the unbending strata of socio-economic classes during the Victorian Era. But this is not merely a sentimental Cinderella Story about the power of love to overcome prejudice: it is a much darker study of the blinding, disorienting power which runaway sexual cravings can wield over intellect and morality, and the vast destruction it can do to even the most authentic person's character and integrity. Sherlock Holmes was famously wary of romance ("love is an emotional thing, and whatever is emotional is opposed to that true cold reason which I place above all things. I should never marry myself, lest I bias my judgment"), though – I would strongly argue – he was hardly a misogynist. In the same manner, this story – which could be mistaken for chauvinistic vitriol – is not so much an assault on or a vilification of powerful *women*, as it is a solemn parable about lustful *men*. Kate comes from genuinely bad stock (note that her wicked ancestor, like Sir Hugo Baskerville, is a *man*), and it is her *soul* rather than her *gender* with which Doyle concerns himself. Oscar Wilde would do the same thing with Dorian Gray, a pansexual, male libertine who used lust to leverage himself socially: the horror of that novel is not so much its homoeroticism or Gray's sexual curiosity, as it is Gray's gradual loss of his humanity and compassion. Erotic emotions terrified the Victorians, not so much because they were prudes as it did because of the threat they posed humanity's higher nature. Lust trumps all social niceties and disciplines; once given into, it can make a murderer out of a humanitarian, a fool out of a genius, a slave out of a king, and a pariah out of a holy man.

II.

Some critics have seen this as a primarily social anxiety: that the Victorians feared romance for its ability to challenge the status quo of social castes by destabilize England's elite families with beautiful albeit low-born social climbers. This may have been a concern of the upper crust, but (for some obvious reasons) it was far from universal, especially among newly socially-mobile middle classes of the Industrial Revolution. Indeed, it was an exceedingly common sentimental trope, and Industrial Era fiction is riddled with poor girls attracting the love of gentlemen through virtue and affection (cf. the novels of Samuel Richardson, Jane Austen, or Charlotte Bronte). *Love* conquering all was perfectly acceptable: after all, it could lead to hard-hearted aristocrats opening their minds to the plight of other classes of humans due to their newfound sympathy with a poor man's daughter. It was impulsive, ignoble *lust* conquering all that was a horror. Whereas love exposes the reality hidden by prejudices (making the lowly seem lovable), lust empowers the wicked and inhumane (making the awful seem alluring). Lust melts resolve, intuition, and decency, leaving society vulnerable to abuse and corruption. It disguises truth and misleads seekers. None of Kate's beaux decided that their physical relationship was worthwhile after being exposed to her nature, so we can sit comfortably with the theory that JBC is not merely a scare-story about premarital sex: it was her *soul* that terrified them, not her *body*. Ultimately, while Kate's demonization is somewhat of a feminist issue, at its heart this is not the classic tale of "sexually assertive women are evil" – it is a *moral* tale not a *social* one: yes Kate empowers herself in the midst of a patriarchal society, but it is a sadistic power, not an assertive one. Doyle's women were often (if not typically) strong, virtuous, clear-eyed, and brave. Irene Adler is also a powerful woman who brings a European kingdom to its knees, but she is characterized as gallant, brilliant, and admirable – "*the* Woman." No, it is not her seemingly modern sexuality that makes Kate a horror, but *what she does with it*, and what her power poses to do to society: corrupt good citizens, wane standards of humanity, and dismiss moral dilemmas: remember that her abuses against the dog and her servant (both of whom are weaker and less powerful than her) are tolerated because of her sexual appeal and rising social power. Throughout the tail end of the 19th century, Doyle's own social community (the liberal, professional classes of Greater London) was haunted by scandal – politicians connected to prostitutes, and medical men accused of murders – and it was hardly a prudish reaction that caused its members to fear the influence of lust, where manipulation rules over affection and libido dominates conscience. With a steady hand, Doyle navigates his readers through yet another disciplined story of the wild and supernatural – a classic vampire story without a single drop of blood.

AS we will mention in our notes to "The Ring of Thoth," Doyle's role in the evolution of the "malevolent mummy" trope was just as fundamental as Stoker's contributions to the vampire, Stevenson's to the werewolf, and Shelley's to the science fiction monster. While "The Ring of Thoth" succeeded in breaking the mummy out of its quaint roles as a romantic curiosity or a satirical mouthpiece – bringing it into the realm of somber supernaturalism – "Lot No. 249" dragged it over the threshold into abject horror. The tale is almost single-handedly responsible for our perception of mummies as potential terrors – combined with the rumors surrounding the Curse of Tutankhamen, and Bram Stoker's horror novella, *The Jewel of Seven Stars* – and was loosely adapted into one of Boris Karloff's seminal roles: the nefarious immortal wizard (and revitalized mummy) Imhotep in Karl Freund's splendid 1932 masterpiece, *The Mummy*. Infused with the romantic plot from "The Ring of Thoth" and the reincarnation device from "Through the Veil, the screenplay was virtually co-written by Doyle, who had died just two years before. "Lot No. 249" is one of my favorite horror stories: it combines the cozy, sitting room atmosphere of Baker Street with the bucolic, intellectual setting of Oxford University, but is subtly darkened by the shadow of a strange and terrible horror that baffles England's brightest and best. It is, however, far from a simple tale of terror, and has the same rich subtext – mostly sexual, cultural, and social – of the Poe and Hoffmann's wildest tales. The story is even more steeped in homoerotic overtones than "The Silver Hatchet," openly brooding – without excuse or artifice – on the nature of British masculinity and its ideal manifestation. The four main characters represent four elements of manhood: the "robust" athlete, the profound scholar, the effeminate victim, and the craven villain. The story revolves around these men as they attempt to define and demonstrate their manliness, at times quite brazenly, fearing all the time that they might be – as Abercrombie Smith puts it – "unmanned." The mummy in question is closeted away in the villain's room, leading to open speculation about his sex life (they assume it to be a "kept woman"), little imagining the truth: it is a revived zombie employed to stalk, dominate, and strangle (a very intimate means of murder) his male enemies. It remains a brilliant commentary on Victorian manhood, with all manner of fascinating symbolism surrounding closeted men, sexual victimhood, and the anxieties of passing as "manly" in a homosocial environment like all-male Oxford in 1884. For Doyle, who stewed over same-sex friendship, masculine rituals, and the "robust" sporting life, it is a vulnerable – if narrow-minded – thesis on the perils, pursuits, and anxieties of the single British male.

Lot No. 249; or, The Mummy

{1892}

Of the dealings of Edward Bellingham with William Monkhouse Lee, and of the cause of the great terror of Abercrombie Smith, it may be that no absolute and final judgment will ever be delivered. It is true that we have the full and clear narrative of Smith himself, and such corroboration as he could look for from Thomas Styles the servant, from the Reverend Plumptree Peterson, Fellow of Old's[1], and from such other people as chanced to gain some passing glance at this or that incident in a singular chain of events. Yet, in the main, the story must rest upon Smith alone, and the most will think that it is more likely that one brain, however outwardly sane, has some subtle warp in its texture, some strange flaw in its workings, than that the path of Nature has been overstepped in open day in so famed a centre of learning and light as the University of Oxford[2]. Yet when we think how narrow and how devious this path of Nature is, how dimly we can trace it, for all our lamps of science, and how from the darkness which girds it round great and terrible possibilities loom ever shadowly upwards, it is a bold and confident man who will put a limit to the strange by-paths into which the human spirit may wander.

In a certain wing of what we will call Old College in Oxford there is a corner turret of an exceeding great age. The heavy arch which spans the open door has bent downwards in the centre under the weight of its years, and the grey, lichen-blotched blocks of stone are, bound and knitted together with withes and strands of ivy, as though the old mother[3] had set herself to brace them up against wind and weather. From the door a stone stair curves upward spirally, passing two landings, and terminating in a third one, its steps all shapeless and hollowed by the tread of so many generations of the seekers after knowledge. Life has flowed like water down this winding stair, and, waterlike, has left these smooth-worn grooves behind it. From the long-gowned, pedantic scholars of Plantagenet days[4] down to the young bloods of a later age, how full and strong had been that tide of young English life. And what was left now of all those hopes, those strivings, those fiery energies, save here and there in some old-world

---

[1] As will be later hinted at, the name is a false one. It is a likely play on New College, which was founded in the ironic year of 1379. Doyle is hinting (knowing that his audience is familiar with New's) that if New's is five hundred years old, then Old's must be thoroughly antique. Here Doyle sets the stage at a worn and crumbling corner of Oxford, dripping with antiquity and wrinkled with history – as fine a setting as can be found in England to play out the drama to follow

[2] Like *Polestar*, this tale is rife with similarities to *Frankenstein*, the first being the introduction of Smith as a capable genius who may have been a great resource for good had he not been corrupted by an impulse to shift the channels of nature and play God

[3] Mother Nature, that is

[4] Lasting from 1154 to 1485, the Plantagenet House was a royal dynasty of Norman kings who ruled England, and included such luminaries as Richard the Lionhearted, the vilified Richard III, Henry "Prince Hal" V, Henry IV, Edward "Longshanks" I, and King John of Robin Hood infamy

churchyard a few scratches upon a stone, and perchance a handful of dust in a mouldering coffin[1]? Yet here were the silent stair and the grey old wall, with bend and saltire[2] and many another heraldic device still to be read upon its surface, like grotesque shadows thrown back from the days that had passed[3].

In the month of May, in the year 1884, three young men occupied the sets of rooms which opened on to the separate landings of the old stair. Each set consisted simply of a sitting-room and of a bedroom, while the two corresponding rooms upon the ground-floor were used, the one as a coal-cellar, and the other as the living-room of the servant, or gyp, Thomas Styles, whose duty it was to wait upon the three men above him. To right and to left was a line of lecture-rooms and of offices, so that the dwellers in the old turret enjoyed a certain seclusion, which made the chambers popular among the more studious undergraduates. Such were the three who occupied them now--Abercrombie Smith above, Edward Bellingham beneath him, and William Monkhouse Lee upon the lowest storey[4].

---

[1] Doyle sets the stage for questioning the permanence of death. For all his eulogizing the generations that have died leaving only wear and tear to remember them by, it is clear that the place is rich with layers of accumulating life that – for all the centuries that have passed – continue to hum and vibrate in the empty corridors. Bellingham, of course, knows all too well that human life is not reduced solely to dust in a moldering coffin – that dust is merely slumbering

[2] In heraldry, a bend is a crossbar running diagonally across a shield (cf. the diving flag) and a saltire is an X-shaped cross (cf. the Scottish or Confederate flags), both of which are used extensively in coats of arms and other devices across the world. As Harry Potter fans know, each school is wont to have its own heraldic device, and within each school there are still more to represent houses, clubs, concentrations, and societies

[3] Again we hear the theme march on: if these things are supposed to be dead – these people, these ideas, these ambitions, these histories – then why do they continue to cast a shadow on modern society? The dead and gone do not cast shadows

[4] The setup is suggestive of three levels of manhood: the manly hero, the jaded villain, and the nervous victim. Smith, the highest, is studious, athletic, stoic, and taciturn – a private, self-reliant, and principled gentleman, the archetype of the British hero – the same as Holmes. Bellingham, beneath Smith but above Lee, is as capable, dedicated, intelligent, and emotionally restrained as Smith, but lacks the principles and virtue Smith shares with Lee. He is craven, selfish, greedy for recognition, desperate for approval, and sorely jaded against the society that emulates Smith and protects Lee. In those respects he is a villain – an enemy of Western civilization whose unmanly sense of inferiority puts him at odds with Smith and sends him on a vengeful mission to subvert the Smiths of the world by victimizing the Lees. Lastly, beneath both the superior Smith and the inferior Bellingham is the effeminate and victimized Lee. Lee is nervous, suggestible, somewhat scattered, and mildly negligent, but above all emotionally expressive and excitable, thus making a less manful appearance – the archetype of the imperiled victim. Sexually the dynamics here are quite interesting: the manly but homosocial Smith (cf. Holmes), the eccentric, domineering, and campy Bellingham, and the rabbity, submissive, and helpless Lee. In this world with only one gender (women are only passingly suggested at – Lee's sister whom Bellingham attempted to seduce) there are three apparent choices: sexless masculinity,

It was ten o'clock on a bright spring night, and Abercrombie Smith[1] lay back in his arm-chair, his feet upon the fender, and his briar-root pipe between his lips[2]. In a similar chair, and equally at his ease, there lounged on the other side of the fireplace his old school friend Jephro Hastie[3]. Both men were in flannels, for they had spent their evening upon the river[4], but apart from their dress no one could look at their hard-cut, alert faces without seeing that they were open-air men--men whose minds and tastes turned naturally to all that was manly and robust[5]. Hastie, indeed, was stroke[6] of his college boat, and Smith was an even better oar, but a coming examination had already cast its shadow over him and held him to his work, save for the few hours a week which health demanded[7]. A litter of medical books upon the table, with scattered bones, models and anatomical plates, pointed to the extent as well as the nature of his studies, while a couple of single-sticks[8] and a set of boxing-gloves above the mantelpiece hinted at the means by which, with Hastie's help, he might take his exercise in its most

---

bisexual villainy, or homosexual victimization. Of course, there is no sex here at all, but as we shall see, Bellingham's secret roommate has all sorts of sexual implications that are impossible to avoid discussing

[1] A name with implications: Smith, the name of the everyman – straightforward, unpretentious, and genuine – and Abercrombie, the name of a high-end sporting goods retailer (in the days before it ministered to posh teens) based in New York. Abercrombie Co, (later joined by Fitch) was founded in June, four months before this story was produced. As a transatlantic gentleman, an avid sportsman, and a great consumer of newspapers, Doyle would have been aware of the advertising buzz surrounding the new chain, and the name seems to suggest health, vigor, and manly vitality

[2] In Doyle, pipe smoking is a masculine rite which denotes thoughtfulness, intellect, and emotional control. Have troubles? Worried? Depressed? Don't talk about it or complain; smoke a pipe, internalize your anxiety, and self-reliance will work it all out. First seen partaking in this ritual, Smith is immediately recognized as a manful, self-controlled character of good standing

[3] A Scottish surname which predicts its bearer's personality: brash, quick-acting, prone to action, in other words, quite hasty. Hastie is the other side of ideal manhood – the Watson as it were. Where Smith is saturnine and thoughtful, Hastie is outspoken and vital

[4] Flannels were the Under Armour of the day, being used in most outdoors athletic events of relative leisure (so not rugby, boxing, or football, but hiking, rowing, shooting, camping). In this case the activity is sculling, or rowing competitively

[5] I think much of the commentary here would frankly be obvious. Simply note that Doyle's codification of manhood is not tremendously subtle

[6] The rower closest to the stern of the boat who sets the pace of the oar sweeps. Their responsibility is establishing the rhythm of the rowing and communicating with the cox

[7] Unlike Bellingham, who is over-committed to his intellectual pursuits, Smith strikes a balance between studies and athletics – which "health demands"

[8] Single-stick is a martial art akin to fencing conducted with wooden cudgels which typically included a leather guard and grip like a saber. Originally designed as a comparatively safe way to practice swordplay, Sherlock Holmes was known to be a master of the craft which came in handy when he was attacked by brigands in "The Illustrious Client" and defended himself with his cane

compressed and least distant form[1]. They knew each other very well--so well that they could sit now in that soothing silence which is the very highest development of companionship[2].

"Have some whisky," said Abercrombie Smith at last between two cloudbursts. "Scotch in the jug and Irish in the bottle."

"No, thanks. I'm in for the sculls. I don't liquor when I'm training. How about you?"

"I'm reading hard. I think it best to leave it alone."

Hastie nodded, and they relapsed into a contented silence.

"By-the-way, Smith," asked Hastie, presently, "have you made the acquaintance of either of the fellows on your stair yet?"

"Just a nod when we pass. Nothing more."

"Hum! I should be inclined to let it stand at that. I know something of them both. Not much, but as much as I want. I don't think I should take them to my bosom if I were you. Not that there's much amiss with Monkhouse Lee[3]."

"Meaning the thin[4] one?"

"Precisely. He is a gentlemanly little fellow. I don't think there is any vice in him. But then you can't know him without knowing[5] Bellingham[6]."

"Meaning the fat one?"

"Yes, the fat one. And he's a man whom I, for one, would rather not know."

Abercrombie Smith raised his eyebrows and glanced across at his companion.

"What's up, then?" he asked. "Drink? Cards? Cad[7]? You used not to be censorious."

"Ah! you evidently don't know the man, or you wouldn't ask. There's something damnable about him--something reptilian. My gorge always rises

---

[1] A convenient visual summary of Smith's dual life – the mental and the physical

[2] This Watson/Holmes dynamic – a quietly intimate homosocial relationship – is a common Doyle ideal based on Greek and Roman values of *philia*, or brotherly love

[3] The name Monkhouse seems to imply infertile isolation and stodgy, introspective impotence

[4] Doyle adores phrenology and physiological personality analyses; thinness indicates intellect combined with reserve, but unlike the spindly but towering Holmes, Lee is a little, wasted man with a little, wasted personality

[5] There is already something fishy to Smith and Hastie about the relationship between these two men: it is impossible to know one without the other, which implies either a sense of indecent dependence, or a parasitic relationship. Even without reading a sexual element into their association, it defies conventional British standards of masculinity for being excessively clingy and dependent

[6] "Bellingham" sounds bombastic, corpulent, and somewhat grotesque with its connotations of clanging bells and fattened pigs

[7] A man who mistreats women – a rake or player

at him. I should put him down as a man with secret vices--an evil liver[1]. He's no fool, though. They say that he is one of the best men in his line that they have ever had in the college[2]."

"Medicine or classics[3]?"

"Eastern languages. He's a demon at them[4]. Chillingworth[5] met him somewhere above the second cataract[6] last long, and he told me that he just prattled to the Arabs as if he had been born and nursed and weaned among them. He talked Coptic to the Copts, and Hebrew to the Jews, and Arabic to the Bedouins, and they were all ready to kiss the hem of his frock-coat. There are some old hermit Johnnies[7] up in those parts who sit on rocks and scowl and spit at the casual stranger. Well, when they saw this chap Bellingham, before he had said five words they just lay down on their bellies and wriggled. Chillingworth said that he never saw anything like it. Bellingham seemed to take it as his right, too, and strutted about among them and talked down to them like a Dutch uncle[8]. Pretty good for an undergrad. Of Old's, wasn't it?"

"Why do you say you can't know Lee without knowing Bellingham?"

"Because Bellingham is engaged to his sister Eveline. Such a bright little girl, Smith! I know the whole family well. It's disgusting to see that brute with her. A toad and a dove, that's what they always remind me of."

Abercrombie Smith grinned and knocked his ashes out against the side of the grate.

"You show every card in your hand, old chap," said he. "What a prejudiced, green-eyed, evil-thinking old man it is! You have really nothing against the fellow except that."

"Well, I've known her ever since she was as long as that cherry-wood pipe, and I don't like to see her taking risks. And it is a risk. He looks

---

[1] Plato argued that the liver was "the seat of the darkest emotions (specifically wrath, jealous and greed) which drive men to action," a belief shared by the writers of the Hebrew Talmud

[2] Doyle may have a prototype for Professor Moriarty here, about whom he said: "He is a man of good birth and excellent education... and had, to all appearances, a most brilliant career before him. But the man had hereditary tendencies of the most diabolical kind. A criminal strain ran in his blood, which, instead of being modified, was increased and rendered infinitely more dangerous by his extraordinary mental powers. Dark rumours gathered round him in the University town, and eventually he was compelled to resign." A brilliant man with a rotten character is indeed a dangerous maverick to deal with

[3] Humanities: literature, history, philosophy, and languages

[4] Playful foreshadowing

[5] Almost certainly a reference to Bellingham's literary kinsman, Roger Chillingworth, the vindictive scholar – who is himself a flabby and toadish dabbler in the occult – from Nathaniel Hawthorne's *The Scarlet Letter*

[6] One of six shallow rapids that are historical landmarks of the Nile

[7] Turks

[8] We would say a rich uncle – someone who stands to benefit them

beastly. And he has a beastly temper, a venomous temper. You remember his row with Long Norton?"

"No; you always forget that I am a freshman."

"Ah, it was last winter. Of course. Well, you know the towpath[1] along by the river. There were several fellows going along it, Bellingham in front, when they came on an old market-woman[2] coming the other way. It had been raining--you know what those fields are like when it has rained--and the path ran between the river and a great puddle that was nearly as broad. Well, what does this swine do but keep the path, and push the old girl into the mud, where she and her marketings came to terrible grief. It was a blackguard thing to do, and Long Norton, who is as gentle a fellow as ever stepped, told him what he thought of it. One word led to another, and it ended in Norton laying his stick across the fellow's shoulders. There was the deuce of a fuss about it, and it's a treat to see the way in which Bellingham looks at Norton when they meet now. By Jove, Smith, it's nearly eleven o'clock!"

"No hurry. Light your pipe again."

"Not I. I'm supposed to be in training. Here I've been sitting gossiping when I ought to have been safely tucked up. I'll borrow your skull, if you can share it. Williams has had mine for a month. I'll take the little bones of your ear, too, if you are sure you won't need them. Thanks very much. Never mind a bag, I can carry them very well under my arm[3]. Good-night, my son, and take my tip as to your neighbour."

When Hastie, bearing his anatomical plunder, had clattered off down the winding stair, Abercrombie Smith hurled his pipe into the wastepaper basket[4], and drawing his chair nearer to the lamp, plunged into a formidable green-covered volume, adorned with great colored maps of that strange internal kingdom of which we are the hapless and helpless monarchs[5]. Though a freshman at Oxford, the student was not so in medicine, for he had worked for four years at Glasgow and at Berlin[6], and this coming examination would place him finally as a member of his profession. With

---

[1] A rough trail on the side of a river or canal used by horses or oxen to tow barges from the shore

[2] A woman who peddles wares – vegetables, goods, soaps, knittings, etc – much in the manner of participants in modern farmers' markets

[3] A little black medical humor from Doyle, who is slowly setting the tone by introducing this macabre vision into a warm and cheery sitting room

[4] Not unlike Holmes' coal shuttle where he stores his cigars. If it hasn't become immediately apparent, Smith is – consciously or unconsciously – as much of a self-pastiche of Holmes as Bellingham resembles Moriarty

[5] That is Egypt. Egypt became a British protectorate in 1882

[6] Berlin and Glasgow were both renowned for being centers of scholarship and hard-headed research during the late 19th century when colleges were moving away from humanities and liberal arts-based classical education and towards a rigorous use of peer review and scientific method

his firm mouth, broad forehead, and clear-cut, somewhat hard-featured face[1], he was a man who, if he had no brilliant talent, was yet so dogged, so patient, and so strong that he might in the end overtop a more showy genius. A man who can hold his own among Scotchmen and North Germans[2] is not a man to be easily set back. Smith had left a name at Glasgow and at Berlin, and he was bent now upon doing as much at Oxford, if hard work and devotion could accomplish it.

He had sat reading for about an hour, and the hands of the noisy carriage clock upon the side table were rapidly closing together upon the twelve, when a sudden sound fell upon the student's ear--a sharp, rather shrill sound, like the hissing intake of a man's breath who gasps under some strong emotion. Smith laid down his book and slanted his ear to listen. There was no one on either side or above him, so that the interruption came certainly from the neighbour beneath--the same neighbour of whom Hastie had given so unsavoury an account. Smith knew him only as a flabby, pale-faced man of silent and studious habits, a man, whose lamp threw a golden bar from the old turret even after he had extinguished his own. This community in lateness had formed a certain silent bond between them. It was soothing to Smith when the hours stole on towards dawning to feel that there was another so close who set as small a value upon his sleep as he did[3]. Even now, as his thoughts turned towards him, Smith's feelings were kindly. Hastie was a good fellow, but he was rough, strong-fibred, with no imagination or sympathy. He could not tolerate departures from what he looked upon as the model type of manliness[4]. If a man could not be measured by a public-school standard[5], then he was beyond the pale with Hastie. Like so many who are themselves robust, he was apt to confuse the constitution with the character, to ascribe to want of principle what was really a want of circulation. Smith, with his stronger mind, knew his friend's

---

[1] Physiologically suggestive of strong character, strong intellect, and stoic but noble personality, respectively

[2] Scots and Prussian have both achieved reputations for their robust intellectualism

[3] The relationship between Smith and Bellingham has parallels with that between Lee and Bellingham – the first being a symbiotic, comforting homosocial relationship defined by absence – by remote proximity – while the later is a parasitic, antagonizing homosocial relationship defined by intrusion – by unavoidable proximity. The comparison shows both how different Smith is in his relationship with Bellingham (read: appropriate masculinity) and how unnervingly similar it is (only a few personal visits would be necessary to transform their complacent remoteness into aggravated intimacy

[4] The "hastiness" of Hastie's more impulsive masculinity is reasserted – while Smith is melancholic and even-keeled, Hastie is sanguine and hot-blooded. While both have their pros and cons, Doyle seems to validate both humors as acceptable interpretations of Victorian manhood

[5] Public school in Britain means the opposite of what it means in the States – a school system funded by donors rather than by government. There is a strong classist element to Hastie's disgust, which seems to begrudge Bellingham's self-educated past

habit, and made allowance for it now as his thoughts turned towards the man beneath him.

There was no return of the singular sound, and Smith was about to turn to his work once more, when suddenly there broke out in the silence of the night a hoarse cry, a positive scream--the call of a man who is moved and shaken beyond all control. Smith sprang out of his chair and dropped his book. He was a man of fairly firm fibre, but there was something in this sudden, uncontrollable shriek of horror which chilled his blood and pringled[1] in his skin. Coming in such a place and at such an hour, it brought a thousand fantastic possibilities into his head. Should he rush down, or was it better to wait? He had all the national hatred of making a scene[2], and he knew so little of his neighbour that he would not lightly intrude upon his affairs. For a moment he stood in doubt and even as he balanced the matter there was a quick rattle of footsteps upon the stairs, and young Monkhouse Lee, half dressed and as white as ashes, burst into his room.

"Come down!" he gasped. "Bellingham's ill."

Abercrombie Smith followed him closely down stairs into the sitting-room which was beneath his own, and intent as he was upon the matter in hand, he could not but take an amazed glance around him as he crossed the threshold. It was such a chamber as he had never seen before--a museum rather than a study. Walls and ceiling were thickly covered with a thousand strange relics from Egypt and the East. Tall, angular figures bearing burdens or weapons stalked in an uncouth frieze[3] round the apartments. Above were bull-headed, stork-headed, cat-headed, owl-headed statues, with viper-crowned, almond-eyed monarchs, and strange, beetle-like deities cut out of the blue Egyptian lapis lazuli.[4] Horus and Isis and Osiris[5] peeped down from every niche and shelf, while across the ceiling a true son of Old Nile, a great, hanging-jawed crocodile, was slung in a double noose.

In the centre of this singular chamber was a large, square table, littered with papers, bottles, and the dried leaves of some graceful, palm-like plant. These varied objects had all been heaped together in order to make room for a mummy case[6], which had been conveyed from the wall, as was evident

---

[1] A portmanteau of *prickle* and *tingle*

[2] British manliness – the stiff-upper lip philosophy

[3] A long stretch or band of decoration, be it sculpture, painting, calligraphy, or bas relief

[4] A semi-precious stone of very deep, pure blue

[5] Three of the most important Egyptian gods: Osiris with his green skin and pharaoh's garb was the ruler of the underworld and the dead, while his consort, the maternal Isis was seen as a goddess of magic and life, and their son, the falcon-headed Horus represented the sun, war, and protection

[6] Mummies, though rare, were not the priceless museum pieces they are today during the 19th century. With the rise of Egyptology beginning with Napoleon's exploits during the European conflicts that bore his name, Europeans consumed Egyptian culture voraciously, and it was not uncommon for aristocrats to purchase mummies with as little effort as one would bid for an armoire or piano. Mummy unwrapping parties were not unheard of, and

from the gap there, and laid across the front of the table. The mummy itself, a horrid, black, withered thing, like a charred head on a gnarled bush, was lying half out of the case, with its clawlike hand and bony forearm resting upon the table. Propped up against the sarcophagus was an old yellow scroll of papyrus, and in front of it, in a wooden armchair, sat the owner of the room, his head thrown back, his widely-opened eyes directed in a horrified stare to the crocodile above him[1], and his blue, thick lips puffing loudly with every expiration.

"My God! he's dying!" cried Monkhouse Lee distractedly.

He was a slim, handsome young fellow, olive-skinned and dark-eyed, of a Spanish rather than of an English type[2], with a Celtic[3] intensity of manner which contrasted with the Saxon phlegm of Abercombie Smith.

"Only a faint, I think," said the medical student. "Just give me a hand with him. You take his feet. Now on to the sofa. Can you kick all those little wooden devils[4] off? What a litter it is! Now he will be all right if we undo his collar and give him some water. What has he been up to at all?"

"I don't know. I heard him cry out. I ran up. I know him pretty well, you know. It is very good of you to come down."

"His heart is going like a pair of castanets," said Smith, laying his hand on the breast of the unconscious man. "He seems to me to be frightened all to pieces. Chuck the water over him! What a face he has got on him!"

It was indeed a strange and most repellent face, for colour and outline were equally unnatural. It was white, not with the ordinary pallor of fear but with an absolutely bloodless white, like the under side of a sole. He was very fat, but gave the impression of having at some time been considerably fatter, for his skin hung loosely in creases and folds, and was shot with a

---

were often sensational events that featured the corpse being unwound in a private fete followed by its rapid disintegration after being carelessly exposed to the air without any preservative efforts. Thousands of mummies were mishandled and destroyed this way (Mark Twain once joked that they were used as fuel for locomotives), and as a result, they are now the rare and well-guarded gems of today's museums. This may explain the lack of shock at Bellingham's having a mummy sitting willy-nilly in his study. In fact, it might even be expected of an Egyptologist just as one might expect a skeleton assembled in the room of an anatomist or a suit of armor in the library of a medieval historian

[1] Recall that Hastie described Bellingham as somehow "reptilian." The parallelism between the metaphorical reptile and the preserved crocodile is thoroughly intentional on Doyle's part

[2] Spanish and Celtic masculinity – excitable, emotional, and undisciplined – is eagerly juxtaposed with so-called Anglo-Saxon phlegm – detached, stoic self-discipline. Such lack of restraint or self-reliance is at odds with Doyle's insular ideal of "robust" manhood

[3] Both Monkhouse and Lee are English surnames. We might assume that Lee's mother was Welsh – possibly Irish or Scottish. This receptiveness to his mother's heritage – though assumed – further fleshes out his portrayal as weak and effete

[4] Idols, though the term "devil" or demon is certainly suggestive of the powers at play here

meshwork of wrinkles. Short, stubbly brown hair bristled up from his scalp, with a pair of thick, wrinkled ears protruding on either side[1]. His light grey eyes were still open, the pupils dilated and the balls projecting in a fixed and horrid stare. It seemed to Smith as he looked down upon him that he had never seen nature's danger signals flying so plainly upon a man's countenance, and his thoughts turned more seriously to the warning which Hastie had given him an hour before.

"What the deuce can have frightened him so?" he asked.

"It's the mummy."

"The mummy? How, then?"

"I don't know. It's beastly and morbid. I wish he would drop it. It's the second fright he has given me. It was the same last winter. I found him just like this, with that horrid thing in front of him."

"What does he want with the mummy, then?"

"Oh, he's a crank[2], you know. It's his hobby. He knows more about these things than any man in England. But I wish he wouldn't! Ah, he's beginning to come to."

A faint tinge of colour had begun to steal back into Bellingham's ghastly cheeks, and his eyelids shivered like a sail after a calm. He clasped and unclasped his hands, drew a long, thin breath between his teeth, and suddenly jerking up his head, threw a glance of recognition around him. As his eyes fell upon the mummy, he sprang off the sofa, seized the roll of papyrus, thrust it into a drawer, turned the key, and then staggered back on to the sofa.

"What's up?" he asked. "What do you chaps want?"

"You've been shrieking out and making no end of a fuss," said Monkhouse Lee. "If our neighbour here from above hadn't come down, I'm sure I don't know what I should have done with you."

"Ah, it's Abercrombie Smith," said Bellingham, glancing up at him. "How very good of you to come in! What a fool I am! Oh, my God, what a fool I am!"

He sunk his head on to his hands, and burst into peal after peal of hysterical laughter.

"Look here! Drop it!" cried Smith, shaking him roughly by the shoulder.

"Your nerves are all in a jangle. You must drop these little midnight games with mummies, or you'll be going off your chump[3]. You're all on wires now."

---

[1] Everything about Bellingham is – physiologically speaking – grotesque, distasteful, and off putting. He appears flabby, overfed, and unkempt, with a sense of wrongness and perversity lingering about him (again, according to conventional ideas of physiological personality readings). He is toadlike

[2] An annoyingly eccentric person – a loon

[3] British slang of unknown origin: mad, balmy, off your rocker

"I wonder," said Bellingham, "whether you would be as cool as I am if you had seen----"

"What then?"

"Oh, nothing. I meant that I wonder if you could sit up at night with a mummy without trying your nerves. I have no doubt that you are quite right. I dare say that I have been taking it out of myself too much lately. But I am all right now. Please don't go, though. Just wait for a few minutes until I am quite myself."

"The room is very close[1]," remarked Lee, throwing open the window and letting in the cool night air.

"It's balsamic resin[2]," said Bellingham. He lifted up one of the dried palmate leaves from the table and frizzled it over the chimney of the lamp. It broke away into heavy smoke wreaths, and a pungent, biting odour filled the chamber. "It's the sacred plant--the plant of the priests," he remarked. "Do you know anything of Eastern languages, Smith?"

"Nothing at all. Not a word[3]."

The answer seemed to lift a weight from the Egyptologist's mind.

"By-the-way," he continued, "how long was it from the time that you ran down, until I came to my senses?"

"Not long. Some four or five minutes."

"I thought it could not be very long," said he, drawing a long breath. "But what a strange thing unconsciousness is! There is no measurement to it. I could not tell from my own sensations if it were seconds or weeks. Now that gentleman on the table was packed up in the days of the eleventh dynasty[4], some forty centuries ago, and yet if he could find his tongue he would tell us that this lapse of time has been but a closing of the eyes and a reopening of them. He is a singularly fine mummy, Smith."

Smith stepped over to the table and looked down with a professional eye at the black and twisted form in front of him. The features, though horribly discoloured, were perfect, and two little nut-like eyes still lurked in the depths of the black, hollow sockets[5]. The blotched skin was drawn tightly from bone to bone, and a tangled wrap of black coarse hair fell over the

---

1 Meaning musty, stuffy, acrid

2 Commonly used in perfumes, religious incense, and essential oils, he refers to benzoin, the hydrocarbon excretions of plants of the Styrax genus. Frankincense is one popular example

3 Being a tad xenophobic, Smith is likely proud of his ignorance

4 Dynasty XI occurred sometime between 2160 BCE and 1985 BCE (estimations vary) during the Middle Kingdom of Egypt, or Period of Reunification, at a time when Osiris became the principle diety, and the kingdom was united under a single, central government in Thebes

5 If we follow the conventional wisdom that the eyes are the windows to the soul, then this corpse is still endowed with a soul, but a corrupted, shriveled, twisted, bloodless soul – a spirit drained of warmth, emotion, and humanity, but living all the same, reptilian and vicious

ears. Two thin teeth, like those of a rat[1], overlay the shrivelled lower lip. In its crouching position, with bent joints and craned head, there was a suggestion of energy about the horrid thing which made Smith's gorge rise. The gaunt ribs, with their parchment-like covering, were exposed, and the sunken, leaden-hued abdomen, with the long slit where the embalmer had left his mark; but the lower limbs were wrapt round with coarse yellow bandages. A number of little clove-like pieces of myrrh and of cassia were sprinkled over the body, and lay scattered on the inside of the case.

"I don't know his name," said Bellingham, passing his hand over the shrivelled head. "You see the outer sarcophagus with the inscriptions is missing. Lot 249 is all the title he has now. You see it printed on his case. That was his number in the auction at which I picked him up."

"He has been a very pretty sort of fellow in his day," remarked Abercrombie Smith.

"He has been a giant. His mummy is six feet seven in length, and that would be a giant over there, for they were never a very robust race[2]. Feel these great knotted bones, too. He would be a nasty fellow to tackle."

"Perhaps these very hands helped to build the stones into the pyramids," suggested Monkhouse Lee, looking down with disgust in his eyes at the crooked, unclean talons.

"No fear. This fellow has been pickled in natron, and looked after in the most approved style. They did not serve hodsmen[3] in that fashion. Salt or bitumen[4] was enough for them. It has been calculated that this sort of thing cost about seven hundred and thirty pounds[5] in our money. Our friend was a noble at the least. What do you make of that small inscription near his feet, Smith?"

"I told you that I know no Eastern tongue[6]."

---

[1] There is something about this which suggests the vampiric. In fact, before the popularization of Hammer horror films, which depicted vampires with elongated canines (per Bram Stoker's description in *Dracula*) vampires were depicted with extended, angular incisors, like rats or bats. This is most famously demonstrated in *Nosferatu*

[2] A term which – in this story – Doyle has indelibly linked to ideal masculinity. The mummy, then, was that of a man with a manly body educated by a simpering, weak civilization. Like Bellingham, he had the beginnings of an exceptional life but – it seems implied – his gifts were misused and corrupted by a cruel personality

[3] A rare variant of a rare word, hodman – the laborer who prepares bricks and mortar and brings them to bricklayers for application

[4] Asphalt made from coal tar

[5] £64,475 or $95,857 in 2015 currency

[6] It is worth noting that he probably knows several Western tongues: German and French, likely, with a good deal of Latin and possibly some Ancient Greek

"Ah, so you did[1]. It is the name of the embalmer, I take it. A very conscientious worker he must have been. I wonder how many modern works will survive four thousand years[2]?"

He kept on speaking lightly and rapidly, but it was evident to Abercrombie Smith that he was still palpitating with fear. His hands shook, his lower lip trembled, and look where he would, his eye always came sliding round to his gruesome companion. Through all his fear, however, there was a suspicion of triumph in his tone and manner. His eye shone, and his footstep, as he paced the room, was brisk and jaunty. He gave the impression of a man who has gone through an ordeal, the marks of which he still bears upon him, but which has helped him to his end[3].

"You're not going yet?" he cried, as Smith rose from the sofa.

At the prospect of solitude, his fears seemed to crowd back upon him, and he stretched out a hand to detain him.

"Yes, I must go. I have my work to do. You are all right now. I think that with your nervous system you should take up some less morbid study."

"Oh, I am not nervous as a rule; and I have unwrapped mummies before."

"You fainted last time," observed Monkhouse Lee.

"Ah, yes, so I did. Well, I must have a nerve tonic or a course of electricity. You are not going, Lee?"

"I'll do whatever you wish, Ned[4]."

"Then I'll come down with you and have a shake-down[5] on your sofa. Good-night, Smith. I am so sorry to have disturbed you with my foolishness."

---

[1] An artless test, no doubt. It is dearly important to Bellingham that Smith not recognize the words on his scroll which consist of a spell for resurrection and mastery

[2] Possibly a cue taken from Poe's cynical mummy ("Some Words with a Mummy") who demeans everything modern life has to offer him except for snake oil cough drops

[3] All of the young men are preparing for rites of passage which promise entry to proper adulthood and manly validation: Hastie's athletic trials, Smith's academic rigors, and Bellingham's comparably gargantuan mastery over death. And yet, his accomplishment, be it ever so tremendous, seems ghastly and revolting compared to his peers' more mundane tasks. The takeaway point here is that Bellingham is usurping and subverting the conventional channels of achievement that Smith and Hastie traverse – as well as the laws of God and Victorian decency

[4] It was a tremendously intimate liberty to call a man by his first name – let alone a boyhood pet name – in public, especially around relative strangers. You notice that even Watson never calls Holmes "Sherlock," unless he refers to him by his full name, or as "Mr Sherlock Holmes," and Watson himself is never called John. This was a very intimate and familiar way to address another man, particularly for young men hoping to establish themselves as adults in the rat race of Oxford

[5] To relax or settle down. Clearly he prefers to leave the mummy's company

They shook hands, and as the medical student stumbled up the spiral and irregular stair he heard a key turn in a door, and the steps of his two new acquaintances as they descended to the lower floor.

In this strange way began the acquaintance between Edward Bellingham and Abercrombie Smith, an acquaintance which the latter, at least, had no desire to push further. Bellingham, however, appeared to have taken a fancy to his rough-spoken neighbour, and made his advances in such a way that he could hardly be repulsed without absolute brutality[1]. Twice he called to thank Smith for his assistance, and many times afterwards he looked in with books, papers, and such other civilities as two bachelor neighbours can offer each other[2]. He was, as Smith soon found, a man of wide reading, with catholic tastes and an extraordinary memory. His manner, too, was so pleasing and suave that one came, after a time, to overlook his repellent appearance. For a jaded and wearied man he was no unpleasant companion, and Smith found himself, after a time, looking forward to his visits, and even returning them.

Clever as he undoubtedly was, however, the medical student seemed to detect a dash of insanity in the man. He broke out at times into a high, inflated style of talk which was in contrast with the simplicity of his life.

"It is a wonderful thing," he cried, "to feel that one can command powers of good and of evil--a ministering angel or a demon of vengeance." And again, of Monkhouse Lee, he said,--"Lee is a good fellow, an honest fellow, but he is without strength or ambition. He would not make a fit partner for a man with a great enterprise. He would not make a fit partner for me[3]."

---

[1] There is certainly an uneasy, awkward tone about Bellingham's unwanted attention, especially concerning the nature of their brief acquaintance: Smith, a medical student, having merely come to attend him at Lee's request, and – having found him all right – coarsely rebuffing his offers of hospitality, rudely parrying his attempts at conversation, and eagerly parting ways without much ado. Clearly there is no reason for Bellingham to expect to find a friend in Smith, yet he pushes the envelope to the point that Smith becomes gruff with his rejection. It has the mood of an unrequited romance about it – of an unwanted admirer pursuing a hopeless crush to the point of disgusting the object of their fixation with their pathetic excuses to share company. In any case, Bellingham's clinginess – homosexual in nature or otherwise – is an unmanly embarrassment by Victorian standards of homosocial conduct

[2] The excuses to see Smith are needless and shameless, and imply that Bellingham finds an equal in Smith – in intellect, not character – thus furthering their relationship as one another's foils: equal in intelligence and industry, but diametrically opposed in every other capacity – a medical superhero and his antiquarian supervillain

[3] This is all quite interesting. Homosexual implications aside, it seems that Lee – who indeed is neither strong like Hastie and Smith, nor ambitious like Smith and Bellingham – has been replaced as the cohort in Bellingham's mind by Smith, whom he has only just met. His attraction – sexual, intellectual, or social – to Smith has all the mood of a man who, unsatisfied with a wife of some years, abandons her for a new, exciting mistress.

At such hints and innuendoes stolid Smith, puffing solemnly at his pipe, would simply raise his eyebrows and shake his head, with little interjections of medical wisdom as to earlier hours and fresher air[1].

One habit Bellingham had developed of late which Smith knew to be a frequent herald of a weakening mind. He appeared to be forever talking to himself. At late hours of the night, when there could be no visitor with him, Smith could still hear his voice beneath him in a low, muffled monologue, sunk almost to a whisper, and yet very audible in the silence. This solitary babbling annoyed and distracted the student, so that he spoke more than once to his neighbour about it. Bellingham, however, flushed up at the charge, and denied curtly that he had uttered a sound; indeed, he showed more annoyance over the matter than the occasion seemed to demand.

Had Abercrombie Smith had any doubt as to his own ears he had not to go far to find corroboration. Tom Styles, the little wrinkled man-servant who had attended to the wants of the lodgers in the turret for a longer time than any man's memory could carry him, was sorely put to it over the same matter.

"If you please, sir," said he, as he tidied down the top chamber one morning, "do you think Mr. Bellingham is all right, sir?"

"All right, Styles?"

"Yes sir. Right in his head, sir."

"Why should he not be, then?"

"Well, I don't know, sir. His habits has changed of late. He's not the same man he used to be, though I make free to say that he was never quite one of my gentlemen, like Mr. Hastie or yourself[2], sir. He's took to talkin' to himself something awful. I wonder it don't disturb you. I don't know what to make of him, sir."

"I don't know what business it is of yours, Styles."

"Well, I takes an interest, Mr. Smith. It may be forward of me, but I can't help it. I feel sometimes as if I was mother and father to my young gentlemen. It all falls on me when things go wrong and the relations come. But Mr. Bellingham, sir. I want to know what it is that walks about his room sometimes when he's out and when the door's locked on the outside."

"Eh! you're talking nonsense, Styles."

"Maybe so, sir; but I heard it more'n once with my own ears."

Bellingham's sights are now on Smith, whom for reasons to be guessed at, he supposes to be a fitting partner in his mummy enterprise

[1] "It's far too late in the evening; you don't know what you're saying." Smith does genuinely find Bellingham's intellect engaging, but wishes to avoid the obvious fixation the fat man has for him, rapidly ascribing his transparent hints to sleep deprivation and musty air

[2] Note that Lee doesn't make the cut, but Hastie (who is in fact *not* one of his "gentlemen") does. Styles ascribes very deeply indeed to the code of Victorian manhood and expects the scholars he serves to be of the "robust" and "manly" variety – not effete and craven like Bellingham and Lee

"Rubbish, Styles."

"Very good, sir. You'll ring the bell if you want me."

Abercrombie Smith gave little heed to the gossip of the old man-servant, but a small incident occurred a few days later which left an unpleasant effect upon his mind, and brought the words of Styles forcibly to his memory.

Bellingham had come up to see him late one night, and was entertaining him with an interesting account of the rock tombs of Beni Hassan[1] in Upper Egypt, when Smith, whose hearing was remarkably acute, distinctly heard the sound of a door opening on the landing below.

"There's some fellow gone in or out of your room," he remarked.

Bellingham sprang up and stood helpless for a moment, with the expression of a man who is half incredulous and half afraid.

"I surely locked it. I am almost positive that I locked it," he stammered. "No one could have opened it."

"Why, I hear someone coming up the steps now," said Smith.

Bellingham rushed out through the door, slammed it loudly behind him, and hurried down the stairs. About half-way down Smith heard him stop, and thought he caught the sound of whispering. A moment later the door beneath him shut, a key creaked in a lock, and Bellingham, with beads of moisture upon his pale face, ascended the stairs once more, and re-entered the room.

"It's all right," he said, throwing himself down in a chair. "It was that fool of a dog. He had pushed the door open. I don't know how I came to forget to lock it."

"I didn't know you kept a dog," said Smith, looking very thoughtfully at the disturbed face of his companion.

"Yes, I haven't had him long. I must get rid of him. He's a great nuisance."

"He must be, if you find it so hard to shut him up. I should have thought that shutting the door would have been enough, without locking it."

"I want to prevent old Styles from letting him out. He's of some value, you know, and it would be awkward to lose him."

"I am a bit of a dog-fancier myself," said Smith, still gazing hard at his companion from the corner of his eyes. "Perhaps you'll let me have a look at it."

"Certainly. But I am afraid it cannot be to-night; I have an appointment. Is that clock right? Then I am a quarter of an hour late already. You'll excuse me, I am sure."

He picked up his cap and hurried from the room. In spite of his appointment, Smith heard him re-enter his own chamber and lock his door upon the inside.

---

1 An Ancient Egyptian cemetery, largely used between the 21st and 17th centuries BCE

This interview left a disagreeable impression upon the medical student's mind. Bellingham had lied to him, and lied so clumsily that it looked as if he had desperate reasons for concealing the truth. Smith knew that his neighbour had no dog. He knew, also, that the step which he had heard upon the stairs was not the step of an animal. But if it were not, then what could it be? There was old Styles's statement about the something which used to pace the room at times when the owner was absent. Could it be a woman[1]? Smith rather inclined to the view. If so, it would mean disgrace and expulsion to Bellingham if it were discovered by the authorities[2], so that his anxiety and falsehoods might be accounted for. And yet it was inconceivable that an undergraduate could keep a woman in his rooms without being instantly detected. Be the explanation what it might, there was something ugly about it, and Smith determined, as he turned to his books, to discourage all further attempts at intimacy[3] on the part of his soft-spoken and ill-favoured neighbour.

But his work was destined to interruption that night. He had hardly caught tip the broken threads when a firm, heavy footfall came three steps at a time from below, and Hastie, in blazer and flannels, burst into the room[4].

---

[1] While it is my interpretation that Bellingham is codified as being sexually queer, the concept of an exclusively homosexual man was not commonly considered a reality until the time of Freud. Before that sodomy was considered a degenerate quirk of behavior, not a biological predisposition or even a serious preference. It must also be noted that Bellingham is engaged to Miss Lee. In any case, Bellingham comes across as bisexual or perhaps even pansexual, and Smith's suspicion need not be written off as mere wishful thinking, niavete, or denial on his part – Bellingham certainly seems like the type to seduce a woman for the power trip alone if for no other reason

[2] A thoroughly prohibited activity – to have a woman in one of the university dorms not to mention allowing one to lodge there. Aside from the school's sexist standards which prohibited women to matriculate the school, or to graduate from it until 1920, the sexual mores of harboring an woman in the room of an unmarried student would have made the secret a career-destroying scandal

[3] The Bellingham/Smith relationship is hardly one-sided. Smith is repulsed by his needy, clingy neighbor, but he continually finds himself shaking Bellingham off his back, only after having allowed him to climb on time after time. Although he is, as he puts it, "brutal" with Bellingham, he finds a strange and somewhat disturbing level of comraderie in his fellow maverick. For all of his exemplary masculinity, Smith lurks on the outskirts of the Victorian society that Hastie drinks from ravenously, and is in some sense vulnerable to Bellingham's asocial allure. Both are unconventional, antisocial, intellectual prodigies, and as much as Smith prefers Hastie to "Ned," there is no denying that the Egyptologist's introverted kingdom of solitude and books has a habit of seducing Smith over to his side on several occasions. This is just one instance where Smith resolves to quit his neighbor's "intimacy," but will ultimately fail in that resolve

[4] Right on time, Hastie appears in the very moment that Smith shifts in his opinion of his new friend, like an angel manifesting once a demon has been spurned. He has virtually been summoned by Smith's rejection of Bellingham's antisocial allure

"Still at it!" said he, plumping down into his wonted arm-chair. "What a chap you are to stew! I believe an earthquake might come and knock Oxford into a cocked hat, and you would sit perfectly placid with your books among the rains[1]. However, I won't bore you long. Three whiffs of baccy, and I am off."

"What's the news, then?" asked Smith, cramming a plug of bird's-eye into his briar[2] with his forefinger.

"Nothing very much. Wilson made 70 for the freshmen against the eleven. They say that they will play him instead of Buddicomb, for Buddicomb is clean off colour. He used to be able to bowl a little, but it's nothing but half-vollies and long hops now[3]."

"Medium right[4]," suggested Smith, with the intense gravity which comes upon a 'varsity[5] man when he speaks of athletics.

"Inclining to fast, with a work from leg. Comes with the arm about three inches or so. He used to be nasty on a wet wicket. Oh, by-the-way, have you heard about Long Norton?"

"What's that?"

"He's been attacked."

"Attacked?"

"Yes, just as he was turning out of the High Street, and within a hundred yards of the gate of Old's."

"But who----"

"Ah, that's the rub! If you said 'what,' you would be more grammatical. Norton swears that it was not human, and, indeed, from the scratches on his throat, I should be inclined to agree with him."

"What, then? Have we come down to spooks?"

Abercrombie Smith puffed his scientific contempt.

"Well, no; I don't think that is quite the idea, either. I am inclined to think that if any showman has lost a great ape lately, and the brute is in these parts, a jury would find a true bill against it. Norton passes that way every night, you know, about the same hour. There's a tree that hangs low over the path--the big elm from Rainy's garden. Norton thinks the thing

---

[1] He reiterates Smith's disconnect from the "robust" activities on campus. Removed from them to this seismic extent, he is prey to Bellingham's steady seduction. Hastie's return is almost a warning to put the books down for a while and to go outside and work up a sweat – like a good Englishman

[2] Smith here redeems his wanderings by partaking in the manly ritual of smoking. Bird's eye tobacco is when pipe tobacco is prepared and cut after being twisted into curly rolls, leaving small "coins" or bird's eyes speckling the tobacco. A briar is a sturdy pipe made from the hardwood of the briar root

[3] The sport in question is cricket. A half volley is a delivery that just misses the block hole. A long hop is a delivery that is far too short to be even considered a good lenth delivery

[4] A type of cricketer who bowls with their right hand with a moderate level of speed

[5] The term varsity – short for university – denoted a member of an official school athletic team, even as it is now applied to high school teams

dropped on him out of the tree. Anyhow, he was nearly strangled by two arms, which, he says, were as strong and as thin as steel bands. He saw nothing; only those beastly arms that tightened and tightened on him. He yelled his head nearly off, and a couple of chaps came running, and the thing went over the wall like a cat. He never got a fair sight of it the whole time. It gave Norton a shake up, I can tell you. I tell him it has been as good as a change at the sea-side for him."

"A garrotter[1], most likely," said Smith.

"Very possibly. Norton says not; but we don't mind what he says. The garrotter had long nails, and was pretty smart at swinging himself over walls. By-the-way, your beautiful neighbour would be pleased if he heard about it. He had a grudge against Norton, and he's not a man, from what I know of him, to forget his little debts. But hallo, old chap, what have you got in your noddle[2]?"

"Nothing," Smith answered curtly.

He had started in his chair, and the look had flashed over his face which comes upon a man who is struck suddenly by some unpleasant idea.

"You looked as if something I had said had taken you on the raw. By-the-way, you have made the acquaintance of Master B[3]. since I looked in last, have you not? Young Monkhouse Lee told me something to that effect."

"Yes; I know him slightly. He has been up here once or twice[4]."

---

[1] An assassin or thief who kills his victims by strangling – often with a wire or cord, called a garrote

[2] "What's on your mind?"

[3] Possibly a reference to Mr. B---, the rakish aristocrat in what many consider to be the first English novel, *Pamela*, by Samuel Richardson. The story, which resembles *Pride and Prejudice, Jane Eyre,* and modern domination narratives such as *Secretary* and *Fifty Shades of Grey,* follows a virtuous servant girl who rebuffs her employer's grotesque assaults on her virginity, ultimately reforming his lustful ways. Such a comparison is apt, because although Hastie is likely thinking of the "dove and toad" relationship between Bellingham and Miss Lee, Bellingham is also the seducer of Lee himself and Smith by degrees – in spite of his ugly appearance, his charisma makes him a successful pied piper to those who fall under his power

[4] By Doyle's account, this is a shamefaced lie, either because Smith is embarrassed due to Hastie's overwhelmingly negative opinion of "B," or because he doesn't even want to admit to himself the bizarre sympathies that exist between himself and Bellingham. Likely a combination of the two

"Well, you're big enough and ugly enough to take care of yourself[1]. He's not what I should call exactly a healthy sort of Johnny[2], though, no doubt, he's very clever, and all that. But you'll soon find out for yourself. Lee is all right; he's a very decent little fellow[3]. Well, so long, old chap! I row Mullins for the Vice-Chancellor's pot[4] on Wednesday week, so mind you come down, in case I don't see you before."

Bovine[5] Smith laid down his pipe and turned stolidly to his books once more. But with all the will in the world, he found it very hard to keep his mind upon his work. It would slip away to brood upon the man beneath him, and upon the little mystery which hung round his chambers. Then his thoughts turned to this singular attack of which Hastie had spoken, and to the grudge which Bellingham was said to owe the object of it. The two ideas would persist in rising together in his mind, as though there were some close and intimate connection between them. And yet the suspicion was so dim and vague that it could not be put down in words.

"Confound the chap!" cried Smith, as he shied his book on pathology across the room. "He has spoiled my night's reading, and that's reason enough, if there were no other, why I should steer clear of him in the future[6]."

For ten days the medical student confined himself so closely to his studies that he neither saw nor heard anything of either of the men beneath him. At the hours when Bellingham had been accustomed to visit him, he took care to sport his oak[7], and though he more than once heard a knocking at his outer door, he resolutely refused to answer it[8]. One afternoon,

---

[1] This teasing, almost flirtatious language is truly bizarre, almost suggesting that Bellingham might have rapine ambitions towards Smith, and that were he not as muscular and fit, there might be a legitimate danger of physical assault. Although the tone is likely sarcastic in nature, it is suggestive: take care of yourself; this man is a serious danger, and not just to women like Lee's sister

[2] In other words, he's not what the British would call a regular bloke, or the Americans a man's man, or a good guy. He isn't, that is to say, the sporting type, and falls short of the Victorian yardstick for masculinity

[3] "A decent little fellow." Hastie doesn't restrain from infantilizing Lee even as he compliments his strength of character (at least when compared to the grotesque Bellingham. He is decent, but he's not a "healthy sort of Johnny" either

[4] He rows against an athlete named Mullins for what appears to be a fictitious cash prize (all references to it that I can find are in reference to this story)

[5] Typically used to mean cow-like, but in this case the sense is cow-like in temperament, not in build – that is, stoic and phlegmatic

[6] Smith continues to protest too much: surely Hastie's disapproval and his own revulsion are enough to discontinue the relationship without producing facile excuses or encouraging himself out loud. It seems that Bellingham's strange spell is resisting Smith's natural self-reliance and the advice of his best friend

[7] A jaunty way of saying "close his door"

[8] This passive aggressive evasion hardly seems natural for Smith who first came across as being unmovable as Gibraltar: if a chap decided to bother him during his studies, wouldn't

however, he was descending the stairs when, just as he was passing it, Bellingham's door flew open, and young Monkhouse Lee came out with his eyes sparkling and a dark flush of anger upon his olive cheeks. Close at his heels followed Bellingham, his fat, unhealthy face all quivering with malignant passion.

"You fool!" he hissed. "You'll be sorry."

"Very likely," cried the other. "Mind what I say. It's off! I won't hear of it!"

"You've promised, anyhow."

"Oh, I'll keep that! I won't speak. But I'd rather little Eva was in her grave. Once for all, it's off. She'll do what I say. We don't want to see you again."

So much Smith could not avoid hearing, but he hurried on, for he had no wish to be involved in their dispute. There had been a serious breach between them, that was clear enough, and Lee was going to cause the engagement with his sister to be broken off. Smith thought of Hastie's comparison of the toad and the dove, and was glad to think that the matter was at an end. Bellingham's face when he was in a passion was not pleasant to look upon. He was not a man to whom an innocent girl could be trusted for life. As he walked, Smith wondered languidly what could have caused the quarrel, and what the promise might be which Bellingham had been so anxious that Monkhouse Lee should keep.

It was the day of the sculling match between Hastie and Mullins, and a stream of men were making their way down to the banks of the Isis[1]. A May sun was shining brightly, and the yellow path was barred with the black shadows of the tall elm-trees. On either side the grey colleges lay back from the road, the hoary old mothers of minds looking out from their high, mullioned windows[2] at the tide of young life which swept so merrily past them. Black-clad tutors, prim officials, pale reading men, brown-faced, straw-hatted young athletes in white sweaters or many-coloured blazers, all[3]

---

a glare and a grunt have been enough to send them away without pretending not to be home? His moods and manners are slightly different, and they resemble the flustered confusion and avoidance of a person in rocky yet unconsummated relationship: they don't turn the fellow away or tell him off, but coldly avoid contact in hopes that the point can be conveyed without hurting the poor thing's feelings to his face

[1] The name given the part of the Thames which flows through Oxford. Although it is technically derived from the Thames' Latin name – Tamesis – it harmonizes well with our story, since Isis is a powerful Egyptian goddess. The Isis was the focal point of Oxford rowing sports, and is always referred to as the Isis in those contexts

[2] A window criss-crossed with framework, often in a series of oblique lines which house diamond-shaped panes of glass

[3] A veritable catalog of British manhood – at least of the gentlemanly sort. Somber, bookish, athletic, important, and waggish, all are flocking to the Isis to witness a combat of honor – a masculine rite of passage which offered a playful, modern response to the medieval joust. This event, which is a focal point of the story, is important because of its

were hurrying towards the blue winding river which curves through the Oxford meadows.

Abercrombie Smith, with the intuition of an old oarsman, chose his position at the point where he knew that the struggle, if there were a struggle, would come. Far off he heard the hum which announced the start, the gathering roar of the approach, the thunder of running feet, and the shouts of the men in the boats beneath him. A spray of half-clad, deep-breathing runners shot past him, and craning over their shoulders, he saw Hastie pulling a steady thirty-six, while his opponent, with a jerky forty, was a good boat's length behind him. Smith gave a cheer for his friend, and pulling out his watch, was starting off again for his chambers, when he felt a touch upon his shoulder, and found that young Monkhouse Lee was beside him.

"I saw you there," he said, in a timid, deprecating way. "I wanted to speak to you, if you could spare me a half-hour. This cottage is mine. I share it with Harrington of King's[1]. Come in and have a cup of tea."

"I must be back presently," said Smith. "I am hard on the grind at present. But I'll come in for a few minutes with pleasure. I wouldn't have come out only Hastie is a friend of mine."

"So he is of mine. Hasn't he a beautiful style? Mullins wasn't in it[2]. But come into the cottage. It's a little den of a place, but it is pleasant to work in during the summer months."

It was a small, square, white building, with green doors and shutters, and a rustic[3] trellis-work porch, standing back some fifty yards from the river's bank. Inside, the main room was roughly fitted up as a study--deal table, unpainted shelves with books, and a few cheap oleographs upon the wall. A kettle sang upon a spirit-stove, and there were tea things upon a tray on the table.

"Try that chair and have a cigarette," said Lee. "Let me pour you out a cup of tea. It's so good of you to come in, for I know that your time is a good

---

gladiatorial importance and because of its subtle sporting of machismo: two young braggarts strut and posturing in a public display of masculine daring and do

[1] There is no King's College, Oxford, although Oriel College was called King's during the middle ages

[2] After having taken leave of Bellingham, Lee is already demonstrating a more conventionally masculine attitude – associating with Hastie, the consummate sportsman, and having an informed and debatable opinion on an athletic feat. His independence has drawn him closer to the masculine ideal, but like the chivalric Long Norton, it has left him vulnerable to Bellingham's vengence

[3] As a part of Lee's manly makeover, he has relocated from living beneath Bellingham – which has psychological as well as sexual implications – to living in a rustic (read: robust), rural cottage that is simple and self-reliant. The fact that Doyle bothers to go into such detail to describe its crude but sturdy features – unpainted bookcases, crackling spirit stove, etc. – testifies to its importance in Lee's transformation from docile doormat to respectable adult male

deal taken up. I wanted to say to you that, if I were you, I should change my rooms at once."

"Eh?"

Smith sat staring with a lighted match in one hand and his unlit cigarette in the other.

"Yes; it must seem very extraordinary, and the worst of it is that I cannot give my reasons, for I am under a solemn promise--a very solemn promise. But I may go so far as to say that I don't think Bellingham is a very safe man to live near. I intend to camp out here as much as I can for a time."

"Not safe! What do you mean?"

"Ah, that's what I mustn't say. But do take my advice, and move your rooms. We had a grand row[1] to-day. You must have heard us, for you came down the stairs."

"I saw that you had fallen out."

"He's a horrible chap, Smith. That is the only word for him. I have had doubts about him ever since that night when he fainted--you remember, when you came down. I taxed him to-day, and he told me things that made my hair rise, and wanted me to stand in with him. I'm not strait-laced, but I am a clergyman's son[2], you know, and I think there are some things which are quite beyond the pale. I only thank God that I found him out before it was too late, for he was to have married into my family."

"This is all very fine, Lee," said Abercrombie Smith curtly. "But either you are saying a great deal too much or a great deal too little."

"I give you a warning."

"If there is real reason for warning, no promise can bind you. If I see a rascal about to blow a place up with dynamite no pledge will stand in my way of preventing him[3]."

---

[1] Americans may mistake this to be commentary on the sculling race, but nay: a row (rhymes with how and sow) is a British term for a fight or quarrel

[2] Another interesting development in Lee's characterization: he implies that his character may be somewhat checkered – that he may harbor some vices or sins. Although we mustn't read too much into it, deviations from sexual mores may be among his activities that move him past a "straight-laced" persona

[3] A vital difference between Smith and Lee – one which is the crucial factor in Smith's characterization as a "robust" man. Holmes was a great one for breaking laws and committing felonies when done in the name of a higher good. This is an example of what Nietzsche called "master morality" – a philosophy which holds that the highest moral evolution in men actually calls for the disobeying of laws in the name of a more fluid, flexible moral code. Robin Hood, William Tell, Rob Roy, and Henry D. Thoreau were all popular examples of this mindset: breakers of civic order who were, shall we say robust enough, to perceive a higher, nobler means of dispatching justice than that proscribed by following convention, laws, protocol, or other such red tape. Holmes and Smith both resemble Nietzsche's description of the Uebermensch, or Super-Man, an individualistic loner who designs his own morality and executes it when necessary in flagrant disregard for the one-size-fits-all approach of modern society. While Smith follows the "master

"Ah, but I cannot prevent him, and I can do nothing but warn you."

"Without saying what you warn me against."

"Against Bellingham."

"But that is childish[1]. Why should I fear him, or any man?"

"I can't tell you. I can only entreat you to change your rooms. You are in danger where you are. I don't even say that Bellingham would wish to injure you. But it might happen, for he is a dangerous neighbour just now."

"Perhaps I know more than you think," said Smith, looking keenly at the young man's boyish, earnest face[2]. "Suppose I tell you that some one else shares Bellingham's rooms."

Monkhouse Lee sprang from his chair in uncontrollable excitement.

"You know, then?" he gasped.

"A woman."

Lee dropped back again with a groan.

"My lips are sealed," he said. "I must not speak."

"Well, anyhow," said Smith, rising, "it is not likely that I should allow myself to be frightened out of rooms which suit me very nicely. It would be a little too feeble for me to move out all my goods and chattels because you say that Bellingham might in some unexplained way do me an injury. I think that I'll just take my chance, and stay where I am, and as I see that it's nearly five o'clock, I must ask you to excuse me."

He bade the young student adieu in a few curt words, and made his way homeward through the sweet spring evening feeling half-ruffled, half-amused, as any other strong, unimaginative man might who has been menaced by a vague and shadowy danger.

There was one little indulgence which Abercrombie Smith always allowed himself, however closely his work might press upon him. Twice a week, on the Tuesday and the Friday, it was his invariable custom to walk over to Farlingford, the residence of Dr. Plumptree Peterson, situated about a mile and a half out of Oxford. Peterson had been a close friend of Smith's elder brother Francis, and as he was a bachelor, fairly well-to-do, with a good cellar and a better library[3], his house was a pleasant goal for a man

---

morality," Lee (a devoted follower, either of people like Bellingham, or – even at his boldest – of social conventions of behavior) is a hopeless devotee of "slave morality," Nietzsche's concept of the rule-abiding citizen who follows law and order even if it conflicts with their values or the present need, in this case breaking his oath with the nefarious Bellingham to prevent accidental deaths or even homicides

[1] Or, as Nietzsche would say, slavish

[2] Lee is growing closer to Doyle's ideal of self-reliant manhood, but he is still a boy in his core: a slave to convention without imagination, conviction, or character

[3] Having an appreciation for both the things of the body and of the spirit – wine and books, respectively – Peterson may not be the robust sportsman that Hastie is, but he is a very well-balanced figure of manhood by Doyle's standards, perhaps even more so than Smith, who is always a little too embroiled in books and a little too detached from the

who was in need of a brisk walk. Twice a week, then, the medical student would swing out there along the dark country roads, and spend a pleasant hour in Peterson's comfortable study, discussing, over a glass of old port, the gossip of the 'varsity or the latest developments of medicine or of surgery[1].

On the day which followed his interview with Monkhouse Lee, Smith shut up his books at a quarter past eight, the hour when he usually started for his friend's house. As he was leaving his room, however, his eyes chanced to fall upon one of the books which Bellingham had lent him, and his conscience pricked him for not having returned it. However repellent the man might be, he should not be treated with discourtesy[2]. Taking the book, he walked downstairs and knocked at his neighbour's door. There was no answer; but on turning the handle he found that it was unlocked. Pleased at the thought of avoiding an interview, he stepped inside, and placed the book with his card upon the table.

The lamp was turned half down, but Smith could see the details of the room plainly enough. It was all much as he had seen it before--the frieze, the animal-headed gods, the banging crocodile, and the table littered over with papers and dried leaves. The mummy case stood upright against the wall, but the mummy itself was missing. There was no sign of any second occupant of the room, and he felt as he withdrew that he had probably done Bellingham an injustice. Had he a guilty secret to preserve, he would hardly leave his door open so that all the world might enter.

The spiral stair was as black as pitch, and Smith was slowly making his way down its irregular steps, when he was suddenly conscious that something had passed him in the darkness. There was a faint sound, a whiff of air, a light brushing past his elbow, but so slight that he could scarcely be

---

pleasures of the flesh. He serves as the Van Helsing for Smith's Dr. Seward: a creative and inspiring father figure who encourages imagination, passion, and gusto in a phlegmatic student who is too dependent on pulseless reason and bloodless books to inform his one dimensional worldview

[1] Already it becomes obvious that Peterson's influence is invigorating to the parts of Smith's character which would otherwise atrophy: his physical, social, and spiritual well-being. Visiting Peterson requires a brisk walk in nature, and leads to good conversation on a myriad of topics ranging from medicine to gossip, all nurtured by strong wine and heated by a warm fire. These visits are vital to Smith's sustained balance between the perhaps overly physical Hastie and the doubtlessly overly intellectual Bellingham

[2] Smith doesn't strike me as a man ruled by etiquette. Is this perhaps an excuse to see his friend without having to go out of his way and confess the affinity that he harbors for him? Surely he wouldn't want Hastie or (by now) Lee to know that he finds camaraderie in Bellingham's company, but no one could blame him for getting tied up in a conversation after dropping off a book

certain of it[1]. He stopped and listened, but the wind was rustling among the ivy outside, and he could hear nothing else.

"Is that you, Styles?" he shouted.

There was no answer, and all was still behind him. It must have been a sudden gust of air, for there were crannies and cracks in the old turret. And yet he could almost have sworn that he heard a footfall by his very side. He had emerged into the quadrangle, still turning the matter over in his head, when a man came running swiftly across the smooth-cropped lawn.

"Is that you, Smith?"

"Hullo, Hastie!"

"For God's sake come at once! Young Lee is drowned! Here's Harrington of King's with the news. The doctor is out. You'll do, but come along at once. There may be life in him."

"Have you brandy?"

"No."

"I'll bring some. There's a flask on my table."

Smith bounded up the stairs, taking three at a time[2], seized the flask, and was rushing down with it, when, as he passed Bellingham's room, his eyes fell upon something which left him gasping and staring upon the landing.

The door, which he had closed behind him, was now open, and right in front of him, with the lamp-light shining upon it, was the mummy case. Three minutes ago it had been empty. He could swear to that. Now it framed the lank body of its horrible occupant, who stood, grim and stark, with his black shrivelled face towards the door. The form was lifeless and inert, but it seemed to Smith as he gazed that there still lingered a lurid spark of vitality, some faint sign of consciousness in the little eyes which lurked in the depths of the hollow sockets. So astounded and shaken was he that he had forgotten his errand, and was still staring at the lean, sunken figure when the voice of his friend below recalled him to himself.

"Come on, Smith!" he shouted. "It's life and death, you know. Hurry up! Now, then," he added, as the medical student reappeared, "let us do a sprint.

---

1 Classic Doyle – and beautifully done. He demonstrates his trademark restraint by only suggesting the awful thing that passes Smith in the dark, leaving our imaginations free to picture the sight and sense the sounds and smells of the mummy lurking in the stairwell. Truly a chilling moment

2 For whatever reason Doyle loves this image, enlisting it in many of his stories (including several Holmes episodes), not to mention earlier in this very story (that time it was Hastie). Perhaps the robust ideal is served by having a man usurp the proscribed tread of others (instead of taking each step he bounds three at a time, subverting convention) in a metaphor for his rule-breaking heroes

It is well under a mile, and we should do it in five minutes[1]. A human life is better worth running for than a pot[2]."

Neck and neck they dashed through the darkness, and did not pull up until, panting and spent, they had reached the little cottage by the river. Young Lee, limp and dripping like a broken water-plant, was stretched upon the sofa, the green scum of the river upon his black hair, and a fringe of white foam upon his leaden-hued lips. Beside him knelt his fellow-student Harrington, endeavouring to chafe some warmth back into his rigid limbs.

"I think there's life in him," said Smith, with his hand to the lad's side. "Put your watch glass to his lips. Yes, there's dimming on it. You take one arm, Hastie. Now work it as I do, and we'll soon pull him round."

For ten minutes they worked in silence, inflating and depressing the chest of the unconscious man. At the end of that time a shiver ran through his body, his lips trembled, and he opened his eyes. The three students burst out into an irrepressible cheer.

"Wake up, old chap. You've frightened us quite enough."

"Have some brandy. Take a sip from the flask."

"He's all right now," said his companion Harrington. "Heavens, what a fright I got! I was reading here, and he had gone for a stroll as far as the river, when I heard a scream and a splash. Out I ran, and by the time that I could find him and fish him out, all life seemed to have gone. Then Simpson couldn't get a doctor, for he has a game-leg, and I had to run, and I don't know what I'd have done without you fellows. That's right, old chap. Sit up."

Monkhouse Lee had raised himself on his hands, and looked wildly about him.

"What's up?" he asked. "I've been in the water. Ah, yes; I remember."

A look of fear came into his eyes, and he sank his face into his hands.

"How did you fall in?"

"I didn't fall in."

"How, then?"

"I was thrown in. I was standing by the bank, and something from behind picked me up like a feather and hurled me in. I heard nothing, and I saw nothing. But I know what it was, for all that."

"And so do I," whispered Smith.

Lee looked up with a quick glance of surprise. "You've learned, then!" he said. "You remember the advice I gave you?"

"Yes, and I begin to think that I shall take it."

---

[1] Here Doyle gleefully demonstrates his ideal of manhood: endowed with both brains (medical acumen) and brawn (the ability to run a five-minute mile), Smith is able to save a life. Had he not the know-how (Hastie) or the physicality (Lee, Bellingham), Lee would not stand a chance. It is due to Smith's well-rounded Victorian masculinity that he is able to prevent an attack from becoming a homicide

[2] Prize money gathered from bets

"I don't know what the deuce you fellows are talking about," said Hastie, "but I think, if I were you, Harrington, I should get Lee to bed at once. It will be time enough to discuss the why and the wherefore when he is a little stronger. I think, Smith, you and I can leave him alone now. I am walking back to college; if you are coming in that direction, we can have a chat."

But it was little chat that they had upon their homeward path. Smith's mind was too full of the incidents of the evening, the absence of the mummy from his neighbour's rooms, the step that passed him on the stair, the reappearance--the extraordinary, inexplicable reappearance of the grisly thing--and then this attack upon Lee, corresponding so closely to the previous outrage upon another man against whom Bellingham bore a grudge. All this settled in his thoughts, together with the many little incidents which had previously turned him against his neighbour, and the singular circumstances under which he was first called in to him. What had been a dim suspicion, a vague, fantastic conjecture, had suddenly taken form, and stood out in his mind as a grim fact, a thing not to be denied. And yet, how monstrous it was! how unheard of! how entirely beyond all bounds of human experience. An impartial judge, or even the friend who walked by his side, would simply tell him that his eyes had deceived him, that the mummy had been there all the time, that young Lee had tumbled into the river as any other man tumbles into a river, and that a blue pill was the best thing for a disordered liver[1]. He felt that he would have said as much if the positions had been reversed. And yet he could swear that Bellingham was a murderer at heart, and that he wielded a weapon such as no man had ever used in all the grim history of crime.

Hastie had branched off to his rooms with a few crisp and emphatic comments upon his friend's unsociability[2], and Abercrombie Smith crossed the quadrangle to his corner turret with a strong feeling of repulsion for his chambers and their associations. He would take Lee's advice, and move his quarters as soon as possible, for how could a man study when his ear was ever straining for every murmur or footstep in the room below? He observed, as he crossed over the lawn, that the light was still shining in

---

[1] Blue mass – AKA blue pill, pilula hydrargyri – was a mercury-based pharmecuetical commonly proscribed from the seventeenth to early twentieth century, given to lift energy and clear the mind and body of toxins and other disorders. First used to fight syphilis, it was given for any number of problems from constipation and toothache to tuberculosis and depression. It was unfortunately somewhat toxic (although it consisted of licorice, marshmallow, glycerol, and rose honey, 33% of it was pure mercury, which if overused could lead to any number of medical problems). Famous users of the treatment include presidents Abraham Lincoln and Ulysses S. Grant

[2] Smith's asocial introversion constantly pitches between an advantage and a problem. On one hand he is objective, committed to his studies, and self-reliant, while on the other he is isolated, self-involved, and immune to the same egotistical demons that plague Bellingham. In this instance he is off to do battle with Bellingham, and the behavior is excusable

Bellingham's window, and as he passed up the staircase the door opened, and the man himself looked out at him. With his fat, evil face he was like some bloated spider fresh from the weaving of his poisonous web[1].

"Good-evening," said he. "Won't you come in?"

"No," cried Smith, fiercely.

"No? You are busy as ever? I wanted to ask you about Lee. I was sorry to hear that there was a rumour that something was amiss with him."

His features were grave, but there was the gleam of a hidden laugh in his eyes as he spoke. Smith saw it, and he could have knocked him down for it.

"You'll be sorrier still to hear that Monkhouse Lee is doing very well, and is out of all danger," he answered. "Your hellish tricks have not come off this time. Oh, you needn't try to brazen it out. I know all about it."

Bellingham took a step back from the angry student, and half-closed the door as if to protect himself.

"You are mad," he said. "What do you mean? Do you assert that I had anything to do with Lee's accident?"

"Yes," thundered Smith. "You and that bag of bones behind you; you worked it between you. I tell you what it is, Master B., they have given up burning folk like you, but we still keep a hangman[2], and, by George! if any man in this college meets his death while you are here, I'll have you up, and if you don't swing for it, it won't be my fault. You'll find that your filthy Egyptian tricks won't answer in England[3]."

"You're a raving lunatic," said Bellingham.

"All right. You just remember what I say, for you'll find that I'll be better than my word."

The door slammed, and Smith went fuming up to his chamber, where he locked the door upon the inside, and spent half the night in smoking his old briar[4] and brooding over the strange events of the evening.

Next morning Abercrombie Smith heard nothing of his neighbour, but Harrington called upon him in the afternoon to say that Lee was almost himself again. All day Smith stuck fast to his work, but in the evening he determined to pay the visit to his friend Dr. Peterson upon which he had started upon the night before. A good walk and a friendly chat would be welcome to his jangled nerves.

---

[1] Perhaps the imagery is particularly directed at Smith: while Norton and Lee have been each momentarily snared in Bellingham's traps, it is Smith who seems to be his ultimate quarry – not his life, but his character, and Smith now fully recognizes the Egyptologist's predatory designs

[2] Smith compares the crimes of sorcery, witchcraft, and necromancy – formerly a capital crime – with that of murder

[3] Smith's ethnocentric chauvinism bursts out of the shadows. Previously he showed disdain at the suggestion that he might know any Eastern languages, but at this point he brazenly juxtaposes England and respectability with Egypt and subterfuge

[4] Purging himself of Bellingham's fellowship, Smith commits himself to his manly smoking ritual

Bellingham's door was shut as he passed, but glancing back when he was some distance from the turret, he saw his neighbour's head at the window outlined against the lamp-light, his face pressed apparently against the glass as he gazed out into the darkness[1]. It was a blessing to be away from all contact with him, but if for a few hours, and Smith stepped out briskly, and breathed the soft spring air into his lungs. The half-moon lay in the west between two Gothic pinnacles, and threw upon the silvered street a dark tracery from the stone-work above. There was a brisk breeze, and light, fleecy clouds drifted swiftly across the sky. Old's was on the very border of the town, and in five minutes Smith found himself beyond the houses and between the hedges of a May-scented Oxfordshire lane.

It was a lonely and little frequented road which led to his friend's house. Early as it was, Smith did not meet a single soul upon his way. He walked briskly along until he came to the avenue gate, which opened into the long gravel drive leading up to Farlingford. In front of him he could see the cosy red light of the windows glimmering through the foliage. He stood with his hand upon the iron latch of the swinging gate, and he glanced back at the road along which he had come. Something was coming swiftly down it.

It moved in the shadow of the hedge, silently and furtively, a dark, crouching figure, dimly visible against the black background. Even as he gazed back at it, it had lessened its distance by twenty paces, and was fast closing upon him. Out of the darkness he had a glimpse of a scraggy neck, and of two eyes that will ever haunt him in his dreams. He turned, and with a cry of terror he ran for his life up the avenue. There were the red lights, the signals of safety, almost within a stone's throw of him. He was a famous runner, but never had he run as he ran that night.

The heavy gate had swung into place behind him, but he heard it dash open again before his pursuer. As he rushed madly and wildly through the night, he could hear a swift, dry patter behind him, and could see, as he threw back a glance, that this horror was bounding like a tiger at his heels, with blazing eyes and one stringy arm outthrown. Thank God, the door was ajar. He could see the thin bar of light which shot from the lamp in the hall. Nearer yet sounded the clatter from behind. He heard a hoarse gurgling at his very shoulder. With a shriek he flung himself against the door, slammed and bolted it behind him, and sank half-fainting on to the hall chair.

[1] Bellingham's puppy/toddler-like attitude – face pressed against the glass as he watches Smith walk away – underscores his pathetic clinginess. What follows even mirrors a toddler's hateful tantrum when spurned by their parent – albeit with homicidal intentions

"My goodness, Smith, what's the matter?" asked Peterson, appearing at the door of his study.

"Give me some brandy!"

Peterson disappeared, and came rushing out again with a glass and a decanter.

"You need it," he said, as his visitor drank off what he poured out for him. "Why, man, you are as white as a cheese."

Smith laid down his glass, rose up, and took a deep breath.

"I am my own man again now," said he. "I was never so unmanned before[1]. But, with your leave, Peterson, I will sleep here to-night, for I don't think I could face that road again except by daylight. It's weak, I know[2], but I can't help it."

Peterson looked at his visitor with a very questioning eye.

"Of course you shall sleep here if you wish. I'll tell Mrs. Burney to make up the spare bed. Where are you off to now?"

---

[1] There is something so tantalizingly Freudian about the mummy and its "unmanning" powers – something rapacious and emasculating. Bellingham is no physical specimen, but he secretly shares quarters with a man who is – a roommate whom he both figuratively and literally keeps in the closet, only releasing him when it is time to "un-man" a victim. Essentially the mummy fills his victims with the same fear that a woman might fear when she walks alone through a dark park. It is not murder that so terrifies them, but who the murderer is, and it is not the threat of death which so "un-mans" Smith but the feeling of being stalked, attacked, and dominated by this secret which Bellingham harbors in his closet. The mummy could be seen as a symbol of male rape, or at the most innocent of fear between peers and gentlemen (a middle classed man might be wary of being attacked by roughs in the dockyards or back alleys, but it would be particularly unsettling to experience fear from a man of his same social station). Smith finds himself emasculated by the fear that he might expect only an assaulted woman to experience, especially since the attack is so dominating: not the threat of a gun or a knife, but the threat of strangulation – a death which is both highly sexualized (the use of brute force, the rape-like stifling, the gasping for air, and the flushing faces as one body crushes down upon another – it is no surprise that erotic and auto-erotic asphyxiation remains a popular sex-play in spite of the many accidental deaths caused by the practice) and highly associated with male-on-female murders (we don't often hear of one man strangling another, although the crime is more among mixed-gender assaults). Unable to bear the thought of being stalked, dominated, and smothered, Smith flees in terror, momentarily losing his manhood in the girlish flight (surely his hyper-English instinct was to stand and fight to the death), but in the long run preserves it because succumbing to the mummy's symbolic rape would have unmanned him in death and hence for eternity, allowing Smith to restore his manhood (specifically through the masculine ritual of consuming brandy) and live to be "robust" another day

[2] With his chauvinistic worldview, it is no surprise that Smith finds his action "weak" – it so thoroughly resembles the plight of a girl who is stalked on her way home and rushes to the door of her nearest friend, who lets her spend the night since she is too shaken to set foot outside. It has all the emotional tension of a targeted rape victim who is harbored for the night by caring friends, an experience which the self-reliant Smith must find overwhelmingly emasculating and feminizing

"Come up with me to the window that overlooks the door. I want you to see what I have seen."

They went up to the window of the upper hall whence they could look down upon the approach to the house. The drive and the fields on either side lay quiet and still, bathed in the peaceful moonlight.

"Well, really, Smith," remarked Peterson, "it is well that I know you to be an abstemious[1] man. What in the world can have frightened you?"

"I'll tell you presently. But where can it have gone? Ah, now look, look! See the curve of the road just beyond your gate."

"Yes, I see; you needn't pinch my arm off. I saw someone pass. I should say a man, rather thin, apparently, and tall, very tall. But what of him? And what of yourself? You are still shaking like an aspen leaf."

"I have been within hand-grip of the devil, that's all. But come down to your study, and I shall tell you the whole story."

He did so. Under the cheery lamplight, with a glass of wine on the table beside him, and the portly form and florid face of his friend in front[2], he narrated, in their order, all the events, great and small, which had formed so singular a chain, from the night on which he had found Bellingham fainting in front of the mummy case until his horrid experience of an hour ago.

"There now," he said as he concluded, "that's the whole black business. It is monstrous and incredible, but it is true."

Dr. Plumptree Peterson sat for some time in silence with a very puzzled expression upon his face.

"I never heard of such a thing in my life, never[3]!" he said at last. "You have told me the facts. Now tell me your inferences."

"You can draw your own."

"But I should like to hear yours. You have thought over the matter, and I have not."

"Well, it must be a little vague in detail, but the main points seem to me to be clear enough. This fellow Bellingham, in his Eastern studies, has got hold of some infernal secret by which a mummy--or possibly only this particular mummy--can be temporarily brought to life. He was trying this disgusting business on the night when he fainted. No doubt the sight of the creature moving had shaken his nerve, even though he had expected it. You remember that almost the first words he said were to call out upon himself

---

[1] Sober

[2] As mentioned in a previous note, fatness is often used to demarcate one of two personalities: broad generosity or gluttonous greed. The professor is a large, round, jolly fellow whose girth is due to a warm and open persona, unlike Bellingham, who is depicted as a self-absorbed egomaniac prone to character vices (gluttony can imply a ravenous appetite for psychological, sexual, and personal indulgence as well as the obvious culinary weaknesses)

[3] Indeed, not even in fiction, this being the first malevolent mummy story that we have on record. It does, however, bear strong resemblances to the myth of the Jewish Gollum of Prague and, of course, to the necromancy of Frankenstein

as a fool. Well, he got more hardened afterwards, and carried the matter through without fainting. The vitality which he could put into it was evidently only a passing thing, for I have seen it continually in its case as dead as this table. He has some elaborate process, I fancy, by which he brings the thing to pass. Having done it, he naturally bethought him that he might use the creature as an agent[1]. It has intelligence and it has strength. For some purpose he took Lee into his confidence; but Lee, like a decent Christian, would have nothing to do with such a business. Then they had a row, and Lee vowed that he would tell his sister of Bellingham's true character. Bellingham's game was to prevent him, and he nearly managed it, by setting this creature of his on his track. He had already tried its powers upon another man--Norton--towards whom he had a grudge. It is the merest chance that he has not two murders upon his soul. Then, when I taxed him with the matter, he had the strongest reasons for wishing to get me out of the way before I could convey my knowledge to anyone else. He got his chance when I went out, for he knew my habits, and where I was bound for. I have had a narrow shave, Peterson, and it is mere luck you didn't find me on your doorstep in the morning. I'm not a nervous man as a rule[2], and I never thought to have the fear of death put upon me as it was to-night."

"My dear boy, you take the matter too seriously," said his companion. "Your nerves are out of order with your work, and you make too much of it. How could such a thing as this stride about the streets of Oxford, even at night, without being seen?"

"It has been seen. There is quite a scare in the town about an escaped ape, as they imagine the creature to be. It is the talk of the place."

"Well, it's a striking chain of events. And yet, my dear fellow, you must allow that each incident in itself is capable of a more natural explanation."

"What! even my adventure of to-night?"

"Certainly. You come out with your nerves all unstrung, and your head full of this theory of yours. Some gaunt, half-famished tramp steals after you, and seeing you run, is emboldened to pursue you. Your fears and imagination do the rest."

"It won't do, Peterson; it won't do."

"And again, in the instance of your finding the mummy case empty, and then a few moments later with an occupant, you know that it was lamplight, that the lamp was half turned down, and that you had no special reason to

---

[1] This especially resembles the Gollum, a clay man which is summoned to life when the Jewish community in Prague required a defender. Certainly this "agent" is far less noble, however

[2] Unlike poor Lee. It is interesting that Lee began the story as a decent-but-pathetic character in Smith's eyes – largely due to his subservience to Bellingham and his generally submissive personality – and that Smith should wind up, even if momentarily, a rabbity, pathetic character himself as a result of his past intimacy with Bellingham

look hard at the case. It is quite possible that you may have overlooked the creature in the first instance."

"No, no; it is out of the question."

"And then Lee may have fallen into the river, and Norton been garrotted. It is certainly a formidable indictment that you have against Bellingham; but if you were to place it before a police magistrate, he would simply laugh in your face."

"I know he would. That is why I mean to take the matter into my own hands."

"Eh?"

"Yes; I feel that a public duty rests upon me, and, besides, I must do it for my own safety, unless I choose to allow myself to be hunted by this beast out of the college, and that would be a little too feeble[1]. I have quite made up my mind what I shall do. And first of all, may I use your paper and pens for an hour?"

"Most certainly. You will find all that you want upon that side table."

Abercrombie Smith sat down before a sheet of foolscap, and for an hour, and then for a second hour his pen travelled swiftly over it. Page after page was finished and tossed aside while his friend leaned back in his arm-chair, looking across at him with patient curiosity. At last, with an exclamation of satisfaction, Smith sprang to his feet, gathered his papers up into order, and laid the last one upon Peterson's desk.

"Kindly sign this as a witness," he said.

"A witness? Of what?"

"Of my signature, and of the date. The date is the most important. Why, Peterson, my life might hang upon it."

"My dear Smith, you are talking wildly. Let me beg you to go to bed."

"On the contrary, I never spoke so deliberately in my life. And I will promise to go to bed the moment you have signed it."

"But what is it?"

"It is a statement of all that I have been telling you to-night. I wish you to witness it."

"Certainly," said Peterson, signing his name under that of his companion. "There you are! But what is the idea?"

"You will kindly retain it, and produce it in case I am arrested."

"Arrested? For what?"

"For murder. It is quite on the cards[2]. I wish to be ready for every event. There is only one course open to me, and I am determined to take it."

"For Heaven's sake, don't do anything rash!"

---

[1] Already self-conscious about his being "unmanned" into running for his life, Smith resents the idea that he be scared off of campus as a "feeble" response, clashing with his dominant, "robust" nature – or at least his perception of it

[2] Likely to happen, fateful

"Believe me, it would be far more rash to adopt any other course. I hope that we won't need to bother you, but it will ease my mind to know that you have this statement of my motives. And now I am ready to take your advice and to go to roost, for I want to be at my best in the morning."

Abercrombie Smith was not an entirely pleasant man to have as an enemy. Slow and easytempered, he was formidable when driven to action[1]. He brought to every purpose in life the same deliberate resoluteness which had distinguished him as a scientific student. He had laid his studies aside for a day, but he intended that the day should not be wasted. Not a word did he say to his host as to his plans, but by nine o'clock he was well on his way to Oxford.

In the High Street he stopped at Clifford's, the gun-maker's, and bought a heavy revolver[2], with a box of central-fire cartridges[3]. Six of them he slipped into the chambers, and half-cocking the weapon[4], placed it in the pocket of his coat. He then made his way to Hastie's rooms, where the big oarsman was lounging over his breakfast, with the Sporting Times[5] propped up against the coffeepot.

"Hullo! What's up?" he asked. "Have some coffee?"

"No, thank you. I want you to come with me, Hastie, and do what I ask you."

"Certainly, my boy."

"And bring a heavy stick with you."

"Hullo!" Hastie stared. "Here's a hunting-crop[6] that would fell an ox."

"One other thing. You have a box of amputating knives. Give me the longest of them."

"There you are. You seem to be fairly on the war trail. Anything else?"

---

[1] This is where Hastie's rash, sanguine manliness falls short of Smith's even-keeled, melancholic masculinity: although he is unsociable, dull, and unclubbable, he is cool under fire, methodical, and precise

[2] Probably a Colt, Enfield, or Webley make, with a .45, .455, or .476 bullet

[3] Centerfire ammunition is ubiquitous today (the primer is located in a depression in the center of the cartridge case head, and can be removed and replaced if needed), but it was only 23 years old at this time. Previously, the entire head of the cartridge was a primer pan, making it dangerous and inaccurate. Centerfire catridges are for persons who don't want to miss what they're shooting at – persons who mean business

[4] At half-cock, the weapon is engaged but on safety. The mere pressing of the thumb on the hammer will drop it into full-cock: ready to fire with live ammunition

[5] Founded in 1865, discontinued in 1932, this weekly British paper was mostly centered on sports (unsurprisingly), especially horse racing

[6] This is no BDSM plaything – a leather crop with a heart-shaped tip. A hunting crop was the favorite weapon of Sherlock Holmes (Six Napoleons), specifically a loaded crop – one with a heavy metal core. The hunting crop resembled a very short walking cane, having a sturdy two or three foot shaft made of heavy wood with a bone or antler grip on one end and a leather flail on the other. Like a cudgel or a shillelagh, the crop could be a murderous tool in the right hands, and would easily be capable of splitting a man's head open given enough force

"No; that will do." Smith placed the knife inside his coat, and led the way to the quadrangle. "We are neither of us chickens, Hastie," said he. "I think I can do this job alone, but I take you as a precaution[1]. I am going to have a little talk with Bellingham. If I have only him to deal with, I won't, of course, need you. If I shout, however, up you come, and lam out with your whip as hard as you can lick. Do you understand?"

"All right. I'll come if I hear you bellow."

"Stay here, then. It may be a little time, but don't budge until I come down."

"I'm a fixture."

Smith ascended the stairs, opened Bellingham's door and stepped in. Bellingham was seated behind his table, writing. Beside him, among his litter of strange possessions, towered the mummy case, with its sale number 249 still stuck upon its front, and its hideous occupant stiff and stark within it. Smith looked very deliberately round him, closed the door, locked it, took the key from the inside, and then stepping across to the fireplace, struck a match and set the fire alight[2]. Bellingham sat staring, with amazement and rage upon his bloated face.

"Well, really now, you make yourself at home," he gasped.

Smith sat himself deliberately down, placing his watch upon the table, drew out his pistol, cocked it, and laid it in his lap. Then he took the long amputating knife from his bosom, and threw it down in front of Bellingham.

"Now, then," said he, "just get to work and cut up that mummy."

"Oh, is that it?" said Bellingham with a sneer.

"Yes, that is it. They tell me that the law can't touch you. But I have a law that will set matters straight. If in five minutes you have not set to work, I swear by the God who made me[3] that I will put a bullet through your brain!"

"You would murder me?"

Bellingham had half risen, and his face was the colour of putty.

"Yes."

"And for what?"

"To stop your mischief. One minute has gone."

"But what have I done?"

"I know and you know."

"This is mere bullying."

---

[1] Although we might tend to trust Smith's assertion that he is not asking for company because he is "chicken" (he might as well relent and say what he is really afraid of seeming: a pussy), he is not so sure that Hastie will understand, and makes a weak attempt to win his friend's confidence in his masculinity

[2] We must suppose this to be a coal fireplace, otherwise Bellingham must have it perfectly arranged with tinder and clippings for a quick light. This marks the deplorable race to the finish of this story. Doyle appears to have tired with it and rushes to the end without adequately resolving several key elements and glossing over some basic logic

[3] Unquestionably this must be Smith's way of defying Bellingham's pagan gods and affirming his own Christian, Anglican worldview

"Two minutes are gone."

"But you must give reasons. You are a madman--a dangerous madman. Why should I destroy my own property? It is a valuable mummy[1]."

"You must cut it up, and you must burn it."

"I will do no such thing."

"Four minutes are gone[2]."

Smith took up the pistol and he looked towards Bellingham with an inexorable face. As the second-hand stole round, he raised his hand, and the finger twitched upon the trigger.

"There! there! I'll do it!" screamed Bellingham.

In frantic haste he caught up the knife and hacked at the figure of the mummy, ever glancing round to see the eye and the weapon of his terrible visitor bent upon him. The creature crackled and snapped under every stab of the keen blade. A thick yellow dust rose up from it. Spices and dried essences rained down upon the floor. Suddenly, with a rending crack, its backbone snapped asunder, and it fell, a brown heap of sprawling limbs, upon the floor.

"Now into the fire!" said Smith.

The flames leaped and roared as the dried and tinderlike debris was piled upon it. The little room was like the stoke-hole of a steamer[3] and the sweat ran down the faces of the two men; but still the one stooped and worked, while the other sat watching him with a set face. A thick, fat smoke oozed out from the fire[4], and a heavy smell of burned rosin and singed hair filled the air. In a quarter of an hour a few charred and brittle sticks were all that was left of Lot No. 249.

"Perhaps that will satisfy you," snarled Bellingham, with hate and fear in his little grey eyes as he glanced back at his tormenter[5].

---

[1] As previously mentioned, valuable but not yet seen as a museum piece. Mummies were fairly easy to obtain if one had enough money, and many members of the aristocracy hosted unwrapping parties during the early and mid-nineteenth century

[2] Ludicrous, absolutely ludicrous. If their dialogue is not separated by long and awkward pauses hardly ten seconds will have passed. Doyle truly disappoints in the finale

[3] An area in a steamship where the furnace was fed coal through a chute. The temperatures could become practically unlivable when the vessels were running under high steam

[4] As one might expect of a veritable crematorium. The grisly description is worthy of Poe's body horror "Hop-Frog" and "The Facts in the Case of M. Valdemar," both of which detail the gruesome destruction of a body (the first by tar-fueled fire and the later by spontaneous decomposition). Important to note Doyle's admiration for Poe

[5] The relationship here has shifted from sadist and victim to victor and prisoner, inverting the previous dynamic by which Bellingham successfully un-manned three of his peers. Their relationship also resembles that of a demon being castigated by an angel – Lucifer and Saint Michael for example – which reinforces the religious, "good vs. evil" overtones

"No; I must make a clean sweep of all your materials. We must have no more devil's tricks. In with all these leaves! They may have something to do with it."

"And what now?" asked Bellingham, when the leaves also had been added to the blaze.

"Now the roll of papyrus which you had on the table that night. It is in that drawer, I think."

"No, no," shouted Bellingham. "Don't burn that! Why, man, you don't know what you do. It is unique; it contains wisdom which is nowhere else to be found."

"Out with it!"

"But look here, Smith, you can't really mean it. I'll share the knowledge with you. I'll teach you all that is in it. Or, stay[1], let me only copy it before you burn it!"

Smith stepped forward and turned the key in the drawer. Taking out the yellow, curled roll of paper, he threw it into the fire, and pressed it down with his heel. Bellingham screamed, and grabbed at it; but Smith pushed him back, and stood over it until it was reduced to a formless grey ash.

"Now, Master B.," said he, "I think I have pretty well drawn your teeth[2]. You'll hear from me again, if you return to your old tricks. And now good-morning, for I must go back to my studies."

And such is the narrative[3] of Abercrombie Smith as to the singular events which occurred in Old College, Oxford, in the spring of '84. As Bellingham left the university immediately afterwards, and was last heard of in the Soudan[4], there is no one who can contradict his statement. But the wisdom of men is small, and the ways of nature are strange, and who shall put a bound to the dark things which may be found by those who seek for them?

---

[1] Meaning "stop," "hold on," "have mercy," literally "stay your hand"

[2] Teeth have often been viewed as phallic symbols, or – at the very least – as indicating power to penetrate, dominate, and overpower. Smith refers to the proverbial lion who has had its fangs pulled out and been rendered harmless consequently

[3] See following discussion for complaints at Doyle's unnecessarily hasty conclusion

[4] Where – we must presume, for Doyle coyly and appropriately leaves out this detail – he died during the ghastly Mahdist War. Sudan was ruled by the Egyptians (themselves ruled by the Turks), who taxed them heavily. War broke out when a Muslim cleric led a rebellion against the government in 1881. It continued for 18 years peaking with the 1885 death of General Gordon (whose portrait is treasured by Sherlock Holmes) at the massacre of Khartoum

---

TRAGICALLY, Doyle appears to have had a word limit to meet, because the story – which had been smooth up to the point where Smith threatens Bellingham – ends on a clunky note. It almost feels as though he misjudged the amount of his writing and suddenly reeled it in. The character of Plumptree serves no real purpose after his final appearance, the final confrontation is rushed and inorganic, and worst of all – for this cozy, character-driven piece – there is no real resolution with the main characters: did Hastie – as would be fitting – marry Lee's sister? How did Lee recover? What of Long Norton? Under what circumstances did Bellingham leave? What did Plumptree think of the whole matter? What about Styles? I have often regretted the fact that Doyle wrote such a weak ending to a short story that may have been better served in novella form. But these are merely my complaints, and we must move on and accept the story for what it is. "Lot No. 249" remains – in spite of its faults – a beautiful narrative rich in setting, mood, character, and subtext, and is perhaps the seminal literary treatment of mummy fiction – as foundational to the genre as *Dracula* or *Frankenstein* are to theirs. The Egyptological craze of the nineteenth century was still burning hot after its commencement with the discovery of the Rosetta Stone in 1799 and would continue to blaze until World War II. Egypt represented something dearly coveted by the Victorians and the Edwardians. It was a grand society of passionate, elegant people, more ancient than Rome, nobler than Greece, more mystical than Babylon, and after Doyle wrote his pair of mummy stories, fantasy and horror writers began to plumb its depths for material. Bram Stoker, E. F. Benson, H. P. Lovecraft, Robert Bloch, H. Rider Haggard, Agatha Christie, Ray Bradbury, Sax Rohmer, and Anne Rice all generated fantastic tales surrounding animated mummies, haunted Egyptian relics, revived curses, and ghostly pyramids. Doyle's hand, unquestionably, was in some way present in all these works.

II.

At the bottom of his tale, however, is the unavoidable conflict between Smith and Bellingham, and with it come questions which are both uncomfortable and fascinating to a modern audience. There is no question that we should rebuke his portrayal of effeminate men as either domineering villains or submissive cowards, his depiction of British manhood as the ideal, or his suggestion that masculinity is a precious commodity not to be polluted with transcultural cross-pollination, but we must also remember that the time in which he wrote was one of deep concern and uncertainty for the British male. As colonial projects continued to yield embarrassing stories of atrocity, rebellion, and shame, and as domestic scandals such as the Cleveland Street debacle, the Oscar Wilde trial, and the exploits of crossdressers Fanny and Stella, long-held assumptions of the superiority, nature, and definition of British manhood suddenly became elusive. Today we often applaud the blurring and – as it were – queering of gender roles, but at the time it was an understandable crisis. The Big Brother of British colonialism (as seen in our next story, "The Brown Hand") had reigned without question for several decades, but by the 1890s it was clear that Anglo-Saxon colonizers had ruined many of the cultures they sought to civilize, had spread disease and misery, and had been agents of abuse and genocide. This was the case in Egypt just as it was in South America, India, and China. H. G. Wells, Joseph Conrad, Sir Roger Casement, and other disenchanted Victorians filled the papers, magazines, and bookstores with tales of colonial negligence, and the myth of the White Man's Burden began to sour in the minds of the British public – and with it their assumptions about British manhood, for if Father truly knew best, then why were his Indian servants dying of cholera, and why were they being mutilated by his overseers, and why did they want to murder him in his bed?

III.

Doyle's tale responds to these concerns with a comparatively light-handed description of "noble masculinity": it need not be domineering or authoritative, but it *should* be "robust" – well-rounded, physically and mentally stable, and hardy to the core, without pretense, dependence, or intrigue. To him, the most stable form of manhood was that which was self-reliant and forthright (*a la* Smith), not clingy and helpless (*a la* Lee) or craven and perfidious (*a la* Bellingham). This range of masculinity can even be seen in the order in which Doyle organizes their apartments in what we must assume to be an evolutionary ascendance. Anemic Lee, who is weak, dependent, and uncreative (a virtual stereotype of a masochistic "sub") is placed at the bottom of the tower. Bellingham, who is intelligent and inspired but jealous, secretive, and physically deficient, is lodged in the middle. Meanwhile, physically and intellectually vigorous Smith – Doyle's Holmesian ideal of manhood – retains the top spot. This depiction of the well-balanced life comes directly from Poe, who also emphasized the perils of imbalance between the spiritual/psychical and the material/physical self. Lee represents the dangers of being both physically and intellectually effete – you are vulnerable to the predations of evil people who will use either intellect or strength to overpower you. Bellingham (intellectually tough but physically and morally deficient) and his mummy (pure strength devoid of a soul) represent the dangers posed by evil people. Finally, Smith and Hastie are charged with the responsibility – as well-rounded men – of protecting the Lees of the world from the Bellinghams: while both are physically and intellectually robust, Smith's strengths are more scholarly and Hastie's lean towards physique. Together, though – like Holmes and Watson – they form a formidable pair, and – most importantly – they share a moral code (one which Lee has, but is powerless to promote, and which Bellingham rejects and actively attempts to subvert. The most telling part of this model is the way in which Bellingham's zone quietly bleeds into Lee and Smith's: he first attempts to convert Lee – who lacks his intelligence but shares his material weakness – but is rejected, causing him to turn up towards Smith, who shares his intellect but also stands to provide the missing ingredient of physical fortitude. Indeed, the similarities between Bellingham and Smith genuinely unsettle the latter: he recognizes that his own anti-social isolation, self-reliance, and nonconformity – traits shared with his downstairs neighbor – could leave him vulnerable to Bellingham's temptations. At the end of the story, in spite of his huff and puff, Smith appears shaken by the similarities between himself and the alchemist.

IV.

Today Doyle's thesis seems chauvinistic and vaguely homophobic, and indeed it is. The soulless, sensual mummy can easily be seen as the physical manifestation of homosexuality: a dark and frightening secret hidden in a closet and released at dark to dominate and "unman" its male victims. But to Doyle this was less of a parable about sexual deviancy than a philosophical discourse on what makes an adult a productive member of society: a person who is strong-willed but compassionate, bold but gentle, idealistic but restrained, imaginative but logical, and balanced equally between the physical and mental experiences of life – neither a roughhousing bully nor a socially detached bookworm. Regardless of gender, class, income, sexual orientation, nationality, or religion, these are the hallmarks of a good citizen of the world, and they needn't be a "robust," heterosexual, white, British male to achieve what Doyle has so carefully described here.

THE brand of speculative fiction for which Doyle is most famous falls under the genre of "lost worlds" – a trope which derives its very name from his 1912 novel *The Lost World*. The first of three novels following the eccentric Professor Challenger, an unconventional explorer who discovers a plateau in the Amazon where prehistoric beasts thrive, unnoticed by modern humanity. Serialized in *The Strand, The Lost World* was astonishingly popular and afforded Doyle a break from Holmes, and a new feather in his literary cap – indeed, the Challenger novels would become his proudest literary accomplishment. The original novel was adapted for film as early as 1925, and Challenger has been portrayed by such stalwart actors as Claude "The Invisible Man" Rains, Basil Rathbone (whose Sherlock Holmes is still considered the most iconic), John Rys-Davies, and Bob Hoskins. The series also inspired *Jurassic Park* (and, of course, its sequel *The Lost World*), and an eponymous Australian produced television series written in the campy vein of *Xena: Warrior Princess* and *Hercules: The Legendary Journeys*. Doyle certainly did not invent the genre that adopted his title – H. Rider Haggard's *King Solomon's Mines* (1885) and *She* (1887) were among its most famous examples, not to mention Jules Verne's *Journey to the Center of the Earth* (1864), Rudyard Kipling's *The Man Who Would Be King* (1888), and the 1820 novel *Smyzonia* (a Hollow Earth novel that inspired Verne and Poe), but *The Lost World* still seemed to galvanize and shape the genre just as Sherlock Holmes did to a tradition that had been pioneered by Poe and Hoffmann. The following story is not one of a lost *world* per se, but of a lost monster – a prehistoric creature which has been capable of evading human detection despite its massive size and horrific features. The story predates *The Lost World* by two years and may be seen as something of a practice run for the novel which expands its scope considerably.

The Terror of Blue John Gap
{1910}

THE following narrative was found among the papers of Dr. James Hardcastle, who died of phthisis on February 4th, 1908, at 36, Upper Coventry Flats, South Kensington. Those who knew him best, while refusing to express an opinion upon this particular statement, are unanimous in asserting that he was a man of a sober and scientific turn of mind, absolutely devoid of imagination, and most unlikely to invent any abnormal series of events. The paper was contained in an envelope, which was docketed, "A Short Account of the Circumstances which occurred near Miss Allerton's Farm in North-West Derbyshire in the Spring of Last Year." The envelope was sealed, and on the other side was written in pencil—

DEAR SEATON, "It may interest, and perhaps pain you, to know that the incredulity with which you met my story has prevented me from ever opening my mouth upon the subject again. I leave this record after my death, and perhaps strangers may be found to have more confidence in me than my friend." Inquiry has failed to elicit who this Seaton may have been. I may add that the visit of the deceased to Allerton's Farm, and the general nature of the alarm there, apart from his particular explanation, have been absolutely established. With this foreword I append his account exactly as he left it. It is in the form of a diary, some entries in which have been expanded, while a few have been erased.

April 17. — Already I feel the benefit of this wonderful upland air. The farm of the Allertons lies fourteen hundred and twenty feet above sea- level, so it may well be a bracing climate. Beyond the usual morning cough I have very little discomfort, and, what with the fresh milk and the home-grown mutton, I have every chance of putting on weight. I think Saunderson will be pleased.

The two Miss Allertons are charmingly quaint and kind, two dear little hard-working old maids, who are ready to lavish all the heart which might have gone out to husband and to children upon an invalid stranger. Truly, the old maid is a most useful person, one of the reserve forces of the community. They talk of the superfluous woman, but what would the poor superfluous man do without her kindly presence? By the way, in their simplicity they very quickly let out the reason why Saunderson recommended their farm. The Professor rose from the ranks himself, and I believe that in his youth he was not above scaring crows in these very fields.

It is a most lonely spot, and the walks are picturesque in the extreme. The farm consists of grazing land lying at the bottom of an irregular valley. On each side are the fantastic limestone hills, formed of rock so soft that you can break it away with your hands. All this country is hollow. Could you strike it with some gigantic hammer it would boom like a drum, or possibly cave in altogether and expose some huge subterranean sea. A great sea there must surely be, for on all sides the streams run into the mountain itself, never to reappear. There are gaps everywhere amid the rocks, and when you pass through them you find yourself in great caverns, which wind down into the bowels of the earth. I have a small bicycle lamp, and it is a perpetual joy to me to carry it into these weird solitudes, and to see the wonderful silver and black effect when I throw its light upon the stalactites which drape the lofty roofs. Shut off the lamp, and you are in the blackest darkness. Turn it on, and it is a scene from the Arabian Nights.

But there is one of these strange openings in the earth which has a special interest, for it is the handiwork, not of nature, but of man. I had never heard of Blue John when I came to these parts. It is the name given to a peculiar mineral of a beautiful purple shade, which is only found at one or two places in the world. It is so rare that an ordinary vase of Blue John would be valued at a great price. The Romans, with that extraordinary instinct of theirs, discovered that it was to be found in this valley, and sank a horizontal shaft deep into the mountain side. The opening of their mine has been called Blue John Gap, a clean-cut arch in the rock, the mouth all overgrown with bushes. It is a goodly passage which the Roman miners have cut, and it intersects some of the great water-worn caves, so that if you enter Blue John Gap you would do well to mark your steps and to have a good store of candles, or you may never make your way back to the daylight again. I have not yet gone deeply into it, but this very day I stood at the mouth of the arched tunnel, and peering down into the black recesses beyond, I vowed that when my health returned I would devote some holiday to exploring those mysterious depths and finding out for myself how far the Roman had penetrated into the Derbyshire hills.

Strange how superstitious these countrymen are! I should have thought better of young Armitage, for he is a man of some education and character, and a very fine fellow for his station in life. I was standing at the Blue John Gap when he came across the field to me.

"Well, doctor," said he, "you're not afraid, anyhow."

"Afraid!" I answered. "Afraid of what?"

"Of it," said he, with a jerk of his thumb towards the black vault, "of the Terror that lives in the Blue John Cave."

How absurdly easy it is for a legend to arise in a lonely countryside! I examined him as to the reasons for his weird belief. It seems that from time to time sheep have been missing from the fields, carried bodily away, according to Armitage. That they could have wandered away of their own accord and disappeared among the mountains was an explanation to which he would not listen. On one occasion a pool of blood had been found, and some tufts of wool. That also, I pointed out, could be explained in a perfectly natural way. Further, the nights upon which sheep disappeared were invariably very dark, cloudy nights with no moon. This I met with the obvious retort that those were the nights which a commonplace sheep-stealer would naturally choose for his work. On one occasion a gap had been made in a wall, and some of the stones scattered for a considerable distance. Human agency again, in my opinion. Finally, Armitage clinched all his arguments by telling me that he had actually heard the Creature—indeed, that anyone could hear it who remained long enough at the Gap. It was a distant roaring of an immense volume. I could not but smile at this, knowing, as I do, the strange reverberations which come out of an underground water system running amid the chasms of a limestone formation. My incredulity annoyed Armitage, so that he turned and left me with some abruptness.

And now comes the queer point about the whole business. I was still standing near the mouth of the cave turning over in my mind the various statements of Armitage, and reflecting how readily they could be explained away, when suddenly, from the depth of the tunnel beside me, there issued a most extraordinary sound. How shall I describe it? First of all it seemed to be a great distance away, far down in the bowels of the earth. Secondly, in spite of this suggestion of distance, it was very loud. Lastly, it was not a boom, nor a crash, such as one would associate with falling water or tumbling rock, but it was a high whine, tremulous and vibrating, almost like the whinnying of a horse. It was certainly a most remarkable experience, and one which for a moment, I must admit, gave a new significance to Armitage's words. I waited by the Blue John Gap for half an hour or more, but there was no return of the sound, so at last I wandered back to the farmhouse, rather mystified by what had occurred. Decidedly I shall explore that cavern when my strength is restored. Of course, Armitage's explanation is too absurd for discussion, and yet that sound was certainly very strange. It still rings in my ears as I write.

April 20.—In the last three days I have made several expeditions to the Blue John Gap, and have even penetrated some short distance, but my bicycle lantern is so small and weak that I dare not trust myself very far. I shall do the thing more systematically. I have heard no sound at all, and could almost believe that I had been the victim of some hallucination, suggested, perhaps, by Armitage's conversation. Of course, the whole idea is absurd, and yet I must confess that those bushes at the entrance of the cave do present an appearance as if some heavy creature had forced its way through them. I begin to be keenly interested. I have said nothing to the Miss Allertons, for they are quite superstitious enough already, but I have bought some candles, and mean to investigate for myself.

I observed this morning that among the numerous tufts of sheep's wool which lay among the bushes near the cavern there was one which was smeared with blood. Of course, my reason tells me that if sheep wander into such rocky places they are likely to injure themselves, and yet somehow that splash of crimson gave me a sudden shock, and for a moment I found myself shrinking back in horror from the old Roman arch. A fetid breath seemed to ooze from the black depths into which I peered. Could it indeed be possible that some nameless thing, some dreadful presence, was lurking down yonder? I should have been incapable of such feelings in the days of my strength, but one grows more nervous and fanciful when one's health is shaken.

For the moment I weakened in my resolution, and was ready to leave the secret of the old mine, if one exists, for ever unsolved. But tonight my interest has returned and my nerves grown more steady. Tomorrow I trust that I shall have gone more deeply into this matter.

April 22.—Let me try and set down as accurately as I can my extraordinary experience of yesterday. I started in the afternoon, and made my way to the Blue John Gap. I confess that my misgivings returned as I gazed into its depths, and I wished that I had brought a companion to share my exploration. Finally, with a return of resolution, I lit my candle, pushed my way through the briars, and descended into the rocky shaft.

It went down at an acute angle for some fifty feet, the floor being covered with broken stone. Thence there extended a long, straight passage cut in the solid rock. I am no geologist, but the lining of this corridor was certainly of some harder material than limestone, for there were points where I could actually see the tool-marks which the old miners had left in their excavation, as fresh as if they had been done yesterday. Down this strange, old- world corridor I stumbled, my feeble flame throwing a dim circle of light around me, which made the shadows beyond the more threatening and obscure. Finally, I came to a spot where the Roman tunnel opened into a water-worn cavern—a huge hall, hung with long white icicles of lime deposit. From this central chamber I could dimly perceive that a number of passages worn by the subterranean streams wound away into the depths of the earth. I was standing there wondering whether I had better return, or whether I dare venture farther into this dangerous labyrinth, when my eyes fell upon something at my feet which strongly arrested my attention.

The greater part of the floor of the cavern was covered with boulders of rock or with hard incrustations of lime, but at this particular point there had been a drip from the distant roof, which had left a patch of soft mud. In the very centre of this there was a huge mark—an ill-defined blotch, deep, broad and irregular, as if a great boulder had fallen upon it. No loose stone lay near, however, nor was there anything to account for the impression. It was far too large to be caused by any possible animal, and besides, there was only the one, and the patch of mud was of such a size that no reasonable stride could have covered it. As I rose from the examination of that singular mark and then looked round into the black shadows which hemmed me in, I must confess that I felt for a moment a most unpleasant sinking of my heart, and that, do what I could, the candle trembled in my outstretched hand.

I soon recovered my nerve, however, when I reflected how absurd it was to associate so huge and shapeless a mark with the track of any known animal. Even an elephant could not have produced it. I determined, therefore, that I would not be scared by vague and senseless fears from carrying out my exploration. Before proceeding, I took good note of a curious rock formation in the wall by which I could recognize the entrance of the Roman tunnel. The precaution was very necessary, for the great cave, so far as I could see it, was intersected by passages. Having made sure of my position, and reassured myself by examining my spare candles and my matches, I advanced slowly over the rocky and uneven surface of the cavern.

And now I come to the point where I met with such sudden and desperate disaster. A stream, some twenty feet broad, ran across my path, and I walked for some little distance along the bank to find a spot where I could cross dry- shod. Finally, I came to a place where a single flat boulder lay near the centre, which I could reach in a stride. As it chanced, however, the rock had been cut away and made top-heavy by the rush of the stream, so that it tilted over as I landed on it and shot me into the ice-cold water. My candle went out, and I found myself floundering about in utter and absolute darkness.

I staggered to my feet again, more amused than alarmed by my adventure. The candle had fallen from my hand, and was lost in the stream, but I had two others in my pocket, so that it was of no importance. I got one of them ready, and drew out my box of matches to light it. Only then did I realize my position. The box had been soaked in my fall into the river. It was impossible to strike the matches.

A cold hand seemed to close round my heart as I realized my position. The darkness was opaque and horrible. It was so utter that one put one's hand up to one's face as if to press off something solid. I stood still, and by an effort I steadied myself. I tried to reconstruct in my mind a map of the floor of the cavern as I had last seen it. Alas! the bearings which had impressed themselves upon my mind were high on the wall, and not to be found by touch. Still, I remembered in a general way how the sides were situated, and I hoped that by groping my way along them I should at last come to the opening of the Roman tunnel. Moving very slowly, and continually striking against the rocks, I set out on this desperate quest.

But I very soon realized how impossible it was. In that black, velvety darkness one lost all one's bearings in an instant. Before I had made a dozen paces, I was utterly bewildered as to my whereabouts. The rippling of the stream, which was the one sound audible, showed me where it lay, but the moment that I left its bank I was utterly lost. The idea of finding my way back in absolute darkness through that limestone labyrinth was clearly an impossible one.

I sat down upon a boulder and reflected upon my unfortunate plight. I had not told anyone that I proposed to come to the Blue John mine, and it was unlikely that a search party would come after me. Therefore I must trust to my own resources to get clear of the danger. There was only one hope, and that was that the matches might dry. When I fell into the river, only half of me had got thoroughly wet. My left shoulder had remained above the water. I took the box of matches, therefore, and put it into my left armpit. The moist air of the cavern might possibly be counteracted by the heat of my body, but even so, I knew that I could not hope to get a light for many hours. Meanwhile there was nothing for it but to wait.

By good luck I had slipped several biscuits into my pocket before I left the farm-house. These I now devoured, and washed them down with a draught from that wretched stream which had been the cause of all my misfortunes. Then I felt about for a comfortable seat among the rocks, and, having discovered a place where I could get a support for my back, I stretched out my legs and settled myself down to wait. I was wretchedly damp and cold, but I tried to cheer myself with the reflection that modern science prescribed open windows and walks in all weather for my disease. Gradually, lulled by the monotonous gurgle of the stream, and by the absolute darkness, I sank into an uneasy slumber.

How long this lasted I cannot say. It may have been for an hour, it may have been for several. Suddenly I sat up on my rock couch, with every nerve thrilling and every sense acutely on the alert. Beyond all doubt I had heard a sound—some sound very distinct from the gurgling of the waters. It had passed, but the reverberation of it still lingered in my ear. Was it a search party? They would most certainly have shouted, and vague as this sound was which had wakened me, it was very distinct from the human voice. I sat palpitating and hardly daring to breathe. There it was again! And again! Now it had become continuous. It was a tread—yes, surely it was the tread of some living creature. But what a tread it was! It gave one the impression of enormous weight carried upon sponge-like feet, which gave forth a muffled but ear-filling sound. The darkness was as complete as ever, but the tread was regular and decisive. And it was coming beyond all question in my direction.

My skin grew cold, and my hair stood on end as I listened to that steady and ponderous footfall. There was some creature there, and surely by the speed of its advance, it was one which could see in the dark. I crouched low on my rock and tried to blend myself into it. The steps grew nearer still, then stopped, and presently I was aware of a loud lapping and gurgling. The creature was drinking at the stream. Then again there was silence, broken by a succession of long sniffs and snorts of tremendous volume and energy. Had it caught the scent of me? My own nostrils were filled by a low fetid odour, mephitic and abominable. Then I heard the steps again. They were on my side of the stream now. The stones rattled within a few yards of where I lay. Hardly daring to breathe, I crouched upon my rock. Then the steps drew away. I heard the splash as it returned across the river, and the sound died away into the distance in the direction from which it had come.

For a long time I lay upon the rock, too much horrified to move. I thought of the sound which I had heard coming from the depths of the cave, of Armitage's fears, of the strange impression in the mud, and now came this final and absolute proof that there was indeed some inconceivable monster, something utterly unearthly and dreadful, which lurked in the hollow of the mountain. Of its nature or form I could frame no conception, save that it was both light- footed and gigantic. The combat between my reason, which told me that such things could not be, and my senses, which told me that they were, raged within me as I lay. Finally, I was almost ready to persuade myself that this experience had been part of some evil dream, and that my abnormal condition might have conjured up an hallucination. But there remained one final experience which removed the last possibility of doubt from my mind.

I had taken my matches from my armpit and felt them. They seemed perfectly hard and dry. Stooping down into a crevice of the rocks, I tried one of them. To my delight it took fire at once. I lit the candle, and, with a terrified backward glance into the obscure depths of the cavern, I hurried in the direction of the Roman passage. As I did so I passed the patch of mud on which I had seen the huge imprint. Now I stood astonished before it, for there were three similar imprints upon its surface, enormous in size, irregular in outline, of a depth which indicated the ponderous weight which had left them. Then a great terror surged over me. Stooping and shading my candle with my hand, I ran in a frenzy of fear to the rocky archway, hastened up it, and never stopped until, with weary feet and panting lungs, I rushed up the final slope of stones, broke through the tangle of briars, and flung myself exhausted upon the soft grass under the peaceful light of the stars. It was three in the morning when I reached the farm-house, and today I am all unstrung and quivering after my terrific adventure. As yet I have told no one. I must move warily in the matter. What would the poor lonely women, or the uneducated yokels here think of it if I were to tell them my experience? Let me go to someone who can understand and advise.

April 25.—I was laid up in bed for two days after my incredible adventure in the cavern. I use the adjective with a very definite meaning, for I have had an experience since which has shocked me almost as much as the other. I have said that I was looking round for someone who could advise me. There is a Dr. Mark Johnson who practices some few miles away, to whom I had a note of recommendation from Professor Saunderson. To him I drove, when I was strong enough to get about, and I recounted to him my whole strange experience. He listened intently, and then carefully examined me, paying special attention to my reflexes and to the pupils of my eyes. When he had finished, he refused to discuss my adventure, saying that it was entirely beyond him, but he gave me the card of a Mr. Picton at Castleton, with the advice that I should instantly go to him and tell him the story exactly as I had done to himself. He was, according to my adviser, the very man who was pre-eminently suited to help me. I went on to the station, therefore, and made my way to the little town, which is some ten miles away. Mr. Picton appeared to be a man of importance, as his brass plate was displayed upon the door of a considerable building on the outskirts of the town. I was about to ring his bell, when some misgiving came into my mind, and, crossing to a neighbouring shop, I asked the man behind the counter if he could tell me anything of Mr. Picton. "Why," said he, "he is the best mad doctor in Derbyshire, and yonder is his asylum." You can imagine that it was not long before I had shaken the dust of Castleton from my feet and returned to the farm, cursing all unimaginative pedants who cannot conceive that there may be things in creation which have never yet chanced to come across their mole's vision. After all, now that I am cooler, I can afford to admit that I have been no more sympathetic to Armitage than Dr. Johnson has been to me.

April 27. When I was a student I had the reputation of being a man of courage and enterprise. I remember that when there was a ghost-hunt at Coltbridge it was I who sat up in the haunted house. Is it advancing years (after all, I am only thirty-five), or is it this physical malady which has caused degeneration? Certainly my heart quails when I think of that horrible cavern in the hill, and the certainty that it has some monstrous occupant. What shall I do? There is not an hour in the day that I do not debate the question. If I say nothing, then the mystery remains unsolved. If I do say anything, then I have the alternative of mad alarm over the whole countryside, or of absolute incredulity which may end in consigning me to an asylum. On the whole, I think that my best course is to wait, and to prepare for some expedition which shall be more deliberate and better thought out than the last. As a first step I have been to Castleton and obtained a few essentials—a large acetylene lantern for one thing, and a good double-barrelled sporting rifle for another. The latter I have hired, but I have bought a dozen heavy game cartridges, which would bring down a rhinoceros. Now I am ready for my troglodyte friend. Give me better health and a little spate of energy, and I shall try conclusions with him yet. But who and what is he? Ah! there is the question which stands between me and my sleep. How many theories do I form, only to discard each in turn! It is all so utterly unthinkable. And yet the cry, the footmark, the tread in the cavern—no reasoning can get past these. I think of the old-world legends of dragons and of other monsters. Were they, perhaps, not such fairy- tales as we have thought? Can it be that there is some fact which underlies them, and am I, of all mortals, the one who is chosen to expose it?

May 3.—For several days I have been laid up by the vagaries of an English spring, and during those days there have been developments, the true and sinister meaning of which no one can appreciate save myself. I may say that we have had cloudy and moonless nights of late, which according to my information were the seasons upon which sheep disappeared. Well, sheep have disappeared. Two of Miss Allerton's, one of old Pearson's of the Cat Walk, and one of Mrs. Moulton's. Four in all during three nights. No trace is left of them at all, and the countryside is buzzing with rumours of gipsies and of sheep-stealers.

But there is something more serious than that. Young Armitage has disappeared also. He left his moorland cottage early on Wednesday night and has never been heard of since. He was an unattached man, so there is less sensation than would otherwise be the case. The popular explanation is that he owes money, and has found a situation in some other part of the country, whence he will presently write for his belongings. But I have grave misgivings. Is it not much more likely that the recent tragedy of the sheep has caused him to take some steps which may have ended in his own destruction? He may, for example, have lain in wait for the creature and been carried off by it into the recesses of the mountains. What an inconceivable fate for a civilized Englishman of the twentieth century! And yet I feel that it is possible and even probable. But in that case, how far am I answerable both for his death and for any other mishap which may occur? Surely with the knowledge I already possess it must be my duty to see that something is done, or if necessary to do it myself. It must be the latter, for this morning I went down to the local police-station and told my story. The inspector entered it all in a large book and bowed me out with commendable gravity, but I heard a burst of laughter before I had got down his garden path. No doubt he was recounting my adventure to his family.

June 10.—I am writing this, propped up in bed, six weeks after my last entry in this journal. I have gone through a terrible shock both to mind and body, arising from such an experience as has seldom befallen a human being before. But I have attained my end. The danger from the Terror which dwells in the Blue John Gap has passed never to return. Thus much at least I, a broken invalid, have done for the common good. Let me now recount what occurred as clearly as I may.

The night of Friday, May 3rd, was dark and cloudy—the very night for the monster to walk. About eleven o'clock I went from the farm-house with my lantern and my rifle, having first left a note upon the table of my bedroom in which I said that, if I were missing, search should be made for me in the direction of the Gap. I made my way to the mouth of the Roman shaft, and, having perched myself among the rocks close to the opening, I shut off my lantern and waited patiently with my loaded rifle ready to my hand.

It was a melancholy vigil. All down the winding valley I could see the scattered lights of the farm-houses, and the church clock of Chapel-le-Dale tolling the hours came faintly to my ears. These tokens of my fellow-men served only to make my own position seem the more lonely, and to call for a greater effort to overcome the terror which tempted me continually to get back to the farm, and abandon for ever this dangerous quest. And yet there lies deep in every man a rooted self-respect which makes it hard for him to turn back from that which he has once undertaken. This feeling of personal pride was my salvation now, and it was that alone which held me fast when every instinct of my nature was dragging me away. I am glad now that I had the strength. In spite of all that is has cost me, my manhood is at least above reproach.

Twelve o'clock struck in the distant church, then one, then two. It was the darkest hour of the night. The clouds were drifting low, and there was not a star in the sky. An owl was hooting somewhere among the rocks, but no other sound, save the gentle sough of the wind, came to my ears. And then suddenly I heard it! From far away down the tunnel came those muffled steps, so soft and yet so ponderous. I heard also the rattle of stones as they gave way under that giant tread. They drew nearer. They were close upon me. I heard the crashing of the bushes round the entrance, and then dimly through the darkness I was conscious of the loom of some enormous shape, some monstrous inchoate creature, passing swiftly and very silently out from the tunnel. I was paralysed with fear and amazement. Long as I had waited, now that it had actually come I was unprepared for the shock. I lay motionless and breathless, whilst the great dark mass whisked by me and was swallowed up in the night.

But now I nerved myself for its return. No sound came from the sleeping countryside to tell of the horror which was loose. In no way could I judge how far off it was, what it was doing, or when it might be back. But not a second time should my nerve fail me, not a second time should it pass unchallenged. I swore it between my clenched teeth as I laid my cocked rifle across the rock.

And yet it nearly happened. There was no warning of approach now as the creature passed over the grass. Suddenly, like a dark, drifting shadow, the huge bulk loomed up once more before me, making for the entrance of the cave. Again came that paralysis of volition which held my crooked forefinger impotent upon the trigger. But with a desperate effort I shook it off. Even as the brushwood rustled, and the monstrous beast blended with the shadow of the Gap, I fired at the retreating form. In the blaze of the gun I caught a glimpse of a great shaggy mass, something with rough and bristling hair of a withered grey colour, fading away to white in its lower parts, the huge body supported upon short, thick, curving legs. I had just that glance, and then I heard the rattle of the stones as the creature tore down into its burrow. In an instant, with a triumphant revulsion of feeling, I had cast my fears to the wind, and uncovering my powerful lantern, with my rifle in my hand, I sprang down from my rock and rushed after the monster down the old Roman shaft.

My splendid lamp cast a brilliant flood of vivid light in front of me, very different from the yellow glimmer which had aided me down the same passage only twelve days before. As I ran, I saw the great beast lurching along before me, its huge bulk filling up the whole space from wall to wall. Its hair looked like coarse faded oakum, and hung down in long, dense masses which swayed as it moved. It was like an enormous unclipped sheep in its fleece, but in size it was far larger than the largest elephant, and its breadth seemed to be nearly as great as its height. It fills me with amazement now to think that I should have dared to follow such a horror into the bowels of the earth, but when one's blood is up, and when one's quarry seems to be flying, the old primeval hunting- spirit awakes and prudence is cast to the wind. Rifle in hand, I ran at the top of my speed upon the trail of the monster.

I had seen that the creature was swift. Now I was to find out to my cost that it was also very cunning. I had imagined that it was in panic flight, and that I had only to pursue it. The idea that it might turn upon me never entered my excited brain. I have already explained that the passage down which I was racing opened into a great central cave. Into this I rushed, fearful lest I should lose all trace of the beast. But he had turned upon his own traces, and in a moment we were face to face.

That picture, seen in the brilliant white light of the lantern, is etched for ever upon my brain. He had reared up on his hind legs as a bear would do, and stood above me, enormous, menacing—such a creature as no nightmare had ever brought to my imagination. I have said that he reared like a bear, and there was something bear-like—if one could conceive a bear which was ten-fold the bulk of any bear seen upon earth—in his whole pose and attitude, in his great crooked forelegs with their ivory-white claws, in his rugged skin, and in his red, gaping mouth, fringed with monstrous fangs. Only in one point did he differ from the bear, or from any other creature which walks the earth, and even at that supreme moment a shudder of horror passed over me as I observed that the eyes which glistened in the glow of my lantern were huge, projecting bulbs, white and sightless. For a moment his great paws swung over my head. The next he fell forward upon me, I and my broken lantern crashed to the earth, and I remember no more.

When I came to myself I was back in the farm-house of the Allertons. Two days had passed since my terrible adventure in the Blue John Gap. It seems that I had lain all night in the cave insensible from concussion of the brain, with my left arm and two ribs badly fractured. In the morning my note had been found, a search party of a dozen farmers assembled, and I had been tracked down and carried back to my bedroom, where I had lain in high delirium ever since. There was, it seems, no sign of the creature, and no bloodstain which would show that my bullet had found him as he passed. Save for my own plight and the marks upon the mud, there was nothing to prove that what I said was true.

Six weeks have now elapsed, and I am able to sit out once more in the sunshine. Just opposite me is the steep hillside, grey with shaly rock, and yonder on its flank is the dark cleft which marks the opening of the Blue John Gap. But it is no longer a source of terror. Never again through that ill-omened tunnel shall any strange shape flit out into the world of men. The educated and the scientific, the Dr. Johnsons and the like, may smile at my narrative, but the poorer folk of the countryside had never a doubt as to its truth. On the day after my recovering consciousness they assembled in their hundreds round the Blue John Gap. As the Castleton Courier said:

"It was useless for our correspondent, or for any of the adventurous gentlemen who had come from Matlock, Buxton, and other parts, to offer to descend, to explore the cave to the end, and to finally test the extraordinary narrative of Dr. James Hardcastle. The country people had taken the matter into their own hands, and from an early hour of the morning they had worked hard in stopping up the entrance of the tunnel. There is a sharp slope where the shaft begins, and great boulders, rolled along by many willing hands, were thrust down it until the Gap was absolutely sealed. So ends the episode which has caused such excitement throughout the country. Local opinion is fiercely divided upon the subject. On the one hand are those who point to Dr. Hardcastle's impaired health, and to the possibility of cerebral lesions of tubercular origin giving rise to strange hallucinations. Some idee fixe, according to these gentlemen, caused the doctor to wander down the tunnel, and a fall among the rocks was sufficient to account for his injuries. On the other hand, a legend of a strange creature in the Gap has existed for some months back, and the farmers look upon Dr. Hardcastle's narrative and his personal injuries as a final corroboration. So the matter stands, and so the matter will continue to stand, for no definite solution seems to us to be now possible. It transcends human wit to give any scientific explanation which could cover the alleged facts."

Perhaps before the Courier published these words they would have been wise to send their representative to me. I have thought the matter out, as no one else has occasion to do, and it is possible that I might have removed some of the more obvious difficulties of the narrative and brought it one degree nearer to scientific acceptance. Let me then write down the only explanation which seems to me to elucidate what I know to my cost to have been a series of facts. My theory may seem to be wildly improbable, but at least no one can venture to say that it is impossible.

My view is—and it was formed, as is shown by my diary, before my personal adventure—that in this part of England there is a vast subterranean lake or sea, which is fed by the great number of streams which pass down through the limestone. Where there is a large collection of water there must also be some evaporation, mists or rain, and a possibility of vegetation. This in turn suggests that there may be animal life, arising, as the vegetable life would also do, from those seeds and types which had been introduced at an early period of the world's history, when communication with the outer air was more easy. This place had then developed a fauna and flora of its own, including such monsters as the one which I had seen, which may well have been the old cave-bear, enormously enlarged and modified by its new environment. For countless aeons the internal and the external creation had kept apart, growing steadily away from each other. Then there had come some rift in the depths of the mountain which had enabled one creature to wander up and, by means of the Roman tunnel, to reach the open air. Like all subterranean life, it had lost the power of sight, but this had no doubt been compensated for by nature in other directions. Certainly it had some means of finding its way about, and of hunting down the sheep upon the hillside. As to its choice of dark nights, it is part of my theory that light was painful to those great white eyeballs, and that it was only a pitch-black world which it could tolerate. Perhaps, indeed, it was the glare of my lantern which saved my life at that awful moment when we were face to face. So I read the riddle. I leave these facts behind me, and if you can explain them, do so; or if you choose to doubt them, do so. Neither your belief nor your incredulity can alter them, nor affect one whose task is nearly over.

So ended the strange narrative of Dr. James Hardcastle.

LIKE Professor Challenger, Hardcastle struggles to earn the trust and respect of the academic community when he relates his shocking experiences. There is a biographical element to this as well, one that would only worsen in the years to come: as Doyle delved into spiritualism and cryptozoology he found that the public were tickled by the idea of the creator of renowned skeptic Sherlock Holmes suiting up to go hunting fairies, ghosts, and giants. It bruised his ego deeply to find his pet interests so disrespected, and he felt that he had been wronged by a stubborn, close-minded scientific establishment. Challenger acted, in many ways, as an anti-Holmes: he was hot-blooded, passionate, imaginative, and mystical. In a sense Challenger gave voice to the part of Doyle which the public had rejected in favor of his colder, more analytic side. Personally Doyle was always more of a Watson than a Holmes: athletic, clubbable, in touch with fashions and current events, extroverted, and warm-blooded – the consummate chap's chap. If Doyle was truly Watson – with Holmes representing the bookish, boorish extreme of his personality – then Challenger was the opposite extreme of Holmes: brash, angry, demanding, and physical. But Hardcastle stands with Watson near the center – an adventurous, brave, intellectually curious busy body. "The Terror of Blue John Gap" is in many ways lands in the overlap of a Venn diagram of the Holmes and Challenger series: from the first it borrows a convalescing doctor with an adventuresome curiosity stomping about the English countryside in search of solutions to puzzling mysteries; from the second it borrows a frustrated believer in the uncanny whose adventures with prehistoric monsters are laughed off as the ravings of an unwell eccentric. Things would only get worse for Doyle in the years to come: his role in the Cottingley Fairies debacle would forever change public opinion of him. During the feverish chaos of World War One, two sisters photographed themselves with "fairies" they had encountered in the woods off of their rural English cottage. In reality they had posed with cut outs of fairies from an Edwardian picture book, and while the hoax was not fully admitted to until well after Doyle's death, his ravenous defense of the girls caused the public to view him with protective pity – like a once-commanding, now senile grandfather. While both "Blue John Gap" and *The Lost World* predate the Cottingley Hoax, Doyle was already feeling public resistance to his support of spiritualism – a trend which had fallen out of fashion by the turn of the 20th century – and seems to have imbued Hardcastle (another well-meaning, open-minded, brave-hearted doctor) with much of his own anxieties and annoyances. Fortunately Doyle, unlike Hardcastle, would survive his humiliation, but it is telling that he chose to lay the brave doctor in his grave – almost as a bitter warning to his critical public.

DOYLE'S final great horror story is truly a worthy swan song – a tale whose science fiction elements maintain their effective awe in spite of having been categorically disproven by aviators within a decade of its publication. And indeed, the tale belongs to the science fiction genre, fitting snuggly on a shelf between the works of H. G. Wells which preceded it, and the cosmic terror of H. P. Lovecraft which succeeded it. Both authors' favorite themes are apparent in Doyle's plot, which resembles elements of Wells' *War of the Worlds*, "In the Abyss," and "The Sea Raiders," and presages Lovecraft's "The Colour Out of Space," "From Beyond," and especially "The Haunter of the Dark" (both share gelatinous predators, barely hidden, misanthropic horrors, and a set of written-out last words that rival Lovecraft's infamous *"I see it—coming here—hell-wind—titan-blur—black wings—Yog-Sothoth save me—the three-lobed burning eye..."*) Where Wells foresaw terrors percolating in the solar system, and Lovecraft under the sea, Doyle predicted the airplane – ten years old at the time – had the potential to discover undetected terrors in the very atmosphere which snuggles the earth and breathes life into our lungs. From this same nurturing comfort could emerge a devilish monstrosity, and all that might be necessary to expose it was for science and technology to continue its upward trajectory into the blue, life-giving skies.

The Horror of the Heights
{1913}

(WHICH INCLUDES *the* MANUSCRIPT KNOWN *as the* JOYCE-ARMSTRONG FRAGMENT)

THE idea that the extraordinary narrative which has been called the Joyce-Armstrong Fragment is an elaborate practical joke[1] evolved by some unknown person, cursed by a perverted and sinister sense of humour, has now been abandoned by all who have examined the matter. The most *macabre* and imaginative of plotters would hesitate before linking his morbid fancies with the unquestioned and tragic facts which reinforce the statement. Though the assertions contained in it are amazing and even monstrous, it is none the less forcing itself upon the general intelligence that they are true, and that we must readjust our ideas to the new situation.

---

[1] At this point in his career, Doyle was becoming involved in the Spiritualist movement, defending frauds, hoaxes, and charlatans against the exposés and criticisms of sceptics. His most famous defense would take place in 1921, when he supported the claims of two girls who became famous for producing five photographs of themselves posing with cardboard cut-outs of fairies which they described to the press as snapshots of legitimate pixies

This world of ours appears to be separated by a slight and precarious margin of safety from a most singular and unexpected danger. I will endeavour in this narrative, which reproduces the original document in its necessarily somewhat fragmentary form, to lay before the reader the whole of the facts up to date, prefacing my statement by saying that, if there be any who doubt the narrative of Joyce-Armstrong, there can be no question at all as to the facts concerning Lieutenant Myrtle, R.N[1]., and Mr. Hay Connor, who undoubtedly met their end in the manner described.

The Joyce-Armstrong Fragment was found in the field which is called Lower Haycock, lying one mile to the westward of the village of Withyham[2], upon the Kent and Sussex border. It was on the fifteenth of September last that an agricultural labourer, James Flynn, in the employment of Mathew Dodd, farmer, of the Chauntry Farm, Withyham, perceived a briar pipe lying near the footpath which skirts the hedge in Lower Haycock. A few paces farther on he picked up a pair of broken binocular glasses. Finally, among some nettles in the ditch, he caught sight of a flat, canvas-backed book, which proved to be a note-book with detachable leaves, some of which had come loose and were fluttering along the base of the hedge. These he collected, but some, including the first, were never recovered, and leave a deplorable hiatus[3] in this all-important statement. The notebook was taken by the labourer to his master, who in turn showed it to Dr. J. H. Atherton, of Hartfield. This gentleman at once recognised the need for an expert examination, and the manuscript was forwarded to the Aero Club[4] in London, where it now lies.

The first two pages of the manuscript are missing. There is also one torn away at the end of the narrative, though none of these affect the general coherence of the story. It is conjectured that the missing opening is concerned with the record of Mr. Joyce-Armstrong's qualifications as an aeronaut, which can be gathered from other sources and are admitted to be unsurpassed among the air-pilots of England. For many years he has been looked upon as among the most daring and the most intellectual of flying

---

[1] Of the Royal Navy, specifically the Royal Naval Air Service, or the R.N.A.S.

[2] A village of 2,600 approximately fifty miles south-southeast of London

[3] There are times when Doyle unwisely tries to write smart-sounding jargon in order to lend his stories validity. He wisely avoids trying to fluff up this story by having the two pages which would include technical detail missing from the manuscript. The omission may be "deplorable" to the narrator, but for Doyle it is a fine touch to lend the tale mystery and avoids the sort of ludicrous lingo that sometimes make his Sherlock Holmes tales cringe-worthy: "Shall I demonstrate your own ignorance? What do you know, pray, of Tapanuli fever? What do you know of the black Formosa corruption?" Nothing, Holmes. Those terms are bogus

[4] Initially more concerned with ballooning than heavier-than-air flight, the Aero Club was a gentleman's sporting society formed for "the encouragement of aero automobilism and ballooning as a sport" in 1901. By 1910 it was thoroughly focused on all matters and modes of aviation

men, a combination which has enabled him to both invent and test several new devices, including the common gyroscopic attachment which is known by his name. The main body of the manuscript is written neatly in ink, but the last few lines are in pencil and are so ragged as to be hardly legible--exactly, in fact, as they might be expected to appear if they were scribbled off hurriedly from the seat of a moving aeroplane. There are, it may be added, several stains, both on the last page and on the outside cover, which have been pronounced by the Home Office[1] experts to be blood--probably human and certainly mammalian[2]. The fact that something closely resembling the organism of malaria was discovered in this blood, and that Joyce-Armstrong is known to have suffered from intermittent fever, is a remarkable example of the new weapons which modern science has placed in the hands of our detectives.

And now a word as to the personality of the author of this epoch-making statement. Joyce-Armstrong, according to the few friends who really knew something of the man, was a poet and a dreamer, as well as a mechanic and an inventor. He was a man of considerable wealth, much of which he had spent in the pursuit of his aeronautical hobby. He had four private aeroplanes in his hangars near Devizes[3], and is said to have made no fewer than one hundred and seventy ascents in the course of last year[4]. He was a retiring man with dark moods, in which he would avoid the society of his fellows[5]. Captain Dangerfield, who knew him better than any one, says that there were times when his eccentricity threatened to develop into something more serious. His habit of carrying a shot-gun with him in his aeroplane was one manifestation of it.

Another was the morbid effect which the fall of Lieutenant Myrtle had upon his mind. Myrtle, who was attempting the height record, fell from an altitude of something over thirty thousand feet[6]. Horrible to narrate, his head was entirely obliterated, though his body and limbs preserved their

---

[1] The Home Office is the center of national security in Britain, and to suggest that they would take an interest in this affair speaks volumes – as much as it would to cite the NSA or CIA in a story set in the modern-day United States. Clearly the government is concerned about this disappearance, and Doyle may even be hinting at a cover up or conspiracy

[2] Perhaps they used the "Sherlock Holmes test" that Holmes develops in *A Study in Scarlet* to identify blood. Karl Landsteiner began developing tests in 1901 to differentiate human blood from that of animals

[3] A village and parish in Wiltshire, in south-central England

[4] At this point in aviation history, he would be a considerably experienced aviator with so many flights at his presumed age (thirty-something)

[5] He shares the same antisocial, Byronic temperament as the late Captain Craegie

[6] The first of many hints that this is not set in 1913, but in the near future. This altitude was not reached until 1919, when Jean Casale achieved it (being 31,230 feet) flying a Nieuport biplane. At this point in history – when the story was published in November of '13 – the flight record was just under 12,000 feet

configuration[1]. At every gathering of airmen, Joyce-Armstrong, according to Dangerfield, would ask, with an enigmatic smile: "And where, pray, is Myrtle's head[2]?"

On another occasion after dinner, at the mess of the Flying School on Salisbury Plain[3], he started a debate as to what will be the most permanent danger which airmen will have to encounter. Having listened to successive opinions as to air-pockets, faulty construction, and over-banking, he ended by shrugging his shoulders and refusing to put forward his own views, though he gave the impression that they differed from any advanced by his companions.

It is worth remarking that after his own complete disappearance it was found that his private affairs were arranged with a precision which may show that he had a strong premonition of disaster. With these essential explanations I will now give the narrative exactly as it stands, beginning at page three of the blood-soaked note-book:--

"Nevertheless, when I dined at Rheims[4] with Coselli and Gustav Raymond[5] I found that neither of them was aware of any particular danger in the higher layers of the atmosphere[6]. I did not actually say what was in my thoughts, but I got so near to it that if they had any corresponding idea they could not have failed to express it. But then they are two empty, vainglorious fellows with no thought beyond seeing their silly names in the newspaper. It is interesting to note that neither of them had ever been much beyond the twenty-thousand-foot level[7]. Of course, men have been higher than this both in balloons and in the ascent of mountains[8]. It must be well above that point that the aeroplane enters the danger zone--always presuming that my premonitions are correct.

---

[1] Suggesting that he wasn't mutilated in the crash: his head was removed from his body

[2] As we will see, this macabre joke is much less gallows humor than it is a genuine question that he is asking himself – a disturbing puzzle disguised as a morbid jest

[3] The chalk plateau in southern England most famous for Stonehenge

[4] A French city of some 188,000 people, laying approximately 130 miles northeast of Paris

[5] False names made to sound like typical European aviators (of which the French were the forerunners – hence Raymond – followed by the Italians – hence Coselli)

[6] Hence it is established that the missing page introduced his theory on what happened to the slain pilots. While we learn the shapes and forms of those monsters, this page's exclusion prevents us from learning their sources or composition – at least as far as Joyce-Armstrong has theorized. Another wise use of restraint by Doyle, developing more mystery than outlandish science fiction

[7] A record first set in 1916. Doyle's educated readers would have understood immediately that this story was set in the future. For a variety of reasons, I propose that the approximate date is 1935

[8] In 1913 the balloon altitude record was 39,000. In 1935 it was 72,000. Everest is 29,029 feet high

"Aeroplaning has been with us now for more than twenty years, and one might well ask: Why should this peril be only revealing itself in our day? The answer is obvious. In the old days of weak engines, when a hundred horse-power Gnome or Green was considered ample for every need, the flights were very restricted. Now that three hundred horse-power is the rule rather than the exception, visits to the upper layers have become easier and more common. Some of us can remember how, in our youth, Garros made a world-wide reputation by attaining nineteen thousand feet[1], and it was considered a remarkable achievement to fly over the Alps[2]. Our standard now has been immeasurably raised, and there are twenty high flights for one in former years. Many of them have been undertaken with impunity. The thirty-thousand-foot level has been reached time after time[3] with no discomfort beyond cold and asthma. What does this prove? A visitor might descend upon this planet a thousand times and never see a tiger. Yet tigers exist, and if he chanced to come down into a jungle he might be devoured. There are jungles of the upper air, and there are worse things than tigers which inhabit them. I believe in time they will map these jungles accurately out. Even at the present moment I could name two of them. One of them lies over the Pau- Biarritz district of France. Another is just over my head as I write here in my house in Wiltshire. I rather think there is a third in the Homburg-Wiesbaden district.

"It was the disappearance of the airmen that first set me thinking. Of course, every one said that they had fallen into the sea, but that did not satisfy me at all. First, there was Verrier in France; his machine was found near Bayonne, but they never got his body. There was the case of Baxter also, who vanished, though his engine and some of the iron fixings were found in a wood in Leicestershire[4]. In that case, Dr. Middleton, of Amesbury, who was watching the flight with a telescope, declares that just before the clouds obscured the view he saw the machine, which was at an

---

[1] The French aviator, hero, and inventor Roland Garros (1888 – 1918) set this record (it was actually 18,405) on September 11, 1912. If we suppose our characters to be roughly thirty-five in age, and their "childhood" to be a descriptor for the years five to fifteen, with a median age of ten, we can suppose that twenty years after a ten year old in 1912 idolized Garros would be a sensible setting – thus 1930-1935. Doyle was not far off the mark: he suggests that 40,000 feet is the altitude to beat in the early thirties, and the record in 1934 was still only 47,354. Considering how rapidly aviation progressed from flimsy canvas biplanes held together by wire to aluminum monoplanes, it is commendable that Doyle had so much of an ear for the trajectory of aerial technology – though not surprising considering his love of all things fast and mechanical

[2] First accomplished four months before this story was published by Swiss aviation pioneer Oskar Bider on July 11, 1913. Further proof of the story's futurity since Doyle treats a feat still ringing in aviation circles as an everyday occurrence

[3] First achieved on June 14, 1919

[4] As if found inedible or – perish the thought – as if having been passed through a digestive system and excreted – like bones found in owl pellets

enormous height, suddenly rise perpendicularly upwards in a succession of jerks in a manner that he would have thought to be impossible[1]. That was the last seen of Baxter. There was a correspondence in the papers, but it never led to anything. There were several other similar cases, and then there was the death of Hay Connor. What a cackle there was about an unsolved mystery of the air, and what columns in the halfpenny papers, and yet how little was ever done to get to the bottom of the business! He came down in a tremendous vol-plane[2] from an unknown height. He never got off[3] his machine and died in his pilot's seat. Died of what? 'Heart disease,' said the doctors. Rubbish! Hay Connor's heart was as sound as mine is. What did Venables say? Venables was the only man who was at his side when he died. He said that he was shivering and looked like a man who had been badly scared. 'Died of fright,' said Venables, but could not imagine what he was frightened about. Only said one word to Venables, which sounded like 'Monstrous.' They could make nothing of that at the inquest. But I could make something of it. Monsters! That was the last word of poor Harry Hay Connor. And he *did* die of fright, just as Venables thought.

"And then there was Myrtle's head. Do you really believe--does anybody really believe--that a man's head could be driven clean into his body by the force of a fall? Well, perhaps it may be possible, but I, for one, have never believed that it was so with Myrtle. And the grease upon his clothes--'all slimy with grease,' said somebody at the inquest. Queer that nobody got thinking after that! I did--but, then, I had been thinking for a good long time. I've made three ascents--how Dangerfield used to chaff me about my shot-gun!--but I've never been high enough. Now, with this new light Paul Veroner[4] machine and its one hundred and seventy-five Robur, I should easily touch the thirty thousand to-morrow. I'll have a shot at the record. Maybe I shall have a shot at something else as well. Of course, it's dangerous. If a fellow wants to avoid danger he had best keep out of flying altogether and subside finally into flannel slippers and a dressing-gown. But I'll visit the air-jungle to- morrow--and if there's anything there I shall know it. If I return, I'll find myself a bit of a celebrity. If I don't, this note-book may explain what I am trying to do, and how I lost my life in doing it. But no drivel about accidents or mysteries, if *you* please.

---

[1] As if being grabbed and shaken up and down

[2] For an airplane to glide down with its engine shut off

[3] To parachute

[4] A fictitious company. By the craft's description, it may be intended to be a Morane-Saulnier monoplane

"I chose my Paul Veroner monoplane for the job. There's nothing like a monoplane when real work is to be done[1]. Beaumont[2] found that out in very early days. For one thing, it doesn't mind damp, and the weather looks as if we should be in the clouds all the time. It's a bonny little model and answers my hand like a tender-mouthed horse. The engine is a ten- cylinder rotary Robur[3] working up to one hundred and seventy-five[4]. It has all the modern improvements--enclosed fuselage, high-curved landing skids, brakes, gyroscopic steadiers, and three speeds, worked by an alteration of the angle of the planes upon the Venetian-blind principle[5]. I took a shot-gun with me and a dozen cartridges filled with buck-shot. You should have seen the face of Perkins, my old mechanic, when I directed him to put them in. I was dressed like an Arctic explorer, with two jerseys under my overalls, thick socks inside my padded boots, a storm-cap with flaps, and my talc goggles. It was stifling outside the hangars, but I was going for the summit of the Himalayas, and had to dress for the part[6]. Perkins knew there was something on and implored me to take him with me. Perhaps I should if I were using the biplane[7], but a monoplane is a one-man show--if you want to get the last foot of lift out of it. Of course, I took an oxygen bag; the man who goes for the altitude record without one will either be frozen or smothered--or both[8].

---

[1] Doyle trying to sound authoritative. In fact, biplanes achieved every single altitude record with only two exceptions until 1936, and monoplanes were universally inferior to biplanes until technology allowed airplanes to be constructed from metals instead of canvas and wood

[2] Jean Louis Conneau (1880 – 1937), alias "Beaumont" was a pioneering aviator, racer, and manufacturer of flying boats. Beaumont earned his pilot's license in 1910, continuing the trend of futurizing this story written only two years after he became an international figure. He flew a Bleriot XI monoplane during many of his most famous races

[3] Another fictitious brand. This one is based on the Le Rhone rotary motor, most famously used in the Sopwith Camel, Nieuport series, and a variety of other allied aircraft. The rotary engine was "an early type of internal-combustion engine, usually designed with an odd number of cylinders per row in a radial configuration, in which the crankshaft remained stationary in operation, with the entire crankcase and its attached cylinders rotating around it as a unit. Its main application was in aviation, although it also saw use before its primary aviation role, in a few early motorcycles and automobiles."

[4] The best airplanes of 1913 could run at just under 50 mph. The Sopwith Camel could hit 115, and the Red Baron's Albatros D.V topped at 116. Some Nieuports and SPADs were making 170-175 mph by 1920

[5] Trying to sound authoritative, Doyle seems to postulate that airplanes will become like automobiles and require gear shifts

[6] A necessary precaution for anyone planning to fly in an open cockpit more than a few thousand feet in the air

[7] Presumably a two-seater

[8] As Doyle well knew, several balloonists had been knocked unconscious – and some killed – by ascending into the oxygen-starved higher atmospheres. This is a thoroughly modern

"I had a good look at the planes, the rudder-bar, and the elevating lever before I got in. Everything was in order so far as I could see. Then I switched on my engine and found that she was running sweetly. When they let her go she rose almost at once upon the lowest speed. I circled my home field once or twice just to warm her up, and then, with a wave to Perkins and the others, I flattened out my planes and put her on her highest[1]. She skimmed like a swallow down wind for eight or ten miles until I turned her nose up a little and she began to climb in a great spiral for the cloud-bank above me. It's all-important to rise slowly and adapt yourself to the pressure as you go.

"It was a close, warm day for an English September, and there was the hush and heaviness of impending rain. Now and then there came sudden puffs of wind from the south-west--one of them so gusty and unexpected that it caught me napping and turned me half-round for an instant. I remember the time when gusts and whirls and air-pockets used to be things of danger--before we learned to put an overmastering power into our engines. Just as I reached the cloud-banks, with the altimeter marking three thousand, down came the rain. My word, how it poured! It drummed upon my wings and lashed against my face, blurring my glasses so that I could hardly see. I got down on to a low speed, for it was painful to travel against it. As I got higher it became hail, and I had to turn tail to it. One of my cylinders was out of action--a dirty plug, I should imagine, but still I was rising steadily with plenty of power. After a bit the trouble passed, whatever it was, and I heard the full, deep-throated purr--the ten singing as one. That's where the beauty of our modern silencers comes in. We can at last control our engines by ear. How they squeal and squeak and sob when they are in trouble! All those cries for help were wasted in the old days, when every sound was swallowed up by the monstrous racket of the machine. If only the early aviators could come back to see the beauty and perfection of the mechanism which have been bought at the cost of their lives!

"About nine-thirty I was nearing the clouds. Down below me, all blurred and shadowed with rain, lay the vast expanse of Salisbury Plain. Half-a-dozen flying machines were doing hackwork at the thousand-foot level, looking like little black swallows against the green background. I dare say they were wondering what I was doing up in cloud-land. Suddenly a grey curtain drew across beneath me and the wet folds of vapour were swirling round my face. It was clammily cold and miserable. But I was above the hail-storm, and that was something gained. The cloud was as dark and thick as a London fog. In my anxiety to get clear, I cocked her nose up until the automatic alarm-bell rang[2], and I actually began to slide backwards. My

---

precaution, however, as pilots didn't carry oxygen on hand until the 1930s, and then only high flying bombers and their fighter escorts

[1] More Doyle bunk

[2] Doyle demonstrates foresight, as alarms, lights, and buzzers were still years off from primitive machines like the Bleriot XI

sopped and dripping wings had made me heavier than I thought, but presently I was in lighter cloud, and soon had cleared the first layer. There was a second--opal-coloured and fleecy--at a great height above my head, a white unbroken ceiling above, and a dark unbroken floor below, with the monoplane labouring upwards upon a vast spiral between them. It is deadly lonely in these cloud-spaces. Once a great flight of some small water-birds went past me, flying very fast to the westwards. The quick whirr of their wings and their musical cry were cheery to my ear. I fancy that they were teal, but I am a wretched zoologist. Now that we humans have become birds we must really learn to know our brethren by sight.

"The wind down beneath me whirled and swayed the broad cloud-plain. Once a great eddy formed in it, a whirlpool of vapour, and through it, as down a funnel, I caught sight of the distant world. A large white biplane was passing at a vast depth beneath me. I fancy it was the morning mail service betwixt Bristol and London[1]. Then the drift swirled inwards again and the great solitude was unbroken.

"Just after ten I touched the lower edge of the upper cloud-stratum. It consisted of fine diaphanous vapour drifting swiftly from the westward. The wind had been steadily rising all this time and it was now blowing a sharp breeze--twenty-eight an hour by my gauge. Already it was very cold, though my altimeter only marked nine thousand. The engines were working beautifully, and we went droning steadily upwards. The cloud- bank was thicker than I had expected, but at last it thinned out into a golden mist before me, and then in an instant I had shot out from it, and there was an unclouded sky and a brilliant sun above my head--all blue and gold above, all shining silver below, one vast glimmering plain as far as my eyes could reach. It was a quarter past ten o'clock, and the barograph needle pointed to twelve thousand eight hundred. Up I went and up, my ears concentrated upon the deep purring of my motor, my eyes busy always with the watch, the revolution indicator, the petrol lever, and the oil pump. No wonder aviators are said to be a fearless race. With so many things to think of there is no time to trouble about oneself. About this time I noted how unreliable is the compass when above a certain height from earth. At fifteen thousand feet mine was pointing east and a point south. The sun and the wind gave me my true bearings.

"I had hoped to reach an eternal stillness in these high altitudes, but with every thousand feet of ascent the gale grew stronger. My machine groaned and trembled in every joint and rivet as she faced it, and swept away like a sheet of paper when I banked her on the turn, skimming down wind at a greater pace, perhaps, than ever mortal man has moved. Yet I had always to turn again and tack up in the wind's eye, for it was not merely a height record that I was after. By all my calculations it was above little

[1] The first scheduled airmail in the UK occurred in 1911 between Berkshire and London

Wiltshire that my air-jungle lay, and all my labour might be lost if I struck the outer layers at some farther point.

"When I reached the nineteen-thousand-foot level, which was about midday, the wind was so severe that I looked with some anxiety to the stays of my wings, expecting momentarily to see them snap or slacken. I even cast loose the parachute behind me, and fastened its hook into the ring of my leathern belt, so as to be ready for the worst. Now was the time when a bit of scamped work by the mechanic is paid for by the life of the aeronaut. But she held together bravely. Every cord and strut[1] was humming and vibrating like so many harp-strings, but it was glorious to see how, for all the beating and the buffeting, she was still the conqueror of Nature and the mistress of the sky. There is surely something divine in man himself that he should rise so superior to the limitations which Creation seemed to impose--rise, too, by such unselfish, heroic devotion as this air-conquest has shown. Talk of human degeneration! When has such a story as this been written in the annals of our race[2]?

"These were the thoughts in my head as I climbed that monstrous inclined plane with the wind sometimes beating in my face and sometimes whistling behind my ears, while the cloud-land beneath me fell away to such a distance that the folds and hummocks of silver had all smoothed out into one flat, shining plain. But suddenly I had a horrible and unprecedented experience. I have known before what it is to be in what our neighbours have called a *tourbillon*[3], but never on such a scale as this. That huge, sweeping river of wind of which I have spoken had, as it appears, whirlpools within it which were as monstrous as itself. Without a moment's warning I was dragged suddenly into the heart of one. I spun round for a minute or two with such velocity that I almost lost my senses, and then fell suddenly, left wing foremost, down the vacuum funnel in the centre. I dropped like a stone, and lost nearly a thousand feet. It was only my belt that kept me in my seat, and the shock and breathlessness left me hanging half-insensible over the side of the fuselage. But I am always capable of a supreme effort--it is my one great merit as an aviator. I was conscious that the descent was slower. The whirlpool was a cone rather than a funnel, and I had come to the apex. With a terrific wrench, throwing my weight all to one

---

[1] Early airplane wings were secured with wires which were attached to fortified struts: braces made of metal or wood which allowed the canvas wings to support the punishment of flight

[2] This is Doyle the ever-optimist shining through as Europe was poised on the brink of mutual destruction. Amidst all the talk of moral degeneracy, corrupt civilization, and human wickedness, Doyle held fast to his belief that mankind strove to be noble and was divine at heart. The advances of science, technology, and exploration only fed his voracious optimism, and where the war machine saw U-boats, aerial bombing, mustard gas, and machine guns, he saw deep sea exploration, new frontiers in the sky, advances in medicine, and mechanized luxuries

[3] French: whirlwind

side, I levelled my planes and brought her head away from the wind. In an instant I had shot out of the eddies and was skimming down the sky. Then, shaken but victorious, I turned her nose up and began once more my steady grind on the upward spiral. I took a large sweep to avoid the danger- spot of the whirlpool[1], and soon I was safely above it. Just after one o'clock I was twenty-one thousand feet above the sea-level. To my great joy I had topped the gale, and with every hundred feet of ascent the air grew stiller. On the other hand, it was very cold, and I was conscious of that peculiar nausea which goes with rarefaction of the air. For the first time I unscrewed the mouth of my oxygen bag and took an occasional whiff of the glorious gas. I could feel it running like a cordial through my veins, and I was exhilarated almost to the point of drunkenness. I shouted and sang[2] as I soared upwards into the cold, still outer world.

"It is very clear to me that the insensibility which came upon Glaisher, and in a lesser degree upon Coxwell[3], when, in 1862, they ascended in a balloon to the height of thirty thousand feet, was due to the extreme speed with which a perpendicular ascent is made. Doing it at an easy gradient and accustoming oneself to the lessened barometric pressure by slow degrees, there are no such dreadful symptoms. At the same great height I found that even without my oxygen inhaler I could breathe without undue distress. It was bitterly cold, however, and my thermometer was at zero Fahrenheit. At one-thirty I was nearly seven miles above the surface of the earth, and still ascending steadily. I found, however, that the rarefied air was giving markedly less support to my planes, and that my angle of ascent had to be considerably lowered in consequence. It was already clear that even with my light weight and strong engine-power there was a point in front of me where I should be held. To make matters worse, one of my sparking-plugs

---

[1] Doyle attempts to pattern the perils of the sky on those of the sea, using maritime terminology, presenting oceanic dangers, and (eventually) casting his adversaries as jelly fish, sharks, serpents, and squids. His hope appears to be to paint the heavens as a new ocean to be explored and adventured upon

[2] No doubt counteracting the benefits of the oxygen

[3] The following is a brief account of that record-breaking ascent: "In 1862 the British Association for the Advancement of Science determined to make investigations of the upper atmosphere using balloons. Dr James Glaisher, FRS. was chosen to carry out the experiments, and at the suggestion of Charles Green Coxwell was employed to fly the balloons. [Henry Tracey] Coxwell constructed a 93,000 cu ft (2,600 m^3) capacity balloon named the *Mammoth*, and on 5 September 1862, taking off from Wolverhampton, Coxwell and Glaisher reached the greatest height achieved to date. Glaisher lost consciousness during the ascent, his last barometer reading indicating an altitude of 29,000 ft (8,800 m) and Coxwell lost all sensation in his hands, but managed just in time to pull the valve-cord with his teeth. The balloon dropped nineteen thousand feet in fifteen minutes, landing safely made near Ludlow. Later calculations estimated that their maximum altitude at 35,000 to 37,000 ft (10,700 to 11,300 m)"

was in trouble again and there was intermittent misfiring in the engine. My heart was heavy with the fear of failure.

"It was about that time that I had a most extraordinary experience. Something whizzed past me in a trail of smoke and exploded with a loud, hissing sound, sending forth a cloud of steam. For the instant I could not imagine what had happened. Then I remembered that the earth is for ever being bombarded by meteor stones, and would be hardly inhabitable were they not in nearly every case turned to vapour in the outer layers of the atmosphere. Here is a new danger for the high-altitude man, for two others passed me when I was nearing the forty-thousand-foot mark[1]. I cannot doubt that at the edge of the earth's envelope the risk would be a very real one.

"My barograph needle marked forty-one thousand three hundred when I became aware that I could go no farther. Physically, the strain was not as yet greater than I could bear, but my machine had reached its limit. The attenuated air gave no firm support to the wings[2], and the least tilt developed into side-slip, while she seemed sluggish on her controls. Possibly, had the engine been at its best, another thousand feet might have been within our capacity, but it was still misfiring, and two out of the ten cylinders appeared to be out of action. If I had not already reached the zone for which I was searching then I should never see it upon this journey. But was it not possible that I had attained it? Soaring in circles like a monstrous hawk upon the forty-thousand-foot level I let the monoplane guide herself, and with my Mannheim glass[3] I made a careful observation of my surroundings. The heavens were perfectly clear; there was no indication of those dangers which I had imagined.

"I have said that I was soaring in circles. It struck me suddenly that I would do well to take a wider sweep and open up a new air-tract. If the hunter entered an earth-jungle he would drive through it if he wished to find his game. My reasoning had led me to believe that the air-jungle which I had imagined lay somewhere over Wiltshire. This should be to the south and west of me. I took my bearings from the sun, for the compass was hopeless[4] and no trace of earth was to be seen--nothing but the distant silver cloud-plain. However, I got my direction as best I might and kept her head straight to the mark. I reckoned that my petrol supply would not last

---

[1] The chances of an airplane being struck by a meteorite are more than one in a billion since they are largely destroyed in the highest climes of the stratosphere, and those that strike the earth are often harmless. No airplane has ever been recorded as being struck by a meteorite

[2] Mumbo jumbo

[3] A fictitious brand of binoculars – the "pair of broken binocular glasses" described found near the bloodstained journal. Germans were renowned for the precision of the lens crafters and glassworks, so the name is suitable

[4] You would have to travel a quarter of the distance to the moon before a compass would cease to work

for more than another hour or so, but I could afford to use it to the last drop, since a single magnificent vol-plane could at any time take me to the earth.

"Suddenly I was aware of something new. The air in front of me had lost its crystal clearness. It was full of long, ragged wisps of something which I can only compare to very fine cigarette-smoke. It hung about in wreaths and coils, turning and twisting slowly in the sunlight. As the monoplane shot through it, I was aware of a faint taste of oil upon my lips, and there was a greasy scum upon the woodwork of the machine. Some infinitely fine organic matter appeared to be suspended in the atmosphere. There was no life there. It was inchoate and diffuse, extending for many square acres and then fringing off into the void. No, it was not life. But might it not be the remains of life? Above all, might it not be the food of life, of monstrous life, even as the humble grease of the ocean is the food for the mighty whale[1]? The thought was in my mind when my eyes looked upwards and I saw the most wonderful vision that ever man has seen. Can I hope to convey it to you even as I saw it myself last Thursday?

"Conceive a jelly-fish such as sails in our summer seas, bell-shaped and of enormous size--far larger, I should judge, than the dome of St. Paul's[2]. It was of a light pink colour veined with a delicate green, but the whole huge fabric so tenuous that it was but a fairy outline against the dark blue sky. It pulsated with a delicate and regular rhythm. From it there depended two long, drooping green tentacles, which swayed slowly backwards and forwards[3]. This gorgeous vision passed gently with noiseless dignity over my head, as light and fragile as a soap-bubble, and drifted upon its stately way.

"I had half-turned my monoplane, that I might look after this beautiful creature, when, in a moment, I found myself amidst a perfect fleet of them, of all sizes, but none so large as the first. Some were quite small, but the majority about as big as an average balloon, and with much the same curvature at the top. There was in them a delicacy of texture and colouring which reminded me of the finest Venetian glass. Pale shades of pink and green were the prevailing tints, but all had a lovely iridescence where the sun shimmered through their dainty forms. Some hundreds of them drifted past me, a wonderful fairy squadron of strange, unknown argosies[4] of the sky--creatures whose forms and substance were so attuned to these pure

---

[1] He refers, of course, to plankton, which is quite alive. Nonetheless, this continues to promote the conceit of the heavens being a new ocean teeming with a complex ecosystem that begins with sky-plankton and culminates in something monstrous

[2] First raised in 1708, St. Paul's Cathedral in London is 365 feet high

[3] The description is quite akin to the Portuguese man-o-war, or the lion's mane jellyfish, both of which are lethal to men, the later even making an appearance as a eponymous villain in the Sherlock Holmes story "The Lion's Mane"

[4] Seventeenth century merchant ships recognizable by their great puffy sails

heights that one could not conceive anything so delicate within actual sight or sound of earth.

"But soon my attention was drawn to a new phenomenon--the serpents of the outer air[1]. These were long, thin, fantastic coils of vapour-like material, which turned and twisted with great speed, flying round and round at such a pace that the eyes could hardly follow them. Some of these ghost-like creatures were twenty or thirty feet long, but it was difficult to tell their girth, for their outline was so hazy that it seemed to fade away into the air around them. These air-snakes were of a very light grey or smoke colour, with some darker lines within, which gave the impression of a definite organism. One of them whisked past my very face, and I was conscious of a cold, clammy contact, but their composition was so unsubstantial that I could not connect them with any thought of physical danger, any more than the beautiful bell-like creatures which had preceded them. There was no more solidity in their frames than in the floating spume from a broken wave.

"But a more terrible experience was in store for me. Floating downwards from a great height there came a purplish patch of vapour, small as I saw it first, but rapidly enlarging as it approached me, until it appeared to be hundreds of square feet in size. Though fashioned of some transparent, jelly-like substance, it was none the less of much more definite outline and solid consistence than anything which I had seen before. There were more traces, too, of a physical organization, especially two vast shadowy, circular plates upon either side, which may have been eyes, and a perfectly solid white projection between them which was as curved and cruel as the beak of a vulture[2].

"The whole aspect of this monster was formidable and threatening, and it kept changing its colour from a very light mauve to a dark, angry purple so thick that it cast a shadow as it drifted between my monoplane and the sun. On the upper curve of its huge body there were three great projections which I can only describe as enormous bubbles, and I was convinced as I looked at them that they were charged with some extremely light gas which served to buoy-up the misshapen and semi-solid mass in the rarefied air.

---

[1] As with many stories of this genre – the lost world type (the name comes from Doyle himself, of course), or any variety of science fiction which explores a newfound ecosystem – the voyager progresses from scenes of deep beauty and awe, to visions of increasingly sinister kinds. In the typically, dinosaur-infused "lost world" narrative (think Jurassic Park), we first see the vegetation, lush and pure and lovely, then the noble but harmless stegosaurus, followed by the sublime, gentle giants, the Apatosaurus and his kind, and while we are distracted by their immensity, we suddenly see the velociraptors and smaller but sinister beasts, only to find Tyrannosaurus staggering onto the stage with his banana-sized incisors, and then the spell becomes a nightmare

[2] If the previous creatures are sky-jellyfish and sky-serpents, then surely this is a sky-squid with its monstrous eyes, covetous tentacles, shifting color, and gnashing beak. It bears a distinct resemblances to H. G. Wells' hideous, beaked Martians

The creature moved swiftly along, keeping pace easily with the monoplane, and for twenty miles or more it formed my horrible escort, hovering over me like a bird of prey which is waiting to pounce. Its method of progression--done so swiftly that it was not easy to follow--was to throw out a long, glutinous streamer in front of it[1], which in turn seemed to draw forward the rest of the writhing body. So elastic and gelatinous was it that never for two successive minutes was it the same shape, and yet each change made it more threatening and loathsome than the last.

"I knew that it meant mischief. Every purple flush of its hideous body told me so. The vague, goggling eyes which were turned always upon me were cold and merciless in their viscid hatred. I dipped the nose of my monoplane downwards to escape it. As I did so, as quick as a flash there shot out a long tentacle from this mass of floating blubber, and it fell as light and sinuous as a whip-lash across the front of my machine. There was a loud hiss as it lay for a moment across the hot engine, and it whisked itself into the air again, while the huge flat body drew itself together as if in sudden pain. I dipped to a vol-plane, but again a tentacle fell over the monoplane and was shorn off by the propeller as easily as it might have cut through a smoke wreath. A long, gliding, sticky, serpent-like coil came from behind and caught me round the waist, dragging me out of the fuselage. I tore at it, my fingers sinking into the smooth, glue-like surface, and for an instant I disengaged myself, but only to be caught round the boot by another coil, which gave me a jerk that tilted me almost on to my back.

"As I fell over I blazed off both barrels of my gun, though, indeed, it was like attacking an elephant with a pea-shooter to imagine that any human weapon could cripple that mighty bulk. And yet I aimed better than I knew, for, with a loud report, one of the great blisters upon the creature's back exploded with the puncture of the buck-shot. It was very clear that my conjecture was right, and that these vast clear bladders were distended with some lifting gas, for in an instant the huge cloud-like body turned sideways, writhing desperately to find its balance, while the white beak snapped and gaped in horrible fury. But already I had shot away on the steepest glide that I dared to attempt[2], my engine still full on, the flying propeller and the force of gravity shooting me downwards like an aerolite. Far behind me I saw a dull, purplish smudge growing swiftly smaller and merging into the blue sky behind it. I was safe out of the deadly jungle of the outer air.

"Once out of danger I throttled my engine, for nothing tears a machine to pieces quicker than running on full power from a height[3]. It was a glorious spiral vol-plane from nearly eight miles of altitude--first, to the

---

[1] Certainly presaging the gelatinous monstrosities of Lovecraft

[2] Lest the wings be shorn off by the G forces – a very real danger

[3] Also accurate. Like an ascending diver (to continue the aerial/nautical theme), he is best advised to return to safety in a slow, steady, consistent manner to avoid the G forces and vibrations of the wrenching engine from shaking the struts and wings loose

level of the silver cloud-bank, then to that of the storm-cloud beneath it, and finally, in beating rain, to the surface of the earth. I saw the Bristol Channel[1] beneath me as I broke from the clouds, but, having still some petrol in my tank, I got twenty miles inland before I found myself stranded in a field half a mile from the village of Ashcombe[2]. There I got three tins of petrol from a passing motor-car, and at ten minutes past six that evening I alighted gently in my own home meadow at Devizes, after such a journey as no mortal upon earth has ever yet taken and lived to tell the tale. I have seen the beauty and I have seen the horror of the heights--and greater beauty or greater horror than that is not within the ken of man[3].

"And now it is my plan to go once again before I give my results to the world. My reason for this is that I must surely have something to show by way of proof before I lay such a tale before my fellow-men[4]. It is true that others will soon follow and will confirm what I have said, and yet I should wish to carry conviction from the first. Those lovely iridescent bubbles of the air should not be hard to capture. They drift slowly upon their way, and the swift monoplane could intercept their leisurely course. It is likely enough that they would dissolve in the heavier layers of the atmosphere, and that some small heap of amorphous jelly might be all that I should bring to earth with me. And yet something there would surely be by which I could substantiate my story. Yes, I will go, even if I run a risk by doing so. These purple horrors would not seem to be numerous. It is probable that I shall not see one. If I do I shall dive at once. At the worst there is always the shot-gun and my knowledge of[5] . . ."

---

[1] A major inlet which cuts into Britain, separating the southern Welsh coast from England

[2] 109 miles west of his hangars in Devizes

[3] Doyle was nothing if not a true Romantic, and as a Romantic he was compelled to respect the sublimity of Nature – the delicate balance of serene beauty and horrific power that mingle in its unrestricted domain. The Romantics were drawn to desolate scenes of natural dominion – mountains, oceans, poles, deserts, wastes, moors, forests, caverns, jungles, etc. – and Doyle sees fit to introduce the heavens as a new source of sublimity, awe, and mystique. He portrays it as being equally thrilling and terrifying, inspiring and frightening, and thus a subject of human wonder and fear

[4] This ill-fated return in search of proof bears a distinct and undeniable similarity to that of Well's tragic protagonist from *The Time Machine*. Other comparisons may be drawn with Doyle's own approval-seeking Professor Challenger. All three characters share with Doyle a sour desire to bring mind-expanding truth to a world of self-involved skeptics. Rejected and written off by the establishment, they return to the perils of their wondrous discoveries on suicide missions to validate the terrors and wonders that they have grown to adore. No great detective work need be done to note the similarities between these scientific outcasts and Doyle, who poured his energies into validating the claims of Spiritualism to a condescending public and a spiteful academy

[5] This presumably – and tantalizingly – refers to the information collected on the first page which has gone missing, made further mysterious by the absence of the following page

Here a page of the manuscript is unfortunately missing. On the next page is written, in large, straggling writing:--

"Forty-three thousand feet. I shall never see earth again. They are beneath me, three of them[1]*. God help me; it is a dreadful death to die*[2]*!"*

Such in its entirety is the Joyce-Armstrong Statement. Of the man nothing has since been seen. Pieces of his shattered monoplane have been picked up in the preserves of Mr. Budd-Lushington upon the borders of Kent and Sussex[3], within a few miles of the spot where the note-book was discovered. If the unfortunate aviator's theory is correct that this air- jungle, as he called it, existed only over the south-west of England, then it would seem that he had fled from it at the full speed of his monoplane, but had been overtaken and devoured by these horrible creatures at some spot in the outer atmosphere above the place where the grim relics were found. The picture of that monoplane skimming down the sky, with the nameless terrors[4] flying as swiftly beneath it and cutting it off always from the earth while they gradually closed in upon their victim, is one upon which a man who valued his sanity would prefer not to dwell. There are many, as I am aware, who still jeer at the facts which I have here set down, but even they must admit that Joyce-Armstrong has disappeared, and I would commend to them his own words: "This note-book may explain what I am trying to do, and how I lost my life in doing it. But no drivel about accidents or mysteries[5], if *you* please."

---

[1] There is a disturbing sense of sentience in their arrangement, especially considering Joyce-Armstrong's claim that they were rarely scene and relatively uncommon. It seems to smack of a vengeful trap organized by the beast he mauled in his first encounter. Waiting for him, they ensured his destruction

[2] Indeed, if we are to take Myrtle's death as an indication of their modus operandi, it would seem that they crush and drain their victims (his head was crushed into his torso, you will remember, and thence obliterated) like a coconut which is first broken and then sucked and carved dry

[3] A shocking distance from Devizes for an early aircraft

[4] So tremendously Lovecraftian. We cannot imagine that the American writer did not treasure this little story amid his vast collection of supernatural literature

[5] Doyle snipes bitterly at skeptics who habitually attributed his pet examples of psychic and supernatural phenomena to simple accidents and unsolvable mysteries

IT continues to surprise me how gripping this story can be. The idea that the atmosphere at 30,000 – 50,000 feet is populated by ethereal jungle-beasts is completely ludicrous, and we now live in a world where we are looking under every rock in the universe to uncover new life without avail. The seas are not peopled by aquatic civilizations, nor is the earth's core a hollow kingdom of subterranean societies, nor are cities thriving on the moon, nor are empires sprawling on Wells' Mars, nor are monsters launching from Lovecraft's Pluto. And yet this story, with its primitive account of cloud beasties, has the ring of genuine horror to it. Perhaps it is the setting, in the infancy of aviation, and the daring of its characters who are fledglings in the sky which is the natural domain of geese and meteors and cumuli, but a brave new world for mankind to toddle into, optimistic, ignorant, and vulnerable. Today we have exhausted so many frontiers that it is perhaps refreshing to enter a mindset where even the white vapor above us has the potential to obscure unseen leviathans. The seas have been plumbed, Everest surmounted, the earth orbited, the moon trodden, Mars sampled, Pluto photographed, and the Solar System escaped. We have accomplished much in five hundred years of active scientific exploration, but our reward is boredom and cynicism: the loss of wonder and mystery. Doyle never lost those qualities. To him the fields of England still harbored the fairy folk of ages past, the spirit world bled into that of the living, monsters roamed forgotten plateaus, and each scientific advance heralded an opportunity to be either astounded or horrified. *Both* are achieved in this story. Joyce-Armstrong flies to his death aware of the risks to prove something that he believed in. It was pure wish fulfilment for Doyle to write a character who was thought a fool – a romantic who dared to gauge the unseen world around our tiny civilization – who, even though his end was horrendous, was ultimately vindicated. To Doyle the world was full of mystery, and so much of its humbling awe could be appreciated if we would only open their eyes to see and their ears to hear. As misguided as his theories may have been, we cannot fault him for being a hopeless and devoted romantic. His self-assigned epitaph sums up his quixotic character: "Blade Straight, Steel True."

—FURTHER READING—
Critical, Literary, and Biographical Works

Belanger, Derrick, editor. *A Study in Terror: Sir Arthur Conan Doyle's Revolutionary Stories of Fear and the Supernatural.* MX Publishing, 2014.

Bleiler, Everett Franklin, editor. *The Best Supernatural Tales of Arthur Conan Doyle.* Dover Publications, Inc, 1979.

Jones, Kelvin I. *Conan Doyle and the Spirits: The Spiritualist Career of Sir Arthur Conan Doyle.* Aquarian Press, 1989.

Klinger, Leslie. *The New Annotated Sherlock Holmes.* W.W. Norton, 2007.

Lycett, Andrew. *The Man Who Created Sherlock Holmes: The Life and Times of Sir Arthur Conan Doyle.* Free Press, 2008.

Stashower, Daniel. *Teller of Tales: The Life of Arthur Conan Doyle.* Penguin, 2001.

About the Editor and Illustrator

Michael Grant Kellermeyer -- OTP's founder and chief editor -- is an English professor, bibliographer, illustrator, editor, critic, and author based in Fort Wayne, Indiana. He earned his Bachelor of Arts in English from Anderson University and his Master of Arts in Literature from Ball State University. He teaches college writing in Indiana where he enjoys playing violin, painting, hiking, and cooking.

Ever since watching Bing Crosby's *The Legend of Sleepy Hollow* as a three year old, Michael has been enraptured by the ghastly, ghoulish, and the unknown. Reading Great Illustrated Classics' abridged versions of classic horrors as a first grader, he quickly became enthralled with the horrific, and began accumulating a collection of unabridged classics; *Edgar Allan Poe's Forgotten Tales* and a copy of *The Legend of Sleepy Hollow* with an introduction by Charles L. Grant are among his most cherished possessions. Frequenting the occult section of the Berne Public Library, he scoured through anthologies and compendiums on ghostly lore.

It was here that he found two books which would be more influential to his tastes than any other: Henry Mazzeo's *Hauntings* (illustrated by the unparalleled Edward Gorey), and Barry Moser's *Great Ghost Stories*. It was while reading through these two collections during the Hallowe'en season of 2012 that Michael was inspired to honor the writers, tales, and mythologies he revered the most.

Oldstyle Tales Press was the result of that impulse. Its first title, *The Best Victorian Ghost Stories*, was published in September 2013, followed shortly by editions of *Frankenstein* and *The Annotated and Illustrated Edgar Allan Poe.*

In his free time, Michael enjoys straight razors, briarwood pipes, Classical music, jazz standards from the '20s to '60s, sea shanties, lemon wedges in his water, the films of Vincent Price, Alfred Hitchcock, and Stanley Kubrick, sandalwood shaving cream, freshly-laundered sheets, gin tonics, and mint tea.

Made in the USA
Middletown, DE
23 September 2024

61218720R00205